He placed the blade in his palm and handed the hilt back to her. She slid it back in its sheath and snapped its strap.

"Weapons are a powerful thing. There's a mind/body connection to what you hold in your hand that adds to your strength when wielding your piece."

Shay arched a brow. "You know more about weaponry than I thought."

Nic shrugged. "I've dabbled here and there."

"Bought into the bad-boy image, hook, line, and sinker, did you?"

He grinned. She read him pretty well. "Bad boy, huh?"

"You have the look."

"What look?"

"Gorgeous, sex appeal, charm, a bit of a dangerous edge. Irresistible to some women."

He tried not to laugh. He had no business feeling this sense of ease, this playfulness with Shay. But he couldn't help it. He tried to keep his distance from her, to hold on to the anger, but something compelled him, drove him to get closer.

"I see. Some women. But not you, of course."

"Of course not. I'm immune to that kind of thing."

Challenge. She'd thrown down the gauntlet and he snatched it up, ready to do battle.

"You're immune," he said.

"Yup."

"Wanna bet?"

Also by Jaci Burton

Surviving Demon Island

HUNTING
THE
DEMON

Jaci Burton

A DELL BOOK

HUNTING THE DEMON

A Dell Book / September 2007

Published by Bantam Dell
A Division of Random House, Inc.
New York, New York

Dell is a registered trademark of Random House, Inc.,
and the colophon is a trademark of Random House, Inc.

ISBN 978-0-440-24336-6

Printed in the United States of America
Published simultaneously in Canada

www.bantamdell.com

OPM   10 9 8 7 6 5 4 3 2 1

Dedication

To my editor, Shauna Summers, who obviously has the patience of a saint. Thank you!

To my phenomenal agent, Deidre Knight, who puts up with my neuroses and loves me anyway.

To Mo, a wonderful friend, whose research materials for this book were incredibly helpful. Thanks so much for sending that huge package from Australia!

To my fellow Bantam babes, Lara Adrian and Sydney Croft, thank you for the cheerleading, for the countless emails back and forth, and for always giving me something to laugh about. It's wonderful to have friends to angst with.

As always, to the BB's—Angie, Shan, Mandy, and Mel—can't get through the day without you.

And to Charlie—thank you for your willingness to discuss plot and action scenes, and for always giving me a strong shoulder to lean on. Love you, babe.

Hunting the Demon

Chapter One

Nic Diavolo stood in the dark place, hundreds of clawed hands reaching for him. They tore at his clothes, the creatures' voices like a cacophony of humming bees. Now the buzzing grew louder, a chant of triumph as they surrounded him.

They'd finally won. All these years the monsters had chased him, and he had always run. Run as hard as he could, slipping and falling, but he'd stayed ahead of them. Always escaped.

This time, he had slowed down. Stopped. Turned and let them catch up, watched as five became ten. Then twenty-five. Then finally there were a hundred or more of the creatures. Horrifying in appearance, with their red eyes and long fangs, their dirty, clawlike fingernails reaching for him.

When they touched him, he expected to scream.

This was it. The moment he had spent a lifetime fearing.

Their nails raked over his skin. He shuddered at the first touch, revulsion and dread filling him.

But they didn't shred him to pieces, didn't sink their dripping talons into his flesh, didn't growl as if they wanted to tear him apart.

They stared at him in awe, stroked him with reverence, bowed their heads.

As if he was their king.

At that moment, Nic realized something monumental.

He felt no fear.

And that was the most frightening thing of all.

Take your place.

He heard the voice, but didn't understand, couldn't see anyone around him but the creatures.

You're home, son.

Recognition struck. It was his father. But Nic was confused, didn't comprehend the command.

These are your people, Dominic. You belong to them, and they to you.

Nic shook his head. Something wasn't right. He didn't belong here, with these creatures.

"Dad?"

All he heard was soft laughter.

"Dad!"

The laughter faded, and he was once again alone with the beasts. They beseeched him wordlessly with their groping hands, their mumbled adoration. They closed in and he felt suffocated, unable to breathe as they pressed against him.

No! He didn't want this. He wanted answers, god-dammit.

"Dad! Where are you?"

The shrill alarm blasted Nic into an upright position. Covered with sweat, his heart hammering his ribs, he slammed his hands onto the mattress and blinked against the darkness, fighting for breath.

What. The. Fuck. Disoriented and shaking, he struggled for time and place.

His bedroom at the house in Sydney. No monsters.

Just the dream.

Man, that was some weird shit.

Constantly the same. Okay, maybe this one wasn't exactly like the others. But still a theme similar to the rest. Monsters, and him, and wandering around in the dark in search of . . . something. Seemed to be every night lately. Would they ever end?

He leaned toward the nightstand and punched the button, watching the slow crawl of the drapes as they opened, revealing a semicircle of floor-to-ceiling windows connecting him with the outside world again. With reality. It was still dark outside, but at least he had the comfort of the lights in the harbor, boats in the water, real things.

Sydney was alive and breathing, even at five in the morning. And that was good enough for now. Sunrise would come soon, banishing the last vestiges of the dream from the recesses of his mind.

He rubbed his temples, sucked in air, and shook off the confusion. So he had dreams. So what? Too much partying is what he attributed it to. And not enough sleep. In every respect, Nic was normal. Healthy as could be for a thirty-three-year-old male.

Right.

"Fucking freak of nature is what you are," he mumbled as he slid out of bed and grabbed his board shorts.

The waves were supposed to be kick-ass right now. It was the only lure that would have brought him home. Not that anyone was here anyway. His father wasn't, which was typical. And even if he had been here, he wouldn't have noticed Nic if he'd paraded naked into the kitchen with a girl under each arm.

He smirked at the shock value of that visual. He might have to try that sometime to see if it got a reaction from his dad or his uncle Bart.

Probably wouldn't.

With a loud yawn, he stretched, then slid into his shorts and white nylon shirt, went into the bathroom to brush his teeth, ran his fingers through his hair, and splashed water on his face, hoping to shake off the nightmare.

One would think he'd downed enough booze at the club last night to afford a dreamless sleep. But oh, no. Sometimes he was lucky enough to remember.

Or cursed. He wished he couldn't recall the dreams with such clarity.

The dreams terrified him. And he was too damned old to be scared of monsters in the dark.

As he came out of the bathroom, the first line of

dawn slipped above the horizon. He grinned, adrenaline pumping blood into his booze-soaked veins.

Time to catch a wave.

And forget about monsters.

Shay Pearson drummed her fingers on the kitchen tabletop of the small house where she and the rest of the demon hunters had been housed for over a month. They'd been plotting and waiting, plotting and waiting. Talking and planning was tiresome. She was ready to get out there and get the job done. The time for all this strategizing was over, at least in her mind.

Try telling that to Lou. He was big on the scheming thing, on making sure there was a plan.

Whatever. This was the reason why she wasn't the one in charge. If it were up to her she'd charge out there on the beach, grab Nic, and haul him off. She still didn't understand why they couldn't do just that. Other than the whole kidnapping-in-public thing.

But if Dominic Diavolo, aka "Nic," was a danger—was a demon—then wouldn't it be better to snatch him now, before he did something...demonic?

"Okay, so we've determined Nic's daily routine." Nic's brother, Derek, rounded the table and pointed to the whiteboard they'd set up. They'd marked routes from Nic's house to the beach to the nightclubs—everywhere Nic had been going for the past month since they'd tracked him down in Sydney. "Which really isn't much so far. He gets up, he drives to the beach, and he surfs with friends for several hours. Then he goes back to the house and stays there until dark, when he typically heads out to one of the Sydney night spots to party."

"And, man, does he know how to party." Punk dragged his hand through his spiky hair and yawned. "The bastard is running us ragged."

Derek grinned. "Yeah, like you hate hanging out in bars."

Punk shrugged. "A man's gotta do what a man's gotta do."

Lou stepped up next to Derek and put up his hands. "It's important to remember that we have two main objectives here. First, to figure out what Nic is up to, and whether or not he's part of the Sons of Darkness. If so, how deep into the demon realm is he?"

"And do we kill him if he is?" Ryder asked, his gaze shooting to Derek.

It was a valid question, Shay thought, though a delicate one. Derek was the right-hand man to Lou, a Keeper of the Light, the prime nemesis to the Sons of Darkness, the demons. Derek was also Nic's brother. Derek was half demon, which meant so was Nic. Derek controlled the dark half of himself. But they didn't know yet about Nic, since he'd been kidnapped by their father when he was just a child. Whether Nic was a good guy or a bad guy hadn't yet been determined.

That was their mission here in Australia.

Derek shrugged in reply to Ryder's question. "I don't know the answer to that until I see Nic for myself and gauge the level of his involvement with the Sons of Darkness."

"I know you all want answers now, but we don't have them yet," Lou added. "You'll just have to be patient awhile longer."

Shay knew she wasn't the only impatient one here. Tensions were high—had been that way since they'd arrived here a month ago.

That's how she, how all the hunters, came to be involved in all this. All of their mothers had been kidnapped by demons, used to make half demons. Except for Derek, of course. His father, Ben, was a Lord of the Sons of Darkness, only Derek hadn't known that until they'd run into Ben on the island recently. And Derek and Gina had killed him. That's when they had discovered that Nic—Dominic, Derek's brother—was still alive. Ben had taken Nic when he was eight years old, and Derek had thought all these years that Nic was dead. Now the hunters had to figure out just how much demon lived inside Nic.

What a mess. But it had strengthened all of them, this knowledge about their mothers, the demons' involvement in all their lives. It gave them resolve to fight, to change their lives and become hunters. To want to battle the demons and ensure the Realm of Light came out victorious.

"We're with you, Lou," Shay said. "Though patience isn't easy for any of us, especially after being holed up together in this tiny little house for a month."

"The ocean view has been really spectacular," Mandy added with a wide grin.

"So has the eye candy from the window," Ryder added.

"And the bar," Punk said.

Shay rolled her eyes. She just wanted out of the house. Some of the guys had taken turns hanging out at the clubs Nic frequented at night. She'd been stuck inside for the better part of a month. Oh, sure, there was a pool and a nice view that came with the house, but something more than that called to her. Some*one*. A pull that she couldn't—wouldn't—talk about, not even with her fellow demon hunters. She just had to figure out how to be the one to get in on this.

"Let's get our heads back in the game," Derek warned. "We have a lot to do."

"Right," Lou said. "Because as I was saying, we have two objectives here. One is Nic. The other is the black diamond. We have to find it before the Sons of Darkness do."

The black diamond. Just the name of it made Shay shiver, though she didn't know whether it was in fear or excitement. The black diamond was some kind of key that the Realm of Light had uncovered after they arrived in Australia, and it was connected to the Sons of Darkness. The Realm knew it was important to the demons, a kind of magical element that was to be used to empower them. The Realm of Light wanted to get to it first, because they felt if the Sons of Darkness managed to uncover and use it, it did not bode well for the future of the Realm of Light and the demon hunters.

"Any clues on that yet?" Shay asked.

"Yes, as a matter of fact. The Realm of Light feels that Diavolo Diamonds is the key to the black diamond. After all, Ben—Derek and Nic's father—was the head of Diavolo Diamonds. As Ben's heir, Nic stands to inherit the bulk of the Diavolo fortune, which includes major stock ownership in Diavolo Diamonds."

"We think the Diavolo mine might be the location of the black diamond. What better place to hunt it down than in the middle of a mine owned by one of the Lords of the Sons of Darkness?" Derek added.

Shay nodded. "Makes sense. I've been studying the research you gathered on Diavolo Diamonds. The mine is rather extensive. They could have been mining for years and not found the black diamond yet. It could even be located on the outskirts of the mine property itself."

"Exactly," Derek said. "Which makes it imperative we get started on our mission. We have to figure out what Nic knows, how much of the demon blood is within him, and if we can pull his loyalties to our side. If we can, then maybe he can help us get to the black diamond before the Sons of Darkness find it."

"And if we can't? What do we do with Nic if we can't get him to come to our side?"

Shay's gaze shot to Ryder. She supposed someone had to ask the question.

"Then I'll take care of him," Derek shot back.

Shay's heart squeezed. Derek had been without his

brother for over twenty-five years. Now he'd found him again, his only tie left to his blood family. To have to eliminate Nic would destroy him. But if Nic was evil, Derek would do what was necessary to protect the Realm of Light.

Gina laced her fingers with Derek's, the love in her eyes evident as she looked up at him. "It won't come to that. I know it won't."

"Let's hope not," Derek said. "In the meantime, we need a plan."

Finally, her chance. Shay had to get to Nic and soon, had to see him, touch him, find out if what she'd been feeling was real.

"I have an idea."

All eyes turned to her.

Chapter Two

He stepped out of the waves like the god Poseidon, at home in his element. Drenched, bronzed, his shorts riding low on his hips showcasing lean six-pack abs, the sculpted body of a man who worked hard at his sport. There wasn't an ounce of fat on him.

His sun-tipped brown hair was cut short and spiked up in all directions as he shook the salt spray from it with a wild twist of his head. Shay held her breath, wondering if the shorts balancing precariously on his slim hips would drop to his ankles.

No such luck. The pictures she'd seen of him hadn't done him justice. Though the photographs showed a charming, handsome man, up close he was just devastating. She exhaled, reminding herself why she was here.

She was bait. Lou and Derek had jumped on her suggestion and allowed her to be the front man, er, woman, on the mission. So now that she'd opened her mouth and volunteered, she had to get the job done. She was equal parts excited and terrified at what would happen when they met, already knowing she was going to feel the telltale zing. She'd been experiencing it for weeks, just glimpsing him from afar.

Hard to believe the water god making his way to the beach, surfboard in his hands, was her quarry. As far as assignments went, this one was pretty damn good-looking.

She licked her lips and tipped her sunglasses down over the bridge of her nose, wishing her knees would stop knocking. She wasn't very good at this stealth stuff. Her heart was pounding, her palms were sweating, and she hoped to God she remembered how to flirt. It had been a really long time. She was out of practice.

So here she stood on a secluded beach in Sydney, Australia, just past dawn, while the most gorgeous man she'd ever laid eyes on strolled out of the ocean toward her.

When he hit the sandy beach he caught sight of her. Positioning herself against the shack where he'd stored his gear, she struck the most seductively casual pose she could manage without looking obvious and smiled as he approached.

"Mornin'," she said.

"G'day," he shot back, tilting his head to size her up.

Oh, that accent. She melted into the sand under his careful perusal of her, and suddenly felt damn near naked in her all-too-tiny bikini, wishing she'd worn a cover-up. But that would hide the lure, wouldn't it? Ugh.

She much preferred killing demons to flirting with gorgeous men.

C'mon, Shay. You're a southern girl. You were born to flirt.

Digging her toes in the sand, she tossed her head toward the ocean. "You looked great out there."

His quick grin showed off white, even teeth. "You surf?"

"A little. Not as good as you."

"You're not from here, are you?"

"My southern drawl gave me away, didn't it? Not quite Aussie."

With a laugh, he said, "No, not quite." He leaned his board against the shack and held out his hand. "Nic Diavolo."

"Shay Pearson." She slipped her hand in his and tried not to shudder. *Zing.* There it was, the rush, the heat, the visions.

Darkness. Nic surrounded by demons, all grasping at him, stroking his feet, treating him like he was their god. She sensed evil and fear, though she didn't know if the fear was coming from Nic, or somewhere else.

As soon as it appeared, it was gone.

"You cold?" he asked, shaking her out of the vision.

She blinked and shook her head. "Maybe a little."

"Get out of the shade and into the sun. It's a little chilly in the mornings." He took her hand and led her onto the beach, into the warm sand and sunshine. Shay used the time to file away the psychic vision that had grabbed hold of her, the one she had known she was going to have as soon as she touched him.

She'd already had visions about him, but none that strong. She knew touching him would bring it out, knew there'd be a connection.

The damn curse, anyway. She hated it. It revealed too much. Things she didn't want to know.

Okay, she always hated it. Who the hell would think being a little psychic was a gift?

"Better now?"

She focused on his face and gave him a bright smile, remembering why she was out here. "Absolutely. Thank you."

God, she used to have such a weakness for good-looking men. And damn, was Nic a prime example of perfection. Piercing blue eyes the same color as the ocean, a square jaw, a straight nose, and a body she could spend days and nights exploring.

And he might just be a demon, Shay. Don't forget that.

Oh, yeah. She had forgotten. Just for a second she had simply enjoyed the company of a delectable hunk of beefcake. When was the last time that had happened?

Too long. Before demons and an utter change in her lifestyle.

Back to work.

"So what are you doing in Sydney, Shay Pearson?"

"Right now? Watching you surf. And hoping I could finagle a lesson or two out of you. I've heard you're the best out here."

He tilted his head to the side and grinned. Oh, man, that was sexy.

"The best, huh?"

"That's what I've heard from the locals around here."

"Are you on vacation?"

"Yes. Enjoying a month in Australia. These waves are spectacular."

"They have been, yeah. Want to come play with me for a while?"

She resisted the urge to drool. Play with him? Oh, yeah. She'd love to play with him. But he'd just taken the bait. "If you mean do I want to surf with you, the answer is absolutely yes. I'd love to. If I wouldn't be imposing."

"Nah, not at all. I just came up for a breather and a quick drink, then was going back to it. I'd be more than happy to give a pretty sheila like you a few lessons."

The bio on him being popular with the women wasn't exaggerated. He was gorgeous; his voice alone made her wet, and she already wanted to lick her way up and down his chiseled abs. To say nothing of wanting to explore what was underneath his board shorts.

Yeah, he was good, all right. Now she had to spend some time with him, earn his trust, and get him to open up to her. She had two days, max. Two days to figure out the vibes she was getting from him and what they meant. The visions were bizarre—different from any others she'd gotten before. They were more surreal, not concrete like something was about to happen. Or at least she hoped what she'd seen wasn't real.

"You warm enough now?" he asked.

"Yes. Very." She dug her toes in the sand.

"Let's go surfing then. You got a board?"

"Over there." She thumbed behind her toward the shack.

"Go grab it and I'll meet you at the water's edge."

She nodded and turned toward the shack, taking a quick glance at the tiny white house nestled within the trees on the hillside. She knew the demon hunters were watching her interact with Nic, and felt a little self-conscious about it, but shrugged it off.

She was doing her job, and nothing more. As far as the visions . . . no one needed to know about those. She'd never told anyone about them, not even Lou and Derek or the other hunters. And she never would.

They were her secret to live with.

Nic relaxed on his board, staying seated and keeping an eye on Shay as she crested a small wave in front of him.

She was pretty good for a novice. A few short hours and she was up and riding comfortably. She had no fear; she relaxed, listened to his instructions, and then put them into play, which was why she got up so easily.

And he had a great view of her ass and legs from where he sat, riding the wave into shore.

Tanned and blond with great curves, she was the kind of woman who fired his jets. And it had been a long damn time since any woman had done that. In fact, he'd sworn off women over a year ago and done the celibacy thing—until Shay's sweet smile and the touch of her hand had sent a shockwave through his body. He wasn't much for karma and destiny or any of that other voo-doo kind of shit, but he knew chemistry, and he definitely felt it with Shay.

They'd been surfing for several hours now, and she was easy to be around. She wasn't flirtatious, just friendly. No expectations other than surfing. She laughed easily, didn't ask him probing questions, and seemed to have no expectations other than having him teach her the basics of riding the waves.

That he could handle. Beyond that? Well, he'd see. But he wasn't ready to let go of her just yet, which surprised him, because he'd lost the taste for the wild life with women a long time ago. Oh, he still hung out at the bars with his mates, but that was as far as it went. He didn't bring women home, and sex was out of the question.

He'd grown tired of the merry-go-round, and needed a mental and physical break from women.

At least until Shay.

He grabbed his board and stepped onto the beach. She had stabbed her board into the sand and was wringing out her hair.

"Did you see that?" she asked, her body visibly trembling with excitement. "Did you see that wave?"

He grinned. "I did. You rocked it."

She laughed. "I did, didn't I? Thank you so much. The pointers you gave were so helpful."

"You have a natural ability, you're coordinated, and you aren't afraid to dump. That's half the battle."

She blew out a breath. "Well, I can't tell you how

much I appreciate this." She held out her hand. "Thank you, Nic."

He slipped his hand in hers and frowned. "Are you leaving?"

"I don't want to take up any more of your time. I'm sure you have things to do."

"I do. I'm starving. Surfing works up an appetite."

"Yes, it does. I'm hungry, too. That's why I figured it was time to quit."

"You want to grab a bite to eat?"

She hesitated for a second. "Uh, sure. If you'd like. But I'm buying. It's the least I can do."

Damn. Didn't she know who he was? No woman ever offered to buy him a meal. She really was unusual. "Sure. You pick the place."

"Oh, I'm not that familiar with what's around here. How about you choose?"

"Sure. If you don't mind a short drive, there's a great restaurant with an incredible view."

Again the hesitation. Her gaze darted toward the hills, then back at him. "Okay."

They stowed their boards on the top of his SUV, Shay grabbed her cover-up, and they were off, heading toward an out-of-the-way restaurant that had the best seafood in the city. Not fancy or expensive, which was probably why he liked it. No pretension, and no one treated him any differently from the average surfer bum off the beach.

They ate fish and chips outside, and talked.

"So where are you from, Shay?"

"Georgia."

"Are you here in Sydney with your family or friends?"

She grabbed a chip with her fingers and popped it in her mouth. He liked to watch her eat. She did it with gusto, unlike the women he usually hung around with, who hardly ever ate anything. "No. By myself."

He arched a brow. "Really."

She grinned. "Yeah. Why? Is that a problem?"

"Not really. It's just quite a distance for a woman to travel on her own."

She snorted. "I'm a big girl. I can handle it. I've been on my own for a long time. I'm used to it."

"You're lucky." He wished he was on his own. There were always too many people watching over him, trying to keep him in line and tracking his whereabouts. Not that it did them much good, since he'd always done exactly what he wanted to.

She sipped her iced tea and tilted her head. "Why am I lucky?"

"That you don't have anyone to answer to."

"And you do?"

"Yes and no."

She laughed. "Ohhh, cryptic, are we? I like a little mystery in a man."

And he liked her. Mainly because he really didn't think she had any idea who he was, how much money he had, or what his last name meant. That was refreshing; she knew him only from the locals and only because of his surfing ability. Most women he met targeted the Diavolo money, so he never really knew if they gave a shit about him as a person or not.

Then again, he never really cared about them, either, so it was mutually beneficial. He got what he wanted out of the deal, and so did they.

Nothing.

No wonder he'd stopped playing the game, for a while, anyway.

He might want to start playing again. But there was another reason he'd stayed away from women for so long.

The dreams. They'd grown darker and more frequent, had started wrapping around his conscious thoughts.

He even thought he'd seen those monsters in his own father's house, in the cellars.

There was something seriously fucked-up about that. Enough that it spooked him into keeping his distance from women. He was afraid of what was inside his mind, of what he was seeing and feeling.

But it had just been that one time, and it had never happened again. Probably a hangover, or the remnants of one of his stupid nightmares. He'd had them so long he'd probably started sleepwalking, or had narcolepsy and was falling asleep and dreaming in the daytime, and that's why he thought he'd seen monsters in the basement talking to his dad.

Because, obviously, that hadn't happened. That was the stuff of kid nightmares, and he was long past childhood. It was time to blow it off and start living again. And what better way to get back in the game than with the vivacious blonde across the table from him?

They finished eating and sat back, quietly enjoying the surf and the beachgoers.

"I'm jealous you get to live this life every day," Shay said, propping her feet up on the wooden railing.

"I don't do this every day."

She turned her head. "Oh. For some reason I thought you were a professional surfer."

He laughed. "I wish. I'm not that good."

"I thought you were."

"You're a novice. You don't know the difference."

She sniffed and lifted her chin. "I rode a huge wave, I'll have you know."

"It was a tiny wave."

"Okay, maybe it was." She laughed. "But I didn't fall off."

"Hey, you did great for a beginner. I was impressed."

She grinned. "Thanks. And I still think you're awesome. I've been sitting on the beach watching you for days. If you don't surf for a living, you should. What do you do?"

"This and that. Business stuff."

She squinted. "More mystery. Do you want me to guess or are you some kind of secret agent and you'll have to kill me if you tell me?"

God, she made him laugh. Genuine, unaffected laughter. "Not a secret agent, trust me. Just an average, run-of-the-mill business guy. I run a company with my father."

"Oh, the family business. How fun. I guess."

"Not really. Pretty boring. I try to stay away from it as much as possible. I'd rather be physical."

"Hence the surfing."

"Right."

"What kind of business is it?"

He supposed if he spent any time with Shay at all she was going to find out eventually, so he might as well tell her. He'd find out soon enough if she was the gold-digger type. "Diamonds. We own Diavolo Diamonds. Ever heard of them?"

"Oh, so you own a jewelry store?"

He snorted at that. "Uh, no. We own a diamond mine."

Shay resisted the urge to jump out of the chair and pump her fist. Bingo! Now they were getting somewhere, though she'd thoroughly enjoyed bantering with Nic.

He'd told her who he was and about the mine. Which meant he trusted her, at least a little. This was a very good thing. The next step was gaining even more of his trust.

She widened her eyes and feigned shock. "Are you serious? A diamond mine? Holy crap."

"Yeah."

He looked disappointed that he'd told her. She'd have to fix that.

"I'll bet that keeps you busy. How do you find time to do the fun things like surfing?"

"I'm in corporate sales, so I travel a lot. It allows me freedom to do the other things I enjoy, like surfing."

"Sales, huh? So you don't get to play with the diamonds in the mines?"

"Uh, no."

"Too bad. I imagine unearthing raw diamonds would be a thrill."

"Not quite. The mines are filthy, dark, and dirty. The process is lengthy and tedious from start to finish."

"I can't even imagine all that goes into mining diamonds. I'll bet it's fascinating."

"It is. The rough diamonds aren't pretty at all. Nothing like what you see at the jewelry stores."

"I'd love to learn about it sometime."

He arched a brow, his eyes narrowing. "Like diamonds, do you?"

She shrugged. "Not really. I'm not a flashy stones kind of girl. To be honest, I don't even wear jewelry." To prove her point, she held out her fingers. "See? Not a ring in sight." Then she pulled her hair behind her ears. "Not even earrings."

"Why?"

"I don't know. I guess I prefer precious stones on other things, not on me."

"What other things?"

"Daggers. I collect them." She had to give him a piece of her history since he'd given her information about himself.

"That's one hell of a hobby. Most women I've known collect knickknacks or antiques or pottery."

"I got interested in them in college when I took a course on ancient civilizations. My professor was into daggers; she showed me her collection, and I was hooked. I have a few of my own now, though not nearly as many as she had. They're like my security blanket. I always carry a few with me."

"Interesting protection. You know how to use them?"

She grinned. "You bet I do."

"You are one fascinating woman, Shay Pearson."

She cast him a half smile. "You have no idea, Nic Diavolo."

He leaned forward in the chair. "I'd like to get more of an idea. Come home with me."

Uh, okay. Now that she hadn't expected.

Chapter Three

"Come home with you?" Shay knew the objective was to get close to Nic and earn his trust. She supposed getting an invite to his house was about as close as she could get. But how much closer?

"I just want to get to know you better. I don't mean anything nefarious by the invite. I'm not a secret agent, remember?"

She laughed. "Not a secret agent. Got it."

"I have a big house. We could hang out by the pool and talk."

"I'd love to go to your place. I was hoping we could...continue our conversation. I like spending time with you."

She liked it for more reasons than just the job she was doing, too. Nic was engaging, beautiful to look at, and her vibes had been zinging for hours now, which was both disturbing and fascinating.

But the main part was her job and she had to remember that. The vibes were just a troubling add-on that she had to figure out.

Like why him and why now? It wasn't as if she got the sensations from just anyone.

Nic stood and pulled out his wallet. "Ready to go?"

Shay put a hand on his wrist, feeling a low hum through her body at the touch. She blocked any visuals—she couldn't handle them right now. "I said I'd buy, remember?"

His brows raised. "So you did."

She paid and they climbed into his SUV. "I'll drop you at your car and you can follow me."

Of course she already knew where he lived, but when he let her off, she got into the car and followed behind him. The Diavolo mansion was surrounded by tall black privacy gates, warning signs plastered on the front making it very clear that the property was secure and well guarded. The main double gates opened as he approached, and he drove through, Shay following and smiling at the guards in the shack. They didn't smile back.

They didn't look like demons, either.

What did she expect? Gruesome hybrid demons guarding the gates of Hell at the Diavolo mansion?

She snorted at her wayward imagination.

They snaked through a twisted path lined with tall trees that shadowed menacingly over the road as if in preparation for attack.

How appropriate, given who owned the house.

Finally, they broke through the trees and faced a sun-lit home.

Not really a home, since it was as big as a freakin' hotel. Four stories tall and equally as wide, the driveway alone constituted a parking lot. Nic pulled up in front of the house and Shay pulled behind him.

"Uh, wow," she said as she exited her car. "Nice house."

He rolled his eyes. "Yeah, right. It's a goddamn mausoleum. My dad likes that ostentatious shit."

She resisted the urge to laugh and followed him up the steps. Two men ran outside and nodded to Nic, who tossed them his keys.

"They'll park your car in the garage," he said. "Give them your keys."

She handed them over, not really liking the idea of being unaware of the location of her vehicle, but not wanting to invite suspicion, either.

Once inside the house, she tried not to gape, but it was difficult considering the house was a showcase. Marble flooring, expansive view of the ocean, jeweled colors from the pillows to the rocks adorning the crystal bowls on the tables—she wondered if those were real gemstones. Fancy furnishings and everything polished and gleaming to perfection. She was afraid to move, certain her tennis shoes were tracking sand onto the floor.

The rooms were so huge her voice echoed when she uttered another "Wow."

Nic sidled her a glance. "I find it kind of cold, myself."

She tilted her head. "Why don't you get your own place, then?"

"Good question. Probably because I'm not here often enough, so staying at Dad's isn't that big a deal when I'm in town."

"I thought you worked in Sydney."

"This is where our corporate offices are, but I'm rarely here." He led her out onto the deck.

Now this she liked. The ocean waves crashed against the rocks below and the soft breeze blew through her hair. The smell of sweet roses trailing upward from the vines surrounding the deck was heavenly. Off to the side of the deck was an Olympic-size pool complete with attached hot tub, a slide, and a tall waterfall. It was breathtakingly beautiful.

"Rarely here, huh? More cryptic stuff," she said as she did a complete turnaround, surveying the area. "Are you sure you're not a spy?"

"Positive. Though if I was, would I really spill all my secrets to a virtual stranger?"

She hoped so. She was counting on it.

"Come on," he said, laughing. "I'll take you on a tour of the house."

The house was massive, and if Shay spent any amount of time there, she'd need a map to keep from getting lost. But she made mental notes. Living rooms and kitchens and the library were on the main floor, the bedrooms on the second floor. The third floor was used for offices, where Nic said his father and his uncle Bart did work at home, and the top floor was for staff quarters and use.

"I noticed a driveway going down when I pulled in. Is that the garage?" she asked as they took the staircase back to the main floor.

Nic nodded. "Garage and cellars."

Cellars. Interesting. She wondered what went on down there. "Don't suppose you have any diamond mines under the house, do you?"

"Uh, no. The mines aren't in Sydney. They're up in the northwest territory, clear across the continent. We just house our corporate offices here."

"Oh," she replied, playing dumb, since she knew exactly where the mines were located. "So do you get up to the mines at all?"

"Not that often. We have people in charge of them. I go up when I need to show them off to buyers. Fortunately it's not that often. Things run smoothly there."

She followed him into the kitchen where he stepped into a wine room.

"Whoa. Nice selection."

"White or red?"

"White. Not sweet."

"Good." He pulled a sauvignon blanc from the rack and grabbed two glasses from a cabinet, opened the bottle, and poured. Then he led her into the great room, where she could still hear the ocean waves through the open windows.

"So tell me about diamond sales. What are you in charge of?"

His half smile was devastating to her senses. He took a swallow of wine. "Global sales. Large accounts."

She nodded. "Do you get to handle the diamonds yourself, take them around with you and show them off, or do any actual mining?"

"I've done it all at one time or another."

"How fun."

"Not really. Like I said, it's dusty and dirty and the mines are dark and dank."

"Still, finding diamonds is probably thrilling."

"Most of the mining is automated. It's not pickaxes and shovels like mining of old."

She frowned. "So no hands-on?" That could be a problem based on what they were after.

"There's some, depending on the location. Smaller groups still do individual mining outside the main mine if they feel there's something to go after. But no, most of it is automated now."

"I see." She leaned back and took a long swallow of the wine, wondering how that would affect their search for the black diamond.

"I think we've talked enough about me for a while. What do you do, Shay, when you aren't taking month-long vacations in Australia?"

"Me? Uh, I job-hop."

"Job-hop?"

"Yeah." She smiled behind her glass. "I'm still trying to figure out what I want to do when I grow up."

"You could surf."

She choked out a laugh and set the glass down. "That was funny."

"Okay, so maybe not."

She shook her head at his sly grin. "Definitely not. But I've tried damn near everything else. I won't even tell you how many majors I had in college."

"Try me."

"Eight."

He didn't seem at all shocked. "Some people like learning."

"Yeah, well, my reasons were a little different than just my love of education. I was . . . unfocused."

"Because?"

"My dad died; I started college, couldn't decide what I wanted to do, so I just rambled along and kept switching majors, figuring I'd eventually find something to fall in love with."

"I'm sorry you lost your dad. That must have been rough."

"Thank you." A topic she wasn't about to get into. It wasn't necessary to her mission.

"And did you?"

"Did I what?"

"Fall in love with something?"

She shook her head. "No." And truthfully, she was still feeling her way, even though she'd stumbled onto the demon hunters and the Realm of Light. She knew she fit with the hunters, that she was supposed to be there. They were her family now. But she wasn't yet settled. Something was missing. She'd made a commitment to the Realm. She was a hunter and that wouldn't change.

Still, there was more. She just didn't know what that was yet.

"You have time. That's why I like the job I have. It gives me enough free time to focus on other things, like surfing."

She shifted sideways in the chair so she was looking at him instead of the water. "So you don't love your career?"

He let out a short laugh. "I'm not one to get stuck in an office twenty-four/seven. That's why I chose global sales. There are too many other things in life I want to do, and my dad doesn't really need me around."

There was an edge to his statement that Shay found curious. Did that mean Nic and his father weren't tight? It begged further exploring.

"Is your father here at the house now?" She already knew the answer. Nic's father was dead. The demon hunters had killed him. But did Nic know that yet?

"No. He's sort of missing right now."

She leaned forward, her eyes widening. "Missing? Oh, my God, Nic. What happened?"

He shrugged. "It's not that kind of missing. He's been out of the country for a couple months, but he usually checks in and he hasn't. Which doesn't really mean anything. He often goes off on treks into far reaches and doesn't bother to call in."

Did Nic really believe that, or was he worried about

his dad? Since he didn't know the truth about his father, Shay felt bad for him. He had to be worried, whether he wanted to admit it or not.

"Do you have people out searching for him?"

"I don't. My uncle Bart said he's trying to track him down." At her look of concern, he took her hands in his. There was that zing again. "It's really okay. I shouldn't even have mentioned it. He'll turn up. He always does."

He won't this time, Nic. And she felt sorry. Not for Ben, one of the Sons of Darkness, who deserved to die. But for Nic, because there was so much he needed to know.

And these revelations weren't going to be easy for him. But the sooner they got to it, the better for Nic. Which meant she needed to step this up so the Realm of Light could get to doing their job, and Nic could be brought into the fold.

If that was the way things were destined to go.

She glanced inside the house. "So where's your uncle? Does he live here, too?"

Nic nodded. "Yeah, but I have no idea where he is. The nice thing about the house being so big is we don't run into each other a lot."

So was Nic's uncle a demon, too? He would almost have to be if he was related by blood to Ben. Then again, Shay didn't yet fully understand all the inner workings of the Sons of Darkness.

She squeezed his hand. "I hope you locate your dad soon." God, she felt a stab of guilt at the lie.

"Thanks."

He slid his hand from hers and Shay felt a sudden chill as his warmth left her.

Strange. Really damn strange. And she'd already experienced her fill of the bizarre in the past couple months.

"So what do you say to a swim and lounge by the pool?"

She grinned. "Sounds great."

"Then maybe later we can have dinner and drinks? Or would you rather go out somewhere?"

She looked down at her cover-up. "I'd need different clothes. I can't hang out in this all day."

Heat flushed her body as Nic perused her intently with a sideways glance, then fixed his gaze on her face. "You look pretty damn good to me like that. But I understand. We can go out. I'll drop you off at your place so you can change."

That wasn't going to work. She needed a little more time with him. "I have clothes in a bag in my car. Unless you want to go out."

"No, that's perfect. I'll have Steve bring your bag up from your car. Is it in the trunk?"

She nodded and followed him out to the pool.

So she'd bought a little more time to figure out if she could bring about any changes within him, before the hunters had to reveal everything. Because once they grabbed him, he'd clam up.

They wasted away the remainder of the afternoon by the pool, swimming and lying about. Nic didn't say anything more, just seemed content to laze around and do nothing. She didn't want to press him and raise his suspicions, so she went with it. One of the servants brought them cocktails and snacks. A girl could get used to this decadent lifestyle. What an incredible lure. No wonder Nic had always been surrounded by women—who wouldn't want to be indulged like this?

By the time the sun shifted, she was feeling like a water-soaked prune. She flipped over on the pool float to face Nic.

He was lying on his back with his arm flung over his face. Quite possibly he could be sleeping. She studied his washboard abs, the defined yet lean muscles of his arms and legs. She was close enough to see the fine golden hairs on his thighs.

She swallowed, chastising herself for ogling him. But damn, he had one hell of a body. And when she touched him, something happened. Something beyond her visions. A primal, instant chemistry that had nothing to do with weird psychic phenomena and everything to do with man/woman attraction.

"I need to take a shower," she said.

He removed his arm and lifted his head. "Aren't you wet enough already?"

She grinned and splashed water at him. "I'm on the pool float and perfectly dry."

His eyes lit up when he gave her a wicked smile. He flipped over into the water. She looked down, but couldn't see him.

Until he turned her float over and she went crashing into the pool. She came up sputtering, dragging her wet hair out of her eyes. He was right in front of her.

"Now you're plenty wet," he teased.

She laughed and pushed at his chest, then swam away. But he was on her in seconds, wrapping one arm around her middle and hauling her up to prevent further escape. She squealed, enjoying the play. He turned her around to face him, pinning her between his rock-hard body and the side of the pool.

Heat exploded inside her, a meltdown of sensation as he pressed full-on against her. Breasts against chest, hips against hips, thighs against thighs. Her internal electricity was going haywire. She stared into eyes so blue she couldn't breathe.

She wanted to say something, but couldn't. She waited for him to say something funny, to crack a joke.

He didn't. There wasn't even a smile on his face. Just hot, hungry intent.

He leaned in, swept his mouth against hers and heat exploded into an inferno. With just the softest touch of his lips, she caught her breath, unprepared for the sensations. Physical and psychic, they wrapped around her like a vortex of lightning and energy.

Stars burst behind her eyes, molten lava settling between her legs as he pressed up closer against her, pinning her with everything hard about him. And everything about him was hard, oh-my-God, was it ever. He breathed into her, slid his tongue inside her mouth, and she gave up trying to fight whatever was assaulting her from the inside out. This was magic and she was going to have more of it.

She pushed off the bottom of the pool and wrapped

her legs around him, fitting herself closer. When her sex hit the target point, she moaned against his eagerly searching lips. Her reward—a hard groan from Nic and a deepening intensity of his kiss. He ground his lips against hers in the same maddening way he rubbed his erection against the pulsing center of her.

Passion had never flared out of control for Shay. She had never wanted so much so fast before, had never completely lost her mind or her senses in this way. This was unexpected, had caught her unprepared. A small part of her was aware that this wasn't in the game plan, but that part was weak, soon gone in a puff of smoke and erased.

She craved. Her sex drive was in charge now and she was a goner, tangling her hands in the thick spikes of Nic's hair. She lifted her hips, surging forward to embrace more of that astounding pleasure.

The buoyancy of the water kept them apart. She squeezed her legs around him, wanting him close. He pushed forward, scraping her back on the side of the pool wall. She didn't care, because he was feasting on her mouth, dipping between her lips and taking her with an urgency that spoke of wild desire, untamed need, an animal hunger she'd never experienced but wanted.

She needed a man to want her that desperately—so much that he growled deep in his throat, one hand sliding under the water to dig into the soft flesh of her hip in order to draw her closer, while at the same time rocking against her until she whimpered her desire for him against his mouth.

He was pulling at her, clenching her, driving his tongue deeply inside her mouth. He moved one hand upward until he found her breast, then pulled the material aside to palm her nipple. Shay gasped for breath. The edge of a vision pounded at her psyche, but she held it at bay. She wouldn't let it in, didn't want anything to disrupt this moment.

Not when Nic had hold of her like he was desperate to be inside her. His fingers were doing wild things to her nipple—exquisite sensation shooting straight to her core—while the rest of him pushed against her, tight, gripping her, and pushing with almost violent force. Oh, no. She wasn't going to stop this. The sensation was like having a front-row seat on a runaway train, a high-speed roller-coaster ride without brakes, and she wanted to take it right off the cliff and into the abyss.

But he suddenly stopped, tore his mouth away, and rested his forehead against hers. He pulled his hand away from her breast and righted her clothing.

His breathing was harsh, as was hers, as she fought to come back to some semblance of reality. Because she didn't know where she'd been in the past few minutes, but it sure as hell hadn't been the real world.

She wanted to protest, to grab his head between her hands and make it go on, but she sensed his hesitation almost as remorse.

Did he regret kissing her?

He blew out a breath. "I'm sorry. That got a little out of hand."

She tilted her head back and offered up a reassuring smile. "It was just a kiss, Nic."

"It was more than that."

Yeah, it was. But he couldn't have felt what she did. He didn't possess the curse that she did.

"It was just a kiss," she said again, wanting to temper any second thoughts he might have about spending time with her. She had to remember her mission, though she'd conveniently forgotten that when Nic had shoved his tongue in her mouth.

He nodded. "How about we shower now, and have some dinner?"

"Sure."

They climbed out of the pool and Shay shivered, though it was still quite warm outside. It was the separation, the lack of heat from his body that caused the goose bumps on her skin.

Nic led her upstairs to one of the guest rooms. Her bag was sitting on the bed.

"I'm just down the hall at the end. Let me know when you're done."

"Okay."

She turned to say something, but he shut the door behind him. With a sigh, she stepped into the bathroom and turned on the shower, peeling off her swimsuit and climbing in under the warm water.

She was shaking and kicked the water temp up, though she knew that wasn't the problem. Fighting the visions always did this to her. She slid down the wall and wrapped her arms around herself, allowing her body to settle, knowing it would pass after a few minutes.

Why had Nic pulled away? She knew from his response to her that he was invested in what they'd been doing, so what made him stop? He had the reputation for being a guy who really got into women, though that had somewhat changed in the past year according to the intelligence they'd gathered. He still went to clubs and hung out with his buddies, but he hadn't been seen with a woman on his arm for a long time.

Is that why he'd pulled back from her? And if so, why? Though she wasn't the type to push a man about what was going on in his head, in this instance she was going to have to. Because if Nic's hesitancy with her had to do with the demon inside him, that was crucial information.

Yeah, like that was the only reason she wanted to know. She could still taste him. Her body still pulsed all over from the feel of his hands on her.

And dammit, she wouldn't have stopped.

Once she got the shakes under control, she finished showering and dried off, then slipped on the top and short skirt she'd folded into her bag. She had spent so much time in camouflage gear the past couple months it felt good to dress like a girl again.

Even if the respite would be brief.

After she combed out her hair, she bagged her wet suit and headed down the hall, determined to gather some intel on Nic.

Time was running out, and there were things the hunters needed to know about him. The sun was setting; it was time for all the demons to come out.

Would the demon in Nic be coming out tonight?

Nic stared into the mirror and dragged his fingers through his wet hair, trying to calm down enough to face Shay again.

Darkness still filtered the edges of his mind. Like the dreams, only infringing on his conscious thoughts.

That was bad. Especially since it had happened with Shay.

Christ. Something had come over him when he kissed her. A driving, animal-like need to take her. This weird, possessive caveman mentality that drove him nearly to the brink of madness

He'd always been a little wild and intense with women, but it had been sprinkled with playfulness and fun. Nothing out of hand. With Shay it had been damned serious. And more than a little frightening, once he'd pulled back and figured out what he was doing.

Though she hadn't complained, thankfully. Then again, they hadn't gone too far yet. He'd withdrawn before he lost his mind completely.

Was he losing his mind?

Shit. Maybe he was. As if the fucking nightmares weren't bad enough, now he was going nuts in the daylight.

He turned at a soft tap at the door.

"Nic?"

Pulling on a shirt, he went to the door and opened it, his breath escaping in a rush.

Her hair fell in soft waves over her shoulders, still wet from her shower. She wore a little scrap of a skirt with a matching top that clung to her body. A body he'd wanted to explore with his hands, his mouth. A body he'd wanted to drive inside of until the hunger went away.

His cock stirred and he fought the urge compelling him. Oh, no. He wasn't going there again. He wasn't about to go round two with these demons battering him from the inside out.

With a rush of disappointment, he realized that after tonight he wasn't going to see Shay anymore. He couldn't handle being around a woman. Especially this woman. Not until he could figure out what was going on in his head.

He cast her a relaxed smile. "Let's go see about dinner."

Chapter Four

Shay was disappointed when Nic grabbed her bag and said he'd changed his mind, that he wanted to go out to eat. And that she could follow him so she wouldn't have to come back here afterward for her car.

She was being dumped.

Man, did that ever suck. Something was bothering him in a big way. They went to a restaurant overlooking the ocean, but he was quiet and withdrawn, hardly saying a word throughout dinner. Whatever information she thought she could drag out of him wasn't going to happen.

After the incident in the pool today he'd pulled away from her, both physically and emotionally.

Something scared him, but what?

She laid her hand over his. "Nic, something's wrong. What is it?"

He smiled. "Nothing's wrong. Probably just a little tired. I'm sorry I'm not good company tonight."

"You're fine company, and I don't require entertaining. I'm just worried that I might have said or done something to offend you."

He cupped his hands over hers and leaned forward. "You didn't do anything, okay? It's just me."

She didn't want to do it, but she had no choice. She opened her senses and let the visions in while he was touching her.

Darkness swirled around her. Scary darkness, a black void that blinded her. It was cold, so cold her teeth chattered. Nic stepped up behind her, his warmth like a blanket. He turned her to face him. He was the only light in the room. Where were they? She felt the evil surrounding them, trying to get at them, trying to get at Nic. They wanted him desperately.

She had to keep them away. But what could she do?

He bent down and kissed her, and it was just like earlier today. A rush of passion, sucking her into a vortex of hungry need. Nic was communicating his desperate need for her, as if only she could save him.

She felt the same desperation, knowing she had to have him, that she belonged to him, that if she didn't do this the monsters would get them both.

When he pulled back, his eyes were red, glowing in the darkness around them. Demon eyes. He smiled at her and said she belonged to him. Now she could see—demons all around them, on their knees, bowing to their king.

Nic was that king.

The strange thing was, she felt no fear.

"Shay? Are you listening?"

She blinked and the vision evaporated. "What? I'm sorry. What did you say?"

"I said I think we need to call it an early night if you don't mind. I have a headache."

"Oh. Oh, sure, I understand." Shit. That she hadn't counted on. Okay, time to think fast. "Can you give me a second? I need to use the restroom."

"Sure. I'll take care of the bill."

She stood, shaking off the vision, filing it away to study later. On her way out to her car she grabbed her phone and called Derek, letting him know she'd be bringing Nic back, that it was time. She tampered with the car to make sure it wouldn't start, then slipped back into the restaurant, meeting Nic at the table. He was signing the credit card slip and stood as she approached.

"I'm sorry to cut the night off early."

"Oh, that's no problem," she said. "I'm sorry your head hurts."

He shrugged. "Too much sun and fun today, probably."

She followed him outside and opened her car door, making sure to try the ignition before he got into his. She turned it and nothing happened. She cranked it again and nothing happened.

Nic frowned. "Pop the hood."

She did, stepping out with him and pasting on her own concerned look. "See anything?"

"No."

Thank God for the tip from Punk on how to make the car *not* start.

"I can call for a taxi back to my house."

He slammed the hood down. "I'll drive you home and have someone pick up your car tomorrow and fix it."

"That's not necessary."

"I want to."

"Okay. Thanks." She grabbed her bag and slid into his SUV, giving him directions to the house.

This was it. The no-turning-back point. Once they had him, everything was going to change for Nic. Everything between the two of them was going to change, too.

Shay felt a hard stab of regret. In about ten minutes Nic was going to hate her for deceiving him.

Nic was surprised at the house, well lit as they climbed the hill leading to its location. Though small, it was set off from the other houses in the area, with a stellar view of the beach.

"You stay there by yourself?"

"Yeah. A friend from college owns it and is letting me use it for the month."

"Hell of a deal. Prime property."

She grinned. "She's a great friend."

He pulled into the driveway and got out, then came around and opened Shay's door, walking with her to her front door.

Part of him didn't want this to be the last time he saw her. The other part of him couldn't wait to put some distance between them. He didn't want to endanger her, and being around him for too long could be hazardous to Shay.

"Would you mind stepping inside with me?" she asked. "I know it's kind of childish, but it's dark in there and it's still kind of unfamiliar territory. As long as you're here . . ."

He smiled and nodded. "Not at all."

She slipped the key in the lock and turned it, then stepped inside, flipping the switch.

"Well, damn. No power."

She moved inside and he followed, though she disappeared and it was damned difficult since his eyes hadn't adjusted, all the shades were closed, and he didn't know the layout of the rooms.

"Shay?"

"In the kitchen. Straight down the hall."

Great. So much for her being afraid to wander through the house alone. He made a beeline for the hallway and followed it, feeling his way along the walls to make sure he didn't bump into any furniture. When he felt the doorway, he assumed he was in the kitchen.

"Are you in here?"

"Yeah, come on in. I'm looking for a flashlight so we can go find the circuit box."

He stepped in and followed the sound of her voice, but was blinded by a flash as the lights flipped on.

Shay turned around, her expression one of sadness and regret. But she wasn't alone. There were a half-dozen beefy-looking guys and a couple women flanking her.

Dread turned his heated body cold. His gaze shot to Shay. "What the hell's going on?"

"Welcome home, Nic."

He started to turn at the deep voice behind him, but the prick of a needle sliding into his bicep made him jerk.

"Hey! What the . . ."

He never got the words out as he began to crumple to the floor. Strong arms circled him before he crashed in a heap. Nausea rolled in his stomach as he fought the dizziness brought about by whatever drug they'd injected him with.

He heard them talking, but it was fuzzy, like an echo chamber.

"Derek, is that going to hurt him?"

Shay's voice. Then the guy's voice behind him responding with "No. Just put him to sleep for a while so we can move him."

Shit, shit, shit. This wasn't good. Kidnapping . . . or something worse? He was losing it, couldn't stay conscious.

He'd been ambushed.

Ah, hell. He knew his dick would get him in trouble one day.

They'd done it. Nic was out cold, bound and seated comfortably—well, she had to assume he was comfortable since he wasn't conscious to say otherwise—on the sofa while they finished the plan. Shay was filling Derek and Lou and the others in on what she knew, which frankly was very little. She'd told them she didn't think Nic was involved with the demons, though she couldn't be certain since they had had to cut their time short. She was going on her gut feelings, even though her visions told her otherwise. She wasn't going to tell them about the visions.

But he admitted his father was missing, and it didn't appear that he knew what had happened to Ben. She'd seen no sign of demonic activity during the time she spent with him at his house. By all signs he was normal and human.

She took another glance into the living room. Nic still hadn't moved, and it had been several hours.

"Derek, is he going to be okay? He hasn't budged an inch."

"He's fine, Shay. He's just knocked out, the way we want him to be."

She scrunched her nose, studying Nic's chest, watching the rhythmic rise and fall as he breathed. So she was worried for nothing. The sooner he was conscious and she could be sure he wasn't harmed, the better she'd feel.

Or maybe less guilty that she'd been the one to bring all this about.

He didn't ask for this. What if he was just a normal human guy and they'd just ripped his life apart? She knew what it felt like to have the rug pulled out from under you. It sucked.

Then again, Nic wasn't just a normal human guy. He

had demon blood in him. Just like Derek. They had to know what side he was on. Light or dark, good or bad. He couldn't be left just wandering around. She shouldn't worry about whether or not he was going to be happy about this. It wasn't her concern.

Oh, who was she kidding? She already knew she was connected to Nic through her visions. Dammit, she didn't like it, either.

Lou stood and faced them. "The first thing we have to do is get Nic out of here before his uncle comes hunting for him and brings demons with him. Derek and I, along with Gina, Shay, Ryder, Trace, and Dalton, will take Nic to the northwest territory, on the outskirts of where the Diavolo mine is. There, we'll work on Nic, explain things to him, try to get him to help us. The rest of you will stay here and see if you can keep an eye on what's happening at the Diavolo mansion. There's a strong demon vibe coming from there, so I know something's going on. Linc, you manage the situation from here."

Linc nodded.

"There's a plane standing by. We need to go—and go now, before Nic wakes up."

They moved fast. Gear had already been packed and stowed in the two SUVs waiting for them. The ones remaining behind would take care of hiding Nic's car and retrieving hers from the restaurant.

Once in motion, everything went down smoothly and they were on board the plane in less than two hours.

She cast her gaze toward Nic, wondering how he was going to react after he was told everything. She couldn't even imagine having her life turned upside down.

Well, yeah, she could. That had already happened to her. Years ago, when her mother disappeared. And again a couple months ago, when Lou revealed her mother hadn't been kidnapped, hadn't disappeared without a trace or abandoned her and her father, but had been taken by demons.

Yeah, she could commiserate with Nic. She'd had a few considerable shocks in her life, and she'd managed to weather them.

Fasten your seat belt, Nic Diavolo. It's going to be one hell of a roller-coaster ride for you.

Bart paced the marble floors of the Diavolo mansion, glaring at the men who were supposed to have kept watch on his nephew.

He could not abide ineptitude. They had lost him.

He turned his anger on those who'd been charged with watching him.

"Why did you let him go with her?"

His voice boomed out over the silence.

They directed their gazes to the ground. "It was a woman. He's done it in the past. He's often gone out to clubs to party. We assumed that's where they were going."

Fury boiled within him, the urge to strike these two down so strong he had to take a step back. Now, more than ever, they needed to keep Dominic close, to make sure he didn't disappear. He'd put his two best on watching him.

But he should have known better. Over the past year Nic had changed his patterns. How could these imbeciles fail to notice he didn't take up with random women anymore?

Idiots. Morons. Such incompetence in his ranks. Oh, they would suffer mightily for their mistake. Of that, there was no doubt. But first, he needed information. "Tell me of this woman," he said, purposely lowering his voice, trying to project calm. The magnitude of his displeasure would hit them later.

"Average height. About five foot four. Curves. Beautiful. Blond hair, shoulder-length. Blue eyes. Drove a compact car registered to one of the airport rental agencies under the name Susan Mitchell. We couldn't track an address anywhere that was verifiable. She and Nic spent the day together surfing, then came here, hung out by the pool, and left early this evening. We tried to follow, but—well, you know how Nic drives. We lost him on one of the turns."

Fucking imbeciles. Assuming was their first mistake. They checked all Nic's regular haunts and he was nowhere to be found. Bart tried his cell phone, but there was no answer.

Nic had been taken. And Bart knew by whom.

Damn Louis and the Realm of Light. Bart knew the

Sons of Darkness should have snatched Nic as soon as Derek and that woman of his killed Ben. But he hadn't known they'd discovered Dominic was alive. He hadn't expected them to trace Nic to Sydney.

He had underestimated the Realm of Light. Now the Realm had Nic, and the Sons of Darkness needed to get him back.

But where had they gone? The Sons of Darkness would figure it out, and they'd get Dominic back. They had to. They needed him. After Ben's death, there was only one choice. Find the black diamond and conduct the ceremony immediately. But they needed Nic to do that.

He was the key.

Nic had never felt so hungover in all his life. His mouth was so dry it felt like it was stuffed with cotton, his head pounded like a thousand hammers were beating against his skull, and the roar in his ears was deafening. Every part of his body thrummed with vibration. No, more like a jolt, a pitching wave of nausea he couldn't stop.

What did he have to drink last night? Even worse, what day was it, anyway? And where the hell was he? Judging from the sharp pain slicing through his head, he wasn't even sure he wanted to know. He slitted his eyes open, then went wide-eyed, his synapses firing as shock waves of awareness slammed into him.

Memories flooded back. He wasn't hung over. He'd been drugged. Kidnapped.

Shay.

Was she here? He winced as he moved to stand and realized he was bound against a chair. He looked around, gauging his surroundings, pinpointing his focus to the tiny square windows across from him, the clouds just outside. Moving clouds. Pitching and rolling.

He was on an airplane.

Goddammit!

He counted about a half-dozen people on the plane, all focusing on him. He stared back at their menacing faces. Unruly lot, too. They looked like thugs. Or ninjas, dressed in dark clothes with strange-looking weapons strapped to their bodies, all of them well muscled and looking mean and wary.

Even the women were in prime physical shape, including Shay, who looked a hell of a lot different from the way she had the last time he saw her. Now she wore the same dark camouflage pants as her counterparts on the plane, along with a snug black tank top. A belt slung across her hips was loaded with some kind of ammunition that didn't look like bullets. She had daggers strapped to holsters tied to her thighs.

The female Lara Croft. Sexy but lethal.

She'd screwed him over but good. He couldn't believe he'd fallen for it. And he wasn't buying the look of concern—of guilt—on her beautiful face.

"Who the hell are you people?"

"I'm Derek." That spoken by the one sitting directly

across from him. Big, steely-looking guy with gray eyes and dark hair. "Do you remember me at all?"

Nic studied him, tilting his head to the side, searching for any sign of recognition. "No. Should I?"

Derek's chest expanded with the force of his indrawn breath. Then he exhaled, disappointment washing across his features. "No, I guess not. But I kind of hoped you would."

"Why?"

"Let's take this slowly, shall we?"

That statement came from an older guy with a thick head of white hair. He left his seat and moved to the empty one across from Nic. "Shay, come over here, please. You're the only face Nic recognizes."

Yeah. The face of the woman who was responsible for him being kidnapped. Did this guy think having her close would offer him some kind of comfort? Fat chance. She sat next to him, still sporting that look of concern.

Earlier, she'd been all smiles and sex appeal. But damn if she still didn't exude sex, with laced-up boots and weapons strapped to her hips. She looked like a warrior. He wanted to be freed of these ropes and see how well she'd tussle with him one-on-one. He'd like to tie her up and make her pay for this.

"Sit next to Nic. Why don't you open a bottle of water and offer him a drink?" He turned to Nic. "You must be thirsty. I'm sorry about the drug, but it was necessary to subdue you so we could get you on the plane. I'm afraid it probably gave you a nasty case of dry mouth."

Shay grabbed a bottle from the minifridge next to her

chair and unscrewed the top. She slid a straw in it and
thrust it under his nose. Nic regarded the water for a
second, then figured, screw it. He was dying of thirst.
They'd already drugged and kidnapped him. If they
wanted him dead they'd have done that by now. He took
the straw between his lips and guzzled the water down.

"I'm sorry we can't untie you yet, Dominic," the
white-haired man said. "My name is Louis. Most people
call me Lou."

He'd said "yet." Okay, that implied Nic had a chance
to be let loose of these bonds, which meant the possibility of escape. Though why they had him tied up on an
airplane was beyond him. What was he going to do?
Jump out?

"Who are you people? Why am I on this plane? If you
want money, my family will gladly pay it to get me back,
and we can get this over with."

"This isn't a kidnapping for ransom, Nic," Derek said.

That's not what he wanted to hear. "Then what is it?"

"More like a rescue," Derek replied with an upward
quirk to his lips.

Nic arched a brow. Were these people insane? Maybe
he'd fallen into some weird cult. Maybe they felt he par-
tied too much and needed saving. Hell, who knew with
weirdos like that. One of the drawbacks with being in
the public eye. The Diavolo diamond mine was well
known. Capitalism and all that. "I didn't need rescuing.
But thanks. You can take me home now."

"Actually, you do," Derek said. "We need to ask you
some questions."

Nic snorted. Like he was going to give them any information?

"Nic, it's not what you think," Shay said, her voice soft and meant to soothe.

He didn't feel soothed. His nerve endings were on fire, anger and betrayal making him wish he had super strength so he could break these bonds and wrap his hands around her lying throat.

"Yeah? What do I think?"

"That you've been kidnapped for money, or because we want to do you harm. That isn't the case. Trust me."

"Trust you? That's a laugh."

Her lashes drifted down and her face colored pink before she looked back up at him again. "I'm sorry. I did what I had to do."

"You did it really well, too. Were you intending to fuck me as part of your job? Because you didn't appear to want me to stop in the pool."

The pink of her cheeks turned red, the concerned expression on her face turning to anger.

"Hey," Derek said. "Enough. Nic, do you know where your father is?"

Nic turned his head to Derek. "What about my father? Did Shay tell you he was missing?" God, he couldn't believe he'd confided in her. That was stupid.

"You tell me. Where is he?"

This was about his dad? Did they kidnap his father? "I don't know where he is. Did you take him, too?"

"He doesn't know, Derek," Lou said, shaking his head. "I really don't think he has any idea."

"Then let's tell him what we know and see where we stand." Derek let out a long sigh.

"Yeah, why don't you do that, since I have no fucking idea what you're talking about." And he hated being in the dark. If he was armed with some information, it might help him escape. Or at least figure how to get out of this predicament.

"It's a long story and you'll just have to listen."

Nic nodded at Derek. "Not like I have much choice. So start talking."

Derek looked to Lou, who nodded and said, "Go ahead. You take the lead and tell him."

Derek turned back to Nic. "You're not going to believe some of this." He blew out a breath, looked down at his feet, and shook his head, then jammed his fingers through his hair. "Hell, you're probably not going to believe most of it. If I were in your shoes I wouldn't."

"Great. Then don't waste my time."

He held up his hand. "Just . . . listen, okay?"

The guy was frustrated. Not angry, not mean, but frustrated. Kind of weird for a kidnapper.

Derek lifted his head and stared at Nic. A spark of something familiar hit him in the stomach, but Nic couldn't place it. He was sure he'd never met this guy before.

"Nic, I'm your brother."

Chapter Five

Nic didn't even know how to respond to Derek's statement, the idea was so ludicrous. "I don't have a brother."

"Yeah, you do. You're looking at him. You just don't remember me. Our father, Ben, took you from our house when you were eight years old, in the middle of the night. I don't know why you don't remember it, or me. Do you have any memories of our mother?"

Nic frowned. "*My* mother died when I was an infant. I had no brothers or sisters. Ever."

"So. Somehow you've blocked it all out of your memories. Everything from before Dad took you."

Why were they trying to get him to believe he'd been kidnapped as a child by his father, and that this guy was his brother? He'd have remembered that. Wouldn't he? Even with the head injury he'd suffered as a kid, his father would have told him about a brother, about his mother.

These people were full of shit. They really were part of some brainwashing cult and were trying to get him to believe in this nonsense. If he fought against it, would they drug him again? He had to stay alert and levelheaded so he could fight them. He wasn't going to say a word, just act cooperative until he figured something out.

"It gets worse," Derek said.

Oh, great. "Go on."

"Our father, Ben, was one of the twelve Lords of the Sons of the Darkness."

"What is that? Some secret organization?"

"You could, ah, say that. He was a demon."

Okay, he *was* gonna need boots for bullshit this deep. "A demon. You mean like, from the fires of hell, devil kind of thing?"

"Yes."

"So that would make you and me demons."

"Half demons. Our mother was human."

"Uh-huh. Does the bullshit stop anytime soon?"

Derek turned to Lou.

Lou shrugged. "It's not like the average person is going to accept this at face value, Derek. Would you, would any of you, if you hadn't seen it yourselves?"

So Lou was the leader. Some kind of prophet or savior in the eyes of the minions here. How in the hell had Nic gotten caught up in all this? Why had they chosen him? And more important, how was he going to get out of it?

"I don't know what to do to convince him," Derek

said. "It's not like I'm going to unleash the beast inside me. You know I won't do that."

At the mention of the beast inside him, Nic's heart began to pound. Coincidence, that's all it was. It wasn't the same thing that Nic was going through, had nothing to do with his nightmares or experiences. It was a turn of phrase and nothing more.

"No one expects you to do that, babe. Not even if it would immediately prove to Nic that you speak the truth."

A woman stepped up behind Derek and placed her hand on his shoulder. Gorgeous, with long dark hair that hung in waves over her shoulders. Even devoid of makeup she was breathtakingly beautiful. Some spark of recognition flashed in Nic's mind. He'd seen her somewhere before, but where? In a magazine maybe?

Derek reached behind him and grasped her hand. "I can't. I should, but I won't let it out unless there's no other choice. I don't trust being able to control it."

Again, Derek's words mirrored Nic's thoughts lately. He brushed it aside as coincidence. It *wasn't* the same thing.

"That's unnecessary," Lou said. "We'll convince Dominic another way."

"You're saying you can turn into some kind of demon?" Nic asked, hating that the question spilled from his mouth.

"Yeah. Or at least it came out of me before. On an island where we fought demons. Where Ben and I fought each other."

A cold chill slid down Nic's spine. Common sense told him not to comment, but he couldn't let that statement alone. "You met my father."

"I met *our* father. I grew up with the same man you did, Nic. At least until I was ten and you were eight and he took you from your bed and away from Mom and me. The two of you disappeared. I didn't see him again until a couple months ago, on an island in the South Pacific. Underground, in a tunnel. We fought, and the demon hunters killed him."

Nic swallowed. "You're saying you killed my father."

"No, he killed a Lord of the Sons of Darkness, a vicious demon who was trying to kill him."

Nic's gaze whipped to Shay. She regarded him with a look that he read as fierce loyalty to Derek, to all of them, he supposed. Her chin held high, her eyes sparkling with fire, her posture dared him to balk at what they said.

Whatever. It wasn't like he believed them anyway. If his father was dead he'd have been notified. His uncle would have told him. He'd know ... somehow.

Not that he and his father had a tight bond. They didn't. They weren't even close.

But goddammit, wouldn't he know if his own father was dead?

None of this was true. He had to hold tight to that. Otherwise his entire world would crumble. They were playing mind games with him, trying to make him believe what they said was fact.

It wasn't. His father was alive. There were no such things as demons.

The dreams he had at night about clawing monsters were just that—dreams. There was no correlation between the two.

Reality was something entirely different.

Shay watched the play of emotions cross Nic's face. Disbelief, shock, anger. She knew he didn't believe them. Who would? When Lou had first told them about the demons, she didn't believe him, either. When he'd explained about their mothers being kidnapped and used to make demon babies, she'd thought him insane. That she'd been played. That it was part of the reality show she thought she'd signed on to do. Only the reality show had been a fake, and the demons had been real.

For a while she hadn't known what to believe.

This wasn't going to be easy for Nic, and it made her heart clench. Guilt and sympathy warred within her.

And he was pissed. Really pissed. Palpable waves of anger vibrated off his body. If he was loose, he'd tear the plane apart. Now she understood why he was bound.

She felt so guilty about being responsible for putting him in this position. But why? She'd done what she was told to do. It was essential they pull Nic away from the Diavolos, especially considering he might be a catalyst for the black diamond. He might be able to get them closer to finding it. And if he wasn't one of the bad guys, then they'd rescued him. If it turned out that his blood was evil . . .

She didn't want to think about what Derek would do. Though she didn't sense any evil in Nic. Evil surrounded him, yes, but there wasn't any within him. None that was trying to get out, anyway. But she couldn't tell anyone that, wouldn't reveal her curse even to the demon hunters. It was her secret to keep; she'd kept it her entire life.

But in her heart she knew Nic wasn't evil.

Derek was a half demon, like Nic. And Derek was an okay guy. Was Nic like him, or was he one of the bad guys like his father? She'd kind of like Nic to be one of the good guys.

The thought of Nic turning into one of those evil creatures made her stomach hurt.

"This will all make sense to you soon, I promise."

He shot her a look of pure venom. "Right. And on Christmas Eve I'll see Santa Claus popping down my chimney. Oh, yeah, and on Easter a six-foot bunny will leave me a basket filled with chocolate eggs."

She laid her hand on his forearm, felt his muscles tense, but left it there anyway. "You have to trust us, Nic. We're not trying to hurt you."

"Oh, really? By telling me my father's dead? That you all killed him? That he was a monster? No, that doesn't hurt at all."

Okay, he had her there. "I'm sorry." She squeezed his arm, felt the heat and strength of him. He clenched his hand into a fist. Would he strike her if he were free? She somehow doubted it.

"Sorry doesn't cut it, babe. I should have ignored the Free Sex sign you had posted all over your body. You're nothing but trouble. I should have left you on the beach."

Ouch. She knew it was his anger and pain talking, but dammit, he was hurting her. She held her head high. "I'm sorry, Nic. I had to lie to you—I had no choice. But I did enjoy spending time with you."

"Yeah, I'll bet you did."

She frowned. "Now you're acting like an ass."

He smirked. "I guess you can think whatever you want, since we won't be fucking after all, will we? I don't need to impress you."

She gave up and walked away, flopping into one of the chairs in the back of the plane. Why did she bother? He was a spoiled rich guy used to getting his way. Arrogant asshole. He was lucky she didn't kick him in the balls. And she hated that she'd just left and let him insult her like that.

Fine. Let him be a jerk about it. He was only hurting himself.

Lou stood and moved to the back of the plane, crouching down in front of her. "He's not taking this well," he whispered.

She shrugged.

"After we land, I'd like you to spend some more time talking to him."

"Me? Why?" she shot back in a harsh whisper. She

glanced over Lou's shoulder at Nic. He still didn't turn his head in her direction.

"Because you connected with him."

She snorted out a quiet laugh. "Lou, he hates my guts."

Lou offered the hint of a smile. "That's still a connection. And I don't think he really hates you. He's very confused right now. And hurt. And angry."

"At me, mostly."

"At all of us. But he has a bond with you. I feel it."

She crossed her arms. "I don't feel it," she lied. Not only did she feel it, but it was growing stronger. That's why she wanted to distance herself from him, not draw closer to him.

He took the seat next to her. "We need to hit the ground running once we land. We need information about the mines. We need Nic on our side. I need you to draw him out, figure out what he knows. He needs to talk to someone about this. And I want it to be you."

She shifted and gaped at him. "You want me to act as his interrogator?"

"Not interrogator. Just talk to him. Answer his questions, honestly. Tell him anything he wants to know about the Realm of Light and the Sons of Darkness. About his father, about Derek, about the demons. Talk about yourself. Just keep him talking. And see if he'll tell you anything. If he exhibits any demon behavior."

She sighed and nodded, knowing damn well she'd do whatever Lou asked of her. It was, after all, her job. "Fine. But I doubt he'll talk to me."

"I think you'll be surprised."

Yeah. She'd be surprised if he said anything other than "Fuck off, bitch."

She didn't want to do this. She wanted to wash her hands of Nic Diavolo and get out there with the other hunters, searching for the black diamond, not baby-sitting an arrogant, possibly demonic, tied-up, uncooperative pain in the ass who hated her.

Wasn't this going to be fun?

They'd landed somewhere in the northwest territory, though not near the coast, according to Lou.

Whatever. Like Shay even knew where she was in this country.

Wherever they landed, it wasn't even an airport, at least not by any standards Shay would recognize. Certainly not commercial and no other planes in sight. From the way the plane bumped and bounced along the ridges in the landing strip, it felt like a cornfield, not a landing strip. More like a long stretch of asphalt that could accommodate their airplane.

All thanks to the Realm of Light.

Those people had connections everywhere.

The plane taxied into a hangar covered with camouflage netting so that anyone flying overhead wouldn't recognize it as anything other than part of the landscape. They all spilled out of the plane, with Nic in front of her, his hands still bound, though at least they let him walk. Ryder and Trace escorted him, one on either side of him. He wasn't going anywhere, though. Right now he looked pretty subdued.

She felt like the air had just been sucked out of her lungs. The humidity was so thick she was suffocating. Instant thirst gnawed at her, her mouth going dust dry. Drawing in a breath of hot air she swore she could see, she descended the steel ladder and landed on hard earth within the hangar, dirt billowing up around her feet.

Shay's gaze caught a group of men covering up the landing field, sweeping dirt and brush over the long strip that had been the pilot's touchdown guideline. Every sign of their recent appearance had just been obliterated.

"Christ, it's hot," Ryder drawled.

"Is it? I hadn't noticed," Trace shot back with a grin.

"That's because you're used to this shit."

"Pussy."

"Fuck off."

Shay snorted.

"I hate to interrupt you two in the middle of such an intimate moment," Derek said, "but we need to grab the gear and get into some air-conditioning before we all turn into dust."

They piled into waiting SUVs, which, thank God, were air-conditioned.

There weren't even any definitive roads, just a dry, bumpy stretch of dirt that the drivers followed. She hoped they knew where they were going. She'd be hopelessly lost out here in the middle of nowhere with no path and no signs.

They drove for over an hour, until the terrain changed from dust and scrubby brush to one of greenery. Trees peppered the side of the road, thickening with every mile. The elevation rose, too. They climbed hills so steep all she could see was the hood of the SUV, then dove down steep valleys, making turns along sharp curves that pitched her empty stomach sideways.

Soon the sunlight was all but obliterated by the dense covering of trees as they dipped into a valley and turned down a very narrow road, finally pulling in front of a two-story white house.

"This town is close to the mines, but not so nearby that Bart might come looking for us here," Lou explained. "We rented a place that's away from the other houses, too, so we'll have plenty of privacy."

It was lovely, actually, not at all where Shay imagined they'd be staying. A screened porch wrapped around the entire first floor, and upstairs there were several rooms that led out onto open balconies.

They piled out of the vehicles. Even here, the humidity was thick. Lou unlocked the white door leading inside the house.

"Wander around and check the place out," Lou said.

At least the air-conditioning worked well inside. Shay breathed a sigh of relief as cool air greeted her. Worn but well-maintained wood floors spread out into a massive main room, fully furnished with comfortable-looking cloth-covered couches and chairs. No television.

A trestle table filled the expansive dining room, with more than enough room for all the hunters to sit and eat together. The kitchen was bright and airy, with windows all around and all the modern conveniences. A door led onto the screened-in back porch. Beyond that, dense trees as far as the eye could see.

Plenty of bedrooms and bathrooms upstairs.

"I'll be putting you and Nic in the bedrooms with the adjoining bath."

Shay's mouth fell open. Okay, that was an interesting assignment. She didn't know whether to be annoyed or intrigued. "Uh, Lou," she started.

He held up his hand. "I know. A bit awkward, but I want you to be able to come and go, to check on Nic and be there for him if he needs you. He'll be well guarded by the others and I'm confident you can take care of yourself."

How cozy. She didn't want to think about how they were going to manage it right now. She'd worry about it later.

Room assignments were settled on, and everyone stowed their gear. Nic wasn't brought upstairs, but the clothing they'd gotten for him was. She unpacked for him and headed downstairs with the others.

The first thing they did was eat, huddled together in the kitchen while Lou laid out the battle plan. Nic was tied up in the living room and couldn't hear what they were talking about.

"We'll start by scouting the perimeter around the mine," Lou said. "There are caves outside the Diavolo mine property. I want them explored. Don't get too close to the mines, and don't let any of the guards patrolling the mines see you. We don't want them to know we're here."

"What are we looking for in the caves?"

"See if there are any miners in there digging, first off. If there are, back off and report. If there aren't, explore. I want to know if we can hunt in there for the black diamond or access to the mine. Second, be on the lookout for demons. They're here."

Ryder raised his brows. "You know this?"

Lou nodded "I know this. I'll be setting up my equipment tonight and see if I can pick them up when we're out tracking."

"About damn time," Ryder said. "We haven't killed demons since the island. I'm getting itchy."

"Now you're talking like a demon hunter." Derek clapped him on the back and grinned.

"You'll all get plenty of opportunity, I'm afraid. This area is rich with demons, from what I've been able to gather. So be careful and pack plenty of ammo."

"And water," Trace added. "You'll dehydrate without it."

They'd all gotten some sleep on the plane, but not a full day's rest, since they slept during the days and hunted at night. Demons hated heat and surfaced only after the sun went down, which meant the demon hunters kept the same schedule.

The sun was going down. It was time to pack up and get ready for the hunt.

"Shay, you'll stay here with Nic. As I said, talk to him

and see what you can find out. Keep your weapons trained on him and don't let him loose."

She nodded, hoping she'd make some headway with him tonight. The faster she could break through with Nic, the sooner she could be out there with the others hunting demons.

While everyone prepped for the hunt, she grabbed a corner seat on one of the sofas. They'd placed Nic on a chair, his arms and legs bound.

He glared at her but said nothing.

Reaching Nic was going to be difficult. His anger at her was still strong. But she was determined to see it through. She owed him explanations. She owed him more than that. She'd felt something beyond her assignment, and she needed to tell him that what they'd shared together hadn't been phony.

Would he believe her, though?

And how many of her own secrets would she have to reveal to get through to him?

Chapter Six

N ic ate what they fed him. He wasn't stupid. He'd need to keep his strength up if a possibility for escape came about. And he was going to get out of here. If they were, in fact, near the mines, he had a place to go when he got free.

He watched Shay as he ate the sandwich one of them hand-fed him, trying to reconcile the woman he saw now with the one he'd met yesterday. She looked different, and there was a cocky confidence about her when she moved that he hadn't noticed before. He had found her kind of sweet and vulnerable when he first met her.

Now he just thought her lethal. Sex and sin wrapped up in a fully armed combat package, ready to kill.

He didn't know her at all.

The others were loading up their odd-looking weapons and heading toward the door.

"We'll be back before sunrise," Lou said to Shay. "Though I'll comm you if something comes up."

"Okay."

"Whatever you do, no matter what reason," Derek said, directing a dead-serious look at Shay, "do not untie him. You can feed him and hold the water bottle for him to drink out of. But he doesn't get those ties anchoring him to the chair even loosened. Got it?"

"Got it," she replied.

Did he look that dangerous? He hoped so. He wanted her to be afraid of him, but she was the one holding all the weapons.

The door closed with a decisive click, the sound making him feel more imprisoned than he already was.

Shay turned to him, sucked in her bottom lip, then moved to the sofa next to his chair and sat. She clasped her hands together and rested them on her knees. Her fingers were slender, her nails short, yet well manicured. She even wore pink nail polish. A demon-killer had time to paint her fingernails?

She smelled like the beach, like sunshine and fresh air, like an ocean breeze at sunset.

Like freedom.

He didn't want to inhale her fragrance. She was the enemy and he wanted no part of her. She wasn't fresh, she wasn't beautiful, and he didn't want to feel this weird sizzle whenever she was nearby. He wanted her to go away. He wanted to go home.

"When are you people going to let me go?"

She shrugged. "I'm not privy to the details on that, Nic. I'm just supposed to watch you."

"Watch me what?" Sit there like a trained monkey?

He was trussed up against the chair. Tied to it, to be exact. The chair was heavy. No way could he stand and hoist it up with him.

"Just watch you. And talk."

"Talk about what?"

"Whatever you want to talk about. I'll answer your questions about all this—your brother, the demons, anything you want to know. We'll talk until you're comfortable."

Her voice was soft and melodic. Mesmerizing, almost. So she was the brainwashing expert? Maybe that was her area, the reason she'd been the one to make contact with him first. She was beautiful, engaging, easy to talk to. He could see how she could draw someone out, lull them into conversing, cajole them into believing her.

He'd believed her when she spent the day with him. He believed her when she offered up her body in the pool. He believed they had a connection.

He was a first-class, A-number-one sucker. He'd fallen for every line she'd thrown.

That wasn't going to happen again.

Nic didn't even shift in the chair, though it was goddamned uncomfortable. His ass was numb and he was tired of sitting there like a prisoner. What a bunch of utter bullshit. Was this what he had to look forward to from now on?

As a baby-sitter, Shay wasn't doing a great job. She seemed nervous and unsettled.

She stood and walked around. Looked out the window a few times. Cleaned those funky-looking weapons.

Unloaded and reloaded the ammo. He was dying to know what the hell kind of ammo it was, too, but he wasn't about to ask her. The last thing he'd do is show interest or talk to her.

When she reached for the dagger at her hip while she gazed out the window again and began to stroke it absently, he damn near lost it. Did she even realize what she was doing? She palmed the handle and slid her hand slowly down the scrolled hilt, then back up again. Back and forth, swirling her thumb over the tip of the dagger every time she got to the top.

Goddamn.

She might not know what she was doing, but his dick sure as hell did. And it liked what it saw. A lot.

Especially the way she drew lazy circles over the intricately carved pattern across the top.

He might hate her, but his body remembered what it felt like being slammed up against her in the pool. Soft curves, the fullness of her breast in his hand, the way her nipple came to life under his questing fingers. If he hadn't pulled away he'd have been inside her, feeling her grip him until he got the release he hadn't felt in far too long.

Goddammit. He broke out in a sweat. Fully hard now, he turned away and stared at the sofa, but damn his male interest. His gaze kept gravitating back to the slow, sensuous movements of her hand over that dagger.

She was way too good at that. He'd bet her hand was warm and soft. He could imagine it gliding over his straining, aching flesh, coaxing the ultimate pleasure right out of him.

Shit.

In his currently bound position, an erection wasn't going to be easy to hide. They'd tied his ankles to each foot of the chair. Which meant his legs were spread. And his shorts were tenting nicely due to his aroused flesh trying to tear its way out of his pants and make its way into Shay's hand.

Why the hell should he be the only one to suffer?

"Stop that."

She whirled and turned to him. "What?"

Her hand stilled, but remained on the hilt of the dagger.

"Stop jacking off that dagger."

"Excuse me?"

Then the lightbulb went on, because she looked down at her hand, then at him. Between his legs, actually. Her eyes widened, her face flamed a really attractive shade of pink. She jerked her hand away and whipped it behind her back.

"If you're bored and restless and want something to do with your hands," he said, letting his sentence trail off but leaving no mystery as to what he was referring to. He looked down at his obvious dilemma, then back at her, enjoying her discomfort. He might be the one tied up, but if he could make her at all miserable, he was going to.

"Um, no."

"You started this."

"I did no such thing." She wrapped her arms around herself and turned back to the window.

He smirked at the telltale blush he'd glimpsed on her face. But maybe he'd have a few minutes now to get his unruly dick under control. Bad idea to get turned on by the enemy. Even if she was beautiful. And he wasn't falling for her innocent, guileless act. She might have looked wide-eyed and naïve a minute ago, but nobody who did what she did was that clueless.

And it was time to stop sitting there like a fucking victim and start figuring out how to escape. Because chances were that if these people were on the up-and-up, there wasn't going to be a call or a note to his family for ransom. Which meant it was going to be more difficult for them to locate him.

He was responsible for getting himself out of this mess.

Nic was on his own. He needed a plan. And the best chance he had of escaping was right now when he was alone with Shay. Her, he could take. When the muscle-bound minions returned, it'd be highly unlikely he could whip all of them at once.

After thinking about it for a few minutes, he grinned. Yeah, he had an idea.

"Hey," he said

"What," she mumbled.

"I need some help here."

She turned to him. "What is it?"

He looked up at her and grimaced, putting on the best act of his life.

"I gotta pee."

Shay stared at Nic, dumbfounded and feeling utterly stupid.

He had to pee. Of course he did. He would have to do ... that, eventually, wouldn't he?

Well, Lou, where were the instructions for handling this one?

Shit.

She couldn't very well untie him and lead him to the bathroom, could she? He'd make a run for the door. She wasn't strong enough to restrain him. Of course she could always shoot him, but the weaponry was a bit advanced for humans. He'd die.

She was fairly certain Derek wouldn't want his brother dead. Not right now, anyway.

"You're doing this on purpose."

He cocked a brow.

Yeah, yeah. Stupid comment, she knew, but this was frustrating.

"Are you going to refuse my request?"

She paced back and forth in front of his chair. "I'm thinking. Give me a minute."

"I really need to go."

She shot him a glare. "Hold it."

"I would hold it, but my hands are tied."

He was smirking at her. Asshole. He thought this was funny.

"I could just leave you there to wet yourself."

"You could, but I don't think you will."

He was right. That would be cruel. Not to mention it would render one piece of furniture completely useless to them. This whole situation would be comical if she wasn't the one responsible for figuring out how to make this work.

Why the hell hadn't Lou given this assignment to one of the guys? Then it would have been easy. She didn't have the muscle for it.

Okay, start thinking. There was a way to deal with this. She stared down at him for a few seconds, tilting her head back and forth, then realized she'd been focusing her eyes between his legs again.

Where he'd been hard not that long ago. Quite impressively hard, too.

Her body flared with a sudden wave of heat and a daunting awareness of him as a damned desirable man. One she had no business thinking about.

She inhaled and blew out a frustrated breath. He had to pee. He didn't want to have sex with her.

And even if he did...

"Still need to go here."

She blinked at his words. "Oh. Sorry." Nothing like a little sexual mind-wandering while he was squirming in his chair with a full bladder. Good going, Shay.

Then it hit her.

"I think I have an idea. I'll be right back." She hustled

into the kitchen, rummaged through the cabinets, nearly squealing with delight when she found something she knew would work perfectly. She hurried out into the living room and thrust it into one of his hands.

"Here. This should work."

Nic looked at the container and back at her. "Huh?"

"You can . . . uhh, go in that."

"You're joking, right?"

"No, I'm not joking. Go ahead."

"I can't move my hands to get things situated."

"Excuse me?"

"You'll have to position it if you want me to go in this bottle, babe. I can't do it."

She studied him. His arms were bound to his sides. He was right. He couldn't . . . maneuver things on his own. If he was going to relieve himself in that bottle, she was going to have to assist him.

"Unless you want to untie me. Then I can do it myself."

Not a chance in hell. "I can't untie you."

His lips curled upward in an arrogantly sexy smile. "Then I guess you'd better get over here and start handling my dick, because we're about to reach crisis level."

Shay knelt down between Nic's spread legs, certain she wasn't going to be able to do this. She weighed his growing discomfort against her abject embarrassment.

"You gonna hold that bottle in your hands all night and wave it in front of me? Is this part of the torture games you people play?"

She didn't even know what he meant by "you people." Right now she was trying to figure out how to relieve him without making this whole act too...intimate.

"Just untie me," he said, his gaze boring into hers. "Then you don't have to worry about touching me."

She looked down at his lap, unable to meet the pleading look in his eyes. "I can't."

"Then undo my shorts and let me do what I need to do."

Oh, God, even the way he said it was...harsh, commanding...exciting.

Dammit, she wasn't supposed to be the one in charge of him! Clearly she was way out of her league here. Some demon hunter.

"Shay."

"Yeah."

"Help me."

She knew it cost him to say that, and she was being a big baby about this. After all, she'd been the one to come up with this solution. So now she just had to buck up and deal with it. Lifting her head, she nodded and kept her eyes on his face. She reached for his shorts, pulled apart the Velcro and jammed her hand inside.

"Wanna be careful while you're rummaging around in there?" he asked, his lips curving into a half smile.

Heat sizzled up her neck and along her cheeks. "Sorry."

His skin was smooth, hot, and she found the intended target with no problem, considering it was so...sizeable.

And hard. And growing. Rapidly.

"Hey. Stop that."

He shrugged. "Can't help it."

"Yes, you can." She let go.

He rolled his eyes. "A gorgeous woman has her hand wrapped around my dick. You expect me to be unaffected?"

"Yes, I do, as a matter of fact. You want to pee or have sex?"

He arched a brow. "Is that an offer?"

She was going to implode any second now. The sides of her breasts brushed his bare legs. She could hear her own panting breaths. Heat fused her insides together.

"You going to hold that thing?" he asked.

"What thing?"

"The bottle. My cock. You remember what we're doing here?"

This was ridiculous. She wasn't a virgin. It wasn't like she'd never seen or held a penis in her hand before. She'd even passed some time as a nursing assistant while in college. She had to think medically, not sexually.

But somehow it wasn't working with Nic. Maybe she could do it with her eyes closed.

Finally she sucked in a breath of courage, reached in his shorts for the offending member, and hard or not, yanked it out and forced it into the bottle.

And waited.

Nothing happened.

She held as still as possible, trying not to breathe. Or look. Instead, she stared into the kitchen and pretended she wasn't holding his hot, hard shaft in her hand. One that wasn't pulsing against her palm.

Still, nothing happened.

Maybe he was shy.

She looked at his face, careful not to look down. "Something wrong?"

"It's hard."

Like she wasn't completely aware of that fact. "And?"

"It . . . prevents things from happening."

She sighed. "What now?"

"Let go of it, for starters. You touching it isn't helping."

She dropped it like a log infected with spiders. Then waited for a few minutes, turning her head to the side.

After waiting what seemed like an eternity, she turned back to him.

He shrugged. "Guess I don't have to go anymore."

She dropped back on her haunches. "You're kidding me, right?"

"No."

"You sonofabitch."

She stood and grabbed the bottle, none too gently shoving his body parts back in his shorts. Part of her hoped she'd jam his penis in the Velcro as she jerked it closed.

No such luck.

She stormed into the kitchen, opened the back door, and tossed the bottle in the trash, then flopped in the kitchen chair and laid her head in her hands, cursing her miserable luck.

No way in hell was she going back there to face him.

She was so stupid. God, how he'd played her. It had been a trick to see if she'd untie him. And she'd fallen for it.

How he must be laughing at her. She felt so immature, blushing and stammering her way through what should have been something simple.

Other than his massive erection, he hadn't seemed bothered by the ordeal. She'd been the one flaming with embarrassment.

What was it about Nic Diavolo that got to her?

Nic's cock throbbed so hard he wondered if he'd explode right there.

Thank God Shay made no attempt to return from the kitchen. His erection tented his shorts and didn't seem to be in any hurry to make a retreat.

What the hell was wrong with him? This hadn't gone at all like he'd expected. First off, he hadn't expected Shay to take him in hand like she did.

Gutsy move. He thought she'd untie him, that she'd be too embarrassed to touch him.

He'd been wrong.

And he hadn't expected his body's reaction to her touch. Hot, pounding, instantaneous hard-on when she'd tentatively wrapped her soft, warm hand around his shaft.

Even now he pulsed remembering how it felt, how smooth her hand was, how her thumb accidentally brushed across the crest and he had to fight back a groan and a shudder to appear impervious.

Her eyes had gone glassy, her lips parted. She'd been affected. Deeply affected, from the sound of her breathing and the pink coloring on her cheeks. He could even scent the arousal on her, something he'd never been able to do with a woman before. Hell, he could still smell her. She was tantalizingly sweet, like cotton candy. God, he wanted to be free, to dive down between her legs and take a long slow taste of her.

But that was a fantasy. She was his captor, his bodyguard. She controlled every aspect of his life at the moment.

He'd never wanted control over a woman more than he wanted it right now with Shay. Primal, hot, animalistic, and hungry. Maybe it was because he was tied to this mother-loving chair and she was in charge. He didn't like it. Or maybe it was because with one simple, tentative touch she had fired his blood and brought him into sharp awareness like no woman before her ever had.

He wanted to fuck her. To sweep her underneath him, bury himself inside her and feel her slick, wet heat surrounding him. He wanted his hands around her wrists, lifting them over her head and making her powerless. He wanted his knees between her legs, nudging her thighs apart so he could drive in deep and hard.

He wanted her as aware of him as he'd been of her.

He wanted her writhing underneath him, begging him to make her come.

And none of these thoughts was going to make his erection go away anytime soon.

"What do you mean, you've lost him?"

Bart bowed his head as he faced his brothers. Ten other Lords of the Sons of Darkness plus him, their evil wrapped around him, their anger palpable. Nic's presence at this time was paramount. Bart had assured them he had everything under control. Failure wasn't an option.

"I will find him."

"You shouldn't have lost him in the first place."

Bart nodded at Badon. "I realize this. It wasn't my intention. He is close. I sense he is still in Australia. I will get him back soon."

Badon raised a dark brow, an icy chill emanating from him. "The ceremony is soon. Timing is everything."

"As I'm well aware." His brother wasn't telling him anything he didn't already know. He was wasting precious time having to endure this "meeting." Yet he knew his brothers needed to be reassured that all would happen according to plan.

"Some of us wish to be present during the ceremony."

Bart nodded at Tase. "As you wish. However, do you not think it dangerous to amass so many Lords in one location? What about the Realm of Light? Chances are they will be either present or close by."

"We do not fear the Realm. They are of no matter to us. Once we harness the power of the gem and Dominic joins us, we will become so powerful they will never stop us."

They hoped. Bart had much to do. He had to find Dominic and locate the gem, then conduct the ceremony.

"It will be done, as my brothers wish."

"We have lost one of our own recently," Badon reminded him. "Find Dominic."

Maybe Bart should have developed a closer link to his nephew when the boy was younger. It would have come in handy right about now. But his gift was the strength and power of magic, to be used at the time the gem was found. It wasn't the gift of sight. He didn't know Ben would be destroyed, that Dominic would be taken. He didn't know the Realm of Light would become such a powerful force.

Changes would have to be made. The gem, the ceremony, would take care of their problem with the Realm of Light. Soon, the Sons of Darkness would have nothing to fear. Soon, they would have no enemies.

Very soon.

Chapter Seven

Ryder swore under his breath. The hunters had been skulking around in the black night for several hours now and he hadn't heard or seen any demons. Lou hadn't commed about any appearing through portals—hot spots in the ground signaling the sudden arrival of demons.

Nothing. Nada. Zero. Waste of fucking time. And mother of Christ, it was hot out here. Worse than that island in the Pacific. Sweat poured down his brow, his neck, and his back. He'd already downed two full bottles of water and he was thirsty again.

The group had split up, getting nowhere bunched up together. Ryder had moved north, following an arcing monolith shadowed against one of the taller sloping hills. Even with the night-vision shades that made it seem almost like daylight, it was still dark and things weren't as clear. Though no way in hell could the hunters do this during the day. As hot as it was now, they'd be toast try-ing to hunt when the sun was out.

Not that there'd be anything to hunt for. He was in the mood to kill, and that meant demons and that meant nighttime.

The itch to kill had been strong lately. It had been al-most two months since he'd last fired his weapons. The urge was getting as bad as it had gotten during his time in the military, one of the reasons he'd gotten out.

He was good at killing. No, he was a goddamn expert at it. And he liked it way too much. He'd been getting just like his father, and he hated it. The last thing he wanted to do was turn into a mirror version of his old man, the heartless bastard.

Then again, maybe it was already too late.

He wiped his brow to keep the sweat from dripping onto his specs, took another long draw of water, and headed straight toward the cave. Thick brush impeded his progress but he pushed through the bushes, slugging through the undergrowth like he was wading waist-high through water.

Something drew him to the cave. Maybe because it was a clear-cut destination instead of wandering the area chasing his own ass with no result. Demons? Maybe. He hoped so. Funny how he'd been so reluctant to enter this whole Realm of Light thing in the beginning. But now it was in his blood—a part of him. And it was a rea-son for killing, for getting those urges out of his system. A good, valid reason. Demons were the ultimate bad guy. And there were more demons that needed destroying. Hopefully he'd find them ahead.

As he drew near, a flash of light within the cave caught his eye. He stilled, frowning, not sure he had really seen it. Demons sure as hell didn't wander around with lights. They hated light.

But then he saw it again. That was no mirage.

He slung the UV laser rifle over his shoulder, then released the sonic guns from their holsters, ready to pull them and fire if necessary. He approached the entrance, crouching down when another light zipped along the walls deep inside.

He heard voices now. Whispers. More lights. He commed the others, gave his location, and headed toward the mouth of the cave. Something or someone was in there and whoever or whatever it was, he couldn't afford to wait. If there were demons, he wasn't about to let them get away.

"Don't go inside before we get there," Dalton warned. "We'll be there in under three."

Bullshit. In under three he'd be in there blasting. He could see the lights swirling all around the cave. No way could that be demons, but then who was in there?

He took another step forward.

The lights stilled. Whoever it was had heard him. He stepped behind a shrub just as a bright ray shined outside. He raised his weapon and crouched down so he couldn't be seen as the light scanned the area where he was located. He held his breath, his finger poised on the trigger of his gun.

One rounded boot protruded from the entrance, just inches away from his location. He could reach out and touch it. But he wasn't about to stand up and announce his whereabouts because he didn't know who'd be prowling about in the cave in the middle of the night. It wasn't demons, that much he knew. Someone affiliated with the demons, maybe? Hell, who knew what those bastards had up their sleeves.

The person took another step out of the cave. Camo-clad leg was all he could see, his vision obstructed by the foliage.

Okay, enough of this hiding bullshit. He stood and heard a gasp.

Whoever stood at the entrance pivoted and ran like hell. The only thing Ryder could see from his position was a braid of dark hair trailing behind as the person hightailed it into the mouth of the cave. The lights went out and the cave went dark. Ryder took off at a dead run after what he assumed was a woman.

He heard the pounding of her boots in the distance and followed the sound, the black cave illuminated by his night vision glasses. He pushed forward, determined to find her.

Who was she? Was she alone in the cave, and if so, what was she doing?

He heard a door slam, saw some light, and rushed back, skidding to a halt as he exited the cave. A small Jeep peeled away at high speed, kicking up rocks in its wake. No way could he catch her on foot.

Shit.

He turned at the sound of running feet behind him. Dalton and Trace caught up, having entered the cave at the front entrance and run clear through to the exit here at the back.

"You see someone in here?" Dalton asked.

Ryder nodded. "Bunch of lights hitting the walls and ceiling of the cave like people moving around with flashlights. Someone came to the entrance. Female, I think. At least I think it was a woman. Didn't appear to be demon, but I couldn't say for sure. I ran after her but she took off in a Jeep," he finished with a shrug.

"Anyone else?"

Ryder shook his head. "I think she was alone."

"Damn. Let's go back in there and see what we can find." Dalton took the lead and Ryder fell in next to him, holstering his gun and grabbing for his rifle.

They followed a set of footprints far into the depths of the cave, the air getting much cooler as they went. The surface of the cave was uneven, littered with small pebbles and hard dirt.

The cave sloped down with every step they followed. The air down here was much cooler. Cold, even. He welcomed the relief from the unbearable heat outside.

"This doesn't seem to be your basic cave," Ryder remarked.

"No demon hideaway, either," Dalton said. "No smell."

He was right. Buried in the dirt were tracks used for hauling. "These are old mines."

Dalton nodded, using his lights to scan the walls.

Scratch marks marred the surfaces, showing they'd been picked apart long ago. "It doesn't look like any recent mining activity has occurred here. Most likely abandoned."

They continued to follow the tracks leading farther into the mines until they came upon freshly dug earth. A deep hole with mounds of dirt on three sides had been left, probably by the person with the lights. But when they searched within the hole, they found nothing. Not even equipment.

"Whoever was in here left in a hurry. And they took everything with them," Dalton said.

Ryder jumped into the hole and squatted in the dig. "It's been shoveled and dug through, but I don't see any remnants."

"Okay," Dalton said. "So somebody's been in here."

Ryder nodded. The footprints were small, like the booted foot he'd seen at the entrance to the cave when he'd been hiding.

A woman's foot.

"What do you think she was looking for?"

Ryder shrugged at Trace's question. "Diamonds would be my guess. Same thing we're all looking for."

"Then why did she run?" Dalton stood with his hands on his hips, scanning the room.

"Either she's doing something illegal or I scared the shit out of her," Ryder said. And he wanted to know. Now they didn't have squat—except an empty underground mine and a fleeting glimpse of a dark braid.

He might have lost her this time, but something told him he'd run into her again.

"Let's get out of here," Ryder said.

Angelique Deveraux stepped out of her Jeep and grabbed her binoculars, peering down from her secluded vantage point on the hill overlooking the cave. She wanted to see who had nearly scared the life out of her and made her run. And to make sure they hadn't followed her.

She focused, but there were too many shrubs in the way for her to get a clear shot at the men skulking around the mouth of the cave.

She counted three of them, but she'd only caught a glimpse of one, and he'd practically given her a heart attack, springing out of the bushes at her like that.

Mon Dieu, she'd nearly swallowed her heart. Instinct told her to run. Good thing she'd already packed her gear. Unfortunately, she'd been doing a last sweep through the cave and her Jeep was on the other side. She'd never run so hard or so fast in her entire life.

What did they want? Why were they there? She'd been told she'd be alone up here. Interlopers would be a problem.

She hoped they were game hunters who just happened upon her location and stopped to investigate. She couldn't afford anyone snooping around and finding out what she was doing.

And she was on a timeline. If the black diamond

really did exist, and she was the one to uncover it, the find would go under her name. Her name would be listed on the display in the museums.

Her mother would have been so proud of her.

And if Isabelle, her twin sister, got wind of this expedition, she'd be on it in a heartbeat, trying to unearth the diamond before Angelique did.

Only Isabelle wouldn't want the diamond for a museum. Isabelle would sell it to the highest bidder.

Angelique had to make sure that didn't happen.

Time was of the essence. Secrecy was paramount. And she couldn't afford anyone, or anything, interrupting her work.

Shay was irritated. And pacing. She had nothing to show for her night in captivity with Nic, and she couldn't very well force him to talk to her.

She finally sat and faced him.

"Don't you remember anything about your time as a child?"

"Of course I do. I remember everything, at least everything after my accident."

"But you don't remember Derek, or being kidnapped."

"No. Because I wasn't kidnapped and Derek isn't my brother."

She rolled her eyes and tapped her fingers on the edge of the sofa.

"Tell me what you do remember about your mother, then."

His gaze narrowed. "My mother died when I was born."

"How convenient of your father to say that."

"What do you want me to say? He's lying? I wish I had a mother."

"You did. Until you were eight years old. You *have* a brother, too. Do you know he's spent the last twenty-five years looking for you?"

"Uh-huh. Sure he has."

"He was afraid you were dead, but he never gave up hope that someday he'd find you. When Gina found the fax in the underground tunnels on the island —"

"What fax?"

"The fax someone sent to Ben, saying you'd returned to Sydney."

"When was that?"

She lifted her gaze to the ceiling. "Right before we blew the tunnels on the island. Probably six or eight weeks ago?"

Nic opened his mouth, then clamped it shut.

"What?"

"Nothing."

"We already know that's when you came back to Sydney from your trip to Singapore."

"You people just know everything about me, don't you?"

"No, not everything."

"So tell me about this whole demon-hunting thing."

Finally. At least he was showing some interest, though

she suspected he wanted to lead her away from the questions she was asking. "What do you want to know?"

"I don't know. Everything. Tell me about you, how you got involved in all this."

She blew out a breath. "I was invited to participate in a television reality show called *Surviving Demon Island*. But it was actually a front to recruit me and the others to become demon hunters. Lou and Derek invited a bunch of us, we went to an island in the South Pacific, he trained us, and we played this game."

"Why did they choose you?"

"Because my mother, all our mothers, had been taken by demons."

"Taken?"

"Kidnapped. When all of us were younger. None of us knew what happened. I thought my mother had disappeared while on a business trip."

"Maybe she ran off."

"She didn't!" she said, realizing she'd raised her voice. "She was very happy, dedicated to her job and to my father and me. She loved us. She wouldn't just up and leave without a word."

"Damn. That sucks."

"Even worse for my father. He was devastated. Left alone with a small child he didn't know how to deal with, pining away for the love of his life. It was like his heart had been ripped from his chest. I watched him disintegrate for fifteen years. He never recovered from losing her."

"He's dead?"

"Heart attack when I was twenty. I think he finally gave up." She stared down at her hands. She hated talking about the past, hated thinking that if she had spoken up when she'd gotten the vision, things might have been different.

Could she have changed things if she'd said something to her father? She'd never know now.

"I'm sorry you lost your mother. And your father."

She glanced up at him. "You don't believe me."

"I didn't say that."

"You didn't have to. It comes through in your tone of voice." Not that it mattered. He asked for her story and she was telling it, whether he believed it or not. "The demons use human women for procreation. Their own females are sterile. So they create these hybrids—half demons. Cunning and lightning-fast."

"So these half demons would be just like me and Derek."

"Not really."

"But if we're supposed to be half demons and they breed human women and demons, why wouldn't we be the same?"

She reached up and massaged her temples. "I don't know. You two are just different. You'll have to ask Derek. The ones I saw on that island weren't the same as you two. I don't know why."

"How are we different?"

"They're . . . cold. There's no humanity to them even though they're half human. You look at them and just know they have no soul. You can see it in their pale blue eyes. I thought Derek was different because he grew up with his human mother. He didn't even know about being half demon until recently." She looked at him, at his silhouette in the darkness. "But you didn't have your mother. You were raised by Ben, one of the Sons of Darkness. Why aren't you—"

"Cold?" he finished for her.

She hadn't meant to put it out there, but now that she had, it struck her that there *was* a big difference between Nic and those half demons they'd battled. With Nic, there was warmth. God was there warmth. More like a bonfire, and it burned hot and furious. It had fired her up from their first meeting and had yet to diminish. She didn't know what it was about him, but there was something that differentiated him from the half demons, and even from Derek.

"You're not cold."

"Well, thanks for that."

His voice had gone low and she felt the darkness even more acutely. The room seemed to close in on her, making her more aware that she was locked up with him. The quiet became unnerving.

"Anyway, back to the demons," she said, needing to hear the sound of her own voice to break the spell of silence. "We played this game of 'capture the demon' with our fake weapons. For a while, anyway. Until the real demons showed up."

"Real demons?"

"Yeah. Lou and Derek hadn't expected actual demons to be on the island. They used some of the hunters as game demons, and those were our intended targets. Their objective was to see how we did playing a laser-tag kind of game with fake weaponry, and then if we passed the test, recruit us into the Realm of Light."

"Okay, explain again this Realm of Light?"

"It's a secret organization that fights the Sons of Darkness. The demons. Lou is a Keeper of the Realm of Light. His bloodline is traced back to the original Keepers from centuries ago."

Nic shifted, and Shay knew he was uncomfortable. She wished she could loosen his bonds, but she couldn't.

"So what you're telling me is this whole demon hunting thing has been going on for hundreds of years? And that supposedly my father is part of these Sons of Darkness?"

"Yeah. I guess so. I don't really know all the particulars, but I do know that Derek is part demon. I've seen him in action."

"What do you mean?"

"I saw him change."

"Into a demon."

"Yes."

"Come on."

She shrugged. "You can believe or not believe. I know what I saw."

He paused before he said, "Tell me what happened when he changed."

"His body seemed to grow larger, more muscular, as if he was doubling in size, and his teeth turned to fangs.

His eyes turned red and glowed. His fingernails elongated into claws and his face turned into this twisted, horrifying..."

Nic held his breath and waited for Shay to continue. She didn't.

"What?" he finally asked, needing to know what she saw and whether it was the same thing he saw in his dreams.

"It's just hard to describe. It's like his cheekbones expanded, his mouth grew wider, his forehead popped out more prominently as if the bones themselves had swelled. It was gruesome as hell."

"Jesus." He didn't want to believe it, but she'd come damn close to describing what he saw in his nightmares.

Coincidence? Maybe.

The stories she told. Good God. Either they were true, or she was one incredibly good liar. They had to be lies. "Why doesn't he just prove to me he's half demon by turning into one? That would be the easiest way."

She sighed, her clear blue eyes gazing directly at him, her full lips parted as she took in a breath.

"Another thing you're going to have to ask him," she finally said. "But he's said before he's not going to let the demon out. He's afraid it's too hard to control."

Too hard to control. Like his nightmares, like the feeling he was holding something back—something bad inside him that wanted to get out. "Wouldn't he want to use his power to fight the demons?"

"If you had that monster inside you, would you let it out?"

There was the million-dollar question, the one that kept him from making love to Shay yesterday. The one that had kept him away from women, that made him doubt his own sanity.

Did he have a beast like that inside him? Wouldn't he be able to feel it if he did? Shit, he couldn't even believe he was halfway buying into this, but what she said came too damn close to his own weird experience. "I think I've had enough for today."

"You don't believe any of this, do you?"

He shrugged. "It's not easy without proof."

She nodded. "Understandable. I was the same way at first, but you start to believe in a hurry once you see them."

"I'm not interested in seeing them. Or staying here." A thought occurred to him, one he hadn't considered before. How stupid of him. "I have an offer you might be interested in."

She raised her brows. "What kind of offer?"

"What would you say to a million dollars?"

She snorted. "Funny."

"I'm serious. You find a way to get me out of here and I'll pay you a million dollars."

"You're not joking, are you?"

Now they were getting somewhere. "Do you have any idea how much my family is worth?"

"No."

"Billions."

"No shit."

"Yup."

"Well, la-di-da." She leaned forward, once again letting him share in her enticing scent. "First, don't ever insult me again by making an offer like that. Second, let me give you some advice. Don't try to bribe anyone else here because they're just as likely to slit your throat for even making the suggestion. And you're better off without your other family. They'll only hurt you. Trust me when I tell you that you're safer with us than you are with them."

She stood and left the room.

That went well.

She didn't want a million dollars. What the fuck? Everyone wanted money.

Blowing out a breath, he tilted his head back and stared at the ceiling, trying to assimilate everything she'd told him.

Could this be real? Did demons really exist, could his father be one of them? Either Shay was one hell of a good storyteller and actress, or he glimpsed real, honest pain in her eyes when she told him her story. He felt her anguish as if it were part of him. And he didn't like feeling that deep a connection to someone he barely knew.

He'd never cared about a woman before. Women were fun. They were toys to be played with, trophies on his arm or a romp in bed. He treated them well, gave them gifts, and they always seemed to be satisfied with the monetary aspect of the relationship. It was a two-way street—he got what he wanted, and so did they. He purposely stayed away from the type of woman who wanted more than that.

Shay was different. He didn't quite know what to make of her. His physical reaction to her was like being struck by lightning, but it went beyond that. And she wasn't even interested in his money. How was he supposed to handle a beautiful woman who wasn't into money?

It didn't matter. He had to get a plan together so he could escape, starting with earning their trust so he could get more freedom of movement.

He needed to get the hell out of here.

Before he began to believe the stories Shay told him.

Chapter Eight

Once dawn approached, the hunters went upstairs to sleep. Nic was locked into his room and each of them took two-hour spells guarding his door.

Shay was grateful for the reprieve, since being around Nic was profoundly disturbing. But she'd still have to do her two hours. Fine with her. She could handle having him on the other side of the door, as long as she didn't have to touch him.

She slept until Trace knocked on her door, signaling it was her shift. Dragging herself out of bed, she dressed, grabbed her weapon, and stumbled into the hallway where Trace was sitting on a not-too-comfortable-looking chair, rifle across his lap.

He yawned and stood. "Enjoy yourself," he said as he headed to his room.

"Uh-huh."

Two hours would go by fast. Then she was going back to sleep, since they wouldn't have to be officially up for another several hours. Sleeping in the daylight sucked enough as it was, and screwed up her normal rest patterns. Having to switch her nights and days to hang out with Nic had only made things worse.

She leaned her head against the wall, trying to focus her thoughts on anything that would keep her awake. But then she heard a sound coming from Nic's bedroom.

A groan, maybe?

She stood and moved to his door, pressing her ear there.

He was talking. Mumbling. She couldn't make out what he was saying, though. Whatever it was, he was angry about it. What the hell was he doing?

He kept talking. And his voice was getting louder.

Dammit, why did this have to happen on her watch? With a disgusted sigh, she cradled her weapon and unlocked his door, inching it open.

It was pitch black inside. She opened the door a little further and slipped in.

"Nic?" she whispered.

No answer.

"No!"

Okay, that was an answer. Sort of. She blinked, forcing her eyes to focus in the darkness, and headed toward the sound of his voice. She made out his shape in the bed. He was rolling around, the sheet tangled around his middle. The rest of him was uncovered.

Now that her eyes were adjusted, she could see he must be asleep. Dreaming? Nightmares? Talking in his sleep, he mumbled incoherently, thrashing around the bed like a maniac.

"Stop. Get away from me!"

His voice was getting louder. She really should do something before he woke everyone up.

Edging toward the bed, she reached out and gently pressed on his shoulder. "Nic, wake up."

His hand snaked out, his eyes shot open, and he grabbed her wrist with a crushing force. "Don't touch me."

Like a tornadic wind, her visions sucked her in. Nic was trying to back away from approaching demons and Shay was right there with him now, against the wall. He took her hand and started to run. They were in a cave— so dark, and hard to feel their way around. She couldn't see, had to rely on Nic leading her.

She felt the demons behind them, and something more. Something evil.

They couldn't outrun it. It was catching up.

The vision evaporated, and Shay looked down at Nic. Adrenaline pumping, she tried to jerk her wrist away from him. But he had a tight hold and wouldn't let go. "Nic, it's Shay. You're dreaming."

He stared at her, but it wasn't malevolence in his eyes. It was downright fear. And he was shaking, a fine sheen of sweat coating his face and body.

She kept her voice calm, low and tranquil. "Nic, do you hear me? It's Shay." She stopped struggling to get away from him, and sat on the edge of the bed. "You must be having a nightmare."

He blinked and stared at his hand, then let her loose,

pushing back to sit up against the headboard. He dragged his hands through his hair and blew out a breath. "Sorry. I'm sorry. Shit."

"It's okay. Are you all right?" His hands were still shaky.

"I'm fine." As if he had just realized it was her, and she was armed, he glanced down at the weapon and back up at her. "I'm hardly in a position to make a run for it."

Shay turned and gaped at the sheet that barely covered the most intimate part of him. The rest of him was uncovered. With the daylight filtering in through the dark shades in the room, she could see plenty. As if she hadn't been ogling his body during the day they'd spent together, having him nearly naked and right next to her in his bed set off pinging awareness that shouldn't be happening.

She stood and looked down at him. "You're sure you're okay."

"I'm fine. You can go now."

"You don't need to take that angry tone with me. I was just trying to help."

"I think you've already *helped* me plenty." He whipped the sheet off and swung his legs over before she had a chance to make a beeline for the door. He stood and started moving. She raised her weapon and he grinned, halting in mid-stride. "I'm going to the bathroom, unless that's an offense you're going to gun me down for."

He was beautiful, standing there naked and unashamed, taunting her on purpose.

But she'd be damned if she was going to run off like a frightened virgin who'd never seen a naked man before. She looked her fill, enjoying every square inch of him, a part of her wishing things could be different. Because, God, did she ever wish she could lay down her weapon and go to him right now, throw herself into his arms and finish what they'd started in the pool. Her body throbbed with instant awareness and need.

But things weren't different. And the anger in his gaze was a bitter reminder of that.

"Go right ahead," she said, waiting until he turned from her and entered the bathroom before she went out, locking him back in and taking her seat.

So what was that all about? Nightmares? And the instant he awoke, he grasped her like she was going to hurt or attack him or something. He was angry, and he was scared.

Nic didn't strike her as a guy who frightened easily. He seemed tough and capable. So what scared the hell out of him in his dreams?

She wished he didn't hate her, because she wanted to explore whatever it was that bothered him. And she wanted to talk about her visions and how they tied into him. Had she entered his nightmare, or was it something else? Because goddamn, it was making her crazy.

It had just been a nightmare, right? Her vision had nothing to do with what he'd been dreaming about. Totally unrelated, and his bad dream was probably just a one-time thing brought about by the trauma they'd all inflicted on him. Hell, if they'd done it to her, she'd be having nightmares, too.

Though she'd always had visions, lately they were all about Nic.

Nic woke with a headache. Great. He sat up and stared at the closed door, wondering who was on the other side guarding him. Most likely not Shay.

Of all people to wake him up having a nightmare. Bad enough she'd been dragged right into the middle of his dream. She'd been standing in the center of a room where the monsters surrounded him—cornered him. She beseeched him to leave with her, told him there was redemption if he would only take her hand. And his father was compelling him to stay. His first thought was that he had to get Shay out of there and get her to safety. Before the monsters got her.

These fucking dreams were killing him. His head pounded, confusion twisting his gut. They seemed so real. And now Shay was in them, her presence reassuring, a soft balm to the madness. For some reason her appearing in his dreams was giving him the impetus to run, the courage to get away from the demons.

But dammit, he didn't want her in his dreams. Or in his life. Fisting his temples, he pressed inward, willing the headache away.

That did no good. With a muttered curse he bounded out of bed and into the bathroom, opening up the medicine cabinet but already knowing what he'd find in there.

Nothing. As if goddamn Tylenol could be used as a weapon.

With a disgusted sigh, he went to the door and knocked on it. Ryder was there, a frown on his face.

"'Bout time you got up. I'm hungry. Get dressed."

Nic closed the door. Friendly sort, wasn't he? He pulled on clothes and brushed his teeth, eager to get the hell out of his bedroom prison.

Derek looked up as Nic entered the kitchen. He was the only one in there, leaning against the counter with a steaming mug in his hand. Nic inhaled, and the smell of coffee made his mouth water.

"Coffee?" Derek asked.

Nic nodded. "Black."

Derek filled a cup and handed it to Nic. "Have a seat. We'll talk."

Ryder filled a mug. "Where's everybody else?"

"Other room. Strategizing," Derek said.

Ryder nodded and headed in that direction, leaving Derek and Nic alone. Nic was surprised they hadn't dragged him into the other room and tied him up. Then again, it wasn't like he was going to get anywhere with all these people around. Or at least not far. He didn't know what kind of weaponry they had on them or what ammo they loaded in those things, but he didn't think he wanted any of that blue liquid shit fired in his direction.

"Sleep well?" Derek asked, grabbing a seat across from him.

"Not really."

"You and Shay talk?"

"She filled me in a bit, yeah."

"You probably have a million questions."

"I have a few."

Derek tilted the chair, rocking it on its back legs. "Shoot. I'll tell you whatever you want to know."

"Tell me what you know about my father. Describe him."

"You do realize I can only tell you what I remember of the man from my own childhood, and that was only until I was about ten or so. Long time ago. It's spotty."

Nic crossed his arms. "How convenient."

Derek shrugged. "He hated sports and never went outside during the daylight hours. Claimed allergies to sunlight, which is why he worked nights. Never ate much. Always seemed distracted. Disappeared for long periods of time. Travel was a big thing for him. He really wasn't much of a father figure, leaving our upbringing mainly to Mom."

Nic blinked. Derek had fairly accurately described his childhood with his father, except for the mother part. How would he know about those things? His father had never once watched Nic surf, claiming he couldn't go out during the daylight hours because the sunlight would fry his skin.

"Do you remember anything before the time Ben took you?"

"He didn't 'take me' anywhere. I hit my head in a fall when I was eight, and as a result suffered amnesia. They thought I might eventually remember, but I never have. I don't remember a thing from my life before that head injury."

Derek arched a brow. "Uh-huh. How convenient."

"What? Do you think my father wiped this alleged memory of you and your mother?"

"*Our* mother. And yes, I think that's exactly what he did. Or maybe you blocked it. Hell, I don't know."

Nic picked up Shay's scent before he heard her enter the kitchen. He turned to see her and that dark-haired beauty who seemed to belong to Derek.

"Are we interrupting?" Shay asked from the doorway.

"No. Come on in," Derek said. "I'm just filling in some of the gaps for Nic."

"Okay."

The dark-haired woman leaned down to press a lingering kiss on Derek's mouth. When she lifted her head, she smiled at Nic. "I'm Gina Bernardi," she said, holding out her hand to him.

He shook it. "You look really familiar. I think you look like an actress or something."

She snorted. "I get that a lot."

"We're going to make breakfast while you two talk," Shay said, casting her gaze at Nic. "You hungry?"

He nodded, and Shay turned away to the stove. She wore the same kind of clothes as before. Dark camouflage and a tank top. Very sexy warrior-like clothing, accentuating her curves. He still couldn't reconcile this woman in front of him with the one he'd met on the beach.

"Look," Derek said, pulling Nic's attention away from Shay, "I know this isn't easy to assimilate, but I'm here to answer your questions. And it's going to take time to figure it all out. But I am telling you the truth. Ben was a full-fledged demon. There's evil out there. The kind most people don't know exist. And that evil lives in our blood."

Nic went silent and so did Derek. He watched the women cook.

"I know this is all hard to take. But trust me, eventually you're going to see a demon and you're going to believe."

Nic shot a disbelieving look at Derek. "Sure. If you say so. But I don't feel a damn thing other than human."

"Neither did I," Derek said. "Or at least I didn't think so. But there are subtle differences." He dragged his hand through his hair. "I don't know. We haven't figured this all out yet. You might even be different from me in how the demon blood manifests itself. Your reactions might be the opposite of mine. Lou says our gifts could be completely unique, whatever the hell that means."

Gina laid a plate in front of Derek and placed her hand on his shoulder. "Lou always seems to know what he's talking about, babe. Trust his instincts on this."

"I know," Derek said, caressing Gina's hand. "I just want all the answers now."

Gina sat next to Derek and grinned. "You're always too impatient."

"Yeah, yeah, I know."

Shay placed a plate in front of Nic and sat next to him.

She was watching Derek and Gina, too, then slanted a look at Nic.

"Thank you for cooking for me," he said, his mouth watering at the plate filled with eggs, bacon, potatoes, and toast.

"You're welcome." She cast a wary half smile in his direction.

Eating was an understatement. He inhaled everything on the plate, and when Shay didn't finish hers, he ate the rest of what was on her plate, too. By the time he finished, he felt a lot better. Now maybe his brain cells would work better.

As far as Derek, he didn't remember the guy. He wished he could recall his life before the head injury, but he couldn't. So who did he believe? This stranger claiming to be his brother, or his father?

He was starting to doubt everything his dad had told him. Maybe his dad never had time for him throughout his life; maybe he never showed Nic any affection, but the Diavolos were the only family he knew. He had to believe in his father. Otherwise his entire life was a lie.

These people were strangers, and he had to fight this mind fuck. Sure, they seemed sincere, but that was all part of their game. He could play that game, too. His only hope was to gain their trust, then, when their guard was down, try to make an escape.

"You're quiet," Shay said.

"Trying to take all this in."

"Look," Derek said. "If I were in your place I wouldn't believe any of it, either. I wish I could make this easy and show you, but I can't. If I could drag a demon to the front door, I would."

Nic laughed. "Not sure I really want to see that."

Derek cracked a smile. "Trust me. You don't."

Now it was his turn. "You're just going to have to give me some time. This is all incredible and hard to believe. I need to adjust to it. I want to believe you, but you're asking me to cast aside everything I've known, everyone I've trusted my entire life. I can't do that overnight."

"No one expects you to," Shay said, laying her hand over his. "We'll give you the time you need. But this is a good first step."

He almost jerked his hand away when she touched him, his irritation at her betrayal front and center on his mind. But the goddamn heat exchange between them was lethal. Instead, he offered up a half smile, almost feeling guilty for deceiving her. Almost.

He owed her most of all for what she'd done to him. This was all about self-preservation, and guilt wasn't part of the game.

After breakfast, Derek invited Nic into the living room. He took a seat while the hunters talked about their plans for that night. Derek didn't have him tied up. A good sign.

"I think we need to go back to the area we were last night," Dalton said. "Ryder spotted a woman and we need to follow up on that, see if she comes back and find out what she was doing out there."

Derek nodded. "Good idea. Plus I want to get into

some of those caves and see what we can discover. It's time to do a little gem hunting."

Nic took it all in, storing the information away for future use.

Lou nodded. "Between looking for the black diamond and hunting the demons I'm sure are in this area, there should be plenty to occupy us. Dalton, take your team in that direction tonight. Maybe a few extra hunters, too, just in case. The rest of the teams can take positions south, east, and west of your quadrant."

"Can I go along?" Nic asked.

Derek studied him. "Man, you have no idea how much I'd like that. But you're nowhere near ready for this."

Dammit. He knew Derek was going to say that. "I can just observe. You want me to believe, then show me a demon."

Derek slanted a gaze at him as if he was considering it, but then shook his head. "No. Not yet. First, I don't have time to watch over you and battle demons at the same time. Second, you can't be trusted yet. Sorry."

Nic affected a shrug, but he had to check the anger wanting to burst through. "I understand."

Derek smiled. "No, you don't. You're pissed and I know it. But that's okay. I would be, too, if I were in your position. Give it a few days. You want to start conditioning, we can work with you each day before nightfall. When I feel like we can trust you, and when I'm confident you can hold your own with the physical aspects of this job as well as the weaponry, we'll take you along on a hunt."

Oh, that was priceless. Derek didn't think he was in shape? He really didn't know shit about him. "You don't think I can handle myself?"

"No, I don't."

"Why don't you give me a try right now?"

Derek frowned, shook his head. "Not a good idea."

"Afraid I'll prove you wrong?" He needed this chance. The sooner he got out there, the faster he'd be able to escape.

"You have no idea what you're asking for, little brother."

The endearment bristled. He let it slide. "I know what I'm doing. You want to train me, then train me."

With a shrug of his shoulders, Derek said, "Okay, but don't forget you asked for this."

Chapter Nine

Shay had no business worrying over Nic's safety, but the idea of him skirmishing with Derek made her stomach tie up in knots. They were about the same height, but Nic was leaner, Derek more muscular. She didn't think Nic stood a chance of holding his own. She'd seen Derek fight. He was incredibly tough. She found herself rooting for Nic to win. How odd.

They'd all gathered outside in back of the big house. A wide arc of open space afforded them plenty of room to move around.

Dusk had settled over the area so the sun wouldn't be in anyone's eyes, having long ago filtered behind the tall trees sheltering the back of the property. But it was still hot enough to melt their feet to the ground. Shay drew in lungfuls of humid air, wondering how long the two of them were going to be able to go at it without passing out.

Derek had taken his shirt off and wore only dark camo pants and his boots. Nic wore a sleeveless tank and shorts.

"This is insane," Gina said, moving in next to Shay.

Shay nodded. "Is this really necessary?"

"It's a guy thing. Derek really wants his brother as part of this team."

"I think Nic has something to prove," Shay added, though she felt a little odd speaking for Nic, since he didn't belong to her.

"I think you're right. Let's hope he's able to do it."

It didn't sound like Gina had much faith in Nic's ability to hold his own with Derek, either.

"Derek's going to kick his ass," Ryder said from behind them.

Shay turned around, saw Trace and Dalton with their arms crossed and smug smiles on their faces. Okay. So she might have thought Nic didn't have a chance in hell of besting his brother, but did everyone else have to think that, too?

"You ready?" Derek asked Nic.

"Just get on with it."

Nic moved his right leg back and bent the front one, raising his fists in a fighting stance. So far so good. He at least had that part down right. Shay admired the muscles in his arms and shoulders as they rippled when he flexed. He might be leaner than Derek, but he was no lightweight—he had some strength.

Derek lunged and Nic sidestepped, circling around to take the spot Derek had previously occupied. Derek smiled and nodded. "Pretty good start."

Nic didn't reply, just kept moving back and forth in the dirt, his gaze focused only on Derek. The others watched, unmoving, staying silent at least for the moment. Derek made another lunge and Nic sidestepped again, but this time Derek didn't follow through. He moved along with Nic and threw his shoulder into Nic's stomach, and the two of them went flying.

Shay held her breath as Nic landed on the ground with Derek on top of him, pinning him. Nic expelled his breath as Derek's weight pressed in on him. Surely it wouldn't be over this fast, would it?

The rest of the hunters began to cheer Derek. Shay mentally pleaded for Nic to do something—anything—to keep this fight going. His lips were pressed in a grim line, the concentration on his face evident in the furrow of his brow and the narrowed eyes. He looked only at Derek, then pushed, hard.

Shay's eyes widened, and she gasped as Derek flew to the side and Nic jumped up, leveling a kick at Derek's stomach. Derek rolled out of the way just in time to avoid being stomped on.

Wow. She'd wanted Nic to gain the upper hand, but never in a million years did she figure he had that kind of strength.

The others who'd previously been cheering Derek on, certain of a quick victory, had been reduced to shocked silence as Nic more than held his own with Derek, avoiding blows and kicks from an obviously better trained hunter and swinging and kicking with a few adept moves of his own.

Shay began to smile, even relaxed her shoulders a little, excited to see a very evenly matched battle. Eventually the two of them fatigued, their movements slowing, their breaths heaving with every punch thrown.

Derek held up his hands, panting heavily. "Okay. You proved your point. You're a damn good fighter."

Nic bent over and rested his palms above his knees, his breath sawing in and out. "You're not too bad yourself."

"I was cutting you some slack."

Nic's head shot up and he grinned. "You're full of shit."

Derek laughed. "Let's go inside and get something to drink."

Relieved that was over with, Shay followed them inside and grabbed a bottle of water. She was sweating and dying of thirst, and all she'd been doing was standing around watching. Derek and Nic downed at least a gallon of water apiece while they sat at the table.

"Did we do that a lot when we were kids?" Nic asked, motioning out back with a tilt of his head.

"Fight? Yeah, we did our share of rolling around our bedroom, though it wasn't quite as brutal. Mom usually put a stop to it long before we drew blood."

Nic took another long swallow of water, smiling as he did. He put the bottle on the table and shook his head as he stared at the clear liquid. "I wish I could remember. I can't."

Shay caught the shadow of pain crossing Derek's face.

Gina grabbed his hand and squeezed it. She knew it must hurt him to know Nic didn't remember him.

"Maybe it'll come back to you someday," Shay suggested.

Nic cast his glance toward her and shrugged. "I don't know why it would. It hasn't yet. The first eight years of my life are toast. My dad took me to tons of doctors. They even tried hypnosis. Nothing could bring it back."

"Uh-huh."

Nic glared at Derek. "What's that supposed to mean?"

"It means either you've blocked them because of the kidnapping, or somehow Ben erased your memories of those early years intentionally. Whatever hocus-pocus bullshit he put you through wasn't meant to return those memories to you. He didn't want you to remember."

Nic opened his mouth, then shrugged. "Doesn't matter, but I want to know about those first eight years. If what you say is true and I am your brother, you're the only one besides my dad who can fill in that missing time in my life."

Derek leaned back in his chair. "Obviously the stories I tell you will be different from what Ben said. They'll include our mother, where we grew up. Ben's were all fabricated."

Nic nodded. "I still want to hear them. If yours are the truth maybe they'll jog my memory."

Derek started talking, and Nic listened, his focus entirely on Derek. Shay was enraptured by stories of the two of them as children. Where they grew up, the games they used to play, where they went to school, and what their mother was like. She sounded wonderful—warm, generous and loving—the kind of mother Shay would have wanted to have.

Oh, she had loved her mother so much, but Terry Pearson hadn't been the warmest woman on the planet. She'd been a good mom, a provider, a hard worker, a career woman. As a role model for working women, she was perfect. Driven, focused, Shay's mother got the job done. She could work ten hours a day, six days a week, and still have food on the table every night. But she hadn't been into cuddling and reading bedtime stories and playing games and all those things Shay fantasized about when she thought about mothers. Terry Pearson had been a mother, but not a nurturer. Derek's and Nic's mother sounded like a nurturer—a woman who played in the backyard with her kids, took them to the park, wrestled with them, hugged them, kissed them, loved them with every part of her heart. A true mother   until she went off the deep end after Nic's disappearance.

"So she became really distant then?" Nic asked.

"After you disappeared, she couldn't keep her lies straight from the truth anymore. I didn't notice it so much when I was younger, but I put the puzzle pieces together when I got older, and they didn't make sense. I was convinced you hadn't died, that what I had seen really happened. A demon carried you away from our bedroom that night. And when I saw those demons in Chicago and followed them, when I met up with Lou and learned about the Realm of Light, I knew then that Mom had lied about you being dead. I knew I really had seen a demon that night. And Ben admitted he was the one to take you away. It was our father who ran off with you. He was in demon form that night. He intended to take you first and come back for me. For some reason he targeted you first. Why he didn't take both of us that night, I don't know. But he grabbed you and didn't come back for me. And then Mom took me and ran. She was never the same after that."

Shay's heart broke for both of them, for what they'd lost—their mother, and the close bond between them that Derek described. Derek seemingly had lost even more, because Nic couldn't remember any of this.

But now Derek had Gina, who held tight to his hand, her chair scooted right next to his, her arm slung around his back. She was the cornerstone for a man who seemingly didn't need a rock, but he needed Gina.

Nic didn't seem at all affected hearing this story about his father and about a mother he couldn't remember, or the brother he was just now learning to know again.

"This must be pretty strange for you," Shay said.

Nic looked at her. "More than strange. I look at Derek and don't see any similarities at all between us."

Shay snorted. Gina laughed out loud.

Nic frowned. "What?"

"You two look alike," Gina said. "Same height, same coloring. The eyes might be a different color, but the shape is the same. Your jawline is similar."

"I don't see it at all," Nic said.

"Me, either," Derek said with a shrug.

"Men," Shay interjected. "It's like shoes."

"Shoes?" Nic asked.

"A woman can bring out three pairs of black shoes and ask you which you like best and you'll think all three look exactly the same, yet there are still subtle differences. You just can't see the forest for the trees."

Nic looked at Derek. Derek shook his head and said, "Don't bother trying to figure it out. It's a woman thing."

"It's more than just physical characteristics," Shay said. "You're both driven and competitive and stubborn. You refuse to yield. Just look at your skirmish outside earlier."

"She has a point," Gina said.

"Maybe." Nic just shrugged.

"It was a pretty evenly matched battle. Better than I expected from you."

The pride in Derek's voice was evident.

"You thought you were gonna kick my ass in the first minute, didn't you?" Nic cracked a smile.

"Where did you learn to fight like that? You're stronger than I thought you'd be."

Nic shrugged. "I've had experience here and there. I don't just surf."

"Obviously. You did good. You'll make a hell of a demon hunter. You've got strength and stamina and a top-notch killer instinct."

"I don't like to lose," Nic said, his voice going low.

"That'll keep you alive in this business," Derek said.

"Amen to that," Gina seconded.

Nic stood. "I need a shower. Do I need a guard for that?"

Derek shook his head. "Go ahead. I think you can be trusted not to jump out the window. But if you're not back down here in fifteen minutes I'm going hunting for you."

Nic grinned. "No worries."

Lou stepped in the room as soon as Nic left. His brows lifted as he looked at Derek. "Your thoughts?"

"I don't sense darkness in him. No sense of evil. He doesn't seem to have a clue about the Sons of Darkness or the demons."

"Good. And he did well fighting against you. *Did* you hold back at all?"

"No. He was a good match for me."

"And you're certainly no slouch in the kicking-ass department," Gina said.

"So test him," Lou suggested.

"Not sure that's a good idea, Lou. I don't want to risk it yet." Derek looked to Shay. "Work with him on weapons tonight."

Shay's eyes widened. "Are you sure you trust him enough to put a weapon in his hand?"

He shrugged. "Do you mean am I stupid enough to trust him completely yet? Hell, no. We'll pull the ammo out of them and let you work with him on identifying, explaining functionality and use."

"Okay. Weapons training it is." Anything would be better than having to baby-sit him while he was tied up.

"Keep a weapon strapped to you, though. A loaded one. If he tries anything or looks at all like he's going to shift or go bad . . . wound him."

Shay nodded at Derek, hoping it wouldn't come to that. She didn't want to be the one responsible for hurting Derek's brother. She'd never be able to live with the guilt of causing Derek more pain than he'd already experienced. What he'd gone through with his father was more than enough.

She'd just have to hope Derek's instincts were right, and whatever demon blood lived inside Nic was held at bay, the same way Derek's had been. And that Nic wasn't playing them all for fools, lying to them and lulling them into a false sense of security so they would let their guard down around him.

Because if that's what he was doing, if he was playing them in the hopes of escaping, she'd personally hunt him down and hurt him in a big way.

Chapter Ten

Ryder's quarry had gotten away last night, and it still grated on his nerves. The woman he chased had escaped. Maybe she was a nobody, and maybe she wasn't.

He didn't often lose, and it pissed him off. When he spotted a target, he went after it with precision and he got it.

Not last night, though.

They'd split up to search the caves, staying in contact, and here he was, skulking around in the general location where he'd spotted the woman last night.

What the hell for? She probably wasn't a demon. If he found her, he most likely wouldn't even be able to kill her. He had to hope there were demons out here and he ran into them instead. They were his target, not some elusive woman he never even got a good look at. What difference did it make whether some stranger got away from him or not?

Because you hate to lose.

He scoffed at the voice inside his head. Wasn't that the damn truth? That's why he had been the military's A-number-one killer. He not only hated to lose—he didn't fail.

The Realm of Light just hadn't yet figured out how good he was. He preferred staying back and keeping to himself, learning from those around him better trained in their area. Until he picked up all the skills he needed to, anyway.

This demon hunting thing was something new, so he'd been working with the other hunters during their off time the past couple months, and spending every available minute training. On the island the weapons had been tossed at him with no time to practice. They'd had to kill demons on the run, still shell shocked to learn they had a common bond, that their mothers had all been taken by demons.

Old reminders that only made killing the demons easier. Not that he needed a reason to kill. It was an assignment and he did it.

He kept his movements slow and steady, staying so silent he couldn't hear the sound of his own footsteps moving about in the all-too-quiet night.

And it was that complete lack of background noise that unnerved him—no night creatures were stirring. It usually meant something bad was about to happen.

The comm was quiet, which meant no one had run into any demons yet. He approached a cave entrance and stepped inside, relief from the oppressive heat immediate. He stopped, took a few long gulps of water, then moved further into the cave, keeping a snail's pace.

If there was one thing he'd learned in special ops, it was patience. You never got the jump on the enemy by charging in like a herd of elephants. His hearing was tuned into the slightest sound, so when he heard the scraping he smiled.

Gotcha.

It could be either demon or human, but no matter which, they weren't getting away. Then again, it could be an animal in the cave, so he wasn't going to comm the team until he knew for sure.

He followed the sound, stepping inch by inch into the quickly sloping center of the cave. The scraping continued, the sound rhythmic, like someone using a tool against the wall.

That wasn't an animal, and he'd never heard a demon make a sound like that. Plus he hadn't received any kind of signal from Lou that demons had appeared. Which meant it had to be human.

He smiled in the darkness. A few more feet and he'd reach the sound.

But then he picked up the scent. Foul, like rotting garbage. In the confined area of the cave, the smell traveled fast.

Hybrid demons, the worst kind.

He moved into the room where he found a woman, using what looked like a small pickax to chop away at the far wall in an open room. A light was set up on the floor, illuminating the wall where she worked. As far as he could tell, she was working alone.

Shit.

He had no idea what she was doing and didn't have time to ask, since he had a fraction of a second to make a decision. He moved in quiet and fast and grabbed her around the wrist with one hand, the other clamping over her mouth and smothering her surprised gasp. Her pickax fell to the ground. As soon as it did, he grabbed her around the waist. She struggled, kicking back against his shins with her boots, her screams muffled by his hand.

He clenched his jaw and held her tight, placing his mouth as close to her ear as he could.

"There's something in this cave with us," he whispered harshly, hoping he could get his point across. "Something bad. I'm not going to hurt you, but *it* will. Now shut up and follow my instructions."

At least she stopped struggling, but her heart pounded like a jackhammer against his arm. He didn't have time to worry about her fear.

"Derek," he commed. "I found a woman in the far thest cave to the east. There are hybrids in here."

"How many?" he shot back.

"No clue. Didn't see them but picked up their scent."

"You got the woman?"

"You could say that."

"Get her out of there." Derek swore. "And don't... tell her anything. We're on the way."

Right. He just had to drag her out of the cave and

hope they didn't run into demons along the way. She probably thought she was being kidnapped, but he couldn't tell her why.

This was going to go well.

Shay held the weapon out in front of her. "This is the UV laser. The blue stuff we inject as ammo is ultraviolet light. When blasted through the barrel part here, it melts the demons on the spot. Really icky, too."

Icky. Now there was a word. Nic had been sitting with Shay for the better part of two hours while she went over weaponry. It was like watching one of those television shows on high-tech military hardware of the future. "This stuff's for real, huh?"

Shay nodded, pride evident from the light in her eyes to the wide grin on her face. You'd think she'd created these weapons herself. "You bet it is. You should see these things in action. I didn't believe it myself at first, but they do work. These babies stop demons in their tracks, melt flesh, explode them from the inside out, and in general wreak havoc on demon physiology. Kick-ass weapons."

She placed the laser in his hands, unloaded of course. Heavy sucker.

"Who created these things?"

"The Realm of Light. I imagine they have scientists who put them together. On the island we were more concerned with heading out into the jungle and killing demons. We were given a crash course in the weapons available and shoved out there to use them. There wasn't much time to ask a lot of questions."

He studied her, wondering how someone who looked like she should be teaching a class of kindergarten kids could be handling the life of a demon hunter. That is, if this was really true. "You seem to have adapted well."

She shrugged. "When you see them, you'll understand. You do what you have to do. I don't want those things roaming the world and killing humans. It's my job now to kill as many of them as I can."

He lifted the gun, peering through the sights and aiming at a target— a potted plant on a shelf near the front door in the living room. The trigger was an easy pull. When he put it down, she was staring at him. "Don't you get scared?"

"All the time. Especially when I'm hunting and I know they're out there somewhere, about to attack. But when they show up, adrenaline kicks in and I'm too busy fighting to be frightened."

Damn, she had guts. "I'm impressed."

Her cheeks colored that pretty shade of pink. "Don't be. The other hunters are the ones who deserve your admiration. I'm just a newbie following along and doing what I'm told."

He laid the gun on the table and leaned back in the kitchen chair, lacing his fingers behind his head. "I don't know about that. You seemed pretty self-confident when you played cloak-and-dagger and lured me into your trap."

She blushed a deeper crimson again. "Like I said. I do what I'm told."

"Was kissing me part of the act?"

Shit. He had to bring it up, didn't he?

"No, it wasn't."

Deciding to change subjects, he motioned to the daggers on her hips. "What about those. They part of the secret weaponry?"

Her hands moved to the knives. "No. They're personal."

"That's right. Your hobby. You mentioned that."

She nodded.

"You know how to use them?"

She arched a brow. "If you're going to own them, you should know how to wield them."

He shook his head. "I guess."

"You want to see one?"

"You trust me with a weapon in my hand?"

She tilted her head to the side and patted the pistol tucked into the holster on her hip. "My gun is loaded, Nic. You come at me with my own dagger and I'm afraid I'll have to shoot you."

This time she wasn't smiling. She never ceased to surprise him. "Duly noted. Sure. Let me see it."

The dagger was sheathed on her other hip. The jewel-encrusted hilt looked to be worth a fortune. He wondered if the emeralds and rubies on there were real.

"Damn. That's nice."

She nodded. "It's my favorite. A bit heavy, but the hilt feels right in my hand. There's something magical about it. I can't explain it, but there's a power to it when I hold it. You probably think that's silly."

He placed the blade in his palm and handed the hilt back to her. She slid it back in its sheath and snapped its strap.

"I don't think it's silly at all. Weapons are a powerful thing. There's a mind/body connection to what you hold in your hand that adds to your strength when wielding your piece."

Shay arched a brow. "You know more about weaponry than I thought."

Nic shrugged. "I've dabbled here and there."

She sat in the chair next to him. "You seem to dabble in quite a few things."

"I've been around."

She drew one leg up on the chair, pulling her knee to her chest. "I would think you'd be too busy with the company business to dabble in much else."

"I do my job and I do it well. But it's not so critical that I can't do other things," he said, picking up the UV laser. He liked the feel of this weapon. Light and compact. But goddamn . . . what did they kill with this thing?

"So your dad kept you out of the more intimate business matters?"

"You could say that."

"Why?"

He laid the weapon down and looked at her. "Probably because he sensed my utter disinterest. Corporate life isn't my thing. I like physical activities better, and Dad didn't push me to get that involved in the diamond business. Then I was too busy with my competitive surfing and he wanted me to pursue that. He was always pushing me to go out and have fun, so I did."

"Bought into the bad-boy image, hook, line, and sinker, did you?"

He grinned. She read him pretty well. "Bad boy, huh?"

"You have the look."

"What look?"

"Gorgeous, sex appeal, charm, a bit of a dangerous edge. Irresistible to some women."

He tried not to laugh. He had no business feeling this sense of ease, this playfulness with Shay. But he couldn't help it. He tried to keep his distance from her, to hold on to the anger, but something compelled him, drove him to get closer.

"I see. Some women. But not you, of course."

"Of course not. I'm immune to that kind of thing."

Challenge. She'd thrown down the gauntlet and he snatched it up, ready to do battle.

"You're immune," he said.

"Yup."

"Wanna bet?"

Heat. Pure unadulterated heat, starting at Shay's toes and steaming its way upward through her limbs, pooling between her legs and staying there.

The way Nic looked at her when he issued his dare, the intensity in his eyes and the way he leaned in, crowding her personal space and capturing every breath she took. It wasn't fair. She was prepared to defend herself if he tried to escape. She wasn't prepared for seduction. And every part of his body language right now screamed his intent.

He hated her. Didn't he? Was he playing some kind of game with her? Or did he have ulterior motives? Dammit, her senses were in hyperdrive and she couldn't think straight.

"What are you doing?"

He stood and so did she, backing away from the kitchen table. He followed.

"I thought you were immune."

"I am. I'm thinking you're after my weapons."

That half smile of his was more lethal than any weapon. "I'm not interested in your gun, babe."

Her lower back hit the kitchen counter. She looked left, then right, thinking it was cowardly to run. Besides, she was assigned to keep an eye on him. "I'm supposed to be teaching you how to use the weapons."

"Lessons learned. I got it. Now I need to know just how immune you really are." He placed one hand on either side of her hips, caging her.

"Back off, Nic." Her protest sounded weak, even to her.

"You don't want me to back off. You're curious. You want to find out just how much of a bad boy I really am. If the image holds true. You want to pick up where we left off the other day in the pool. Do you know how sorry I am that I backed away from you? That I didn't do what I really wanted to do to you?"

Oh, God, that was so unfair. Could he hear her heart-beat? She could. Her palms were sweating, her throat was dry. So were her lips. She licked them and tried to swallow. His gaze dropped to her mouth and followed the movement like a predator. She felt like prey, too—like a morsel he intended to swoop down and take.

Did she want him to take? Yes, she did. They'd been circling around this insane attraction from the moment he'd stepped out of the ocean. She'd been hit by a ton of bricks that morning and hadn't recovered, despite her duty to her job, his kidnapping and subsequent anger. Her psychic vibes had been ringing like the Salvation Army bells at Christmas—nonstop and insistent.

She could tell herself a hundred times that there was nothing special about Nic Diavolo, but she already knew that was a lie. There was a connection between them she couldn't deny any longer, and the closer he got, the more she realized that he was danger with a capital *D*. Not just because he put her job in jeopardy, but because she couldn't get a handle on her visions whenever she touched him. She needed to keep her distance, but God help her, she didn't want to fight this any longer.

Shay gripped the edge of the counter and he moved in. His lips touched hers and she inhaled a ragged breath, held it, then exhaled on a moan as his mouth took pos-session.

She hadn't expected an explosion of sensation when he pressed his mouth firmly over hers, slid his tongue in-side, and turned her world upside down. Her stomach did flip-flops and flames shot between her legs, roaring like gasoline thrown on an already raging bonfire. Her legs began to shake and she forced them to still.

Good God Almighty, it was an inferno. Nic surged forward, his body pressed up against hers in every intimate way possible, the hard ridge of his erection shocking her as it hit the sweet spot of her sex. Her body wept in response, needing that joining in a way that stunned her.

She wasn't prepared to have sex with him. She'd allowed a kiss. One simple kiss.

How stupid could she be? Didn't she remember what it had been like before? Nothing about Nic was simple. The way he moved his mouth over hers, plunging his tongue inside and weaving it around hers, ravaging her lips with careless abandon, and rocking his body in a very obvious invitation—oh, no. All these things were clearly meant to disrupt every synapse in her brain, to complicate her life in ways she couldn't begin to fathom. Because all she could think was sex. Sex, sex, sex. She wanted to be naked and on the kitchen table, laid bare to be touched and kissed and licked. She needed him inside her in a way she'd never needed before.

No, this was not simple. This was complicated with a capital C.

And scary as hell. More terrifying than a horde of demons in the dark in the jungle. Because he wasn't just taking. She was offering. And she wanted to offer up everything. Mind, body, and soul.

And along with the searing passion came the tunnel

rushing toward her, threatening to suck her inside and carry her along.

No! No visions. Not now. She pushed them away, knowing she'd pay for it later, but she didn't care.

When he finally broke the kiss, she sucked in huge gulps of air, only to die once again when he planted his hot mouth on her neck and licked along her throat.

She wanted to beg for mercy. Or beg that he never, ever stopped his assault.

"Nic."

Whose voice was that? Throaty and hoarse and sexy. Surely not hers.

"Mmm" was his response. His hands were all over her now, smoothing down her bare arms. Despite the warmth, she broke out in goose bumps, the feel of his calloused hands turning her on in a big way. She wanted his fingers gliding over the more sensitive flesh of her body. Rough, insistent, demanding. She'd had a small taste of his hands before. Now she wanted it all.

Could a woman pass out from too much pleasure?

"Nic, please."

He lifted his head, his pupils dilated. The teasing smile was gone. He was dead serious now. "You're trembling." He moved his hands up and down her arms, encircling her waist and letting his fingers rest on her hips.

That so wasn't helping, especially when he pulled her hips closer to his body. Heat scored her there. Incendiary heat.

"What do you need, babe?"

That was a loaded question. She needed him to stop.

She didn't want him to stop. She wanted him to take the decision out of her hands so she didn't have to make it.

She was such a coward. Why didn't she just say the words? The way he breathed heavily, knowing he was as affected as she was—oh, wow, that excited her. How could she possibly put an end to this? The last thing she wanted right now was coherent thought or logic. There were a million valid reasons not to move forward, and no good ones to continue.

A slant of his head to the side, a quick study of her expression, and he nodded.

"Never mind. I know what you need."

He kissed her again and her mind went to mush. Probably a good thing, since the first thing that went after that was the belt with all her weapons. Then again, if he'd wanted to disarm her, he could have done that a while ago. The belt clanged to the counter. She was dimly aware of its location should she need to get it, but was more interested in Nic's ability to now move in closer to her body.

He didn't. Instead, he drew his hips away from hers, though his mouth still performed magic over hers, his tongue like some kind of brain-fogging drug, raking velvety strokes against hers. She hardly noticed that he'd unsnapped her pants and drawn the zipper down until a cool rush of air greeted her hips as he pushed her camos down her legs.

"Boots," he murmured against her lips.

"Damn." They were laced. This was inconvenient.

"Ah, fuck it. Don't want to wait." He squatted in front

of her and pulled her camos to her ankles, then wrapped his hands around her calves, smoothing his hands upward.

Shay looked down at him, this golden god between her shaky legs. His fingers crept ever upward, his gaze matching the movements of his hands. When he reached her buttocks and caressed them, pulling her hips forward, she released the whimper she'd been holding.

He raised up and buried his face in the V of her panties. Then he exhaled, and the heat from his mouth covering her sex nearly skyrocketed her to the ceiling.

"Nic!"

He didn't look up at her now. Instead, he focused between her legs, drawing the edge of her panties aside, revealing the most intimate part of her to his gaze.

She didn't know if she was more embarrassed or aroused. She barely knew him. He might be a demon. She wanted his mouth on her in the worst way. How could she be thinking of this while he was kneeling between her legs? Why, oh, why couldn't she get her mind to focus on one thing at a time? What was wrong with her?

"You're so pretty down here. Warm, wet, and you smell so good."

He was killing her. Tingles of anticipation swelled the bud nestled there, silently begging for a sweet swipe of his tongue.

"I'll bet you taste like honey."

The tone of his voice—dark, delicious—made her insides quiver.

Then he licked her, and the quiver rocked her like an earthquake. Her body shuddered all over as warm wetness swept over her throbbing cleft. She couldn't believe she was letting this happen. Yet it was, and she wouldn't stop it now if demons came crashing through the back door.

She brushed her hand through his hair. She wanted to touch him everywhere, to feel his skin under her hands, to explore every muscle and learn his body. But then he stroked upward with his tongue again, covering her with his mouth to gently suck, and she lost all focus.

The harsh lights in the kitchen denied her the intimacy that should have come with this act, yet it didn't matter. She was compelled to watch every movement of his tongue along her flesh, fascinated by the movement of his mouth, by her body's reaction. And oh, did it ever react. She'd never gotten this close so fast, never climbed that precipice in such record time. Yet here she was, ready to go off like a screaming rocket on the Fourth of July, and wanting to hold back, but she couldn't. She was there, her fingers tightening on the edge of the countertop, every muscle tensing as he quickened his pace, seemingly sensing she was nearing the end.

"Yes," she whispered, pulling his head closer as she drew to the very edge. Then the floodgates burst and she came, rocking her pelvis toward him. She had no control over her body, just gave it up to Nic. He grabbed her buttocks and pulled her against him, devouring her like she was a feast until she had no breath left, no strength. She sagged against the counter and gasped for breath.

Nic stood and leaned his hip against hers, watching her, smiling down at her as he cupped her moist sex. The intimacy was shocking, yet comforting. He didn't leave her there to come down off this alone, but held her, continued to touch her as she pulsed against him.

"You're quivering. I like that."

He cupped her sensitized flesh, caressing it with gentle motions until she felt the renewal of desire. How could he do this to her, how could he take her from exhausted completion to frantic need in such a short time? He slid two fingers inside her, her body gripping him from the inside, latching on to his fingers as he moved them in, then out, mimicking the movements of sex.

His smile devastated her.

"You're hot inside, babe. Like a melted furnace."

She didn't know what to say. He was right. She was hot and shaky and more uncertain of herself than ever. This was foreign territory. She didn't know Nic, and yet he was more familiar to her than most men she'd been with. She'd changed relationships like she changed majors in college—like she changed careers—never sticking with one long enough to decide whether she wanted to keep it or not.

Yet Nic didn't feel like a stranger to her. He felt comfortable. He was so much like her it was uncanny. She felt close to him. She needed him, and Shay never needed anyone, hadn't needed anyone for a very long time.

"You're tensing. Relax and let me make you come again. I like it when you come apart for me."

His words thrilled her, and yet they put him in power, in control over her. Maybe that's why she had such lousy sex in the past. She never let go. Though she didn't seem to have that problem with Nic. She'd placed her body and soul in his hands and he'd worked magic on her, just like he was doing now.

Quit thinking and let it happen.

She really had to start listening to her inner voice more often, because Nic had the best hands, ever. And either he must have had a lot of sex in his lifetime, or he really knew his way around a woman's body, because she never came more than once. But here she was, ready to go off again.

The man really was a magician. She grabbed his wrist, met his gaze, and let him take her there, panting like a wild thing while he found that perfect spot, and with a few strokes of his fingers she was climaxing again, crying out this time, certain if he wasn't holding on to her she would fall on the floor because her legs would no longer support her.

Turned out it wouldn't have mattered. As soon as the tremors subsided he swept her into his arms and carried her upstairs.

"Where are we going?" she asked when she could manage to find her voice.

"Bedroom. I want you naked."

Holy hell. Maybe he was trying to kill her.

Chapter Eleven

Ryder swore under his breath. The woman did not go easily, and he was in a damn hurry. Though hybrid demons didn't move fast, he needed to get her out of the cave before the demons discovered them. The bad news? He had no idea where the demons were, and trying to wrestle the struggling wildcat meant he couldn't exactly make a stealthlike exit.

She wasn't a weakling, and she had one hell of a kick. She was slowing him down. But he couldn't hoist her over his shoulder because that meant he'd have to release his hold over her mouth and she'd start screaming. Which would alert the demons, and that he wouldn't risk. He wasn't about to get killed over an uncooperative woman.

So he'd deal with the painful shins and just drag her. Hand clamped over her mouth, the other around her waist, he focused around him and moved as fast as possible through the cave, hoping the foul smell would decrease in the direction he was going. That would mean he was heading away from the demons, not toward them.

As he proceeded down a narrow tunnel, the demon smell didn't grow stronger, nor did he hear the familiar shuffling of slow hybrid feet. Good. But it didn't mean the demons weren't going to pick up their scent and start heading in their direction, so speed was vital.

If she'd cooperate just a little he could get them out sooner. Then again, why would she? She didn't know he was trying to save her life.

Finally he saw light. The cave entrance. He picked up the pace and hauled her outside, but didn't stop once they got out. He turned around, backing into the brush, keeping his eyes peeled for signs of demons following. He wasn't going to take any chances until they were well out of sight.

Moving into a thick grouping of trees and bushes that he felt offered protection, he stopped, resting his back against a thick trunk. He caught his breath and leaned his head against the woman's.

"Don't scream or they'll know we're here. I'm going to remove my hand. You let out anything but a whisper and I'll knock you out cold. You got it?"

A short nod. Good enough. He let loose and she tilted her head back to look at him.

Wide-eyed shock mixed with fierce anger emanated from her eyes. "Who are you?"

Damn, she was pretty. "Your rescuer."

"Bullshit. Let me go."

Mouthy, too. And she had an accent. Something odd and unrecognizable. A mixture of cultures. American and maybe a tinge of French. "Sorry. Can't do that."

She pushed against him, trying to break his hold on her. He had to give her points for effort. She was a fighter. And as long as she wasn't screaming, he could handle her struggles.

"I don't know what you think you're doing, but you need to let me go."

"You're safer here with me. You'll just have to trust me."

She elbowed him in the stomach. He grunted, then maneuvered her so that wouldn't happen again. Nice shot.

"I don't trust you and there's obviously no danger in the cave, so why don't you tell me what you want? I don't have any money on me, so if your plan is to rob me you're wasting your time."

She was tough, but there was an edge of fear in her eyes she was trying hard to mask. He'd done enough combat duty to recognize it. She couldn't hide it from him. "Look. I'm not going to hurt you, but I can't let you go."

"Then you need to start talking because I'm not going to let you hold me."

"Darlin', you don't have a choice." Where was Derek? He could handle her. Or Gina. Another woman around would be much better. Women knew how to deal with women. Ryder's experience with women was limited to one thing only, and that wasn't conversation.

She was about to open her mouth to argue, but they both turned their gazes toward sounds coming from the mouth of the cave.

Low mumbling. Shuffling sounds.

Shit. Demons.

"Oh, my God, there *is* something in there," she said, her surprised gaze flitting to him.

Ryder resisted the urge to say "I told you so." "We need to move. Now." He grabbed her arm and dragged her along the path, away from the cave.

This time she didn't resist. "Who's in there?"

He didn't answer, just took her by the hand and pulled her farther into the brush. In the darkness, he could easily see with his night-vision shades. She couldn't. He knew she would have to rely on him, and without him, she'd be lost. He hoped that would be enough impetus for her to come along willingly. That, and the unknown entity in the cave.

He stopped, held his fingers to his lips to signal the woman's silence, and listened.

There were enough twigs and leaves on the ground for demons to make noise if they were following. He didn't hear anything.

This was good enough. They'd stay put for now.

"Okay, you want to tell me now what's going on?" she whispered, her gaze darting around the brush.

"No."

She heaved a frustrated sigh. "I don't know who you are. I don't know why you dragged me out of that cave other than someone else was in there. For all I know they could be after you and you're some kind of thief, or murderer."

She was right. He *was,* just not that kind of killer. "I'm not going to hurt you. If I was, don't you think I'd have already done that?"

"I don't know what to think because you're not telling me anything."

"The less you know the better."

"*Mon Dieu,* you're difficult. What's your name? Can you at least tell me that?"

"Ryder."

"I'm Angelique."

Definitely French, her name rolled off her tongue. Sexy, like her voice. If he'd met her under different circumstances he'd be interested.

Oh, hell, who was he kidding? He was interested now, and that was bad.

"So tell me something, Ryder. Anything, besides your name."

It was bad enough he'd told her that. "Why don't you tell me what you're doing wandering around these caves at night by yourself?"

Her eyes widened. "It was you last night. You were the one who chased me."

"How did you know that?"

"It's not like I'm always interrupted or that there are a lot of people in this remote area. I've been working completely undisturbed around here for weeks. Now suddenly two nights in a row there are people around?

Besides, I watched you and your friends from the ridge after I took off. It was you. What are you after?"

Don't tell her anything. Yeah, right. "I was just checking out the cave. Saw you. You ran so I went after you. Do you have something to hide?"

"No, I don't have anything to hide. You scared the shit out of me. Of course I ran. You jumped out of the bushes like the bogeyman. What did you expect me to do? Stand around and wait to see what you wanted?"

Good point. Still, he wanted to know what a woman was doing in a cave all alone. It didn't seem . . . normal.

Then again, what the fuck was *normal?*

"You still haven't told me what you're doing out here all alone." He wanted to keep her talking, so he didn't have to give her answers.

"I'm doing my job."

"Which is?"

"I'm an archaeologist."

"Ah." That told him nothing. "What are you looking for?"

Her gaze narrowed, suspicion evident in her frown. "That's between me and my employer, and I don't know who you are."

He hoped she'd never find out. "I'm the guy who saved your ass."

"So you keep telling me. For all I know it could have been the authorities back there in the cave, looking for you."

He snorted. "It wasn't."

"And I'm supposed to believe you . . . why?"

"You can believe whatever you want to believe." God, he really needed to offload this woman and soon. He killed things. He didn't offer up explanations.

Her gaze narrowed. "Who hired you to come after me? I haven't found it yet but I will, you know. Did Isabelle send you? I can't believe she'd do that. She usually does her dirty work herself."

She'd started pacing. And Ryder had no idea what the hell she was talking about. But now he was curious.

"No one hired me to come after you, I don't know Isabelle, and what is this 'it' you're referring to?"

She glared at him. "You can stop pretending. I'm not stupid and I don't believe in coincidence. Izzy and I have played this game for too many years for me to be fooled."

Okay, she'd lost him, but as long as she was rambling and the suspicion was cast somewhere else, he was fine with that.

Where the hell were Derek and Gina?

"Derek, are you going to be getting here anytime this millennium?" he commed. "This baby-sitting thing is getting old."

No answer.

Shit.

He signaled again, but got no response.

Great.

"I don't need to be baby-sat. You can let me go. And who are you talking to?"

"The people I work with. And I can't let you go. You're in danger out here by yourself."

Hands on hips, she tilted her head to the side. "Uh-huh. So far I haven't seen much evidence of danger. Except from you."

He'd really like to set her straight. Too bad he couldn't show her just how much danger she was in.

He also wasn't going to lurk out here in the bushes all night. No telling when a demon or a dozen of them were going to pop out of the ground, and he wasn't prepared to take care of Angelique and fend off demons at the same time. He had to find the others and figure out what to do with her.

"Let's go."

"Where?"

"We're going to find my friends."

"Then can I get some answers?"

"Sure." Whether that was true or not, he didn't know, but once he found the others, Angelique would no longer be his problem.

Angelique had no idea why she was following Ryder, other than she had no clue where she was and wasn't too thrilled with the thought of being left out in the pitch-black darkness alone.

Though she doubted he'd just leave her there anyway. And something about him made her doubt he was going to do her harm. Like he said, if he wanted to he'd have done it by now. He dragged her out of the cave in a hurry. And something had been in there, but what? Or who?

If Isabelle had hired Ryder to come after her in the hopes of stealing the black diamond, this would be the last straw. She had put up with her sister's scheming for years, mainly because she loved her. And yes, in many ways she understood Izzy's motivations.

Typically, Isabelle's antics were harmless. Irritating, but harmless. She could put up with it. But not this. Not resorting to kidnapping to prevent Angelique from doing her job. That she wouldn't abide.

She'd promised Mother she would look after Isabelle. That didn't mean she'd let her sister run amok and do what she pleased. It also didn't mean she'd allow Isabelle to interfere in Angelique's career.

Blood ties were sacred, but that only went so far. Isabelle had always been devious, but would she really do this? Angelique didn't want to think so, but the past few years had seen a change in Isabelle. Not good changes, either. Treasure hunting had always been a game to Izzy. She'd never taken archaeology seriously—not like Angelique and their mother had. To Isabelle the finds were loot, to be held only until she found the highest bidder.

What had started out an amusing game between the sisters had turned into something else entirely—a competition. Who would get the prize first? Angelique and her clients, typically a museum or private foundation who would showcase artifacts and share them with the world? Or some rich benefactor, Izzy's clients, who would profit monetarily, as would her sister?

Angelique wrinkled her nose in disgust, following

along behind Ryder. She held tight to his hand, wishing she didn't have to be so tied to this stranger, but having no choice at the moment. This darkness and unfamiliar territory was not where she wanted to be lost, but he'd taken her out so far she'd lost her bearings. Without her bag, her GPS, she might never find her way out. She didn't even have water with her. She had to make her way back to the cave and grab her things.

God help you if you're playing me, Isabelle. On our mother's grave, if you're involved in this, I'll make you pay.

"Are we going back to the cave?" she asked as Ryder moved her along at breakneck speed. Where was he going in such a hurry?

"Not yet."

"All my things are in there. Important things. I need to retrieve them."

"You'll get them, I promise."

She'd better. She couldn't afford to lose her equipment. She was hardly a rich woman, though the finder's fee her client promised for locating the black diamond was significant. Not that the money mattered. It bought basic things to help her do her job, and that was all. The money never mattered. The find was what counted.

Finally, they came out of the brush and trees and into the clearing. The row of caves was like a welcome home, but Ryder was veering away from the cave—her cave.

"Ryder, please." She tugged on his hand. "I need my things."

He shook his head and kept walking. "We can't go

back there right now. Too dangerous. The dem—they might still be in there."

"*Who* might still be in there?" Again, she resisted his pull on her hand. "Please tell me."

He stopped and turned to her. Now that she had a moment to look at him, her breath caught. Such a fierce, handsome man. Tall, though she already knew that from walking beside him. And solid, because her body had been pressed intimately against his when he'd held her. He had very dark hair and equally dark eyes. Rugged chin with a day's growth of beard stubble. Mustache. Very sexy. Full lips. He didn't smile, and seemed to appear as if a growl would spill from his throat any second. She wondered what made him so angry?

Her mother had always told her she liked people way too much, that Angelique had never known a stranger. She couldn't help it. She studied living things as much as she analyzed those that were buried under ancient dirt and rock. Everything made her curious, including people. Especially mysterious people.

And Ryder was gorgeous, rugged packaging clouded in mystery. What was he doing wandering around out here? What was he after?

"I can't tell you. Sorry. We need to keep moving."

He made her curious, all right. He was also really irritating her. She didn't see danger. There was no one else about. And he had an iron grip on her hand that was becoming rather annoying.

"Let me go. I've had enough."

"You're coming with me."

"No, Ryder. No more. I'm not going."

He stopped and heaved a disgusted sigh. So he was unhappy. Not her problem. She had a job to do and he was preventing her from doing it.

"You don't get it, do you?" he asked, his brows knit in a tight frown as he cast a quick glance at her before turning away and continuing his forward progress.

"Obviously not, since you won't tell me anything."

"You're in danger out here by yourself."

"Prove it."

"I can't."

"Then let me go. I can take care of myself."

"You can't be out here at night by yourself anymore."

"I work just fine alone, and it's too damn hot to be in the caves during the daylight hours."

"Angelique, you don't understand—"

"Then help me understand, Ryder. I'm a reasonable person. Explain it."

She heard his frustrated exhale. Good. She didn't want to be the only one.

"There they are."

She froze and scanned the area, saw nothing. "Who?"

"My . . . friends."

Angelique didn't know whether to be relieved or worried. Now she was really outnumbered, though she hadn't been doing such a hot job of wrestling away from one man.

She saw them coming now. Five of them. Three

younger guys, one woman, and an older man. All carrying the same strange-looking weapons as Ryder had. And staring her down like she was the enemy.

A very tall, dark-haired man approached, inclining his head toward her but speaking to Ryder. "This the same woman you chased out of the cave last night?"

"Yeah," Ryder said.

The man looked her over. "Let's talk," he said to Ryder, pulling him off to the side and away from her.

Angelique couldn't hear what they were saying. The rest of them surrounded her in a semicircle, cutting off any chance she had of running.

Ryder and the guy talked for a few minutes, every now and then looking in her direction, then headed back toward her.

"We'll escort you back to the cave to get your things, then you can get back in your Jeep and head out," Ryder said.

She lifted her chin. "I don't know who you people are, but I have as much right to be here as you do."

The dark-haired man said, "Angelique, is it?"

She nodded.

"My name is Derek and I'm in charge here. I wish we could tell you more, but there are bad...people running around here. People who will hurt you if they find you. That's really all I can say."

"Who are you?"

"My name is Louis," the older man said. "We're with an international government organization that I'm sorry we cannot identify for security reasons. The...people we are after are armed and extremely dangerous, and we have to cordon off this area. You will have to leave, and right now. That's all we can tell you. Ryder, Dalton, take her back to the cave, let her gather her belongings and escort her to her vehicle, and see that she gets safely off."

Angelique wanted to object. Something wasn't right about this. She felt it deep in her bones.

But they had the weapons and Ryder had hold of her arm, leading her toward the cave. She glanced over her shoulder at the group of them standing there, weapons held, looking around as if they expected someone, or something, to spring out at them any second.

They really were on the lookout for someone. Maybe they were legitimate.

But she was curious. Damned curious, now. Who were they after? Who the hell would be out here in the middle of nowhere and on the run?

Ryder held on to her arm, stopping her as they entered the cave. "Let me go in first. Stay between Dalton and me."

Shrugging, she let him go in ahead. Right now she just wanted her bag. When he led her to where he'd grabbed her, she picked up her things, loaded everything in her canvas bag, and hauled it over her shoulder.

"Is that everything?" he asked.

She nodded.

"Where's your vehicle?"

"Back side of the cave."

He led the way until they got to the opening of the cave. Then he and the other man—were all these guys impossibly tall and muscular?—walked her to her Jeep and surrounded her until she got in and started it up.

"Stay away from this area, Angelique," Ryder warned. "It's for your own safety. I'd hate to see something bad happen to you."

She gave him a curt nod and floored it, angry and still curious.

Mystery was her livelihood, and she'd just left a huge secret back there.

She wasn't finished with Ryder and his crew. Not by a long shot.

Chapter Twelve

Nic reminded himself as he carried Shay upstairs that he was doing this to fool her, to get her to trust him so he could escape. But the way she responded to him down in the kitchen, her sweet body rocking against his hand, the way she tasted, the way she came for him—he wasn't so sure who he was fooling now.

"Your room or mine?" he asked as he reached the top of the stairs."

"I don't care."

He kicked open the door to her room, wanting her to be comfortable in her own environment, aware of what he was planning but pushing the thought out of his head for now.

The wary trust in her eyes was like a gut punch. He wasn't much for guilt; hell, he never felt it before. He and women had an understanding. He got what he wanted, and they got what they wanted. No apologies necessary. Yet studying her sweet, guileless eyes, the way she looked at him as if she was saying she was doing this, but he damn well better not hurt her—and that's exactly what he was planning to do.

Or at least he thought he was.

He laid her on the bed and stared down at her.

Right now he was rock hard, his balls strung up tight and aching for release. He could fuck her all night and fall asleep in her arms and never want to leave this place, never leave her.

But that wasn't his strategy.

Because he didn't want to fuck her. He wanted to make love to her, wanted to touch and kiss and lick every intimate spot on her body until she strained against him and screamed for release. He wanted to give her what no man had ever given her, so she'd remember him— always remember this time with him, so no man would ever replace him.

A rush of possessiveness came over him. The thought of another man touching her made angry blood rush hot through his veins. Unfamiliar sensations to say the least.

Why did he have to start caring about her? Why did he have to feel a connection to Shay when he'd never felt one with any woman he'd been with before? This would be a lot easier if he didn't give a shit about Shay. The problem was that he not only wanted her, he was starting to feel strange emotions for her. She was in his dreams now as well as in his thoughts, tying into his emotions, clouding his judgment. And Nic didn't really know what to do about it.

Now he was thinking when he should be ripping her clothes off and sliding inside that hot, tight part of her just begging for his cock. What a dumbass he was.

He leaned down, unlaced her boots, and slid them off, jerking her camos and panties from her legs. Damn, she was gorgeous, lying there half naked and looking at him with obvious desire in her wide blue eyes. And when she smiled up at him, so tentative and yet so sexy, he wanted to drop to his knees and worship every inch of her.

Too much thinking was a bad thing. He peeled off his shirt and tossed it on the floor, then shrugged out of his shorts, enjoying the unabashed way she watched the unveiling, especially when she sat up and reached for him.

"I've been wanting to touch your body," she said, running her hand along his hip. His cock jerked in response. She drew her bottom lip between her teeth and tilted her head back to meet his gaze.

She drew up on her knees and faced him. "When you got up from your bed last night and you were naked, I was riveted, you know."

"Is that right?"

"Yes. I love the way you look and I wanted to touch you. But I knew I shouldn't, even though I wanted to. God, how I wanted to. I've been wanting to touch you since I first saw you step out of the ocean that morning. That moment we had together in the pool...interrupted...too short. We need to finish it."

Honesty. Goddamn. Something he wasn't used to from a woman. Shay never ceased to surprise him.

"Touch away, babe." Hell, he'd let her do anything she wanted as long as it involved her hands or her mouth on his body.

She eased her hands alongside his thighs, then behind him, caressing his ass before trailing her fingertips up and along his back. He gritted his teeth and let her explore, ignoring his mind telling him to push her down on the bed and bury himself inside her. If she wanted to play, he was going to let her play.

She stood on the bed so she could reach his shoulders, smoothing her hands down the front of his chest and over his nipples. She hovered over them, seemingly enjoying herself as she flicked them until they hardened. The sensation shot south and his cock lurched. He sucked in a breath and fought back a growl.

Impatience roared like a wild beast. He wanted to throw her down and impale her on his dick. Instead, he leveled a smile at her. "I like your hands on me. I like your mouth on me even better."

She knelt again in front of him, focusing between his legs, on the part of him aching to be inside her. She grasped him between her hands, tentatively stroking.

"Grip harder. I won't break."

She glanced up at him, then smiled, encircling him with a firm grasp. Oh, yeah, he liked that.

Liked it? Hell, he arched his back and let out a groan while she rolled her hands over him. Unlike his own hands, hers were soft—like liquid silk sliding over his shaft. One hand, then the other, she stroked him until his balls tightened in a vise of need and he wanted to cry out for mercy. Just watching her touch him was a turn-on.

And she studied his cock like she was fascinated by it. Until she tilted her head back and looked at his face, keeping her focus on his eyes as she leaned forward and pressed her lips to him, taking him in her mouth, her tongue darting out to taste him.

It was sweetest torture—the best agony he'd ever experienced. The hot wetness of her mouth surrounded him, her tongue swirling around the head like she was savoring her favorite piece of candy. Then she sucked him until he thought his spine was going to burst through his back. Tension coiled throughout and he held firm while her mouth worked magic on him, drawing him in deep, her hot breath sailing across his balls when she released him and licked the length of him.

Christ, he was going to let go in her mouth if she kept this up. And that's not where he wanted to finish. He pulled her away.

"Damn, babe" was all he could say.

She smiled up at him, her mouth wet and ripe as he leaned in for a quick, hungry taste of her.

When he pulled back, he reached for her hair, releasing the clip binding it back and tangling his fingers in the softness of the waves, drawing them forward so they draped over her shoulders. Like honeyed gold, it fell over her creamy skin. He raised the tank top up and over her head and pulled it off, revealing a surprisingly sexy black satin bra filled to overflowing with generous breasts that rose and fell with each breath. He skimmed the swells with his fingertips, watching her eyes darken, her breath catch and hold when he pulled the straps down her arms.

Releasing her breasts from the cups of her bra made *his* breath catch next. Every inch of her skin was beautiful. Her breasts were full and round, her nipples pink and puckered, signaling her desire. Now that he had her completely naked, the rush to finish this had eased somewhat. He wanted to look, to touch.

But first he had to kiss her again. He could never get enough of pressing his lips to hers. She tasted like his favorite shot of whiskey. Shay was a drug in his system, making him act strange, do things he wouldn't normally do. Like make love to her instead of just taking her weapon, tying her up and getting the hell out of here while he had the chance.

Instead, he palmed her breast, feeling her heart beat a high-speed rhythm against his hand as he teased her nipple with the pad of his thumb. And those little sounds she made—moans and whimpers in response to his touch—now those were pure torture. They made him even harder, if that was possible, since he was already suffering pretty damn badly.

And if his touch made her react this way, what would his mouth do to her? He bent and flicked his tongue over the distended bud. She arched into his mouth, feeding him her nipple, then writhed against him with a loud moan when he flattened her nipple against his tongue and the roof of his mouth. Even her skin tasted sweet, and he wanted to devour her. Strange sensations surged through him . . . the need to possess her, in some way ensure she was his. These were fierce, incredible needs, nearly overpowering in their intensity.

These feelings were what kept him away from women for over a year. And with Shay, they were doubly intense, almost uncontrollable.

"You're shaking," she whispered, concern furrowing her brow. She brought her hands up along his arms and shoulders.

"I want you." Man, wasn't that an understatement, because it was so much more than that. He felt possessive of her. Like if he didn't get inside her right now and brand her, there was a chance she could belong to someone else, that he could lose her. A total caveman mentality, but the urges pounded from within and he couldn't push them away. He'd never felt this need with another woman. Why with Shay?

"Then take me, Nic. What are you waiting for?"

What was he waiting for? For sanity to return.

He wanted to take things slow, to make this special so she wouldn't think he was—

Oh, hell. But he was. So fuck it. He growled and moved over her, using his knee to spread her legs. She arched her back, showing him she was more than eager.

He hesitated. Poised on his palms over her, he stared down at this beautiful creature, wondering who the hell he was and what he was about to do.

Was this a mistake?

But then she raised her knees and he looked down at her, lost. Gripping her legs, he pulled them apart more roughly than he should, but she continued to smile at him. He surged between her thighs, desperately trying to maintain control, the silken softness of her sex a sweet invitation as he entered her.

Nic closed his eyes and just allowed himself to absorb the feel of Shay. But she consumed him. Warm, wet, and tight, the feel of her was a sweet burn. Scorching heat enveloped him, sizzling and seductive as hell itself. His breathing grew more harsh and rapid. He groaned and kissed her, desperation only growing in intensity as he moved against her, feeling her grip him as he buried deep. His fingers dug into her hip, not at all tender. She gasped, threading her fingers through his hair, lifting against him. She was so wet inside, so hot, a welcoming inferno; he was lost in her.

"More, Nic," she murmured against his ear. "More."

Christ. Bone-crushing agony wrapped around his spine with each thrust—a painful pleasure that ripped through his nerve endings and settled in his cock, driving his pleasure with a fury he could barely rein in. She was heaven and hell and this joining was going to kill him. Every time she raised her hips he wanted to power his shaft balls deep and come inside her, roar out completion and rage until he was empty. He wanted to wrap his arms around her and shield her from this animal trying to claw its way out from inside him, because he didn't know what was happening. It felt good. Too damn good. And he was afraid if he released it, everything he'd been told would come true.

There was a beast inside him, and Shay had just let it loose.

"Can't stop." He panted now, no longer in control of anything. His mind, his body, these sensations tearing through him. The pleasure was unbearable. He didn't want it to stop, yet begged for it to end. Was he hurting her?

"Don't . . ." he heard her say, and he stilled.

"Don't stop," she continued, her voice no more than hiccupping gasps. "Don't stop."

She moved with him, lifting up, meeting every thrust, and pressing against him, taking everything he had to give. When she tightened around him and cried out with her orgasm, he followed her, and he did roar, tilting his head back and letting out a bellow that had to scare the shit out of her, because it slashed chills down his spine. The voice was deep, dark. And didn't sound like his at all.

He fell on top of her, exhausted and satiated, taking Shay with him and rolling her to the side, feeling her body for scratches.

She purred against him, caressed his chest with the palm of her hand, and laid her head on his shoulder. He took a peek. Her eyes were closed, her breathing a bit fast, but she was smiling.

Fuck. What the hell had just happened? Who—or what—had he just become?

He slowed down his breathing, forced reality. It was just sex, right? Really great sex, but it was just sex. Some women just brought out the animal in a guy. Granted, no woman had hit his hot buttons like this before. He'd just gotten lucky with Shay. She was a good match for him.

Which was really too bad, because he had to get the hell out of here. Tonight.

Her deep, even breathing and relaxed state indicated now was the time.

Didn't that just figure? He'd finally found a woman he cared about. One he enjoyed being with, one he obviously had seriously good sexual compatibility with, and he had to dump her. Hell, he had to more than dump her.

He had to tie her up so he could make his escape.

And he had to do it right now.

The guilt gnawing its way through his gut would just have to stay there, because if he was ever going to get away, it would have to be this moment or not at all. And damn if he wasn't actually having second thoughts about leaving.

How stupid was that?

Think logically here, Nic. Get out, and get out now.

He slid out from under her. She moaned, shifted, but kept her eyes closed. He kissed her forehead. "Going to the bathroom, babe. I'll be right back."

She mumbled, but didn't open her eyes. He covered her and went into the bathroom and shut the door, then opened the adjoining door to his room and crept downstairs in a hurry, finding what he needed. Hightailing it up the stairs, he went inside her room through the bathroom.

He stood still a moment and just looked at her, huddled up under the sheet, her hair a tangled mess from their lovemaking. Her face was turned toward him, her lips swollen from his kisses.

Under different circumstances he'd crawl back in bed with her and do it all over again. Hell, his dick was already twitching, wanting round two. And three, and four. The draw he felt toward Shay was enormous, as if they shared a bond that couldn't be broken.

Bullshit. His freedom was what was important. He leaned over her and slipped his hand under the covers, locking his fingers around her wrists. Her eyes blinked open and she smiled up at him.

"Hey," she said, her voice soft and sleepy.

He sat on the edge of the bed and raised her arms over her head, ignoring the stab of guilt. "Hey."

When he tied the rope around her wrists, she jerked. "Nic. What are you doing?"

He looked down at Shay, regret tearing at him.

He couldn't stay with her. He didn't belong here.

"Sorry, babe." He wound the rope tight around her wrists, hoping it wasn't so tight it would cut off her circulation, then threaded the rope through the steel bars of the headboard on her bed.

"Nic. Don't do this."

"I have to get out of here, Shay."

"No, you don't." She wriggled and kicked out, but her legs were tangled in the cover. He finished the knot on her wrist and grabbed at her feet just as she freed herself from the cover. He grabbed the other rope and fastened it around her ankles.

"Goddammit, Nic, stop this. You don't know what's out there. You'll never make it on your own."

"Gee, thanks for your faith in me."

"You don't understand. Demons are out there."

He shook his head at her wide-eyed look of terror, almost wanting to believe she was afraid for him. But he recognized it for what it was: an act—a way to get him to release her. Or maybe she was afraid what would happen to her when the others came back and found her tied naked to her bed and Nic gone.

He couldn't think about Shay right now. It was time to think about himself.

"This isn't funny. Untie me."

He walked through the bathroom and into his room, gathering up his clothes.

"Nic!" she screamed. "Untie me right now!"

He thought about taking extra clothes, but he didn't intend to be wandering around in the desert for long. Just camos, a shirt, socks, and boots should do it.

"How could you do this to me? What we just did meant nothing to you?"

He paused, closed his eyes for a brief second.

Don't go back in there. You have nothing to say to her.

He clenched his fists and turned, stalking through the bathroom and into her room.

"I didn't ask to be kidnapped. I didn't ask for any of this to happen to me."

"You used me."

Her voice was a whisper, her eyes wet with tears but her face harsh with anger.

He shrugged. "Maybe I did. But didn't you do the same thing to me? How does it feel, Shay?" He turned on his heel and closed the bathroom door, locking it.

"Nic!"

She was cursing now. Pretty inventive curses, too. He moved to her bedroom door, locking it from the outside, and hurried downstairs. He grabbed Shay's gun—the one with real ammo—and was out the door, searching the area to make sure none of the others were returning.

Somewhere around here there had to be a town. A phone. Either way, he was out of here. He'd get to a phone and call his uncle, figure out where he was, and arrange for retrieval.

Shay absolutely would not panic. Anger and frustration and hurt warred, barring her ability to think straight.

First things first. She had to get out of here. She tilted her head back and surveyed the ties around her wrist. He'd tied her to the bottom part of the bars. Wriggling her fingers, she knew there was no way she could get to those knots, and with every minute that went by, Nic was getting further away.

She had to get to him. For his own protection, and to bring him back. He had no idea what he was doing out there, or what he might run into.

Dumbass.

She wouldn't even think about what he had done to

her, how he had used her. That was personal; she'd file that away in the back of her mind.

For now.

She used her shoulder to push away the pillow. Not easy, but she managed, using her body to scoot it to the side. Because underneath it was her dagger, the one she kept there for protection.

The cool metal hit her shoulder and she breathed a sigh of relief. It was still there, hadn't been knocked away by their...

No. She wouldn't think about what they'd done. Grateful the dagger was still in place, her only thought now was how to maneuver it toward her fingers. She had to use her body, shifting to her side, then push it up. Painstaking work that took patience she simply didn't have.

Not like she had a choice. So she took her time and maneuvered the dagger inches closer until she could finally stretch her fingers out and touch it.

Got it! Exhaling a sigh of relief, she unsheathed the blade and flipped it around, then set to work cutting through the ropes. The blade was sharp, so it didn't take long. Once free, she sliced the ropes at her ankles and let loose the anger she'd been holding inside.

The adrenaline rush was exhilarating, but quickly fizzled away as fury boiled within her.

Dammit! How could Nic do this to her? And even worse, how did she let it happen?

She jerked on her clothes, mentally cursing her own stupidity and hormones. No wonder she didn't have sex that often. It made her stupid. So much for not falling for his bad-boy image.

She'd fallen for it all right. Right into bed and big trouble.

Even now, mad as hell and imagining the satisfaction of finding him and melting him down like a demon, her body remembered his touch, the way he felt inside her. And it was so damn good she could fall to the ground and weep.

Conflicted much, Shay?

She needed to get out of there. Her thin-point dagger might do the trick on the door. She rifled in her drawer and found it, the blade sharp enough that she slowed down walking to the door. She knelt, slid the tip in between the doorjamb, and started jimmying the lock.

"Think I'm some dumb blonde, do you? Lock me up in here like freakin' Rapunzel in the tower. I'll show you, dickhead."

She felt a little better grumbling at him out loud, even though he couldn't hear her.

After a few minutes of concerted effort, the lock gave. She smirked, gave the blade a soft kiss, and placed it back in the drawer.

She hurried downstairs, already knowing her gun would be gone. He wouldn't have taken the other weapons because he didn't know where the ammo was. She did, though. In a few seconds her rifle was loaded, her holster was strapped to her hip, and she was out the door.

The air was stifling. She didn't care. It felt good to be hunting again, even if she was hunting a human.

And God help him when she found him.

She commed Derek to let him know Nic had escaped and she was heading out after him. Of course Derek said it wasn't a good idea, but Nic couldn't have gotten too far ahead of her, and she was going to bring him back herself. She assured Derek she'd stay in contact, and that she was well armed.

Derek indicated they were meeting up with her as soon as they could. She was so embarrassed giving Derek that report. And no way was she going to tell him exactly how Nic escaped.

She'd been listening to Lou and the others talk about the geography out here. There was nothing and no place for him to go without a vehicle. The house was remote enough and too far away from other homes in the area. Hopefully, if she was lucky, he hadn't headed in the direction of civilization.

She'd find him soon enough. He didn't have night-vision glasses like she did. And she was rather proud of her hunting skills. It didn't take her long to find his tracks in the dirt and follow them.

He'd headed northeast, toward the caves. And the farther she got, the more irritated she became. Not only because of all he'd done to her, but because she was tramping out here in the dark. Alone. Where demons might be.

And just like her connection to Nic, she felt them all around her. An explicable sensation of being watched, of knowing demons lurked nearby. The closer she got to the caves, the more she felt their presence.

It was probably just atmosphere—being alone in the dark, caves all around her, their entrances ominous. There could be anything hiding in there.

She slowed her pace, moved from bush to bush, and stayed low, convinced someone or something was watching her. She could swear she saw movement in the one cave straight ahead. Then again, maybe not.

Damn you, Nic. This is all your fault.

It would be just her luck to run into a dozen demons while she was searching by herself.

Now that she was out here, she had to investigate. What if there were demons hiding in the cave and the hunters hadn't found this spot yet? She could at least report demon activity. She backtracked and circled around, coming to the front side of the cave where she heard the noises. Flattening herself against the wall, she inched toward the mouth of the cave, intending only to listen, then possibly peer inside. Nothing more than that. She knew better than to face demons on her own.

Just a few inches more and she'd reach the entrance. She didn't hear a thing now. Didn't smell anything either, which was good. That meant no hybrid demons.

But then she heard a noise from the cave next to the one she was about to search. Maybe there was something out there, after all, only it wasn't in this cave. She took a quick peek around the corner of the cave, and when she didn't see anything, decided one more look in the next cave, then she was heading back.

She made it halfway past the mouth of the cave entrance when something clamped down over her mouth and dragged her inside. Her heart skidded and she screamed, the sound muffled by whoever or whatever held her and pulled her into the darkness.

Fighting against it, she clawed at the hand over her mouth. A steel band of strength held her arms at her sides, preventing her from reaching for her weapon. She couldn't move. She couldn't breathe as waves of panic crashed against her chest. God, no. Not demons. She couldn't let this happen to her! She had to stay focused, had to fight.

"Shay, it's me."

Panic stilled as the recognition of Nic's voice entered her stream of consciousness.

"Don't scream. There's something else out there. I need you to stay calm when I take my hand away so you don't let them know we're in here. Okay?"

That she understood all too well. She nodded and he removed his hand from her mouth. She pivoted, making out his features in the darkness. Relief warred with the fierce desire to deliver a swift kick right between his legs. She decided to delay killing him because at the moment she was deliriously happy to see him, considering what might have grabbed her instead.

"What are you doing in here?" She kept her voice low, which meant she had to whisper in his ear, which also meant she had to get close to him, something she wasn't very happy about. The thought of the dagger at her hip was an attractive possibility. But then she'd be alone again.

"I *was* trying to make an escape. I got sidetracked by creatures."

"Creatures?" She ignored the "escape" part. For the moment anyway.

"Ugly fuckers. Big, too. And they stink."

"Oh, shit. Wind must be coming from the other direction. I didn't pick up their scent when I was tracking you."

"What are they?"

"Probably hybrid demons." She stepped to the cave entrance and peered out, saw nothing, and moved back, facing Nic again. "Tell me where they are."

"Demons? C'mon. What are they?"

"Demons, goddammit. What the hell do you think those things are? Trick-or-treaters? Now tell me where you saw them."

He gave her a look that said he didn't want to believe she was telling the truth. She didn't care what he believed or didn't. She just wanted a location.

"Cave directly northeast of this one. Wait a few minutes and keep watching. You'll see them."

She focused where he'd pointed. It didn't take long. They were hybrids all right. Good thing Nic had stopped her before she'd made it too far in that direction. She counted ten of them at least. They were removing huge boulders from the cave, piling them outside, then going back in for more.

"What do you think they're doing in there?" he whispered over her shoulder.

She held up her hand, motioning him to be silent. The last thing she wanted was to alert the demons to their presence. No way could she take on that many by herself, and Nic sure as hell wasn't prepared to fight them yet.

She waited until the demons went back in the cave, then turned to Nic. "We've got to alert Lou and Derek to the presence of demons here."

"What were they doing?"

"No clue."

She commed Derek and let him know about the demons. He instructed her to stay put and not engage the demons on her own. And to keep an eye on Nic. They were on the way.

"Derek and the rest of them are coming."

"Good."

She thought she'd have to fight with Nic to get him to stay, that maybe he'd want to take off. He didn't say a word, and surprisingly stayed close to her as she kept an eye on the demons. Maybe he figured it was better to be captive with the hunters than out there alone with demons.

"Nic, come here."

He stepped toward her and she wrapped her arms around him.

"Whoa," he said, drawing his arms around her. "What's this for?"

God, this felt good. And dammit, it shouldn't. But

that wasn't why she was holding him. She slid her hands down his rib cage, ignoring the steely strength of his body. What she was after was tucked into the back of his pants. She grabbed it and pushed away, holding the weapon on him.

"Shay, what are you doing?" He started forward.

"If you think for one second I won't melt you down with this thing, you're mistaken."

He stopped. "I can't believe this. Why?"

She let out a sharp laugh. "I don't think I need to explain why. Get to the other side of the cave. Do it now because my patience is as thin as thread."

She kept her voice a whisper, one eye on Nic, the other watching the demons.

"You need my help."

"I need nothing from you. Move."

He shrugged and backed away, settling against the other side of the cave, looking at her in disbelief and— she could hardly fathom this—actual disappointment. How dare he look at her that way. This was his fault.

Now all she had to do was wait and keep an eye on Nic until Derek and others got here. Then Derek and Lou could deal with Nic. She was finished with him.

Chapter Thirteen

Nic couldn't believe Shay had grabbed his weapon, was training it on him as if he'd try to make an escape. It wasn't as if he had any intent of running off again. Not after what he'd seen.

Now he had questions. Legitimate questions he wanted answers to. And these people were the ones to give them.

Demons really did exist. Goddamn. His mind was still trying to process the whole thing. It was dark, damn near moonless. He wished he had a pair of those cool night-vision glasses Shay and the rest of them wore, but he hadn't been able to find those when he'd torn out of the house in a hurry, so he'd had to rely on stumbling around in the dark.

But once his eyes had adjusted to the darkness, he could make out shapes okay. Big ones, anyway. Trees, bushes, the caves, and hills.

And when he'd run into the demons while he was

creeping along the series of caves, the first thing he'd noticed was the smell. Damn good thing they gave off an odor, or he'd have smacked into the foul-smelling fuckers. Instead, he'd stopped, sniffed, wondered what the hell had died out there, and while he was pausing and trying to figure out where the dead carcass was, he'd seen them —fortunately before they spotted him. Ducking into the cave entrance, he watched them carry giant-sized boulders out of the cave, but he was horrified at their appearance, thinking his mind was playing tricks on him.

He couldn't deny that demons existed. What else could those things be? Tall; thick, mottled skin; hideously long, dripping claws and fangs . . . there was nothing human about those things. He shuddered, wishing he hadn't allowed Shay to take the gun away from him. He felt better being armed. But she didn't appear to be thinking rationally, and the thought of being nuked from the inside out with one of those weapons wasn't very appealing.

Now she leaned against the cave wall, her UV laser cradled in her arms and pointed right at him. Her expression was blank, but her eyes gave her away. Anger and hurt swirled and mixed in those deep blue depths.

He wanted to tell her he was sorry, give his explanation for what he'd done. He'd had a good enough reason for escape at the time, but not for what he'd done to her. In this case, the end hadn't justified the means.

What was he going to say that was going to make her feel better? *I'm sorry I fucked you then tied you up and locked you in the room so I could escape? I'm sorry you think I used you, because that's not true?*

There were no good excuses, no satisfactory apologies. He *had* used her, though that hadn't been his intent. Had there been another way to get what he wanted, he'd have done it. Things had just gotten out of hand between them. He'd handled everything badly. He'd hurt her. He knew it. And he didn't know how to make it better. The worst part was, he felt like shit about it. His stomach still gnawed with guilt. He wanted to wrap his arms around her and force her to listen, to apologize over and over and do whatever it took to make it up to her.

He didn't want to see that look of pain furrowing her brow and know he was the one who caused it.

Way to go, asshole. All the steps he'd taken to earn the hunters' trust, he'd obliterated in an instant, because he hadn't believed them. And they'd been right. He'd been wrong. Now he had to start over again.

A sound outside the cave drew his attention.

"Shay, give me a weapon."

She shot him a glare. "Not on your life."

Derek, Lou, and the others slipped into the cave. Nic breathed a sigh of relief and relaxed the tension coiling his muscles.

Derek took one look at him and shook his head.

"Bad move, huh?" Derek asked.

Nic shrugged. "I found the demons, didn't I?"

Derek quirked his lips. "Yeah, I guess you did. Too bad you didn't believe us in the first place."

"Would you if you hadn't seen it yourself?"

Derek paused. "Probably not."

"I believe it now."

"Good." Derek looked to Shay. "How many?"

"I saw ten carrying the big rocks outside and piling them up. My guess is there's more of them in the cave."

Derek nodded. "All right. We're going in."

"What about him?" she asked, inclining her head toward Nic.

Derek slanted a glance at Nic and frowned. "I guess you get to come along. But you're not exactly trustworthy yet, so I'm keeping you bound." He pulled a set of handcuffs—an honest-to-God set of steel handcuffs—from his pack.

"What do you carry those around for?"

"Never know when I might need them." He motioned to Shay, who pulled Nic's arms forward. Derek fastened the cuffs around Nic's wrists.

Frustration ate at him. "This isn't necessary. I'm not going anywhere."

"And you're not exactly in a position to argue, are you?" Derek faced him, only inches away. "You want to see how this goes down? You want to see demons in action?"

"Yeah. I do."

"Then this is how it happens."

"Fine." He supposed he deserved this. His gaze shot to Shay, expecting to see triumph in her eyes. Instead, he glimpsed the same emotions he'd seen earlier. Maybe even more pain than anger now, but she jerked her head away as soon as she caught him looking.

Yeah, he deserved this all right. And it felt like shit.

"Try not to run off," Derek said. "Because I'm not sure anyone will go after you, and you won't last long out there."

"I'm not going anywhere," he reiterated.

Derek gave Nic a pair of those cool night-vision shades. Like sunglasses, they were wafer thin, but allowed him to see clearly. He also gave him an ear communication device, allowing him to talk to and hear the other hunters.

"Let's go," Derek said. "Keep it quiet, and get ready to engage."

They moved out, each stride quiet and careful. Nic followed along, stepping where they did so he made no noise.

They approached the cave entrance and Nic tensed, certain demons were going to jump out at them. If they ran into demons they might as well thrust him up front as a target, since he was otherwise useless.

After a quick inspection determined there were no demons lurking just inside the cave entrance, they moved in. Nic was in the middle of the throng of hunters who were tightly packed together, weapons raised, each of them turned in a different direction as they traveled deeper into the cave.

"The tunnels here look man-made," Dalton said. "We're going to have to split up."

Derek nodded. "Shay, Gina, Ryder, you're with me on the right. Dalton, Lou, take the rest and go left."

Nic followed along with Derek's group. They headed off down the right tunnel, one by one, Nic stuck in the middle. Shay was in front of him, right behind Derek and Gina. Ryder was behind Nic, Ryder's weapon occasionally poking Nic in the back.

Nic got the idea Ryder wasn't very happy having Nic along.

Tough. Nic focused on Shay's swaying behind in front of him. Now that was much more pleasant. Her pants stretched over her sweet ass, outlining every curve, reminding him of what it felt like to touch her body.

Something he'd not likely get to do again. Because he was exceptionally stupid.

The tunnels went on seemingly forever, taking them into the depths of the cave. At least it was cooler down there. Nic was grateful for the night-vision glasses because it was midnight dark without even the sliver of the moon to light their way now. And Derek had said the hunters couldn't turn on their lights because it would alert the demons to their presence. So when they heard a shuffling noise to the left, they all stopped in their tracks and raised their weapons, and Shay pivoted, nearly slamming him against the far wall of the tunnel.

"Don't move," she warned, immediately turning away from him to focus on the unknown threat.

Where did she think he was going to go with her body pressing back against his? And he didn't need her protection, dammit.

Especially when they realized the threat was the other hunters.

"Shit," Derek said.

"The tunnels obviously meet up here," Dalton said, lowering his weapon.

"You can get off me now, unless you enjoy grinding your ass against my dick. Because I sure don't mind it a bit," Nic whispered in Shay's ear.

She practically leaped away from him. He grinned as she distanced herself as much as she could, which really wasn't that far given their proximity in the tunnel.

"Let's move on," Lou suggested. "There's only the one path from here."

Single file once again, they progressed even farther downward. How deep did this damn cave go anyway? The walls and ceiling were perfectly smooth and arced, which meant they had to have been created by humans. Or demons.

"I hear something up ahead," Derek said, raising his hand.

Shay stepped back and turned toward Nic. "I'll let you know what's going on. But if something happens, you need to be ready to get the hell out of the way and fast. Either flatten yourself against the wall or hit the dirt, okay?"

"If you'd uncuff me and put a weapon in my hands, you'd have another hunter."

She glanced at his wrists, then back up at him, almost as if she was considering it. "Not my call. Just do what I said."

He wanted to argue. He felt impotent tied up like this. Adrenaline pushed his heart rate up, anticipation making him anxious. He stayed in line with the rest of them as they headed toward the noises.

Derek held up his hand to stop the team. "Demons ahead. Hybrids. They're in a room just down there, pulling more of those big rocks loose."

"So now what?" Nic whispered to Shay.

"We engage them. Destroy them. Then we figure out what they were after." She turned toward him. "Remember what I told you. Stay out of the way."

She wavered for a second, her gaze locked on his. Then she turned, inching forward with Gina. The others brushed past him, pushing him toward the back. He didn't like this. Not at all. He could help, be useful. He had to get to Derek so he could get these cuffs unlocked. He started to push his way up front, but it was too late. The demons spotted them and the hunters advanced, running toward the creatures with weapons ablaze, leaving him behind.

They left his field of vision but he heard growls and weapons fire. He pushed off the wall and hurried to the opening, needing to see this.

Damn. It was like a video game—totally unbelievable—yet it was really happening. Blue light shot across the room from someone's laser, hitting a demon who was lifting a boulder over its head in an attempt to hurl it at a hunter. The demon stopped, dropped the boulder, and began to melt, disintegrating in a puddle of putrid flesh.

Hunters were engaged with demons twice their size. The stench of the creatures was overpowering, making Nic gag, yet the hunters showed no fear, no revulsion, going toe to toe with the things, only inches away from them.

And there he stood, cuffed and useless, while a battle waged around him, leaving him with nothing to do but watch. He hated this. Frustration ate at him as the battle grew more fierce. He counted twice as many demons as hunters. Dammit, they needed him.

And Shay—she was amazing, firing a UV laser with one hand and a sonic handgun in the other, targeting two demons who were heading straight for her. One began to melt, the other twitched as its insides began to boil. She didn't even pause to watch, just turned and went after another, backing up one of the other hunters.

But she didn't see the demon coming up behind her, and neither did the others. Good thing the fuckers were slow. Nic had just enough time to do something.

"Shay!" he hollered as he broke out of the entrance to the cave, grateful they hadn't shackled his ankles together.

Through the noise of battle she didn't hear him on the comm, but he kept rushing the demon, its long, clawlike fingers extended and reaching for her. It was only a couple feet away. Nic pushed himself harder, hoping like hell he was going to make it in time, hoping someone would at least see him and realize where he was headed.

He didn't know if he was strong enough to do any

damage, but he'd be damned if he was going to stand there like a pussy and watch this go down. Even unarmed, he could at least push the demon away, or knock it down—dammit, he could do something.

He hit the demon at full speed. Shay turned at that moment, her eyes widening as Nic rammed the demon. Hell, the damn thing didn't even budge, but at least he'd gotten Shay's attention. As soon as Nic rolled out of the way, Shay lifted her rifle and fired.

Nic kept rolling, away from the gelatinous mess bubbling down near him. Two strong arms lifted him. He looked up to find Derek and Dalton on either side, and carnage all around him.

A couple more shots and the last demon was down.

"That's it, I think," Ryder said, coming up to stand next to Dalton. He looked at the remains of the demon Nic had run into, then back at Nic. "Nice shot, Shay," he said before walking away.

"I wouldn't have shot him at all if Nic hadn't yelled and knocked the demon's hands away from me," she said, shuddering. "The thing would have touched me, and if its claws embedded in my skin, the toxins could have paralyzed me."

She frowned at Nic. "You were supposed to stay hidden."

"And if I had, you might have died. Sorry. I wasn't going to let that happen."

"We could have used you out here, weapon in hand," Derek said.

"I told you I'd have fought."

"If we could trust you."

"You can, dammit. I fucked up, okay? I didn't believe any of this shit existed. Now I do. Now I've seen it. I had to see it."

Derek clapped him on the shoulder, then reached into his pocket and unlocked the cuffs, removing them. "Okay. Let's give this another try."

"Thanks."

"I'm only going to say this once, though. You try to escape again, and brother or no brother, I'll hunt you down myself. And you won't like it when I find you."

"You won't need to hunt me down. I've seen these things now. I believe you. I want to fight them."

"What about our father?"

"What about him?"

"You believe what I told you about him?"

"Which part? That he's dead, that he was a demon? That we're demons?" Nic brushed his fingers through his hair, this time giving an honest answer. "I don't know. I haven't heard from him in months. I don't know where he is."

Derek arched a brow. "What about you? How do you feel?"

Nic shrugged. "I don't feel any different than I always did." That part, at least, wasn't a lie. "I guess you're just going to have to show me what it is about me that makes me different, or I'll have to fumble along until I figure it out." He looked around. "But I do know that so far you haven't lied to me."

"That's a start. The rest we'll take a day at a time.

Trust doesn't come easy within our ranks, Nic. You'll have to earn it. And you *will* be watched." Derek tilted his head to the side then held out his hand. "Welcome to the Realm of Light, brother."

Just like that, as if nothing had happened, Nic had been welcomed with open arms by Derek.

Okay, maybe not exactly like that, but to Shay, it seemed too damned easy.

She wasn't as forgiving as Derek. Then again, she had a more personal, intimate reason for her anger. Of course, no one knew what had happened between her and Nic, and it was going to stay that way. One didn't publicly admit to such stupidity. She had a hard enough time mentally acknowledging her decision to have sex with the man she was supposed to be guarding.

Good sex though it was. No, great sex. Phenomenal, mind-blowing, best-sex-of-her-life kind of sex. Maybe even more than physical kind of sex. The kind that left you all warm inside. The kind that made a woman start thinking that a man might actually care.

Ha! He cared all right. He cared about fucking his way into an escape plan. And she'd fallen for it because she was stupid.

She'd let herself become so tied into Nic, allowing her visions to rule her heart, that it had blinded her. She'd thought there was an emotional connection between them, that he felt the same way.

She'd been wrong. And now she was stuck having to

face that mistake every day, because Nic was part of the team. A demon hunter. A member of the Realm of Light. And Derek's brother.

Needing some distance from all of them, she came upstairs and locked the door between the bathroom and Nic's room. She stayed in the shower a long time, letting the heat and steam pour over her, hoping it would wash away the remnants of Nic.

But it couldn't wash away her memories, no matter how hard she scrubbed. She crawled into bed, physically exhausted but emotionally aching and unable to sleep.

She heard the knock on her bathroom door, knew who it was, and ignored it.

"Shay. I need to talk to you."

"Go away, Nic. We have nothing to talk about."

"I brought you a sandwich. You didn't eat."

"I'm not hungry."

He turned the knob and walked in, flipping on the light. Shay shot up in bed and grabbed the dagger under her pillow while at the same time clutching the sheets to her naked body.

Nic arched a brow. "You'd kill me because I brought you food?"

"Don't tempt me." She wished she'd thrown on some clothes. Now she felt vulnerable, naked underneath a thin sheet. "Get out, Nic. I don't want you here."

"I thought we'd eat together. Talk."

He leaned against the doorway, looking sinfully delectable dressed all in black. He'd come upstairs to shower and change right after they'd come back to the house. As soon as he came downstairs, she'd headed up, wanting to keep as much distance between them as possible. She hadn't even looked at him then. She did now.

How dare he make her stomach do flip-flops? How dare he look at her as if he'd like to eat *her* for dinner rather than one of the sandwiches on the plate? He didn't even have the decency to look ashamed of himself. He was smiling. Bastard.

Nic pulled the chair out next to her bed and sat.

"What part of 'get out' don't you understand?"

He balanced the plate on his knees and grabbed one of the sandwiches. "I'm not leaving, so you might as well eat. Demon hunters need their strength. We can eat while we talk."

She really should stab him. But her traitorous stomach grumbled. And dammit, now she was hungry. She clutched the sheet tighter to her breasts and snatched half a sandwich from the plate, concentrating on the food.

"I don't have anything to say to you." She didn't even look at him, didn't trust herself to gaze into those gorgeous blue eyes of his, afraid she'd be lost if she did.

"So don't talk. Just listen."

Listen to what? Lies? There was nothing he could say that would make any difference in how she felt. She reached for the other half of the sandwich. Obviously misery didn't dampen her appetite.

"I'm sorry. I hurt you and I know it. I didn't intend for this to happen."

She slanted a look of disbelief at him. "Which part? The sex or the escape or locking me in here?"

"All of it. But I never set out to seduce you with the intent to escape. You have to realize I was a prisoner. I had to try to escape. Yeah, I did want to get out of here, but having sex with you wasn't in my plan."

"Good to know. That makes me feel much better. You can go now." She brushed bread crumbs off the top of the sheet and turned away from him.

"Shay, look at me."

She yelped when he grabbed her arms and turned her around, forcing her to face him. His hands held tight to her shoulders, and unless she planned to let go of the sheet, she had no choice. She was trapped. Dammit.

"I'm sorry. I screwed this up. But I'm not going to apologize for making love to you. I'm never going to apologize for that. I shouldn't have tied you up and escaped. That part was wrong. But touching you, being inside you . . . nah, babe, I can't say I'm sorry about that." He skimmed his fingers over her cheek. She drew back, not trusting her body's reaction to his touch.

Dammit. How could she think about being angry when his words evoked memories of the two of them moving together, his mouth on hers, his skin against her skin . . . oh, God, she was losing it. She hated him. She had to remember she hated him.

Didn't she?

"Have you ever made a mistake, Shay?"

She sucked in a breath. "Of course I have."

"Have you ever hurt someone you cared about?"

Did he care about her? Is that what he was trying to say? "I never cared about anyone other than my parents."

"I've never been close to anyone, not even my dad. I never cared about anyone. Until now."

She didn't know what to say to him, so she said nothing. But she felt the loneliness emanating from him and wanted to wrap her arms around him and hold him close. Instead, she forced herself to remain where she was.

"I feel like hell for hurting you. My gut's all twisted up inside."

"Good."

His lips twitched. "Make you feel better?"

He might be smiling over this, but it would be a while before she could. "Somewhat."

"Can we start over?"

"There's nothing to start over. There is no 'us,' Nic."

"What if I want there to be?"

His gaze was intense, his face so close to hers she could feel his breath across her cheek. His touch evoked images, that sense of closeness she'd always felt with him. She fought the visions, not wanting to feel connected to him now. "You threw away any chance of that when you used me as part of your escape plan."

Nic let out a breath and looked away.

Shay refused to feel bad. Words of apology from him didn't heal the hurt inside.

"Look," he said, "I'm confused as hell and trying to

sort through this demon stuff and figure out what's going on between you and me. But I do know I don't want to hurt you again."

"No chance of that. And you can start by letting go of me."

He did, moving away and sitting down.

"Don't ever come near me in an intimate or personal way again."

"Are you sure that's what you want?"

No. Her body was crying out for him right now. "Yes."

"If that's what you want, then I won't."

"Okay."

"We both need sleep. I'm sure we'll be on the hunt again when we get up."

He nodded and grabbed the plate.

"Thanks for the sandwich."

"You're welcome."

He closed the door behind him, and Shay got up and flipped off the light.

She didn't know what to think of her conversation with Nic. He seemed sincere enough, but she knew better than to believe him. Then again, what reason did he have to try to make up with her? He already had his freedom from Derek. No more cuffs, no more lock-ins.

So what could Nic possibly hope to gain from her by apologizing, by being nice? What did he want from her?

Now he was in the next room. They still shared a bathroom—though that was as intimate as it was going to get between them. Whatever physical thing they'd had before was over. This psychic connection she felt with Nic was just going to have to remain unsettled, because she simply couldn't risk the heartache that went with getting close to him.

Derek might trust Nic, but she didn't.

Or maybe she just didn't trust herself.

Chapter Fourteen

N ic, come with me. We have to hurry!"

Nic shook his head. Something wasn't right. It was dark, and though he heard the familiar voice, it seemed strange to him. Not . . . normal.

"Dominic, I said come with me. Now."

That authoritative, commanding voice, one he'd heard all his life. Normally he'd snap to it, but this time, he couldn't.

"Don't listen to him, Nic. Don't go. He's lying to you."

Shay. He turned at the sound of her voice. Her light was strong. He saw her, holding her arms out to him.

"Come with me. We have to get out of here."

"Don't go with her, Dominic. Stay here with me. I need you."

His father's voice. His father needed him.

"He's dead, Nic. He's evil. You can't go to him," Shay beseeched. "Come with me. I can save you."

Nic pressed his hands over his ears, trying to block

them both out. He didn't know what to do, which way to go. And all around him, monsters. Only this time, it was clear what they were.

Demons. Their hands outstretched, claws reaching for him, muttering in some unintelligible language, paying him homage.

"You're their king, Dominic. They need you. I need you."

Nic looked to his father, shook his head, backed away as his father began to turn into one of the demons.

"No.

"No.

"*No!*"

He had to run. Had to grab Shay and get out of here. She was right. They were all right.

His father was evil.

"Dominic, come to me." His father's hands were bony, skeletal claws, dripping with a sticky substance. He reached out for Nic, only inches from reaching him.

"Get the hell away from me. Don't touch me!"

"Nic. Nic, wake up."

Something shook him. He blinked and there she was, hovering above him.

Shay. He reached for her, shooting upright and clutching her to him.

Sweating, panting, she was his lifeline, his light in the darkness.

She smoothed her hand across his brow. "You were having another nightmare. I heard you yelling."

Nightmare. The dreams. Again? Shit. They were becoming so real he couldn't tell the difference anymore. "I get them a lot."

"So I gathered."

He focused on her, obliterating the dream into the recesses of his mind. She had on a T-shirt. His, actually. The light was on in the bathroom behind them, silhouetting her. The T-shirt only reached her thighs, and the outline of her nipples was clear through the thin material. He fingered the hem, trying to ignore the quick swelling of his cock in response as his fingers brushed her skin. "Where did you get this?"

She looked down at the shirt. "I . . . ran in here in a hurry and tossed this on before I woke you."

"Sexy." He grinned. She smiled back. Good start.

She started to get up. "If you're all right, I'll—"

He reached for her wrist. "I need to talk to someone about these dreams."

He couldn't believe the words had spilled from his lips, but as soon as he said them he realized it was true. He did need to talk out the dreams—they were puzzling and getting way too close to what was happening with the Realm of Light, with all of this.

She sat back down on the edge of his bed. "Okay."

He scooted up against the headboard. "I've never told anyone about the dreams. This is kind of a big thing for me, but they're confusing the hell out of me and you're the only one here I'm—or I was—close to."

Shay looked down at her lap for a second, then back

up at him. "Whatever happened between us, Nic—I'm still here for you if you need to talk."

"Thanks." He really was going to tell her about the nightmares. This would seal the deal for sure. She would think he was insane after he told her.

And now that he had her here, now that he was supposed to spill, how was he going to do it?

"Just spit it out, Nic."

"I've been having nightmares for years."

She climbed onto the bed, pulling her legs behind her. "About?"

"Monsters. Darkness. Hell, I guess you'd say. My dad is always in them. And I'm surrounded by these creatures."

"What kind of creatures?"

"I didn't really know how to explain them, until tonight."

"Your nightmares have been about the demons," she said.

"Yeah."

"So do you think your dreams are more like a premonition of what you might face in the future?"

"Maybe. I don't know. I just thought they were remnants of my head injury or some recurring nightmare that my psyche conjured up. Because it's a running theme in my dreams. The same monsters, and my dad is always in them; the creatures surround me like I'm some kind of fucking deity and they want to worship me."

"Worship you, like you're their leader or something?"

"I guess."

"That's freaky."

"Yeah. And lately, you've been in the dreams."

Her eyes widened. "Me?"

"Yeah."

"That's . . . interesting. Tell me what you see in your dreams."

"They've been a little different every time, but basically my dad is pulling me one way, and you're pulling the other. He's trying to draw me in, and you're trying to pull me out."

Shay inhaled and blew out a breath. "That's intense."

He shrugged. "It's probably nothing."

"It's not . . . nothing, Nic."

"You don't think so? I've always thought I was a freak."

She held out her hand. "Welcome to my world."

Nic stared at Shay's hand. "I don't understand."

"I've experienced something similar. I have . . . visions."

"Visions?"

"Yeah. Psychic visions. I felt you before I even met you."

Shay waited for Nic to look at her like she was some kind of oddball or nutcase. Part of her couldn't believe she'd just told him she was psychic. She'd never even told her own father about it. She'd never told the other hunters about it, even though her so-called gift might be useful to them. So why now, and why Nic, of all people?

The one man she could really care about, a man who'd just betrayed her, and she'd shared her deepest, darkest secret with him.

What was she thinking?

"You're psychic?"

She shrugged. "I guess so. I'm not really sure."

"Have you been tested?"

"I've never told anyone before."

"You mean Derek and the others don't know about this?"

She shook her head. "I told you. No one knows."

"Not even your parents?"

She shook her head, looked down at her hands. "I've had this since I was a kid, since . . ."

"Since when, Shay?"

"Never mind." She'd never told anyone what she'd seen, what had happened so long ago. She wasn't going to say it, couldn't dredge up the past hurts. She'd buried it so well. Why was it resurfacing now?

He tipped her chin, forcing her to meet his gaze. "Tell me."

God, she'd wanted to tell someone for so long. It burned inside her, desperate to get out. Nic had just confessed his deep, dark secret to her. If he could trust her with his, then she could share, too. "I saw demons taking my mom. When she kissed me good-bye before she left on her business trip, I saw the whole thing. In my head. It was a vision."

"Christ. How old were you?"

She looked up at him. "Six."

He slipped his hand in hers. She didn't pull away. "You were so young. Why didn't you tell your dad?"

"I couldn't. When my mom didn't come home, when she was determined to be missing, I knew my vision was real. But I didn't equate the demon thing with reality. I just assumed it signified something bad had happened to her. Then I felt guilty because I could have stopped it."

"How could you have stopped it?"

"If I'd said something—to her, or to my dad—begged her not to go, or warned her that something bad might happen—she might still be here."

"You can't know that, babe."

Tears filled her eyes. She couldn't hold them back. The pain she'd held inside for so many years rushed forward, the ache like a knife in her heart, reopening the old wound. "I could have stopped it. I knew in advance something was going to happen to her, but I didn't say anything."

Nic pulled her into his arms and held her. She was supposed to hate him, supposed to be angry at him for betraying her. But right now she needed the solid wall of strength he gave her, needed the kindred spirit that his own personal torment represented to her.

They were alike in so many ways it was uncanny. Was that why she felt the connection?

"You couldn't have stopped it, Shay. You were a child. They wouldn't have believed you."

The adult in her knew that, but the child within still wanted to see what would happen if she begged her mother not to go.

"I often asked my mother not to leave on a business trip. She would smile, kiss my cheek, and say she had to." She leaned away from his embrace, embarrassed that she needed him so much.

"She wouldn't have stopped that time, either." Nic brushed his thumb over her cheek, wiping away the tear that escaped.

Shay shook her head. "No, she wouldn't have. She always went anyway, no matter what. She always left."

Shuddering out a sigh, she reached over him and grabbed a tissue from the nightstand, hating the weakness within her. Now that it was out, she felt vulnerable She'd told Nic her secret.

There were reasons she'd kept this to herself all these years. The vulnerability was a huge issue. If people knew, she could be used. Even Derek and Lou and the other hunters—she hadn't told them, too afraid they might want to tap into her abilities to track demons. She couldn't handle willingly going into these nightmares and confronting the creatures head-on. And she knew holding back the information made her weak, hated herself for it, because this so-called gift was a valuable tool to the Realm of Light. But still, she just couldn't do it.

Until Nic. With Nic she had plunged headlong into the visions again, allowed them to rule her. And now look where she was. Knee deep in demon madness, taking her just where she hadn't wanted to go. And dredging up old memories and pain in the process.

For years she'd been a prisoner to the visions. It was as if the Sons of Darkness had controlled her life from the moment they'd taken her mother away. They had made her afraid, and that fear had made her hide her psychic abilities, something she could have been using against the demons. No more.

It was time to get a grip and face what she was—face this gift or curse or whatever had been given to her, and tell Derek and Lou about it. It was time to use it to fight the Sons of Darkness.

"Tell me about you and me," Nic said. "What do you see? Do these visions come on you all of a sudden?"

Shay took a deep breath. "It's hard to describe. When I saw you from the beach I had one, before we met. When I touch you, they're very strong."

"Every time we touch?"

She knew the question he asked. "No, not every time. Sometimes I can push them away."

"You can control when you have them."

"So far, yes. But it's difficult. Resisting them makes me really shaky for a while afterward."

"What do you see?"

"Pretty much the same thing you see in your dreams."

Nic stared at her, then shook his head. "I knew I felt connected to you, but I didn't understand it. That's why you suddenly started appearing in the dreams."

"I still don't know what it means. The visions aren't clear, only suggesting that you and I seem to have some objective together, and your father is involved. But your father is dead, Nic. I saw it happen."

"I think I need to start believing that." He looked away.

Shay felt his pain, and all the anger she had for him evaporated. Like it or not, they did share a connection, and she couldn't walk away from it, or from him. Whatever had happened between them last night was water under the bridge. He'd screwed up and admitted it. In his position she'd have done whatever it took to gain her freedom, even using him. So could she blame him for doing the same thing?

"I'm sorry, Nic. I know this must be hard to take in. Your father, the demons, you and me . . ."

"I can take it. I'm tougher than you think. I might have been stupid at first for not believing all of you, but I'm grabbing a clue now. My father is dead. He was a demon. That's bad shit. I might not like it, but it is what it is and I have to face it. Derek is a brother I never knew I had, and you and I have some kind of weird psychic connection. This is going to take awhile, but yeah, I'll assimilate it all eventually."

"When you put it like that, I'm not sure I'd be able to face it all at once," she said, offering up a smile.

He cupped her cheek, smoothing his hand down the column of her throat. "You've been through hell and back yourself. If you and the rest of the hunters can do it, so can I."

How could she care about a man who'd hurt her so badly? Shouldn't she be strong enough to resist his lure? Was it the psychic pull, or something else?

The way he looked at her now, a mix of strength and determination coupled with vulnerability, was her downfall.

He needed her. And she needed him. Whatever was happening, they were destined to do it together. She didn't know what or when, but she knew it had to do with the two of them.

"So now that we know about this connection between the two of us, should we go with it and see what happens?"

Her first instinct was to say no. But that was something she'd have to get past. With new resolve, she shrugged. "I suppose we could try. I'm game if you are."

"If we can control it, rather than let it just happen, we can gain some focus on it. Maybe it'll give us some clues. Tell us what we're supposed to do next. Because I'm damn tired of wandering around clueless in the dark—dreamwise, that is."

She adjusted herself on the bed, kneeling, then reached for his hands. "Let's do it." Because he was right. They needed to take charge of whatever was happening between them, rather than let it control them.

"How is this going to work?" he asked.

"I have no idea. I'll open up my mind to the visions. I don't know if you'll be able to share them or not. No one ever has."

"I'm not about to let you do this alone, dammit. Surely these dreams will help me go there with you."

"No clue. Let's just do this and get it over with."

Nic slid his hands in hers and Shay opened herself to the visions.

"I'm right here, Shay. I'm not leaving you."

He had no idea how much that meant to her right

now. Because the room went dark and suddenly they
were no longer in the house.

It was cold, wet. Shay felt the evil around them in-
stantly.

"Nic, are you here with me?"

She didn't hear him, couldn't see him or feel his touch.

"Right with you, babe." He threaded his arms around
her, his body solid and reassuring behind her.

She smiled, relaxed a little, and opened herself up
more.

They were in a cave, much like the one they found
the demons in, only the walls seemed darker. Something
compelled her to move forward, toward a small light she
saw off in the distance. Nic took her hand and walked by
her side.

"Do you see that light up ahead?" she asked him.

"Yeah. I hear voices, too. Lots of voices."

Now she heard them, too, and quickened her step,
anxious to see what was up there. The light grew stronger,
as did the sounds of voices. Then it hit her. Shay pulled
on Nic's hand as they approached the entrance to a
room.

"Don't go in there."

"Why not?" he asked.

"They're in the room."

"Who?"

"The demons."

"No, they're not. We're safe. Come on, Shay."

She tugged on his hand. "We have to get out of here,
Nic. Now." Something told her they were in danger. She

felt the presence of evil like a heavy cloak surrounding her body.

"We have to see what's in there. I have to finish this."

"Not now." Warning bells screamed in her head. Her skin prickled. "Nic, we have to go!"

She tried to break the vision but she couldn't. Was Nic tying her in here, forcing her to remain?

Then she felt it, this time all around them. She turned, already knowing what she'd see.

Demons. Surrounding them, moving in, mumbling, their soulless eyes giving her the creeps, their clawlike fingers reaching out toward them. Toward Nic.

"Nic, we have to go. Now!"

She turned to Nic, and screamed.

He was demon, his father at his side. Bloodred eyes stared out at her with evil intent.

"You're too late," Ben said. "He's mine now."

Nic smiled at her, reached for her. "And now you're mine, Shay."

"No!" Shay pushed at him, screamed, but he held tight to her. Her mind screamed with the betrayal, the thought that he'd used her again, had brought her into this to capture her. Reason warred with abject terror, and she fought for control of her sanity.

"Nic, fight this! We have to get out now!"

She pummeled his chest and kicked at him, but he laughed at her.

"I will *not* do this!"

She beat at his chest, refusing to believe this was real.

The instant before she was propelled back to the bedroom, she could have sworn she saw regret in Nic's eyes.

She sucked in a lungful of clean air.

"Hey, are you all right? What happened?" Nic squeezed her hands.

"What do you mean what happened? Weren't you there with me?"

"No. Nothing. I was just sitting here, watching you breathe. You went dead silent, like you were sleeping, then you started frowning, and twitching, and raising your voice. I had to shake you to get you to snap out of it." He smiled. "Kind of like one of my nightmares."

He hadn't been there with her. He didn't know what she'd seen.

"So what happened?"

Struggling to calm down her jackhammering heartbeat, she breathed in, then out, finally settling. Could she even tell him what she'd seen? Could he handle it? She chewed on her bottom lip and deliberated.

"Just tell me, Shay. I can deal with whatever it is."

His smile was comforting, and she nodded. "We were in a cave, following a light. I felt the evil and I wanted to go but you insisted we keep moving toward it. Demons surrounded us. When I looked at you, you were standing next to your father, both of you turned to demon. Your father said you were his, and you said I was going to be yours. You grabbed me and I screamed, and then I was out of the vision and back here on the bed."

"Christ." He dragged his hand through his hair and looked down, not meeting her eyes.

Shay allowed him the moment, knowing he had to be as shook up as she was. When he lifted his gaze to her, she felt a pang of remorse at the pain she glimpsed there. Pain she had caused.

"I'm sorry, babe," he said. "That must have been really frightening for you."

"And not too pleasant for you to hear about, either."

He shrugged. "No worse than the dreams I've had for years. But still, it reaffirms that these nightmares might be foreshadowing my future. Because that's what you see, isn't it? The future?"

Hesitantly, she nodded. "I haven't had that much experience with the visions, other than the one about my mother, and that one definitely came true. I've fought them so long I never even wanted to know if what I saw came true. But yeah, typically they seem to foretell the future."

He blew out a long breath. "Then that fucking sucks. Because I don't intend to become a demon like my dad."

Shay didn't know how to help him. Had that vision been accurate? "Maybe there's something off about the vision. I don't know. Maybe my visions are just warnings of what could happen, instead of what will happen."

He frowned. "If your vision is accurate, I don't like it. I don't want that to happen. And if we can somehow stop it, I'm all for figuring out how to do that." He leaned forward and reached for her, dragging her across his lap.

Shocked into silence, she could only stare up at him as he held her in his arms.

"I've already hurt you once. I don't intend to ever do it again."

He pressed his lips to hers and she was lost in him. Just like that, everything bad that had happened between them was gone. Like fire in a drought-stricken forest, her body caught flame and burst.

Nic captured her and took no prisoners, his hands roaming over her body with deliberate intent. When he stroked her thighs, skimming his fingers under the hem of the T-shirt, she stretched, eager for more of his touch.

He seemed ravenous, pulling her closer, touching her everywhere, his hands inside the shirt now, capturing her breasts. She arched into his palm, rubbing her nipples against his hot skin.

Now she didn't know who was hungrier for this—him or her. He pulled her into a sitting position, jerking the sheet away from his lap. She straddled and faced him, bending down to capture his mouth and slide her tongue between the warmth of his lips.

She was shivering, needing the heat of his body on her, inside her, desperate for a joining between them. His cock, raging hard and inches from her sex, beckoned. With a forward surge she impaled herself on the solid, throbbing heat of him.

He plunged upward and she cried out into his mouth, finding his tongue and sucking on it hard as he plundered her body with harsh thrusts. She lifted up, then crashed down on him again, harder this time, wanting him deeper, scraping her nails along his back to urge him to drive inside her with more force. She didn't understand what compelled this raging passion, only that she needed it. Maybe she was feeding off the hunger she felt from him. Whatever it was, she loved it, and him, and the way she felt whenever she was with him.

Nic dragged the T-shirt off her body and flung it to the floor, bringing her breasts to his hungry lips. He fed from her nipples, nibbling and sucking on the throbbing peaks as he continued to assault her with punishing upward thrusts. She rocked against him with wild abandon until he took her mouth with a groan.

He brought her to the brink so fast her eyes flew open. His gaze was dark and intense, focusing on her face as she climaxed. Watching him was so intimate, so open, and he gave as good as he got, staying with her as he tightened, whispering her name while he came, then grinding against her while she continued to spasm around him, this closeness between them almost unbearable in its beauty.

He moved against her, slow and easy, taking them both down a notch after that quick, wild ride, then pushed her onto the bed and dropped down on top of her to kiss her with gentle sweeps of his lips.

"Stay with me tonight," he whispered, sweeping his hand over her sweat-dampened hair. "Sleep with me."

He smiled down at her, but when she looked into his eyes the vision came rushing back to her, mixing with the here and now. His eyes, that inhuman, awful red, stared back at her, and he was no longer Nic.

She shuddered and went ice cold, pushing at his chest. "Let me up."

His smile died and he frowned. "Shay, what's wrong?"

She cleared her head of the vision. Of course, Nic stared back at her. It was just Nic. Human, normal, beautiful blue eyes. Nothing demon about him. But she was shook up, and her passion evaporated along with her vision.

"Nothing's wrong. I . . . I just can't stay with you." She hated the vision that had come between them, the awkwardness that now settled between them. She slid off the bed, needing distance to gather her composure. "Not right now, Nic."

He came after her, put his hands on her arms. "What happened?"

Though she knew it was just her mind playing tricks on her, she couldn't handle him touching her. She shook him off. "I'm just tired. The visions wiped me out, and I need some sleep. Alone." She was lying, but she couldn't tell him he scared her. He wouldn't understand.

He reached out, but something in her face must have given him pause. "You're right. I'm sorry. You went above and beyond for me tonight and I appreciate it. Go get some sleep. We'll talk in the morning."

She fled through the bathroom, closing and locking her side of the door.

She leaned against the closed door, her heart pounding so hard she could feel it slamming against her rib cage. She pushed her hair out of her face and climbed into bed, pulling the sheet and blanket over her shivering body.

Cold seeped into her and she shut her eyes, hating the tears that escaped, hating that the moment between them had been lost.

Lovemaking had been beautiful. Heated and passionate and...connected. Then her memory of the vision had ruined it. She could be in his arms right now instead of alone in this bed, dammit.

She hated the visions, knowing what would happen to Nic, hated seeing the part of him that could become dark and evil.

He wouldn't be like that. Nic had strength and he didn't want to become demon. She would help him. Derek would help him. They'd have to tell Derek what she saw.

That meant she'd have to reveal what she was. To everyone. She didn't want to do it, but she had no choice. They had to know.

And she'd have to do it again—she'd have to get close to Nic. She wanted to get close to him, had to get past what she'd seen tonight.

Because she refused to believe that what she'd seen was Nic's future.

Or hers.

Chapter Fifteen

Angelique had been cooling her heels at the campsite for twenty-four hours. That was long enough. The clock was ticking, and she'd already lost valuable dig time.

Cell phone service out here was useless, so she couldn't even try to track down Isabelle unless she drove into town, and that would take too long. Not that her sister would tell her the truth anyway.

Was Isabelle out here somewhere? Was she in some way tied into Ryder and his group? She hoped not, for Izzy's sake.

She'd gone back to the site last night, and found nothing. Perched on a hill overlooking the caves, she'd peered through her scope until she'd squinted herself into a massive headache, and hadn't seen anyone or anything. She'd half expected to see Ryder and his team, but hadn't.

And then she'd been surprised by her own disappointment.

She laughed, knowing it was her curiosity. Though it was better for her project to work alone, she still couldn't help but be curious about him and his people. He intrigued her on an intellectual level, and that was all.

Who were they, really, and what were they doing out there? If they were, in fact, some kind of secret government organization, what was the big secret?

She rolled her eyes and started packing up her things.

Like she didn't have enough on her plate already, she'd started to wonder about Ryder. She was busy and she had to worry about Isabelle's interference. Ryder was an unknown, inconsequential, and it needed to stay that way.

She grabbed her bag and threw it in the Jeep.

It was time to go back to work.

Something about the way Nic held a laser in his hand was unnerving to Shay.

She didn't know if it was because he looked so damned hot, traipsing through the thick brush with a rifle cradled in his arms and ammo strapped across his chest, or if it was the way he was dressed—in camos and boots, sweat dripping off his body, muscles rippling and glistening in the moonlight, and looking dark, dangerous, and ready for action.

She might as well just have a visual orgasm right now.

The man walking next to her now looked completely different from the one who'd stepped out of the ocean only a few days ago. From water god to warrior. Both sexy as hell and devastating to her self-control.

And she knew so much more about him now than she had then. They'd shared so many things together in a few short days—intimate things, both physically and emotionally

She felt bad about running away from him earlier this morning. They'd made love again, had taken another step in bridging the gap that had stood between them.

A lot stood between them. Things she didn't want, and he probably didn't, either. But now wasn't the time to talk about them.

Now they were on the hunt.

The heat tonight was unbearable, even worse than usual. She was drenched through and through, the humidity so thick it seemed she could reach out and touch it, as if it were visible in the air around them.

"Storm's coming," Trace said in answer to her unspoken thoughts. "Big rains are due, and when they hit, they're going to be bad."

"Rain sounds good about now."

"You'd think so, but when they come, they're like monsoons. And then you have to watch out for flooding. And it rains so damn hard you can't see; everything's washed out and the mud is awful. You can't even drive in it."

"Lovely. I don't know which is worse, though right

now I think I'd take my chances with rain. At least it might cool things off."

"Makes the humidity even worse, honey," he said, winking at her before moving off.

Great. She didn't think it could get any worse. As it was now she couldn't breathe. How were they supposed to fight demons?

"You okay?"

"I'm fine." She smiled at Nic, hoping he didn't bear any grudge from her nearly hysterical departure from his bedroom. They hadn't talked about it yet. She hadn't been able to get Nic alone tonight. But she owed him an explanation.

"Did you bring water?" he asked.

"Yes. You?"

"Plenty. I have extra if you need it."

"I'm okay. Thanks." Though she'd already downed two bottles since they started their trek into the hills. Derek wanted to explore the higher elevation caves tonight. They'd already torn into the ones on the lower hills and found nothing.

"You ready for this?" she asked him.

"For what?"

"Demons."

"More than ready. I didn't like being cuffed last night, unable to fight."

She kept her gaze focused on the path ahead. "You shouldn't have thrown yourself at that demon. You could have been clawed."

"You're welcome."

Now she did look at him. His lips were curled in that smile that never ceased to make her legs turn to jelly. The night grew even warmer. She turned away and tried to concentrate on the task at hand.

"When do I get more training?" Nic asked Derek.

"If we run into demons tonight, you'll get on-the-job training, like the rest of the hunters got," Derek shot back.

Nic snorted. "Great."

Shay laughed. "Welcome to the Realm of Light. Trial by fire."

"You could help me out when we aren't in battle."

Shay slanted Nic a dubious look. "I doubt you need my help. Ask one of the other guys. They're much better at this than I am. I'm still learning."

"Actually, that's a really good idea." Derek moved alongside Nic.

"What's a good idea?" she asked.

"You and Nic working together."

Was Derek out of his mind? "I hardly have the depth of experience to train him."

Derek slung his arm around her shoulders as they walked. "You don't give yourself enough credit, Shay. You're an ass kicker. You're adept and focused and you picked up weapons and physical combat like a pro."

Okay, so she beamed under Derek's praise. Ass kicker? Her? Hardly. "Thanks."

"Hopefully we'll engage some demons tonight and we'll see what Nic's got. That should give you a fair idea of how much work he needs. I'll leave it up to you, okay?"

Nic's expression remained impassive, but she caught the glint of amusement in his eyes.

He thought this was funny.

Figured.

Derek moved up ahead of her and Nic.

"Ass kicker, huh?"

"So he says."

"I believe it. I can't wait to go one-on-one with you. Again."

He'd lowered his voice, leaned in so only she could hear him. Somehow she got the idea he wasn't just talking about training.

So maybe he had forgiven her for running out on him.

After a long, arduous climb that left Shay feeling like she'd just scaled Mount Everest, they reached the top of the hill. Long rows of caves stood side by side, their yawning mouths like bodiless monsters lying in wait to devour them. She shivered and stopped, letting the others move ahead. Goose bumps broke out despite the blistering heat of the night.

"What's wrong?" Nic asked, staying behind with her.

"Something's going to happen."

"Are you getting a vision?"

She shrugged. "I feel it."

"Do you think it's time to tell the others?"

She nodded, a swirling of dread in the pit of her stomach. "I suppose now would be as good a time as any."

They caught up with Derek as they entered the mouth of the first cave. "I think something is going to happen."

Derek shot a frown in her direction. "What do you mean?"

"I don't know. It's just a feeling. You probably think I'm crazy, but ever since I was a kid, I've had these weird sensations that pop up every now and then. Premonitions of things to come. Now's one of those times."

Derek nodded. "Any idea what's going to happen?"

Just like that, he believed her. No weird looks or laughs or questions. "No clue. Just . . . something."

"Thanks for the warning."

Lou had stayed back at the house to monitor demon activity via the laptop thermal imagery program. So Shay knew he was listening and it was only a matter of time before he replied.

"Shay," Lou said, "it's not unusual for those who experience paranormal phenomena to come away changed in different ways. We've all been affected."

"You think so?" Shay hadn't considered that.

"You may have always been clairvoyant, or had the ability to sense otherworldly things, but you weren't adept at tapping into your talents until the island. Now you're more focused and in tune with what's on the other side."

"Uh-huh." Understatement. She'd always been in tune, though she'd tried to block it out after her mother's disappearance. Since Nic had come into the picture, the visions were coming hot and heavy, and more frequently.

She supposed she was going to have to sit down with Lou at some point and discuss it.

Shay's attention was diverted by a sense of foreboding. "Something's in here."

Derek halted and pivoted. "You sure?"

"Yes."

Derek tapped his comm. "Lou, you picking up anything?"

"I've got nothing here," Lou said. "Either the caves are interfering with the imaging system, or the demons aren't using portals to make their appearance. We might not be able to get an advance warning system like we usually do. But I trust Shay's senses. Go with them."

"You heard the man," Derek said, releasing the safety on his microwave rifle. "Let's go find some demons."

Derek and Dalton led the teams. Shay slanted a quick glance at Nic, wondering if he was at all nervous. He seemed steady as a rock, just like his brother, his expression determined, his back straight, and his weapon cradled, cocked, and ready to fire as they marched into the black cave.

Instant relief from the blistering heat greeted her as they entered. There was even a breeze—a cold one. Shay sighed, ending on a whispered moan that elicited a deep-throated laugh from Nic.

"That good, huh?" he asked.

"That good." She hoped it would take a while to find the demons so they could linger in the caves. This was heaven.

But it didn't take long for hell to make an appearance.

They zoomed in front of her eyes, so fast she had to blink in rapid succession to focus. Shay knew what that meant—the presence of demons.

"They're here," she commed, mainly to Nic. "Pure demons. They're fast, and just as likely to come up behind you. Be alert and do *not* let them touch you."

"Got it. If they sink their claws into you, they secrete a paralyzing toxin. Then they can go in for the kill. I remember what you told me at the house."

He started to move in front of her, but she grabbed on to his shirt. "I'm going to be too busy to watch out for you."

"I can take care of myself, babe. But thanks for worrying."

He leaned in and kissed her, a quick brush of his lips across hers, and then he was gone.

Dammit, she hadn't expected that. Heat coiled low in her belly. At a time like this she had a physical response to a peck on the lips. Lord, she was hopeless. She pivoted and moved forward, meeting the demons head-on.

There weren't that many—maybe thirty or so—which surprised her. In fact, she inhaled repeatedly, searching for the scent of hybrids, thinking maybe they'd bring up the rear behind the pure demons, but she caught no telltale odor.

The demons circled the hunters, their cold, pale blue soulless eyes never ceasing to give her the creeps. There was nothing behind those eyes, glowing light in the dark; they were vacant, devoid of any life. As the demons rushed the hunters, Shay began to fire, hitting one with the blue light of her laser. It stopped, tilted its head, then began its mournful cry before it melted to the ground.

Advancing outward, the hunters beat the demons back, firing round after round of laser and microwave fire. Smoke filled the tiny cavern, the scent of charred demon worse than the stench of hybrids, making Shay cough. She searched the room for Nic, found him working alongside Derek to battle back the last two demons. Derek was using hand signals to direct Nic where to go. The two purebreds after them were faster than the UV light—switching positions, staying one step ahead of the rapid-fire lasers.

So these demons had decided they weren't going to rush Nic and Derek and end up toast like their brethren. They were avoiding laser fire, self-preservation more important than attack at this point. And Derek and Nic had them backed up with nowhere to go.

The zigzagging demons were making Shay dizzy. She didn't know how Nic and Derek were able to keep up, but they kept firing. It was like watching shooters blasting ducks at one of those midway shooting galleries at the fair. Neither man gave up, backing up a step as the demons approached them while moving sideways, then forward, then sideways, then forward. The demons were trying to disorient them. It didn't work. Derek stopped, letting the demon draw closer. He fired again, hitting one and stopping it in its tracks. Nic hit the other and they both melted down, the howls rending the air around them.

That was it. Demons done for.

Almost too easy, actually.

"So where are the rest of them?" she asked.

"Way too easy," Ryder said, grimacing.

"That was easy?" Nic asked, reloading his laser as he came up to her.

"Yeah. Usually there's a lot more. There weren't that many this time. We handled them pretty fast."

"I'll make a mental note."

She wanted to say it, needed to say it. "You did good."

He grinned. "Thanks It was fun."

She shook her head. "That's because it was easy. Wait till you get involved in a real battle."

"Okay, let's take a look farther into this cave," Derek said. "See where they came from and if there's anything else down here."

Once again the tunnels went down to a formidable depth. An open room showed the presence of demons, the stench remaining from hybrids. Huge chunks of rock had been torn from the walls, the ground ripped up.

"They've been here. It's like they're looking for something," Derek said.

"It has to be the gem." Shay took her dagger and scraped at the walls, coming away with small, strange-looking rock formations. "I'm no geologist or expert, but these look like diamonds."

"Let me see those." Nic took a sample from the palm of her hand and clicked his shoulder light on, flipping his shades up and examining it closely. "They *are* diamonds."

"You shitting me?" Ryder leaned over Nic's shoulder. "Honest-to-God diamonds."

"Yeah."

"Let's take those samples back to Lou," Derek said.

Diamonds. Shay shook her head.

A demon's best friend?

Bart didn't need to look up from his work to know one of his brothers had arrived.

"Tase."

"Bart. Have you found Dominic yet?"

"Not yet. But I'm confident he's close by."

Tase emanated heat, an extremely unusual character- istic for a Lord. His nearness caused great discomfort, which meant Tase enjoyed getting into Bart's personal space.

"And how do you know this?"

Actually, Bart had no idea where Nic was. Tase already knew this or he wouldn't have come. Bart straightened and met Tase's dark gaze head on. "He's blocking my ef- forts at contact."

"What efforts are those?"

"Obviously I can't reach him by phone, and I don't have a psychic link to him. That was Ben's area, and Ben can't do that any longer, as you well know. So I have my people searching for him. We're tracking the scent left by the Realm. It's only a matter of time."

Tase circled him. "Time is of the essence, brother."

"I realize it. I'll have him here before the ceremony."

"Let's hope so." Tase looked around. "Preparations going well?"

"Yes."

"And what of the woman?"

"I'm working on that, too. I have it under control."

"I'm thinking you need my assistance."

"That's unnecessary." And unwanted.

"Nevertheless, the others feel a sense of urgency. I will remain and assist you."

Bart resisted the urge to argue, knowing the power of his brother was much stronger than his own. When Ben was alive, the two of them together were formidable, their bond unbreakable. Since Ben's death, Bart had dropped a rung or two in the Sons of Darkness hierarchy. Tase knew this, too, and was using it to his advantage. Sonofabitch!

Bart couldn't afford to make any more enemies. "I would welcome your assistance."

Tase smiled, though there was no brotherly connection there. He craved power and nothing more. He wanted Bart's downfall. If Bart failed at this task, Tase would rise even higher.

Bart would do everything in his power to make sure that didn't happen. And as soon as this ceremony was finished, he'd have Nic at his side.

Another ally. One even more powerful than Ben had been. Then he'd be on top again. Where he belonged.

Chapter Sixteen

Nic estimated that the hundreds of diamonds they'd seen in the cave were worth millions. The demons had dug through enough depth of rock to uncover a rich vein.

But they'd left it all. And that was the strangest thing. He sat in the living room and listened to Lou and the others hypothesize about the find and what it meant. They'd searched the other caves and the surrounding area, but had come up empty, so they'd returned to the house, showed Lou the diamonds, and grabbed a bite to eat.

"All these diamonds," Nic mused. "Do you think that's what they're after?"

Lou shook his head. "They're after something called the black diamond."

"Which is?"

"Some kind of gem that brings a mystical strength to

the Sons of Darkness. Their search is for power, not riches."

"They sure as hell left a lot of riches behind."

Lou nodded.

"Maybe the demons we happened upon were the tail end of the cleanup team," Derek suggested.

"Could be. You saw no other evidence of them?"

"Nothing. In that cave, the other caves on the hill, or the entire area. It was like the demons disappeared completely."

"Maybe they found the black diamond so they had no reason to remain," Ryder suggested.

Lou shook his head. "I don't think so. If they had, something major would be happening by now."

Ryder scratched his head. "Well, that's good to know, I guess. So now what?"

"We track them. It's a given they're not underground here, because there is no portal signature. We'll have to track them aboveground, the old-fashioned way."

Lou was skirting glances in Nic's direction, and so was Derek. Then it hit him. "Diavolo Diamonds. You think it's in the mine."

"The thought has occurred to us, yes," Lou admitted.

"That's why you wanted me." He was so stupid. He knew they were near the mines, searching the caves in the area, but for some reason it hadn't clicked. Of course.

"Partly," Derek said. "And also because you're my brother, you're half demon, and we needed to know whose side you're on."

"I'm on your side. Or haven't you figured that out yet?"

Derek shrugged. "Jury's still out."

Nic shook his head but didn't argue the point. He knew he still had to prove himself. "So what do you need from me?"

"Not sure yet. I still think we need to explore the caves. The presence of demons means something. I want to get out there and figure out what they're after. But we might need to get into the diamond mine. Can you do that?"

"If we need in, I'll get us there."

Derek's lips curled into a smile and he nodded. "You said 'us.'"

"Well, yeah."

"That's a good thing."

Nic stared at him, confused.

Derek laughed. "Let's get some sleep. We have a long night ahead of us and the sun's coming up."

Nic stood and started upstairs.

"Nic."

He turned at the sound of Derek's voice. "Yeah."

"You did good out there."

"Thanks."

"How are you handling all this?"

Nic shrugged. "As well as I can, and one day at a time." Which was the truth, surprisingly. He headed upstairs, not feeling too bad. He'd proven himself fairly adept at fighting demons. Or at least he'd managed to hold his own without being killed. Admittedly, he'd felt a surge of pure excitement when he battled the demons.

And not an ounce of fear—only the typical adrenaline rush he felt when surfing or skydiving or any one of the other types of sports or physical activities he engaged in. Anything to let off steam or break the boredom.

He got to expend energy, which he'd needed badly. He'd been pretty wound up after what happened this morning with Shay.

Something about the vision she had really freaked her out. That had to be why she'd pulled away from him and run back to her room. Had she told him everything, or had she held something back? Because after the vision she'd looked scared as hell—and he didn't want her looking at him that way.

He took a quick shower . . . a cool one, letting the water wash away the sweat and dust that clung to his body. He palmed the tile wall and lingered, not wanting to get out.

After she left his room this morning, the scent of her shampoo filled the room—hell, the scent of *her* filled *him*. He smelled her in his bed, on his pillow, and it made him crazy. He could still feel her skin—it was like surfing across satin. He could still taste her on his lips, a particular flavor of cinnamon that lingered in her mouth. But the worst torture was that he clearly remembered what it felt like to be inside her. Every sound she'd made was burned in his memory.

He might have to stand under the cold shower all day. Maybe he could sleep in here.

"Hey, you gonna be in there forever?"

Her soft voice penetrated his thoughts, reminding him that even in here, she could get to him.

"Sorry. Be right out."

Except now he was hard, the cold shower doing nothing to eliminate that problem. Sonofabitch, he was screwed. He shut the water off and thought about stinking demons in an effort to make his erection go away, then brushed his teeth and tossed on a pair of shorts. By the time he unlocked the bathroom door on her side, he was in a pretty foul mood.

"All yours," he grumbled, returning to his room.

She popped open the door. "Thanks. Sorry to bother you. I thought maybe you'd drowned in there."

He should be so lucky. He shut his side of the bathroom door, fell onto the bed and pulled the pillow over his head, trying to muffle the sounds of her showering. His imagination was wild enough without going into hyperactive overdrive and visualizing her soaping her naked skin, rivulets of bubbles snaking their way down the valley between her breasts, continuing on toward her belly, making a slow trek as they disappeared into the cleft between her legs.

He groaned, his cock rising in appreciation of his fantasies.

How old was he, anyway? Twelve? He rolled over on his side and faced the wall. The shower turned off and he imagined her stepping out and drying off. He heard her door open. God, his hearing was so damn acute lately. The rustle of sheets was followed by a sigh.

Did he have to hear every sound she made? Were the

walls that paper-thin? He needed rest, dammit. Or at least to stop thinking about her. Pretending to be asleep was a start. If she fell asleep and stopped moving in there, maybe he could, too.

Yeah, right. His blood rushed south and stayed there, parts of his anatomy demanding things that weren't going to happen.

Maybe he'd count demons in his head and hope for oblivion. Even the nightmares were preferable to this torment.

Shay wasn't even tired. Pent-up, anxious, needy—yeah, she was all those things. But definitely not sleepy.

Nic was right next door, no doubt sleeping naked with only a sheet on him. Maybe he wasn't even wearing the sheet. Yesterday weighed heavily on her mind.

Loneliness wrapped around her like a blanket, nearly smothering her in its intensity. She hadn't felt it in a long time, had successfully pushed it away, but tonight it crept in and surrounded her and she couldn't escape it. Pushing Nic away yesterday brought it all back again. She hadn't even realized how close she'd gotten to him until she separated from him. Without her anger at him as a shield, she really felt it now.

She was tired of being lonely; of feeling isolated. From the time her mother disappeared and her father retreated into his shell, she'd been on her own, independent, making her own decisions. Even as a child she remembered making her own meals, taking care of her father when he should have been taking care of her. She'd learned to be self-sufficient and street-smart, to make choices based on no one's opinion but her own.

Doing the reality show on the island had been her choice. Becoming a demon hunter had been her choice. She had no family, no friends besides the other hunters. She had no lovers...none that were long-lasting, anyway. No one had ever appealed enough to make her want to tie herself down, and the visions always made her keep her distance from men. She was afraid of what would happen if she allowed herself to get too close.

She'd held her secret inside her entire life, had told no one. Until Nic. What was it about him that drew her, that made her feel like he was the right thing? She wanted him. Like right now. Wanted to go over to his room, crawl in his bed, and wrap her arms around him. She ached for the feel of his mouth of hers, wet and hot, taking her to places no man ever had. She wanted to make love with him, and this time, she wanted to stay with him.

Why couldn't she stop thinking about him? She'd always spent way too much time thinking; that was her biggest flaw. She knew what she wanted at this moment—why didn't she just take it? She'd never once in her life waited for things to happen to her. Not since her mother disappeared. From that moment on she'd been fully in charge of her life. Yet for some reason she'd been sitting back and reacting, instead of acting, like she should be.

Instinct. She'd always relied on it and it had never

been wrong. Instinct was screaming at her right now—to be bold, to take what she wanted instead of being afraid of getting hurt. Her life had changed in the past couple months. It was fleeting. She could die. If she wanted something, she had to make it happen.

But the vision . . . it still haunted her, made her pause. Damned frustrating. In her heart she knew it wasn't Nic that she'd seen in her vision. It couldn't be. He wasn't a coldhearted demon.

She exhaled, wondering if she'd be able to sleep at all. The draw toward Nic was increasing, as if there was some kind of magnet pulling her toward him. Not that she was complaining about it. She clearly wanted him. And she knew he wanted her. It was in every look he gave her, in his body language, in his voice. His message was clear.

So why did she hesitate? She could wake him; he wouldn't mind.

Shay hadn't feared anything in years. Even the demons, thoughts of death, didn't frighten her.

So why did one man scare the hell out of her?

She tossed over onto her back and exhaled, knowing the answer. Because she was falling in love with Nic. And he might very well be turning into a demon—the bad kind. If his destiny, the one she saw in her visions, proved true, she was falling in love with a man she might have to kill.

But was that enough to keep her away from him? Even knowing what could happen in the future, she still ached for him. Her heart was invested, her connection to him too strong.

It might already be too late.

The rains started that night.

Trace told them the light rain outside was just the beginning of what would undoubtedly become a downpour, making their search for both demons and the black diamond even more difficult. With the roads becoming treacherous and heavy rain expected, the hunters packed up heavy, knowing they probably weren't going to make it back before dawn and would have to camp out.

Shay just prayed the rain would cool things off while they hunted.

It didn't. She and the others were still sweltering hot, only now they were wet, too. The rain came down in a mist, the air around them still thick with heat, and Shay felt like she was walking through a steam room. She might die of suffocation before the night was over.

They traveled by vehicle as far as they could, but the roads at higher elevations were washed out and they had to head out on foot after that. They parked on a precipice overlooking a fast-moving river, which just yesterday had been a dry, empty gulch. And even though there was only a light rain falling here, the creek beds were already swollen from the rains up north. From what Trace told them, those rains were headed their way, and fast. They had to be on the lookout for flash floods and lightning storms.

Wasn't this going to be fun? Not only could they be killed by demons, but it was also possible they could drown or be struck by lightning. So either God or the devil could destroy them out here. Nothing like having the odds stacked against you.

Though they'd managed to kill some demons, they hadn't found the black diamond. Shay was getting frustrated. She could well imagine the others were, too.

Each of them loaded down with supplies, they moved on foot for over three hours. The rains steadily increased, the path the hunters traveled becoming more treacherous. Wet dirt became slippery mud and they were forced to slow their forward progress. Shay's boots were sinking, the mud sucking them down. She no sooner extracted one foot from the muck than the other one sank down deep.

"We're getting nowhere here," she commed, frustrated, tired of stair-stepping through this stuff and standing ankle-high in another hole.

"No shit," Derek shot back. "There are caves up ahead though. Can everyone make it?"

Caves were better than sinking in the mud. It took another hour to make it to the caves, which of course just had to be uphill. Climbing up the rain-slickened slopes was damn near impossible, though with ropes they managed it. By the time the hunters reached the top of the hill, they were all covered in mud.

Shay longed for a bath. There was mud in places on her body that had no business having mud in them. The rains were coming down so hard now she could barely see the person in front of her. Tiny rivers had formed in the grooves on the path. Everything was filling up with water; the hunters were slipping and sliding like they were in a water park.

At least they were on level ground now, not that it did much good. But the cave ahead promised dry shelter, and that was the closest thing to heaven Shay had seen in hours. She didn't even care if there were demons in there. At least there wouldn't be rain and mud.

"Stay alert," Derek commed. "We're heading in."

With the rain blinding them, they'd long ago abandoned their night-vision shades, relying instead on their shoulder lights. Once they entered the dry cave, the lights went out and Shay slipped on her glasses, illuminating the darkness around her. The only sounds she heard were the movements of the hunters and the pouring rain. She inhaled, trying to scent hybrid demons. Nothing. They moved farther inward, weapons raised and ready. This time she decided to keep her psychic senses open, but she didn't pick up anything but dead airwaves.

The cave was long, but this one didn't descend like the others they'd inspected. It did have quite a few channels, though. They broke into teams and searched each one. No sign of demons or any activity. And it was dry. Completely and utterly dry, with the exception of an opening at the top of one of the tunnels that allowed rain to create a lovely pool of clear water in a deep, hollowed-out basin. It looked like a giant bath. Shay had fantasies of jumping in and rinsing off.

"We'll set up base in this cave since it's clean," Derek said. "Take turns guarding the entrance and rear of the cave to make sure no demons enter from either side. We'll have to sleep during daylight. We may be out here for a couple days."

Oh, joy of joys. Sleeping in a cave.

Derek assigned teams. Trace and Dalton stayed behind in the cave with Lou to guard the base. The rest of them went out together.

Back in the rain, which still came down as hard as before. And the caves weren't as close to each other as they had been in the other location, which meant trekking a bit. Because of the rain the hunters chose the cave closest to their home base, and even that one was going to take a while to get to.

They slugged through the thick glop of runny muck at a snail's pace. Nic stayed close to Shay's side the entire time. She didn't even question why, grateful to have him nearby. Twice he'd pulled her up by her belt when she slipped and nearly fell face first. Nothing like demonstrating grace in motion. Her boots were weighed down with water, so heavy she could barely raise them with each step.

"Having fun?" Nic asked, wrapping an arm around her waist.

She tossed a grimace his way. "A ball."

Glancing ahead of her, she saw that Derek was helping Gina along the trail, too.

"I could think of a lot of things I'd rather be doing right now," Nic said.

"Me, too. Starting with a bath."

"I thought women loved mud baths. You pay good money at those fancy spas for what you're getting for free out here."

"Very funny. And not at all the same. Or at least I don't think it's the same. I wouldn't know."

It seemed strange to be toting high-tech weaponry and at the same time having Nic's arm around her. It was like being on some kind of rainy, muddy, romantic, futuristic date. Oddly comforting, actually. This was the first time she'd felt relaxed in a while. Was it having Nic's body pressed against hers that did it? Because it sure as hell couldn't be the ambience of their surroundings.

An ambience that changed in an instant when she felt blanketed by a sensation of evil. She shivered, goose bumps pricking her sweltering skin. She halted and raised her weapon, aiming it toward the darkness around her.

"What's wrong?"

She shook her head, focusing on the feelings, trying to pinpoint the location.

"Derek," she commed. "Demons."

Derek stopped, let go of Gina. Ryder halted, too. They raised their weapons, each of them swiveling to survey the area. "Where?" Derek asked.

"I'm not sure. Close."

"Be more specific," he cut back.

"I don't know!" She turned a full three-sixty.

"Lou," Derek commed. "You got anything?"

"No," Lou returned. "I'm picking nothing up as far as

portals, but as we discussed they're probably not under-ground."

"Fuck." Derek looked to Shay. "You sure?"

"Yes!"

"Then concentrate and tell us where."

"I just sense them," she said. "I don't know where they are."

"Anybody see anything?" Derek asked.

"Nothing," Ryder said. "Just a lot of fuckin' rain."

"Keep moving then," Derek commed. "But maintain weapons ready and eyes sharp."

Shay felt like an idiot. They didn't believe her. She knew demons were here. She could feel them watching her. But a careful scan of the terrain showed nothing. Then again, who could see a damn thing through all this rain? If they were, in fact, headed toward a cave, she hoped Derek knew where it was, because she couldn't see a thing in front of her other than the hunters.

Step by achingly slow step they trudged along, and Shay still felt as though they were being watched. Though she tried to shake off the sensation of demons hiding in the nearby brush and behind every tree, she couldn't. At least the hunters were keeping a watchful eye on their surroundings. Weapons raised, heads turn-ing in both directions, they made their way down the slick path toward the cave, which finally came into view—a shadow in the distance.

Finally—refuge from the pounding elements.

Shay sighed in relief as they drew closer to the cave. Maybe she was just tense about being out here, the rain, her thoughts about Nic—everything piling up and screwing with her senses. There were probably no demons around and she was just stressed.

"Shit. Demons!" Gina commed.

"Where?" Derek asked.

"Coming out of the cave."

Shay squinted, trying to see through the rain that seemed to have increased in intensity.

"I see them, too," Ryder added. "More of them coming around from outside the cave. Look over on the eastern side."

"Western side, too," Derek said.

"They're behind us," Nic commed. "And there's a lot of them."

Shay pivoted, seeing only a blob of dark shapes moving in slow motion toward the hunters.

Hybrids. The rain had masked their foul stench. Oh, God.

"Sonofabitch. We're surrounded," Ryder growled.

"Move! Into positions," Derek commed. "Back each other up and get ready."

As they drew near, the demons came into focus. Huge, lumbering, slow and steady. Hybrids were meaner, tougher to kill, and their stench alone could knock you over. As they got closer, Shay was overwhelmed with their smell, fighting back the nausea that always assailed her when the creatures came in such high numbers.

God, they reeked. Like decay—and death. Every time Shay saw these things she wondered what her mother had endured. Did she have to live with these hybrids, too? Captured and forced to coexist with demons, used as nothing more than a breeding machine to create half-human monsters... She shuddered at the thought, her hatred of the creatures renewing her strength.

This is what she'd dedicated her life to after Lou had dropped the bombshell revelation that her mother had been taken by demons. To destroy as many of them as she could, so they couldn't take another child's mother away. No child should have to live the life she had—the uncertainty, the feeling of abrupt loss, the loneliness. These bastards were going down, and she was taking their brethren with them. As many as she could hunt and kill, for as long as she lived.

Frustration ate away at the last of her patience. The hybrids were slow. She was tired of waiting. She wanted them dead.

"You okay?"

She didn't look at Nic, just nodded. "Fine."

"Take deep breaths. Visualize melting these fuckers — what they look like all gooed down to nothing but jelly. It'll make you smile."

Despite the irritation boiling up inside her, she did allow her lips to curl upward. Then she shot a glance at Nic. "How do you do that?"

"What?"

"Make me smile in a situation like this?"

He shrugged. "You dig me, baby. You can't help it."

Then she laughed, shook her head, and refocused on the approaching demons.

"Now they're close enough," Derek commed. "Move

forward, but keep your positions tight. Stay together. You need help, I better hear you holler for it."

Finally. She forced her mud-laden boots through the slime. This battle wasn't going to be easy with the elements against them. Then again, even the demons' progress seemed to be slowed by the rain. But now she could do something. She could see them, visualize her targets, plan her attack.

She was excited to be in battle.

"There are six within our line of sight," she said to Nic. "Focus on the three to your left; I'll take the other three."

"Got it."

The laser took down the first one with ease, melting it. She had a little internal chuckle at Nic's reference to goo. Yeah, that described what it looked like, all right. The other two demons ducked behind the trees, making it difficult to hit them with the laser. Shay reached into her hip pouch.

"Grenade!" she commed as a warning to the hunters. She pulled the pin and launched a sonic grenade. Sound waves sent the demons running, their arms flailing as they lumbered and grimaced before falling to the ground. The ear protection the hunters wore, which also doubled as their communication system, protected their hearing, rendering them immune to the disastrous effects of the sonic waves. Not the demons, though. The two began to liquefy and disintegrate from the inside out, just as if she'd fired the sonic bullets into them.

God, she loved technology. Gross, but very effective.

She turned her attention to Nic, who'd managed to melt down two of his three demons. The third had come close. Too damn close. And Nic wasn't backing away. Instead, he was moving forward, an expression of pure malice and intensity on his face.

"Nic. Back off."

He didn't listen, still heading toward the demon. Shay raised her laser to fire, but now Nic and the demon were too close to each other. She risked hitting Nic.

"Nic, you need to step back. I can get a clear shot."

"Hold this," he said, tossing his rifle at her.

She grabbed the laser in midair. Oh, God, he'd engaged the demon. It came at Nic, claws outstretched. Nic swung his torso under the demon's arms and barreled into its chest. Shay couldn't believe Nic's strength. The demon went flying backward, losing its balance in the mud and nearly toppling over. She made a quick turn to see if the others had noticed. The battle raged on, everyone involved in their own fight. Nic was on his own, with only Shay as his backup.

There were no other demons about to threaten Nic. Shay decided that rather than joining the others, she was going to stay here and guard Nic. If he'd break away from the demon long enough to gain some distance, she could fire her laser at the demon and free Nic from its hold.

The strange thing was, she didn't think that's what Nic wanted. It was as if he *wanted* to fight with the demon. But that couldn't be, could it? So what the hell was he doing?

Holding his own, amazingly. The demon was twice Nic's size and had to be double his strength, yet Nic was tossing kicks and punches at the demon and the demon was reacting as if in pain, raising its arms to ward off Nic's blows. And Nic was adeptly avoiding the demon's claws and fangs, the parts that secreted paralyzing toxins. Either that or the demon was deliberately not biting or scratching him, which made no sense.

"Shay, what the hell is Nic doing?" Derek commed.

Shay arched a brow as she watched. "It looks like he's kicking the shit out of this demon."

"Tell him to back away so you can shoot it!"

"*You* tell him to back away." She didn't know what was possessing Nic, but she wasn't going to tell him a thing.

Derek was by her side in an instant. Shay tore her gaze from Nic long enough to see Derek's openmouthed look of astonishment.

"He really is beating the hell out of that thing."

Shay glanced behind her. Piles of melted demon flesh sizzled in the rain. The hunters were starting to assemble to watch Nic.

She had had no idea he was so surefooted, so adept, so damn strong. But it was more than human strength, she realized. The same fierce determination, the odd surge of superhuman strength and abilities they'd all witnessed in Derek on the island, was manifesting itself in Nic now. Pride shone on Derek's face.

"Is this what happened to you?" Shay asked Derek.

"Sort of. But I didn't go hand-to-hand with them. I

can't believe he's strong enough to fight a hybrid with his hands and body."

So Nic's demon side, the part of him that made him different from humans, was surfacing. And he was turning those strengths against the demons.

"Do you think you should step in and pull Nic away from that thing?"

"No. Leave him be. I want to see what he's got." Derek hefted his rifle and kept it aimed at the demon.

Gina laid a hand on Shay's shoulder "Trust Derek. He'll stop this if it gets dangerous for Nic."

Shay knew that Derek would look out for his brother. And he probably did know what was best, because as the demon reached for Nic again, it became obvious that Nic was merely toying with it. He even laughed and kicked it away.

"Rifle, Shay," Nic hollered, half turning toward her.

She tossed his UV rifle to him and he grabbed it with one hand, backing a short distance away from the demon.

"Time for you to die, fucker." Nic aimed, fired an array of laser light, and melted the creature on the spot.

The satisfaction on Nic's face was priceless as the demon's body slid to the ground, reduced to nothing but gelatinous mass.

This was why they had traveled to Australia. To find Nic, to determine which side he was on. Maybe the Realm of Light hadn't made that determination yet, but Shay had. She knew. She felt it. Nic wasn't evil. No one who took such joy in killing one of the demons could be with the Sons of Darkness.

Her vision was wrong.

Nic shouldered his weapon and turned toward the hunters, his breath sawing in and out with exertion. "Are we done here?"

Derek nodded. "You have fun?"

"Hell, yeah. Are there any more?"

"Not at the moment. Let's keep moving."

They headed onward. Derek didn't say any more, but Shay had the idea there was plenty he wanted to talk to Nic about later.

Chapter Seventeen

Nic felt great. Weird, but great. He wasn't sure what had happened back there with the demon, but he didn't really care. He was exhilarated, full of energy, and ready to kick more demon ass as they made their way toward the cave.

The others were giving him pretty strange looks. Except for Shay. She was smiling at him.

"What?" he asked as she stepped up beside him.

"You amaze me."

"I do?"

"Yes. What were you doing back there?"

"Fighting demons?"

"We don't fight demons that way."

He shrugged. "It just felt natural to me. The damn thing kept coming at me. After I killed the first two, the other one got too close so I threw down and went after it."

"You're not supposed to wrestle with them."

"Huh. I must have missed that section in the demon handbook."

"Smart-ass."

"Better than being a dumbass."

She snickered.

They entered the cave and found no demons lurking just inside or around the mouth of the cave. Derek halted their progress for weapons check.

Nic did his inventory, reloaded, and was ready to go. Admittedly, he realized he was into this demon-hunting thing. He enjoyed killing them. He didn't know what it was, but some internal force told him what he was doing was right. Eliminating the bad guys—that's what he was supposed to be doing. And every time he killed a demon, he felt more powerful, almost like he gained in strength throughout the battle, as if he was absorbing their energy in some way.

Odd. And probably baseless. It was just an adrenaline rush and nothing more. Though he didn't understand it, he wasn't about to turn down these sensations flowing through him.

He liked feeling a part of the Realm of Light. If his father was truly evil, and if Nic carried that blood within him, he was determined to fight it. He wasn't going down on the dark side of this game. No way. And if his father had lied to him all these years—the thought of it made his blood boil.

He may not have spent his life as a Boy Scout, but he'd never hurt anyone. From what he'd been told, his father had.

Demons. Christ, it was still hard to wrap his head around it all, but he had to believe it. He'd seen it with his own eyes.

And now that he'd been given the keys to the demon-hunting kingdom and realized he was pretty damn good at it, he figured he might as well pump himself up in any way he could. He'd always had strength; had always enjoyed sports and physical activities. If that meant he could fight these demons one-on-one, then that's the way he was going to do it. He'd never been much of a rule follower, anyway.

"Little brother."

Nic sized up Derek as he approached. The man wasn't happy, the muscles of his jaw clenched. Uh-oh. Lecture time. "Yeah."

"Don't do that again."

"Do what?"

"Put yourself within reach of the demons."

"Why not?"

"Did Shay explain to you about their claws and fangs and the toxic substance that can paralyze you if they bite or scratch you?"

"She mentioned it."

Derek slanted a glare in his direction. "Isn't that enough?"

"I didn't let it touch me."

"Which doesn't mean one won't next time. That's why we have weapons."

"I like the hands-on better."

"Maybe you're not listening. I've been at this a long

time. I know what I'm talking about. Hands off. We use weapons to maintain distance, for protection, and so we can keep moving."

Nic could tell Derek was going to be hardheaded about this. "In case you didn't notice, I handled that demon just fine."

"And what if four or five of them had surrounded you? What then?"

Nic shrugged. "That hasn't happened yet. I guess I'll see what goes down when the time comes."

"No, you'll do it my way, and now." Derek's nostrils flared and a spark of memory sailed across Nic's mind. A strange bedroom, and Nic was arguing with a boy who had the same angry expression on his face that Derek sported right now. They were fighting over some toy. Nic wanted that toy; wanted it really bad. So did the other boy. Tension was high and a fight was about to break out. Nic started yelling and the boy yelled back. A woman came into view. She leaned against the doorway, her arms crossed as she watched them argue. She shook her head and told them to work it out without bloodshed, then she smiled.

She had a nice smile. Warm, comforting, like a blanket in the winter. She made him feel safe.

The vision evaporated.

Sonofabitch! Nic blinked and rubbed his temples, shaking his head to clear the dusty memories.

What the hell was that?

"Are you listening to anything I say?"

Derek's voice penetrated, but Nic kept it at bay, not

wanting to deal right now. Not after what he'd just experienced.

"Yeah, yeah."

"This is for your safety, Nic."

Derek's voice had softened, no longer laced with the hard edge of anger it had held earlier. Nic looked up, and instead of fight in Derek's eyes, he saw only concern.

"I just found you again. I don't want to lose you."

He could tell Derek wasn't comfortable saying it, any more than Nic was comfortable hearing it.

Nic nodded. Derek pivoted and walked away, thankfully, before this entire scene got any weirder. He thought for a minute his brother was going to hug him.

His brother. *Was* Derek really his brother? Had the vision he'd just experienced been a memory of the two of them from his childhood? Had the woman been their mother? Nic's mother? He fought to regain the memory, to visualize the woman's face again, but it was lost.

"Are you okay?"

Nic shuttered his eyelids at the sound of Shay's soft voice behind him. "I'm fine."

"I heard you and Derek arguing."

He sucked in a deep breath and turned around, shrugging. "And?"

She blinked. "You want to talk about it?"

"Not particularly." He shouldered his weapons and looked ahead. "We're gearing up to explore this cave. I think the psychoanalysis will have to wait."

She laid her hand on his forearm. "Something else

happened while Derek was talking to you. You had this expression on your face like you were somewhere else, and then like you were in some kind of pain. I could feel these weird vibes—"

"Hey, you know what? I've had enough," he said, cutting her off before she came too close to the truth. "First you want to analyze me, now you want to practice your newfound psychic powers on me? Go find another test dummy, Shay. I'm not in the mood."

Her face showed the pain he caused with his words. Pain he couldn't deal with right now. Yeah, he was harsh, but he couldn't handle her sympathy and he sure couldn't let her delve too deeply into his psyche. Not when even he didn't know what was going on in his head. So she'd just have to deal with him being an ass.

She should be used to that by now.

He pushed past her and moved into the middle of the group next to Ryder, who looked him up and down but didn't say a word.

Perfect. Just the right guy to walk next to while they trekked through the cave. Ryder wouldn't want to talk to him. He might glare, but there'd be no arguing, no psychoanalysis and no discussions.

Which was exactly what he wanted.

Okay, so something happened back there. Shay didn't know what it was, but it had been something profound. She and Nic had been getting along fine. In fact, he'd been working double time to make up for his mistakes.

No way would he take two steps backward by acting like a complete moron.

Which was what he'd just done.

Irritation prickled her skin, but she fought it back, refusing to believe he was simply being a dickhead for no reason. Instinct told her something major had happened to him while he was arguing with Derek, but what? Maybe the danger he was in when he fought that demon just hit him. Or was it something else?

She wished he'd talk to her, open up. Keeping his feelings bottled inside wasn't helping him. Or her. Or them.

If there was, in fact, a "them."

She should never have become involved, should never have started caring about him. The problem was, she did care. She was wrapped up in the who, what, where, when, and why of Dominic Diavolo and had taken it upon herself to help him delve into his past, present, and future, whether he liked it or not. Demon or no demon, brother of Derek, what did he remember or not remember, how dangerous was he?

Yeah, that was the operative word here. He was dangerous all right. To her. Hazard signs flashed in her head, warning her to remain aloof and uninvolved, just as she'd been with every other man in her life so far. She'd escaped heartache because she'd never let anyone get close enough. She'd never had to worry about a guy wriggling his way deep enough into her heart to cause her any pain.

But the one man she shouldn't get involved with was the one who melted her butter and made her want to know more, the one she was literally melded with, psychically. Didn't it just figure?

She should leave him alone, let this thing go between them. But she couldn't. Something told her he was worth fighting for. And she'd learned over the past few years to start listening to that little voice inside her head when it talked to her.

You don't walk away from people you care about. She was just going to have to risk the hurt. And he *was* going to talk to her. Sooner or later.

But he was right. Now wasn't the time. Not when they had caves to explore, demons to kill, black diamonds to find.

How was a girl supposed to have a decent romance in the midst of all this chaos?

They explored the inner recesses of the cave. This one was rocky and uneven. Their footing was unsure as they moved along narrow corridors one by one.

"This doesn't feel stable," Shay said, not sure whether it was vibes or her own equilibrium making her feel so uneasy. The ground felt mushy under her feet, though the cave ceiling was solid. No water from the rain was getting in. The floor was dry, so it wasn't mud causing the wayward tilt of the ground.

"No, it doesn't," Derek said. "Keep your eyes sharp and watch where you're walking."

They moved along, one person barely able to squeeze through the narrow opening. No way could hulking hybrid demons fit through here. Pure demons could, though, so they had to check it out.

Derek held up his hand. "I heard something."

They stopped, raised weapons. Shay readied her finger on the trigger of her laser. As they moved out of the passage, the cave opened into three tunnels.

"Split up. Ryder, I don't want you going in alone. Take Shay and Nic with you. Comm if you find anything."

Ryder led the way into the tunnel on the right. "This floor sucks," he mumbled. It felt like they were walking on marshmallows.

"Do you think there's something under this floor?" Nic asked.

"Possibly," Ryder said. "I just know I don't like it."

They moved along much more slowly than normal. He felt like he was going to fall through the dirt, which didn't make any sense at all. It was eerie.

"We're not alone in here," Shay said.

Ryder stopped, made a half-turn. "You picking something up?"

"Yeah, but I don't know what it is. It's not an evil presence, but there's definitely someone else in here with us."

"Great. Just what we need. Stay sharp." Shay's advance signaling system was better than nothing. Ryder turned back and headed down the tunnel again. They didn't have to wait long. There was a light in one of the channels off the tunnel.

"You see that?" Nic asked.

"Yeah. Let's see who it is," Ryder said, lifting his laser. He peered around the corner, his body relaxing as he stood upright and lowered his gun. He wasn't surprised to find Angelique standing there, pickax in hand.

"Shit. You again?" He shook his head.

"You scared the hell out of me!" She dropped the ax, wiped her hands on her pants, and crossed her arms.

"What are you doing here?" Obviously the woman didn't grab a clue from the other night. She was still here, working alone.

"I'm working. I can't believe *you're* here," Angelique said with a sharp frown. "I'm not even in the same cave as the other night, so you have no excuse to pull me out of here."

"Wanna bet?" Ryder strode toward her, throwing a glance over his shoulder at Shay and Nic as they entered. "Guard the entrance."

"Who's she?" Shay asked.

Ryder sidled her a glance. "Her name's Angelique. She's an archaeologist."

Nic shrugged and turned toward the tunnel entrance. Shay kept her eye on them.

"I told you this area wasn't safe," Ryder said. "Pack up your things. You're leaving."

She didn't move. "Do you get off on giving people orders? Because that's all you seem to do."

"For good reason." Ryder slung his rifle over his shoulder and bent down, tossing Angelique's things into her bag.

"Stop that," Angelique said, bending down with him and taking them out.

Ryder grabbed her hand. "You're leaving."

"Unless you give me a compelling reason to, I'm not. Your telling me there's danger isn't going to stop me from doing my job."

"I've got a pretty damned compelling reason heading in this direction."

Ryder's head shot up at Nic's statement. Shay moved to Nic's side.

"Oh, shit," Shay said, looking at Ryder. "We've gotta go. Now."

Ryder knew what that meant. Demons. They couldn't get stuck in this room with no exit. He grabbed Angelique's hand and hauled her to her feet. With one look he communicated to her that this was no time to argue.

She was smart and caught on quick. She flew out of the room with him, Shay and Nic right behind them. Ryder made a quick turn around the corner in the opposite direction of the approaching demons.

"Derek, we've got company bearing down on us," he commed.

"We'll catch up," Derek commed back.

He had to put some distance between the demons and them. He didn't want to be cornered in these narrow tunnels or rooms with no exits.

They couldn't get out the way they came in, since that's where Nic had spotted the demons. Ryder hoped there was another exit.

Nothing like all hell breaking loose. His pulse raced as his feet tore up the soft dirt underneath his boots. He turned his head every few seconds to gauge the distance between them and the demons.

They weren't hybrids. They were moving fast. Damn.

"We've got to find an exit or a place to stop and fight, Ryder," Shay commed.

"What do you think I'm doing? Looking for a picnic spot?"

He still had hold of Angelique's hand. She hadn't screamed or said a word, nor had she tried to fight Ryder's grasp, thankfully. He had enough to think about right now.

They all did. He wasn't sure how many demons were behind them, but there were only three hunters. And he had an idea there were more than a handful of demons after them. He just hoped they didn't run into a dead end, because then they'd be really screwed.

They came out of the tunnel into a room with two exits. Ryder stopped and pulled Angelique behind him. Shay halted, Nic drawing beside her. Everyone pulled weapons.

"This is as good a spot as any," Ryder said. "Let's do it."

He turned to Angelique. "Don't move."

She nodded and backed up against the wall, a look of fear on her face.

Fear was good right now. It might keep her alive. Ryder turned back to the tunnel where the demons were coming. Nic and Shay were positioned to his left. Ryder stayed in front of Angelique. Dammit, he didn't want to have to worry about her and battle demons at the same time, but it looked like he had no choice. He had to keep her safe. She was unarmed and untrained.

The ground rumbled under his feet. Christ, how many demons were coming?

This was bad. Really bad. The tremors were increasing. He rebalanced his body as the cave floor shook with the intensity of the approaching horde.

Then he looked down, saw the dust rising.

Where were the demons? And why was the ground moving under his feet now? He backed up toward Angelique, not sure what was happening but wanting to protect her in case demons were coming up from the ground. She moved in beside him and he wrapped an arm around her.

What the hell was going on?

"Ryder, you still there?" Derek commed.

"Yeah."

"This whole place is falling down. Get the hell out of there!"

Ryder rolled his eyes. Yeah, easier said than done.

"Derek's right," Nic said. "I don't even see the demons anymore. Let's move."

Move where? The whole place was pitching, dirt from the ceiling raining down on top of them. He supposed the best tactic was to turn tail and run, look for an exit. He grabbed Angelique's hand, shouldered his rifle, and took off down one of the tunnels, hoping he had made the right choice. This tunnel was wider, so he and Angelique were side by side, crashing into each other as the floor pitched up and down like ocean waves. Keeping their balance was damned difficult.

But he finally saw light. The exit!

A fraction of a second too late, as the floor underneath them gave way and the fast clip they were running at didn't allow him to stop in time.

He had a millisecond to grab on to Angelique as they pitched straight down into the open hole.

Chapter Eighteen

Amazing. They weren't dead. Ryder could have sworn, after the hole opened up and they fell, that that would have been the end.

But the drop was shorter than he expected and the ground soft at the bottom. He landed on his feet, taking the brunt of the impact and bringing Angelique on top of him. He rolled over, clearing them both of the falling debris and covering his body over hers until the shaking stopped.

A cloud of thick dust settled around them. Ryder waited until he was sure nothing more was coming down on top of them, then lifted himself off Angelique.

Coughing and sputtering, she sat up.

"Are you okay?" he asked.

She nodded. "What was that?" She took the hand he offered to help haul her to her feet, then looked around while dusting off her pants and shirt.

Ryder shook his head. "Earth tremor, cave-in or something. Hell if I know. The cave is obviously old and unstable."

At least whatever it was had caused the demons to scatter. He looked up, but the hole they'd come through had closed, buried under dirt and rock. So he concentrated instead on where they were. There was one opening, leading down a dark passageway. "That looks like another tunnel."

"Great. So is that the way out?"

"Good question." At least Angelique wasn't panicking. He gave her credit for keeping a cool head. "Derek, can you hear me?" he commed.

"Ryder! Are you okay?" Derek shot back.

"Yeah. We're fine. But it looks like we're stuck down here."

"We caught up with Nic and Shay. But there's a sizeable pile of boulders up here blocking where you fell in, so we can't get to you."

"Wouldn't matter anyway. The hole has closed up so you couldn't throw a rope down. But there's a tunnel. I'm hoping it has an exit. We're going to follow it and see where it leads."

"Do you still have your weapon?"

"Yeah. And plenty of ammo." At least all his stuff had fallen with him.

"Keep your eyes sharp. We're going to see if there's a way down to you. Comm if you need help."

Like that would do any good. He turned his gaze to Angelique. "Let's go exploring."

She nodded and they moved down the tunnel. Ryder

turned on his shoulder lights, noticed Angelique kept a light attached as she turned hers on, too. It was actually cold down here, which was a huge relief from the sweltering heat topside. At least they weren't bathing in sweat. And the walls were made of a different material. Harder, darker, almost black; it kind of reminded him of coal. Even the floor was more solid. He hoped there wouldn't be shaking going on down here. The thought of the entire upper cave falling on them wasn't comforting. Now if they could just find a way out.

When they reached a dead end, he cursed.

"Now what?" Angelique asked, turning around the small rounded room that had ended their exploration.

"No clue. Looks like we're stuck."

Her eyes widened. "I don't like the sound of that."

"Me, either. Derek, can you hear me?"

"I'm here. Find anything yet?"

"Yeah. I found that all roads lead to nowhere."

"Shit. We'll figure some way to get to you. Make your way back to where you fell in."

"Will do."

They trekked back to the room where they'd fallen in.

"Might as well sit and get comfortable. We could be here for a while." He slid down the wall and rested his arms on his knees.

Angelique did the same, taking up a spot next to him. Ryder pulled his canteen and offered her water. She opened it, took a sip and handed it back to him. Other than the layer of dust that covered her, she didn't look injured in any way, or in shock or panicked.

Good. He wasn't prepared to deal with a woman who got hysterical at every little thing. Not that this was a little thing, but then again his life wasn't typical these days. He would imagine that for Angelique this wasn't an average day.

She stayed silent for a few minutes, but he knew it wasn't going to last. He knew the question was coming.

"What was after us up there?" she asked.

Damn. "Bad guys."

"What kind of bad guys?"

"The kind you don't want to skirmish with in a room with no exit."

She laughed. "Typical response. That doesn't tell me anything."

"Some things you don't want to know."

"I'm an archaeologist, Ryder. I want to know everything. And you can't scare me. I've seen strange things in my lifetime. Really strange things. Unexplainable things."

"Like what?"

She shrugged. "Ghosts in the darkness. The feeling that I'm not alone when I'm working, as if someone or something is watching me. I work around the ancients. Oftentimes, things that are buried don't want to be uncovered."

"You don't scare easily, do you?"

"No."

"What are you searching for out here?"

She tilted her head as if she was trying to decide whether to trust him with her secrets, then said, "Something called the black diamond."

Holy shit. "What's that?"

"It's supposed to be a large rock, a raw diamond. Ancient, magical, if you believe the lore surrounding it. I'd never heard of it before, which intrigued me since I tend to know about most undiscovered treasures. But the people who hired me assure me it's around here somewhere."

"Who hired you?"

"A private foundation. Philanthropists. They've researched and uncovered information on the diamond and were worried treasure hunters would find it before it could be located and placed in a museum. It's said to be priceless."

"So you're not in it for the money."

She lifted her chin as if he'd insulted her. "I'm never in it for the money. If I were rich I'd have scores of people hunting for the black diamond with me. I work alone. The fewer people involved, the less chance of word spreading about what I'm hunting for."

That made sense. "So why tell me?"

She blinked, shook her head. "I don't know. I shouldn't have. I promised them I wouldn't tell anyone."

He wondered who the "them" really were. Probably the Sons of Darkness. Wouldn't it be interesting to tell her she'd been hired by demons?

He had to tell Derek. Which would mean bringing Angelique into all of this. He hated to do it, but then again she might end up being a valuable asset in their quest to find the black diamond.

"So is what I'm doing tied into what you and your

friends are hunting for or what was chasing us up there?" she asked.

Screw it. He was tired of trying to keep secrets. She was smack in the middle of this clusterfuck. She deserved to know what was going on.

"Probably."

"Who or what was after us, Ryder? Why do you need those strange weapons? They aren't typical, and whatever is in that rifle isn't a bullet, so you must be hunting something unusual."

He laid the laser across his knees. "I can't explain them. They're not . . . human."

"What do you mean?"

"It's a really long story."

She looked around the room, then back at him. "It appears we have a lot of time."

Maybe an eternity, if they didn't figure out a way to get out of this hell hole.

"Angelique—do you believe in demons?"

Her brows went up in a flash. "Demons? You mean like the devil, or something evil?"

"Yeah."

She looked away. "I'd like to say I don't believe in them, but I know there's evil out there. I've felt it before." When she looked back at him, curiosity mixed with fear.

He knew that look. She wanted to know, but she was afraid of the answer. "Is that what you're chasing? Demons?" she asked.

"Yes. And I'm guessing that's who hired you to find the black diamond, too."

Her eyes widened. "You know about the black diamond?"

He nodded. "The Sons of Darkness want it. They want it bad."

"Who are the Sons of Darkness?"

Ryder exhaled. "You aren't going to believe this."

She shifted to face him. "Just tell me. Tell me everything."

Lou had sent Trace and Dalton out to help the rest of them. Nic had already begun moving boulders he shouldn't be able to lift, but somehow he managed. He and Derek had sizeable strength that could be put to pretty good use in times of dire need.

This was one of those times. One of their own was buried underground, and they had to get him out. With Shay and Gina taking care of the small rocks, they were making some actual headway in clearing the blocked passageway.

"This would be a hell of a lot easier if we could bring in machinery," Trace said, pushing a boulder out of the way, then blowing out a breath filled with the frustration Nic knew they all felt.

Derek dropped an equal-sized boulder next to it. "Yes, but we're kind of remote for that, and it's raining in biblical proportions out there, so even if we could get a digger up here, it would never make it through the mud. Just keep grabbing rocks. We'll get it done."

Two hours later, they weren't even close.

Derek dropped a boulder, using his arm to wipe away the sweat dripping down his face. "It's not working. And I don't like Lou being back at the base cave by himself. Gina, you and Shay head back there. We'll keep working at this."

Nic took a quick glance over at Shay, who looked like she wanted to object, but kept her mouth shut and nodded. She and Gina grabbed their weapons and headed out.

It made sense. The men had most of the muscle, and this was backbreaking work. Not that it was going to do any good.

"We're not going to be able to dig them out," Nic said, feeling the need to voice what he knew they were all thinking.

"We have to keep trying. For as long as we can," Derek shot back, not even stopping to look at him.

Nic nodded and continued to shove, push, and lift boulders, but it was a futile effort.

"Derek!"

Nic turned at the sound of Gina's voice, Shay right behind her, both out of breath as they ran in and stopped in front of Derek.

Derek frowned. "What's wrong? Why aren't you heading back to Lou?"

Gina panted as she got the words out. "Demons out there. Headed this way. Hybrids."

"Are you sure they're coming in this direction?"

Gina nodded. "Right toward this cave."

Nic straightened and grabbed his weapon.

"Shit." Derek looked at the rock wall, then at the rest of them. "Ryder, you hear me? We've got demons approaching. Stay put."

"We're fine down here," Ryder commed back. "You take care of the demons. We'll find a way out."

"Let's go fight some demons," Derek said, leading them out of the cave. He paused and took one last look at the rock wall where Ryder was holed up.

Nic didn't want to leave Ryder behind, either. And from the look on Shay's face, neither did she. The thought of being stuck underground . . .

He didn't want to think about it. He wanted to kill demons. One crisis at a time.

They left the cave and headed outside.

Gina was right. There were hybrids lumbering slowly toward the cave.

"We made it halfway back to Lou when we saw them and figured they might be coming in your direction," Shay said. "No way were we going to let you all fight them without us. We're already one hunter down without Ryder."

"You're right. We need you both," Derek said, lifting his laser and quickening his pace.

Nic felt the rush of adrenaline, the increase in power that seemed to come from somewhere inside him whenever they came in contact with demons. Shay shot a glance in his direction and arched a brow. He wondered if she could sense it.

They hadn't had a chance to talk since he'd brushed her aside after he had that weird memory about his childhood, his mother. He owed her an apology for that.

She smiled at him and nodded, and he breathed a sigh of relief.

It was all starting to make sense, this whole symbiosis they seemed to have. He had to stop trying to figure it out. He'd never believed in destiny before, but the pieces were all falling into place now: his father; meeting up with the hunters and with his brother; having Shay in his life, and the connection he'd forged with her.

This was all *supposed* to be happening. All roads led to . . . somewhere. He figured that would fall into place sometime soon, too.

But right now, he was itching to melt down some demons. And they were drawing close.

Demons. After Angelique had listened to Ryder explain about the demons, she'd tried to absorb it in stunned silence. Could she believe the fantastic story he'd told her? Had she been hired by a Lord of the Sons of Darkness to find a diamond that could wreak havoc on mankind? What had she gotten herself into?

But when she told Ryder the name of the man who hired her, he nodded, saying Bart was one of the twelve Lords.

She shuddered at the thought of shaking hands with the man. He'd seemed so . . . normal, so human.

"How in the world did you get involved in all this?" she asked.

"That's a long story, too."

She let out a short laugh. "Like I said before, it doesn't appear we're going anywhere soon."

Ryder told her about the reality show, and what happened on the island. Angelique listened intently, her eyes widening at the thought of being trapped on a tropical island, forced to battle creatures from the underworld.

"It seems so surreal. This can't be happening."

"It is."

"How do you deal with it?"

Ryder shrugged. "Patiently. By killing them one at a time."

She shook her head. "You make it sound so simple."

"Human or demon, it doesn't matter. Bad guys have to die."

"You've been in the military, haven't you?"

He shot her a curious look. "Yeah. How did you know?"

"You seem to have that fierce mentality. Inner strength. And it's in your bearing. I'll bet you did special ops."

His brows knitted together in a tight frown. Obviously she had hit the mark, and Ryder wasn't happy about it.

Angelique grinned. "I'm a good study of people."

"Too good, I think."

She'd take that as a compliment.

"Who's Isabelle?"

"My twin sister."

"You're pretty pissed at her."

Angelique nodded. "She and I are both archeologists, but Izzy sees the treasures we uncover a lot differently from the way I do."

"How so?"

"She's in it for the money."

Ryder smiled. "And you're not."

Damn, he had a nice mouth. Her body tingled as she studied him. "No, I'm in it for the history."

"Uh-huh."

"You don't believe me."

He shrugged. "I don't really care one way or the other. I was just curious, since you seemed to be ranting about someone named Isabelle."

For some reason it bothered her that he thought of her as a treasure hunter. Though many people had misconceptions of people in her field, thought they were in it to uncover riches and to capitalize on those finds. Angelique wasn't like that. "There's something so exciting about finding a piece of long-buried history, of uncovering it with your bare hands, of being the first person to see it and reveal it to the world. When I make a find, time just stops. So does my breath, while I wipe away centuries of dirt and bring the past into the present."

She inhaled, remembering some of her favorite finds, feeling that thrill shoot through her. Even now, it made her body tingle.

She realized he wasn't responding, so she turned to look at him. He was watching her.

"What?" she asked.

He shook his head. "Nothing." He stood, brushing off his pants. "We need to get out of here. I'm going to take a look around again."

Why had he been studying her as if she was somehow . . . unusual, or fascinating? And why did heat soar through her when he shot her that look?

Okay, Angelique. Time to snap out of it. Ryder wasn't the least bit interested in her. And he probably found her rattling on about archaeology utterly boring.

She got up and inspected the cave and tunnels, desperate for something to do. She wished she had her tools. Even digging would pass the time, though there was nothing to dig for.

"I see something," Ryder said.

She hurried over to him. He was on his knees, his face nearly against the floor and the wall. "What?"

"A hole here in the wall."

She got down and looked.

"Feel that?"

"What?"

"Put your face closer to the wall."

She did. "I feel a rush of air!" She lifted and looked at him.

He grinned. "Exactly."

Angelique was beyond relieved at the possibility of escape.

Finding a potential exit had been a stroke of luck. It

was black down there, and the walls were like a moon-less sky at midnight. They'd missed it the first time.

Ryder picked at the tiny hole with his fingers, and pieces of the wall fell into his hands. He bent down and took a look in the hole.

"There might just be a tunnel in there."

"Really?" She refused to get her hopes up, but couldn't help the quiver of excitement.

"Yeah." He did it again, and more came off. Soon he had enough to slide his finger in the hole. He kept at it, finally pulling his knife to work into the hole and pry more rock loose.

He worked painstakingly at it for about an hour, pick-ing at the hole piece by piece. When he had enough of a hole that she could help, she dug her hands in and helped him.

"Get back," he said.

She moved out of the way. Ryder sat and kicked at some of the rock he'd loosened with his knife. He scooted backward in a hurry as the wall started to crum-ble, then fell. He stood and pulled her away as debris poured from the hole.

They waved at the smoky dust to clear the air, then stepped into the large hole.

"It *is* a tunnel!" she said.

Ryder directed his lights into the passageway. Long and fairly narrow, it stretched beyond what they could see. But cool, fresh air greeted them, and that was worth checking out. He turned to her and grinned. "Let's go exploring."

She nodded and followed, excitement at their release from the cave warring with curiosity about everything having to do with these demons. As they walked down the tunnel, she tried to formulate some coherent sentence that would convey the confusion in her mind. She had questions. Millions of them.

What did she really know about Ryder and his friends? What if he was working for Isabelle and this was all a trick to get to the diamond before she did? A rather convoluted method, granted, but she wouldn't put anything past her sister. Angelique had seen some strange things in her world travels. Things that couldn't be explained away with science and fact.

But demons walking on earth and threatening humans? Stealing mothers away from their children and using them to make half-demon babies? She shuddered, feeling the chill in the cold tunnel even more now.

"You don't believe anything I told you, do you?" Ryder asked as they stepped carefully along the tunnel passageway.

"It's a pretty far-fetched story."

"Yes, it is."

"Hard to fathom without proof."

He nodded but didn't say anything else. What was he supposed to do—conjure a demon out of thin air to prove it to her? She'd rather not see that, even if he could.

The tunnel narrowed and she had to move behind Ryder since they could only traverse single file now. She stayed close, feeling the hairs on the back of her neck rise as if someone or something was watching her.

Ridiculous, of course. No one was down here but the two of them.

Just keep walking. Walking meant they were getting somewhere, and they might yet find a way out of this hellhole.

Hell. Great choice of words, Angelique.

She didn't know how long they walked, but it seemed like hours. The tunnel seemed to go on forever, with no side channels and no break. And no exit. But there was also no turning back.

"This thing has to lead somewhere, doesn't it?" she asked, tired of the silence and her own thoughts.

Ryder stopped and uncapped his canteen, offering her a sip before taking one. "Yes. There's air circulating here, and it doesn't smell stale or musty."

She knew that. She'd explored thousands of caves before. Her mind wasn't working, too filled with thoughts of demons and evil lurking in the darkness.

He slanted a half-lidded gaze at her that was way too sexy given their dire circumstances. "You scared?"

"Not at all."

Then he smiled. "Liar." He turned and continued to move on, leaving her standing there gaping at him. She caught up with him.

"Look," she said, "how many times do I have to tell you this? I work alone in caves all the time, and have since I was a teenager. I don't get scared."

He didn't turn around. "That was before you found out about the demons."

She didn't even have to see his face to know he was smirking. He reminded her of the smart-ass who liked to frighten the hell out of everyone telling ghost stories.

She didn't spook that easily. "Do you think there's a chance we might run into demons down here?"

"They tend to hide out underground, so it's possible."

"Got any more of those weapons on you?"

He half turned and arched a brow. "I have a rifle and a gun, and no, you can't have either."

She couldn't help but pout. "I'd like to be able to defend myself. You know, in case you get eaten or something."

He laughed, the sound echoing off the walls. "I'm not going to get eaten, unless you had something in mind."

She stopped, shocked at the visual his words provoked. Her body heated despite the chill in the cave.

Ryder stopped too, looking at her over his shoulder. "What are you doing?"

Did he have any idea what he'd just said, or was that just a guy thing? Did sexual commentary spill from their lips without thought? It probably did.

"Are you coming?" he asked.

"Not at the moment, but it might relieve the stress." She'd be damned if he was the only one who could toss out innuendo.

And now it was his turn to look shocked. He turned fully around, his eyes narrowing.

Then he walked—no, he stalked back to her, jerked her into his arms, and planted his mouth over hers.

A rush of heat filled her as his mouth plundered hers, and that was really the only word she could think of to describe what he was doing: plundering. Okay, a couple more came to mind—pillaging, taking. His lips were soft but demanding as he slid his tongue between her lips and licked at hers. Maybe it was the stress of everything that had happened, all she had discovered since she'd met Ryder, but she gave in to the madness. She needed this. She moaned and grasped at his shirt as he pushed her against the cave wall, driving his body against hers.

She was helpless against her own response to him. It was primal and immediate and she could only hold on for the wild ride as he tangled one hand in her hair and wrapped the other around her waist to pull her closer.

She'd never been kissed like this—not with such hunger and purpose, such demand and need. She'd never felt so incredibly female before, and she welcomed the sensation. Her body tingled ... everywhere, and she longed for hours and hours of intimate exploration as she felt the hard planes of Ryder's chest against her palms.

But he pulled his lips from hers, his gaze dark and penetrating as he studied her face. The hard length of his erection pressed against her hip.

"I'd like nothing more than to strip you down and lick every inch of your body right now, then fuck you until you scream for me."

She couldn't speak, couldn't find her voice. Her throat had gone dry, her heart pounded so hard she could hear it, and oh, dear God, she really wanted him to do those things to her. Right now.

His breathing was shallow and fast as he said, "But we need to keep moving, so I'm filing that thought away for later."

He pushed away, but dragged his thumb over her bottom lip. "You have one sexy mouth, Angie." He turned away and headed down the tunnel.

Holy merde. She was in way over her head with this man. Grappling for some semblance of sanity, she pushed off the wall and joined him, trying to gather her bearings. Time to think about something else besides Ryder's mouth on hers, his hands roaming her body, and the heat that had exploded between them.

What were they talking about before she'd totally lost it, anyway? Oh, that's right . . . a weapon.

"So about that gun. I think you need to give me one so you're not the only person armed. Just in case."

He slanted her a sideways glance. "Thanks for your confidence in my ability to protect you."

"I don't need protection. I just need a weapon."

"If I die, feel free to grab one."

"You could show me how to use them."

"I could . . ."

He kept walking. Damn, he was frustrating. In more ways than one.

Chapter Nineteen

Carnage. There was no other word to describe the battle they'd just been through. Fighting hybrid demons in the rain wasn't fun. Not that any clash with demons was enjoyable, but the rain slowed them down and made the whole skirmish more difficult.

They won, but not without considerable effort. Demons were all dead.

Shay was exhausted, covered in mud; either the hunters were getting weaker or the demons were getting stronger. Of course, it had been a damn long night. Thank God the first rays of dawn were beginning to creep across the horizon, because she'd had it. She needed rest, and the rest of them did, too.

They walked, asses dragging, back to the home base cave, Derek in contact with Ryder along the way. He and Angelique hadn't found a way out yet, but they were walking along a tunnel that Ryder was sure had an exit. He told them there was no way to even determine his current location, so the rest of them might as well get some sleep. He'd comm when he had something to report.

Derek didn't like leaving one of them behind, but they had no choice. And Ryder kept insisting they were fine. They had enough water and they were going to rest and trudge on later.

Nothing to do but the same thing now.

Shay cleaned up and felt immensely better, even if said cleanup meant standing underneath the cave ceiling opening and letting the rainwater sluice down over her mud-caked body. It had given her the opportunity to rinse out her clothes, remove the dirt and grime from her hair and skin and change into something dry.

Not quite the comforts of home, but it had done the trick. At least physically she felt better. Emotionally, not so good. She was exhausted. She'd tried to curl up and catch a few hours, but that wasn't happening. Instead, she'd lain awake thinking about Nic. Worrying about him, to be more precise. He'd showered the mud off and headed into the depths of the cave for some sleep. Something was going on, and she wanted to help. And since everyone else was getting precious rest and she wasn't, she might as well go check on him and make sure he was okay.

If he was sleeping, maybe she could, too. She maneuvered her way down the dark caverns. The nice thing about sleeping in the caves was the complete obliteration of sunlight, though with the rain still beating away outside there was precious little of that anyway. Still, it made everything cozy dark, and perfect for sleeping. And there were plenty of little channels within the cave for everyone to find their own niche for a bit of privacy if they wanted to.

They all spent so much time together that most of them wanted to at least sleep alone. The funny thing was, Shay didn't. She wanted to sleep curled up against Nic, to feel his body next to hers.

Oh, yeah. She was a total goner where he was concerned. They were so connected now she didn't even wonder why anymore.

After searching every tunnel, she began to wonder if he was even there. Then she found him in the farthest corner of the cave. Wrapping her arms around herself to ward off the chill, she pointed her light downward so as not to wake him.

Not that she could. He seemed to be sleeping soundly, though he appeared restless, frowning and twitching a bit. She pressed her back against the wall and scooted down to her haunches, content just to watch him. Even in sleep he exuded a beautiful strength she couldn't help but admire. His body all chiseled angles, like a lean warrior, a bronzed angel. The way he fought demons reminded her of the classic battle of good against evil. He really got into hand-to-hand combat. It scared the crap out her, but she admired it at the same time.

And now, though asleep, he seemed to be battling something, his lips turned down and his brows slashed in a frown.

Nightmares again? She wanted to touch him, to crawl

into his dreams, but the thought of it scared her. She wasn't sure she was ready to go there again.

She startled at the sound of Nic's voice. His eyes were still closed.

"Where are you?"

"I'm right here, Nic," she answered.

"Dad? What are you doing here?"

He wasn't talking to her; his whispered voice was tight with strain. He was dreaming and talking in his sleep. She switched off the flashlight and pushed off the wall so she could get closer.

She stopped next to him, tossing on her night-vision sunglasses, clarifying his facial expression. He was frowning.

"No. Don't . . . not that. You can't be that."

Shay reached out, wanting to soothe the furrow of his brow, but snatched her hand back and dropped it in her lap. Indecision plagued her. He needed to rest. But was he really resting? He was turning from side to side as if he were bound and trying to wrestle free from something holding him.

She wanted to help him. She had to help him. She reached out—

"Don't touch me . . . don't!"

The first touch was like lightning, sending instant heat sizzling through her. She was there then, the vision surrounding her. Nic was in the darkness, demons all around him, reaching for him, just as she'd seen before, but this time she couldn't get to him—the crowd of demons was so thick, and she was outside the circle.

Standing next to Nic was his father, in demon form, though still recognizable.

The look of horror on Nic's face was heartbreaking.

"How could you do this to me? How could you expect me to become one of them?" he asked his father.

"You already are one of us, my son."

"I will *never* be one of you!"

His father reached out, his hand clawed and dripping with that sticky substance that, even from a distance, made Shay recoil.

"Get away from me!" Nic shouted.

Pulling away from the vision, Shay released her hold on Nic. Reality returned and she looked down at him, still in the throes of his nightmare.

She realized he was getting louder. She was going to have to wake him or he'd have the hunters running, thinking he was in trouble.

"Nic," she whispered, keeping her voice low.

His chest rose and fell with deep, pushing breaths. He was panting, sweat beading on his brow.

"No. No, goddammit, Dad, how could you do this? No!"

"Nic, you have to wake up now." She shook him, gently.

Nic bolted to a sitting position and pushed back, slamming against the wall, his hands flailing out in front of him. He began to kick. Shay straddled him and reached for his hands.

"Nic! Wake up. It's Shay. You're having a bad dream."

She tried to keep her voice calm, but he was starting to scare her. Was he going to come out of it?

His eyes flew open. She ripped her glasses off, knowing it was dark and he couldn't really see her.

"Shh, it's okay. It was just a dream."

She could hear him breathing. Rasping, heavy, and harsh. His fingers were laced within hers, nearly crushing them in his tight hold. She wasn't even certain he was fully awake yet until he spoke.

"Shay." He relaxed his grip on her fingers, but still held on to her hands.

Relief washed over her. "You were dreaming. Then you started to yell."

"The dreams again."

She smoothed her hand over his hair, still feeling his tension. "Yes. A bad one. With your dad and demons."

"You went into it with me, didn't you?"

"Yes."

He let out a breath. "It's just weird, having the same one over and over again. I always felt like a freak. And I couldn't tell anyone about them. Monsters in the dark, ya know? Who would believe that shit?"

She smiled. "Well, obviously I would. We all would."

"Yeah, I guess you would."

"You're not unusual in this group, Nic. We've all had our nightmares. Trust me. No one who's experienced what we have gets through it without freaking out a bit. Maybe your nightmares are one way you're trying to remember who you are."

"Or maybe who I'm supposed to be."

She understood what he was saying. "King of the demons? I hardly think so. If I felt any danger from you, would I be sitting on you right now?"

He slanted a half smile at her. "Not without a laser pointed at me."

She laughed. "You're right."

He stopped talking, but she felt the tension in his muscles ease. "Are you okay now?"

"I'm fine."

She started to rise up, but he let go of her hands and reached for her hips. "Don't leave yet."

"I wasn't. I was just going to get off of you."

"No. I like you where you are. You ran the last time we were alone, and I was worried about you."

"I know. I'm sorry. The vision freaked me out."

"I figured it did. And for that, *I'm* sorry."

"Don't be. I'm not going anywhere now."

"Good."

So he liked her where she was. Sitting on top of him. On top of a very intimate spot on his body, something she was quite aware of, especially since things underneath her were starting to harden, making her soften and warm.

"Nic."

"Shay."

He squeezed her hips, something intense laced within his grip. Now that they were talking, she should bring up the two of them and where they stood in this craziness that couldn't even be defined as a relationship. He'd snapped at her earlier, pushed her away: Something else troubled him beyond her running off the other day.

But all that could wait. She sensed his reluctance to explore further conversation, and frankly, she didn't really want to talk anymore, either. She could try to rationalize her reason for being there, but she'd come here to be with Nic. Because she missed him when she wasn't next to him. Because she couldn't sleep when he wasn't right there with her.

Because she was falling in love with him, because he had become an integral part of her existence, her life's breath.

He lifted his hips, the hard ridge of his erection surging against her soft, wet center.

"Tell me what you want," he whispered.

Any resistance fled. Though they had no privacy, no one would venture back here. Too remote, too dark— and if someone did come this way, then she supposed they were about to get one hell of a show, because she wanted Nic and nothing was going to stop her now.

She leaned forward, resting her hands on his shoulders, rocking against him, needing him so much it hurt. "Make love to me, Nic."

His low growl was an erotic purr that shot through her core, tingling her nerve endings to fiery awakening. Suddenly there were way too many clothes between them. She wanted to feel his skin against hers, wanted to rub against every inch of him with every part of herself, wanted to lie fully on top of him and stretch her body over him, feel his hands explore her back and buttocks.

Instead, he reached up and wrapped the palm of his hand behind her neck, pulling her face down to his. His lips met hers in a rush of expelled breaths and tangling tongues, igniting the flame to a combustible inferno, dragging a low moan from her throat that spoke of need, of hurry, of desperation to join.

Pulling apart from him long enough to undress was agony. Though it was dark in their cavern, she could see him watching her as she pulled off her boots, pants, and shirt, tossing her clothes to the floor while she watched him tug at his own clothes. He never once took his eyes off her.

Naked, she stood over him, wishing for more time, more privacy, a place of their own where she could play with his body. He sat once again and leaned against the cave wall, holding his hand out to her, but this time his gaze drifted between her legs. He reached to the side and flipped on the light, shining it against the far wall but illuminating them.

Shay gasped as she realized she was fully on display, all her secrets at eye level to Nic. The look on his face was rapture, making desire sizzle hot inside her.

When his gaze met hers again, she felt the pounding of her own heart, her pulse thumping against her wrist. Her entire physiology was going haywire, and all from one look.

"I need you, Shay. Slide down on me and fuck me."

Arousal pooled, a warm, liquid heat settling between her legs. She began a slow descent, taking her time to get there. Nic gave her a warning glare, but she smiled, laying her hands on his shoulders, delaying the moment when she'd envelop him.

Such a sweet torment, but she wanted to take his mind off the dream and whatever else bothered him. She wanted to make this good for him, make him forget their surroundings and all the turmoil in his life.

She wanted him to think only of her.

Nic gazed up at the golden-haired goddess straddling him and wondered if she was a dream—a much better dream than the one she'd awakened him from. Edges of that monstrous nightmare still filtered in his mind, but he cast it aside to concentrate solely on the lush visual of full hips, slender thighs, and a thatch of pale hair between her spread legs.

He licked his lips, swallowed past the huge lump in his throat. Instinct made his hips rise, his engorged cock desperate to fit between the plump lips slowly descending over him.

The scent of her bewitched him, her wicked smile captivating, tearing away the last of his patience. With a swift move he reached for her hips and pulled her the rest of the way down, sheathing her over his throbbing cock.

A hiss escaped his lips as her heat surrounded him, her body swelling, gripping him in a stranglehold. She arched to rock against him, offering up her breasts to his hungry lips. He captured one peak—it was so soft, but hardened quickly under his tongue. He splayed his fingers across her back as he licked and sucked the bud, wishing they were completely alone and he had all day to do this. His room in Sydney, with the shades open and sunlight streaming across her body, where he could lay her out and take his time looking at her, then lick his way from one end of her body to the other.

He wanted to make sex special for her, wanted this to be slow, easy, in a place where they'd have privacy and time to explore each other. Instead, they sat on a hard, cold cave floor, where anyone could walk in on them. There was no ambience here. No wine, no music, no soft bed, no hot tub or shower, no champagne and strawberries.

Shay stilled, caressing his forehead. "What's wrong?"

"Nothing."

"You're frowning. Am I doing something wrong?"

"God, no." He cupped her face in his hands, kissed her, savoring the taste of her before reluctantly pulling away. "You make me crazy. I just wanted this to be special. Look where we are."

She smiled and surged against him, making him gasp for breath. "Yes, look where we are. You're inside me, filling me. I couldn't ask for more."

How could he think straight when she was moving against him like that? "I wanted it to be perfect."

Her eyes glittered with unshed tears. "It is perfect. Being with you, having you touch me and kiss me, is absolute perfection, no matter where we are. I don't need a hotel suite or a fancy bed, Nic. I just need you."

She grasped his hands and laid them over her breasts. His balls tightened at the intimacy, of knowing she was giving him access to everything.

"Lean back, let me touch you."

She arched and he swept his hands over her ribs, the softness of her belly, then lower. As she moved upward, he caressed the desire-soaked bud with his thumb, rewarded with soft cries and her body squeezing his.

Shay was his woman. As much his woman as if he'd branded her. Her golden body was bathed by the dim light as she rocked with wild abandon, and the sudden urge to mark his possession overwhelmed him. He kept his hand against her sex, caressing her, but clasped her to him, licking the slender column of her throat, reveling in the rushed beating of her heart against his chest.

He wanted to come inside her, to make her his in every way possible, to ensure that no other man would ever touch her again. And just like the last time he was with her, he felt this urge to claim her, to shout that she belonged to him and no other.

Though he didn't understand the driving force, he recognized he could do nothing about the urge. Nothing but hold her tight while he lifted toward her, felt the storm surge building as she began to tighten against him. When her moans increased and she began to shudder and rock, when her body began to milk him from the inside, he knew he couldn't hold back. Blinding, white hot light took hold of the base of his spine, shooting outward to every nerve in his body. He sank his teeth into the tender flesh between her neck and shoulder as he erupted, her orgasm a cataclysm to his own, rocketing him against the wall of the cave with the sheer force of it.

He bit her. He knew it, but he couldn't let go.

She didn't cry out or complain, just shuddered against him with a moan, finally settling, her body still quaking around him long after the first jolt of her climax had passed. And still he held his mouth around her flesh.

He really should let loose, but he didn't want to.

Finally, sanity returned and he eased back, examining the area where he'd clamped his teeth down on her skin. Dark marks scored her flesh.

Christ, what was he, some kind of animal?

"Shay."

"Mmmm."

Fuck, how was he going to apologize for that? The crimson taste of her blood still filled his mouth. "I bit you."

Her deep, shuddering inhalation thrust her breasts against his chest. "So you did."

"I bit you hard."

"Yes."

"I made you bleed."

"Really?"

"You might scar."

She didn't say anything for a few seconds. He waited, tense, feeling a hundred times an asshole.

"It really excited me, Nic."

"It did?"

"Yeah, I like the idea of you putting your mark on me."

Holy shit. She'd read his mind.

"You probably think I'm a pervert now," she whispered.

He laughed. "That would be like the pot calling the kettle black, I think."

She threaded her fingers through his hair and laid her head on his shoulder. "Good. Then we're both a little kinky."

Ah, hell. He didn't know what to say. Shay was like no other woman he'd known—self-assured and eager to please, yet with an innocence that belied any subterfuge on her part. She was exactly what she showed on the surface. She wasn't a game player. She was straightforward and honest and always said what was in her heart.

He owed her the same. Would he be able to deliver, to tell her what he felt?

He didn't know. But he could show her, and hope she understood. Because she was special to him. Hell, she was his, and he'd never felt a possessive streak toward a woman before.

Was this love? He didn't know it, had never felt it, wasn't even sure he'd be able to recognize it. Was it fair to love her when he didn't know what lurked inside him?

Ryder heard Angelique's stomach growl. Yeah, he was hungry, too. And tired, and dirty. They'd finally had to sit down and settle against the wall to get some sleep, having walked until he knew she was dragging.

She wasn't a complainer, though. He was the one who'd finally made the decision to stop, to make her sit and rest. She'd have kept going. He gave her credit for being tough, and he was damned impressed at her stamina.

He had a few energy bars in his pack, so they ate some, took a few sips of water, sat silently together, and stared at the nothingness of the dark walls. He was thinking—about a lot of different things, mainly about whether or not they were going to make it out of here. He figured she had a lot on her mind, too, with what he'd told her about the demons. She'd probably stay up all day.

But she surprised him. In a matter of minutes Angelique slumped against him, her head nestled on his shoulder. She was out cold. Strange feelings enveloped him—protectiveness, the fierce need to make sure nothing bad happened to her.

He'd kissed her. What the hell had possessed him to kiss her? Oh, sure, she'd tossed out that taunt about having an orgasm in reply to his one-liner about a blow job, but Jesus, that didn't mean he had to stalk her down and devour her like a hungry animal, did it?

Just thinking about what happened back there made his cock twitch. Sure, Angelique was a beautiful woman. Intelligent, strong, and capable. And not a whiner. There was definite chemistry between them. So what? That didn't mean he had to act on it. Wrong woman, wrong place, wrong time.

So why was he getting a hard-on sitting here thinking

about that kiss and what she felt like in his arms? Why was he thinking of waking her up and finishing what they'd started earlier? Why did primal need coil up inside him, demanding to be fed?

Big mistake. He was on a job, and that meant no pleasure. One didn't interfere with the other.

And why the hell did she feel so good nestled against him like this? He didn't know a damn thing about her.

He had the other hunters' backs. That was his job. But he didn't do it because he cared for them. They were all nice people, but he felt no sense of family or loyalty or caring toward them. This was just his work, like being part of a military unit: You protected your own.

Having Angelique down here with him was different. He found her fascinating, and for a guy who didn't care much for women other than the occasional sex release or as battle partners, this was an unusual feeling.

She was intriguing, like a puzzle he couldn't quite fit together. He didn't like that. Attraction got in the way of keeping his head in the game. There were times when you let your dick rule, and times when you let your head rule.

His dick was going to lose this battle, because right now he needed his brains to be in charge. Though the beautiful woman snuggling closer to him for warmth for the past several hours had made that choice damned difficult.

Good thing he got by on very little sleep.

He shifted and she stirred, blinking up at him.

"Did I sleep long?" she asked, still resting her head against his chest.

"A few hours."

"Sorry." She pushed off and stood, then pressed her hands at her back and stretched. He tried to ignore the way her clothes stretched with her, outlining her breasts, but there was no way he could avert his gaze. She was too damn tempting.

"I didn't think I'd be able to sleep. Guess I was more exhausted than I thought."

"No problem." He looked away and dug for his canteen. They took a few sips of water and a couple bites of an energy bar, but both were going to run out soon. He had to find an exit, and fast.

"So now what? More walking?" she asked as she looked at the black wall in front of her.

"Yeah."

She squinted then, and walked toward the wall, practically sticking her nose against it to inspect it.

"What?"

She didn't answer, just kept staring at the wall.

"What are you looking at?"

"This rock wall. Do you have something sharp, like an ax?"

He laughed. "Yeah. Just call me Paul Bunyan. I carry one around with me all the time."

She shot him a glare. "Smart-ass. What do you have, then?"

He pulled his long knife out and handed it to her. "How's this?"

"It'll do." She picked at the rock with relentless precision. Enough that he grew bored and irritated. Tiny pieces of rock fell to the ground. Not enough to dig a hole by any means.

"What are you doing?"

"Mining."

"For?"

"This tunnel looks like it contains a vein. It's old and probably abandoned, but it's deep enough that it might have once been mined for diamonds."

He rolled his eyes. "We don't have time for you to be mining for diamonds right now."

She turned around and waved the knife in his direction. "Don't you think I know that? But if this sunken tunnel is part of the big mine a few miles from here, maybe it's a way out. I'm just testing a theory. So give me a minute."

"Fine." Damn, she was testy when she worked.

He leaned against the wall and waited while she picked, and picked. She was meticulous and precise, scraping and gouging out the wall in one spot. She had to have the patience of a saint to do this kind of work. He was ready to get moving, and he was giving her exactly one more minute before he dragged her down the tunnel.

But just then a chunk of the wall fell into her hand, about the size of a golf ball. She inspected it, moved to Ryder, and shined her shoulder light on the piece.

"Well?" he asked.

She squinted, wrinkled her nose, turned her head from side to side.

"Diamonds."

"Where?"

Using the tip of the knife, she pointed to what looked like a piece of rock salt embedded in the black rock. "There. Not big, but definitely a diamond."

"Okay. So?"

"This cave is part of the Diavolo mine."

He looked from the hunk of rock to her. "How do you know that?"

"Because the Diavolos have annexed every vein within hundreds of miles. Trust me. It's theirs. They've mined here, which means there's a connection to their mine. We just have to find it. Let's go."

Finally. They moved on down the tunnel and Ryder commed Derek, reporting what Angelique had found.

"So she's convinced there's a way out that'll lead into the Diavolo mining operation?" Derek asked.

"Yeah."

"We've got to get on that property, then. And I think you've just given us a good reason. I'll be in touch."

Great. That meant two things. One, they'd be getting out of this dark hole soon, and two, they'd probably be killing more demons when they got there.

Things were starting to look up.

Chapter Twenty

At Ryder's news, everyone woke up and sprang into action. It was time to get moving.

Shay and Nic hurried to meet the others at the entrance to the cave. The rains had stopped, thankfully, which meant that when they left the cave they could at least see where they were going.

"As long as the Sons of Darkness don't have possession of the black diamond, we're on equal ground with them." Lou looked to Nic. "But I think our best bet at this point is to get into the diamond mines. We've delayed long enough."

Nic nodded. "I told you I could get us all in there."

Lou looked to Derek, question in his eyes. Shay knew that letting Nic into the mine meant taking a great leap of faith. Once Nic was on his home turf, he could turn the tables on them, have them arrested for kidnapping. Or something even worse.

If they were ever going to trust Nic, now was the time.

Derek turned his gaze to Shay. She knew what he wanted from her. She was closer to Nic than any of them right now, including Derek.

There was nothing Nic could say to convince them. But Shay could. She slipped her hand in Nic's and nodded at Derek.

Nic squeezed her fingers. She glanced over at him and smiled. Yes, he had her confidence. And her heart. She hoped she was doing the right thing, because Derek and Lou were putting their trust—and the fate of all the hunters—in her instincts.

"Okay," Derek said, "how do you get us in there?"

"That's easy. First, I tell them we were out on a little diamond expedition. You're prospective clients and wanted to see the area, do a little fun spelunking in non-restricted caves. I've done it before, so it's not unusual. Second, I'll indicate that while we were exploring, there was a cave-in and a couple of our people fell into the old mine shaft. Then we'll launch a search within the compound and retrieve Ryder and Angelique. Trust me, they'll get right on it. They don't want anyone wandering unattended within the mines."

"You're pretty good at this," Shay said, amazed he could concoct a plausible story so quickly.

Nic shrugged. "I'm in sales. Always need to have bullshit prepared."

She laughed.

"Let's get ready and go. Nic, from here on out, you lead the way," Derek said.

Nic nodded and started to move away.

"And Nic."

He paused at Derek's words.

"Yeah?"

"Don't make me regret this."

Nic didn't smile. "You won't. This time, you're going to have to trust *me*."

They packed up and trekked to the SUV. After loading up, they headed toward the Diavolo Diamonds mines.

Anticipation and excitement soared through Nic's blood. This was his chance to prove himself to the hunters, to show them he could be trusted.

The terrain grew more familiar, the valleys narrowing, each hill jutting up in jagged splendor like rust-colored monoliths. He remembered his first view of the strange-looking objects from the airplane when his father had brought him out here years ago. He'd never forget it.

"We're close. The mines are centered within the valley surrounded by these hills. There's an opening straight ahead if you stay on this road."

Dalton nodded, and Nic looked out the window once again. With the departure of the rains, the heat had returned, making it unbearable, even with the air conditioning going full blast. Waves of heat shimmered along the roadway like a mirage in the desert. It had to be in the hundreds outside, baking the landscape to a crisp brown. He longed to be back at the ocean, to smell the tang of salt in the air and feel the cool spray and whipping breeze across his face. He missed taking his board out and sailing through the waves, king of his domain, mastering the monster as it roared above him.

This desert shit wasn't for him at all. Being landlocked sucked.

The mines came into view; tall fencing surrounded Diavolo land.

"Electrified?" Derek asked.

"Yeah. With camera surveillance and motion detectors around the entire perimeter, providing added security. With this many diamonds, we have to make sure the area's impenetrable. The wall's insurmountable except by air and the main entrance gates are manned by several armed guards at multiple checkpoints."

The gated entrance loomed ahead, guards already spilling out, rifles held loosely in their arms. Nic remembered how ominous the scene looked when he was younger—like something out of a movie. Of course his father had flashed a grin, placed his thumbprint on the screen, and zipped them right through.

"You ready for this?" Shay asked.

Nic shrugged, affecting a calm he didn't really feel. This had to work. He had the hunters to protect now, and it was up to him to get Ryder and Angelique out of the closed-up part of the mine. "Sure. Should go down easy."

The SUV stopped and Dalton rolled down all the windows, allowing the guard to approach.

"This is a restricted area," the guard said, then arched

his brows as he spotted Nic. "Oh, Mr. Diavolo, I didn't see you back there."

"It's okay, Dave. We need entrance. These are prospective clients, and we've had a bit of an accident in one of the caves east of here. There was a cave-in, and two of our people are stuck down in the tunnels."

"Yes, sir. I'll need your thumbprint first."

Nic exited the SUV and the guard led him to the scanner. He laid his thumb on the screen and waited while the identification software pulled up his name and recognition information.

The guard nodded. "I'll alert everyone at the house that you're on your way up."

"Thanks, Dave." Nic slid into the seat and Dalton drove forward.

"Slick," Derek said as moved through the gates.

Nic shrugged. "That part was easy."

But at least they'd gotten inside. Now they had to find Ryder and Angelique, and figure out if the gem they were searching for was within the mines.

"You do realize it's a high probability your uncle is here," Lou said.

"It wouldn't surprise me," Nic said. "If what you say is true and he's part of all this, he has to be expecting the Realm of Light to show up here at the mines, especially if he thinks you kidnapped me."

If his uncle Bart was a Lord of the Sons of the Darkness, he was embroiled in this evil shit up to his beady eyeballs, the shifty fucker. Nic never had trusted his uncle. Bart had always been whispering in his father's ear, hanging close and leering at Nic as if he knew secrets about Nic that even Nic didn't know.

Nic hated that shit. He just hoped Bart wasn't at the mines. They had enough to deal with right now.

The first thing Shay realized when the SUV pulled in front of the house was that her perceptions of a diamond mine weren't at all correct. She had pictured dirt and more caves, not this sprawling paradise and huge mansion.

Nic had told her the mine and the house were at the top of the far hill. They were heading to the house first, a rambling drive along twisting roads that made her stomach pitch. But once they'd finished climbing, she felt the air change. There were trees and lots of them, dense, crowding out the heat and surrounding the house, providing a shady shelter as they exited the vehicles. Shay tilted her head back to survey the four-story structure, which stretched high above the treetops and as wide as she could see.

Wow. It was a gorgeous piece of architecture. Modern and angular, it signaled a cheery welcome to her weary body. They stepped up onto the expansive porch that wrapped around the entire front of the house and through the double doors leading into the entry.

The house was bright and open. Pale marble tiles spread across the expansive living area that splayed out toward floor-to-ceiling windows overlooking a deck out back. More greenery in the back, a pool, every possible modern convenience. Nothing like a little luxury in the midst of the desert.

"Disgustingly lavish, isn't it?" Nic whispered over her shoulder.

"Unimaginable." Shay's gaze wandered over the antiques, the modern mixed with the old, wishing she could take the time to explore every room, every ancient piece of furniture that must be worth a fortune. Swords and daggers hung on the walls, their blades gleaming bright in invitation. Shay salivated at the thought of taking them down and inspecting them, of tracing her fingers along their gilded and jeweled edges and absorbing their history, because she didn't for a second doubt their authenticity.

The first thing Nic did was grab the phone and make a couple calls while the rest of them stood around. When he hung up, he turned to them.

"The head of security for the mines is on his way here," Nic said. "We'll see what's happening with the search for Ryder. My uncle Bart is on the mine property. He'll show up shortly."

Derek arched a brow. "Was he surprised to hear from you?"

"Shocked was more like it. We didn't talk. He said he was coming right over and hung up."

Derek crossed his arms and smirked. "This should be fun."

Shay didn't know if fun was the right word to use.

A spark of nervousness flickered to life at everything

going on. Much was at stake, and this was a critical time. She could feel it churning inside her.

The front door opened and a tall, burly man in camouflage entered the room. He looked military. Close-cropped blond hair, beefy thick neck, and muscles to spare. Based on the monster-size gun in his belt, Shay assumed he had to be the head of security.

Nic walked over and shook the man's hand, then turned to them. "This is Denton Luellen, head of security for Diavolo Diamonds." He turned back to Denton. "Anything on our missing friends yet?"

Denton shook his head. "Nothing yet. Scanners are running the length of the unused tunnels, but our equipment isn't set up in every abandoned shaft. We're sending in search teams."

Nic nodded. "Thanks. Keep me posted."

"Aye, sir." Denton swiveled and walked out of the room, closing the door behind him.

Derek approached Nic. "Can that guy be trusted?"

Nic shrugged. "Who the hell knows? Until I met you people I thought everyone here could be. Now I don't trust anyone. But as far as security knows, you all are potential diamond buyers, and Ryder and Angelique are clients. They'll hustle their asses to find them."

"I wish we could go look for them," Gina said, standing to pace the length of the room. "I don't like sitting here doing nothing."

"I agree," Nic said. "But it would look suspicious for diamond buyers to crawl down into abandoned tunnels to hunt for missing persons when we have trained security staff for that. Let them do their jobs. They'll find Ryder and Angelique."

Nic allowed entrance to whoever knocked on the door. It opened and a man entered the room.

"Mr. Diavolo, I'm so pleased you've decided to visit us and that you've brought guests."

Dressed in casual attire, the man who spoke nevertheless carried himself with authority. In his fifties, she would guess, with dark hair graying at the temples, he had lined, tanned skin and was very tall and lean.

"This is James Waters, manager of the estate here," Nic explained to them. "James, these are my guests. Can you have rooms arranged for everyone? We'll be staying a few days at most."

James nodded. "Rooms have already been prepared for your guests."

"Thank you, James. I knew I could count on you."

James nodded and motioned to one of the staff standing by. "Take everyone's things upstairs. I've taken the liberty of putting you in the master suite, of course, Mr. Diavolo."

"Of course," Nic replied.

Shay fought back a grin at the way Nic had shifted to an air of pompous, in-charge rich man. Even the way he carried himself changed. Shoulders back, chin high, and nose in the air, like he deserved James's fawning all over him. If she didn't know it was an act she'd be gagging at his attitude.

"You all might as well clean up while we're waiting to hear about Ryder," Nic suggested. "We can meet back downstairs afterward, get something to eat and see if there's any word."

"Good idea," Derek agreed. "I'd like to get this ten pounds of mud off me."

James had the staff hustling and showing the "guests" to their rooms, no questions asked. Shay was surprised to discover her things had been taken to the master suite along with Nic's. That she hadn't expected.

The other hunters followed, surely noticing her belongings being taken into the master suite along with Nic's.

Frankly, she didn't care what they thought. Her only thought was that Nic wanted her in his room. When she walked in and found him standing at the foot of the bed, she waited while the servant laid down her bags and closed the door.

"I wanted you to have the best room, and this one is it," Nic said. "I hope you don't mind."

"No, I don't mind at all." The bedroom was phenomenal. The size of a small house actually, with a separate sitting area, an obscenely large bathroom with separate tub, shower, and two sink areas, all in the same pale marble. Windows everywhere, floor-to-ceiling, and a private deck overlooking the pool. The focal point of the room was the king-size bed, though. She could already envision rolling around on it with Nic. "Nice room," she said when she finished walking around.

"I wanted you to be comfortable."

She smiled. "I doubt there's a bad room in the house."

"All right. I wanted you with me. Is that a problem?"

She twined her arms around his neck. "Hell, no." Just being near him made her temperature spike. Knowing he wanted her aroused her. The way he looked at her melted her feet to the cool marble floor.

She sighed, wishing they had time. "I need to take a shower."

He smiled. "Go ahead."

With great regret she untangled herself from his embrace and stepped into the bathroom, undressed, and turned on the water in the expansive stall.

A real, honest-to-God shower. Shay let the water pour over her head for a good five minutes before reaching for the shampoo to scrub the mud out, then worked over her body until it felt clean again. She groaned at the sheer pleasure of not feeling mud caked all over her.

"You look good."

She shrieked and whirled around as cool air hit her skin and Nic's voice invaded her shower. He was leaning against the shower door, naked and with an appreciative smile on his dirt-streaked face.

"I'm sorry I took so long. I hadn't had a shower in a while and I was en—enjoying this one," she stammered, tripping over her own tongue as she ogled his body. In the bright light she got a nice long look at his lean muscled abs, strong shoulders, and biceps, and as her gaze dipped below his waist . . . oh, my.

For the love of God. It wasn't as if she hadn't seen his body before, but he'd scared the hell out of her. She hadn't expected him to pop in on her like this.

"I'm not here to complain about you taking up shower time. Scoot over."

She moved and he stepped in, closing the door behind him.

The shower had just gotten a lot smaller.

"I hope you don't mind." He stood in the water, letting it spray over his head.

"Not at all." Naked man in the shower with her? Hell, no, she didn't mind.

"Give me a second to wash up."

He washed. She watched, leaning against the wall and looking her fill of him as he raised his hands over his head to wash his hair. Perfectly proportioned in all the right places. *All* the right places. Her nipples tightened, as did parts south, remembering the feel of him inside her, the touch of his lips to her breasts, the way his hands felt when they skimmed over her body. Though she hadn't set the water on hot, her body temperature rose. Every time she looked at him she was reminded of that first time she'd seen him, walking out of the ocean.

"Enjoying the view?"

She gazed into his eyes. He was staring at her, grinning, his hands planted on either side of the shower wall. Water rained over the back of his neck, rivulets pouring down the front of his chest. She followed the trail as the rivers snaked lower, over his flat abdomen and lower belly and between his legs, down his powerful thighs and onto his feet.

Shay realized she could admire his body like one would a sculpture, study it from all angles and look at it for hours on end, never tiring of the view. He was absolute perfection, at least to her.

"Yes, as a matter of fact I am." She pushed away from the wall and moved closer to him. "You have an incredible body."

"And here I thought you liked me for my sharp wit and sense of humor."

She swept her hand over his shoulders and down his chest, following the trail of water. "Those, too."

"I don't believe you. You're just using me for sex."

He sucked in a breath when she mapped his abdomen with her fingertips. She liked knowing her touch affected him, liked it even more when she circled his erection and he surged into her grasp. "You think I'm using you for sex?" she asked, stroking him with long, leisurely movements.

"Oh, hell, yeah." He palmed the side of the shower, moving his hips forward, thrusting into her hand.

"Hmm, you may be right. I've never used a man for his body before. This could be fun."

She dropped to her knees. Nic shifted and the water sprayed over her head, against her face and in her mouth. She welcomed the sensation of being submerged as she captured his shaft between her lips and devoured him. She was drowning in sensation, in carnal delights. The pounding water against her, the sound of his groans as she tasted his velvet softness between her lips, the salty flavor of him spilling onto her tongue.

"Use me, baby," he growled, pushing between her lips

with more force each stroke, taking control away from her as he held her head and used her mouth.

And she loved it. God help her, she loved his mastery of her this way. She wasn't submissive by any stretch of the imagination, but this position, the way he touched her, the look on his face as he drove between her lips, was so enticing she could barely stand it. His face was contorted into a grimace that looked like pain but which she knew to be the utmost pleasure. She reached underneath to cup the twin sacs strung tight and hard beneath his shaft, squeezing them with gentle pulses.

"No," he said, withdrawing and pulling her to a standing position. His gaze was hot as he looked into her eyes. "I don't want to come in your mouth, but goddamn, I'm close to it."

He pushed her against the wall and drew one of her legs up, reaching down to cup her sex. She opened her mouth to cry out, but he swallowed her gasp with his lips against hers, kissing her with a force that slammed her head against the tile wall.

She didn't even feel the pain, she was so lost in the sensation of his hand between her legs, doing magical, sinful things to her, things designed to take her to the brink and over. He knew just where to touch her and how—slow at first, then increasing the motions, circling the taut bud with his thumb just as he drove his fingers inside her, drinking in her moans of climax as she tore over the edge like quick lightning. She shuddered against his hand, spilling her liquid heat. He groaned against her lips, licking her tongue with his, making her absolutely insane with pleasure.

Relentless, he didn't stop, just kept moving inside her, swirling the palm of his hand over her pulsing nub until desire blazed hot as fire again. His cock replaced his fingers, driving inside her with a quick thrust that left her breathless. He lifted her other leg, suspending her in midair while he pumped hard against her, slamming her back against the wall.

Shay opened her eyes. Nic's gaze was dark, intense, as he thrust forward, pulling out of her only to drive to the hilt again. She sensed his desperation, as if this might be the last time they'd connect this way. For a while, possibly forever? She didn't know, but the same sense of need wrapped itself around her. She tangled her fingers into his hair and met his mouth with fervor, kissing him with a longing she prayed showed him how she felt. Because she couldn't say the words, couldn't speak past the blinding pleasure he gave her. She could only feel, and hopefully give him in return.

When her orgasm gripped her he let go of her legs and she wrapped them around his back, squeezing him, trying to become part of him as she shattered and trembled and cried through intense waves crashing inside her. He stilled, then thrust deeply, shuddering, kissing her with a softness that belied the savage passion they'd just shared.

Panting, she let go, her shaky legs sliding down him until her feet hit the floor. Nic held tight to her until she was certain she could maintain her footing. She looked up at him and gave him a tentative smile.

He kissed her with gentle sweeps of his lips, then moved to her neck. "I see the bite I gave you didn't leave any lasting marks."

She smiled. "No, it didn't. Guess you're not a vampire after all."

He didn't let go of her for the longest time. Shay felt like he wanted to say something more, but he didn't, eventually turning the water off and grabbing towels for both of them.

He grinned. "Now we really need to get downstairs."

"I guess we do."

But she was pretty sure that wasn't what he was about to say.

Nic had been about to tell Shay he loved her.

Something stopped him. The words had hovered on his tongue, ready to spill. He'd been inside her, her body still quaking around him, and he hadn't said the words.

He should have. That might have been his only chance. He had a feeling something major was about to go down, and it involved him. And the feeling had a lot more to do with just being on Diavolo property. A lot more. A gut feeling that told him whatever was about to happen was going to change him in a big way. Maybe that's what stopped him. He didn't want to risk Shay, to put her in the middle of whatever was going on.

Plus, he still hadn't quite figured out this whole demon thing inside him, what part was good and what, if any, was bad. He couldn't subject her to loving someone who had evil inside him. First he had to determine who and what he was. Then he'd get the love part out in the open.

Because he was pretty certain that she returned his feelings. She hadn't said the words, either, so maybe she was as uncertain about everything as he was.

What a pair they made. Probably why he didn't like being separated from her for even a short period of time, why he'd had her bags brought to his room. He wanted her with him.

Forever.

Pretty big turnaround for someone who'd never even had a long-term relationship. Now he wanted to bond with Shay in an eternity kind of way. But he couldn't do that until this mission was over with—that much he knew. So first things first.

They dressed and headed downstairs to meet up with the others. Nic hoped they'd find Ryder and Angelique quickly. There were things to be done, loose ends to wrap up.

And he had his uncle to deal with, too.

"Did you hear that?"

Ryder stopped, listened, then shook his head. "No."

"Are you sure? I heard pounding, I know it."

"I didn't. Let's keep moving."

Angelique blew out a sigh, but followed him. He

hoped what she heard wasn't the rumbling of another cave-in. As tight as this tunnel was, they wouldn't survive it. There was nowhere to go if the roof started falling in on them. As it was, he'd had to prod her every step of the way, since she was now convinced they were standing in the middle of a diamond vein. After all that had happened, she still wanted to do her job and find the black diamond. Even knowing who her client was.

Maybe she didn't believe him after all. Whatever. She could diamond hunt on her own time. After this mess with the Sons of Darkness was taken care of, and after the Realm of Light found the black diamond. Now that Ryder knew who Angelique worked for, there was no way she was going to be allowed to go free and secure the diamond for them. She'd have to come along with the hunters.

Or something. Hell, he didn't know what Lou and Derek were going to do with her, but once they got out of this tunnel, she wouldn't be Ryder's problem anymore. And he could gain a little distance between them.

Which made rescue even more appealing. He didn't want to look after anyone but himself. In the demon-hunting business, keeping yourself alive was a full-time job. Keeping an untrained civilian safe who didn't know jack about demons or how to kill them was an added burden he didn't want to assume.

Lou and Derek could handle her.

He stopped when he heard the pounding.

"You heard it that time, didn't you?" she asked, coming up so close behind him her breasts brushed his back.

"Yeah, I heard it. Stay quiet."

They'd long ago lost touch with Derek. Either the batteries were dead in Ryder's comm or he and Angelique were too far underground for the system to make contact. Maybe the hunters were out of range. Either way, he had no way of knowing what was going on topside, so he had to rely on his own instincts.

"What do you think—"

He silenced her by raising his hand, wanting to listen to the sound, track its location, and see if he could figure out what it was.

The sound drew closer. Someone . . . or something . . . was definitely heading their way. He turned to Angelique, lowering his voice to a whisper.

"Back up around that corner and slip under that overhang we just passed through so whoever's coming can't see you. Until we figure out who it is, I don't want you to be found."

"Why?"

Because something bad could happen to her and he didn't like the thought of that. Disgusted with the way his mind was working, he said, "Because I can't fight and worry about protecting you at the same time."

She frowned. "I don't need protection. I can help. If you'd just give me a weapon like I asked—"

"Not now, Angie! There's no time to show you how to use this weaponry. Just do as I ask. Please," he added.

With a sigh, she said, "Okay."

"If I holler at you to run, try to get past whatever's

happening and head for the exit. I'll keep them engaged so you can get through."

She nodded. After she'd moved around the corner, Ryder raised his laser, pointing it in the direction of the approaching sounds.

He was ready for whatever it was. Worst-case scenario—demons. Best case—rescue.

The rumble grew louder, closer still. Ryder's finger rested on the trigger, ready to let loose with an array of UV light if it was demons.

He really hoped it wasn't. Not when he had Angelique to protect. He didn't have a problem dying doing this, but putting her life at risk wasn't his call to make. He moved forward, toward the sound, putting distance between himself and Angelique. As he quickened his step and rounded a corner, he saw lights approaching.

Demons didn't have lights. That could be a very good thing. He still maintained caution, though. When a flash hit his face, he froze.

"Ryder?" someone called out.

Whoever it was knew his name. "Yeah."

"We're with the Diavolo Diamonds security team. Mr. Dominic Diavolo sent us after you. Are you okay?"

He saw them now. There were five of them. Weapons strapped to their belts, not in their hands. He hurriedly bagged his laser as they drew closer. "Fine. We're fine. Glad to see you people. We thought we'd be down here forever."

"Let's get you out of here. Where's the woman?"

"She's farther down the tunnel. I came up here to investigate the noise."

They followed while he went to retrieve Angelique.

"Angelique," he yelled as he made it halfway down the corridor.

She didn't answer.

"It's okay, Angelique. We've got rescue personnel here. You can come out now."

He kept walking toward the corner where he'd told her to stay put, but she still didn't answer or come forward.

Shit. An odd tingle rumbled in his gut. He had a bad feeling and hurried along the tunnel to the spot where he'd left her.

She wasn't there.

"Angelique!"

Nothing.

Goddammit, where was she?

"Is there a problem?"

Ryder turned to the head security guy. "Yeah, there's a problem. Angelique is missing."

The man arched a brow. "Missing? Where would she go? I thought the cave-in blocked any exit."

"It did."

"Then how could she disappear?"

Excellent damn question. One Ryder didn't have an answer to.

But Angelique was definitely gone.

Chapter Twenty-One

Missing? You searched everywhere for her?" Lou asked.

Shay couldn't believe Angelique had disappeared in the tunnels. But Ryder had confirmed it.

"We trekked all the way back to the cave-in. No sign of her. It was like she vanished into the goddamn walls."

Ryder looked exhausted, dragging his hand through his hair, dark circles under his eyes. Shay had never seen Ryder look worried.

But he wasn't just upset. He was angry.

"That is most unfortunate. And definitely suspicious." Lou sighed. "But we're happy to have you back."

"Damn glad to get out of that dark hole. I just want to know why and how Angelique disappeared."

"So do I," Derek said. "You don't think she'd make an escape on her own, do you?"

Ryder shrugged. "It's not like I know her all that well.

But I don't think so. And where the hell would she go? There were no exits down there."

"That you know of," Lou reminded him. "Maybe she did, and was just waiting for an opportunity to get alone and take one."

Ryder stared at Lou for a few seconds, his glare intensifying. "Shit."

"We don't know that to be a fact," Shay said. "Someone could have taken her."

"Or she could be working with the Sons of Darkness. Great. And I told her everything." Ryder shook his head. "I should know better than to trust a damn woman."

"Gee, thanks," Gina said, arching a brow.

"Present female company excluded," Ryder grumbled.

Lou held up his hands. "Let's not jump to conclusions. Any number of things could have happened. Yes, Angelique could be working with the Sons of Darkness, or they could have taken her when Ryder left her alone. We don't know."

"I'm going to take a shower," Ryder said, stalking out of the great room.

"He's pissed," Nic said.

Shay nodded. "Most likely at himself. But if Angelique is with the Sons of Darkness, he didn't tell her anything she didn't already know, did he?"

"Other than alerting them that we're after the black diamond," Dalton offered.

"I highly doubt that's a secret to the Sons of Darkness." Lou stood and paced the great room. "They know we're here. They know what we're after. Nothing Ryder said to Angelique would be a surprise to the demon Lords."

The front door opened again and everyone turned. Shay knew immediately who the man was. Late fifties, salt-and-pepper hair, but very fit; the resemblance was still there.

He looked a lot like Ben.

"Uncle Bart," Nic said, moving toward the man.

Bart's eyes widened with concern as he wrapped Nic into an embrace. "Dominic. We've been so worried about you."

Nic stepped back after a quick hug. "I'm fine. I've been working. Lost my damn cell phone, and you know the things don't work in the caves anyway."

Bart shifted his gaze from Nic to the rest of them. "Of course. I'm glad you're all right."

Nic made the introductions, claiming they were all potential diamond buyers, with Lou as the head. Shay knew Bart wasn't buying into it, but the charade was playing out on both sides at the moment.

"So happy to meet you all. Welcome to Diavolo Diamonds," Bart said, greeting them each individually with an enthusiastic handshake.

"His hands are freaking icy," Gina whispered to her after Bart moved away. "Just like a demon's."

Shay nodded, resisting the urge to wipe her hands on her pants.

Bart turned to Nic. "I heard you had a cave-in. Anyone hurt?"

Nic shook his head. "No. Two of our guests fell into

one of the abandoned tunnels. One recovered. One still missing."

Bart arched a brow. "Missing? How can that be?"

As if he didn't know. Shay wanted to ask him where Angelique was and if she was part of all this, but bit her tongue.

"We don't know. Security said they'd keep searching, but it's a mystery. There wasn't any other exit."

Bart laid his hand on Nic's shoulder, but looked at Lou. "I'm so sorry about this. I assure you our people will do our utmost to find your friend."

Lou nodded. "I'm certain you will."

Returning his gaze to Nic, Bart asked, "How long will you be staying, and what are your plans for our guests?"

"A couple days. They would like the tour of the mining operation."

Bart nodded. "Of course. I'll be happy to assist."

"That's not necessary. I'm sure you're busy. I'll see to *my* clients, as I always do. But thank you for the offer."

Nic's demeanor was stiff. Shay could feel the tension pouring from him as he faced off with Bart. The room was soon filled with it. Would Bart call him out now, in front of them and here at the house?

But Bart gave a curt nod. "As you wish. If I can help in any way, give me a call."

"Are you heading back to Sydney?" Nic asked.

"No, I have a few matters to attend to at the mines, so I'll be here awhile longer." Bart turned to Lou. "It was a pleasure to meet all of you. I look forward to seeing you again."

After he left, Shay exhaled, feeling the taut energy drain from the room.

"Damn," she said to Nic. "He's intense."

Nic shrugged. "He's always like that. Pain in the ass, too."

"In what way?" Derek asked, coming up beside Nic.

"Very in-your-face kind of guy. Probing, curious, always prying into my business. Kept very close tabs on my clientele, my projects, my trips. He always had to know what I was doing, who I was going to be with, where I was going and when I was due back. Damned annoying."

"You're a critical component to the Sons of Darkness, Nic," Lou said. "Bart is no doubt charged with keeping track of you."

Nic dragged his hand through his hair. "I don't know anything about that. I always assumed he didn't trust me to do my job, and it annoyed the fuck out of me."

"Has his observance of you escalated recently?" Lou asked.

"Hell, yes. Even worse over the past couple months. I received urgent calls from him asking me to cancel all my appointments and return to Sydney. He wanted me to work some special project with him, said it was vital I appear at the mines."

"You said no," Derek said with a smirk.

When Nic's expression mirrored Derek's, Shay couldn't get over the similarities between them.

"I said no. I don't answer to Bart. I run my portion of the corporation and he doesn't tell me what to do. And when I need downtime, I take it. Which is why you found me surfing," he said, turning his gaze to Shay.

Why did Shay get the feeling this was all preordained? That they were in this place right now because they were supposed to be? That maybe Bart had Nic right where he wanted him, despite Nic's refusal to toe the line?

She shuddered as a vision tried to appear.

Not now. She didn't want to deal with it, and pushed it away by rubbing her temples with her fingers.

"Shay, what's wrong?" Gina asked.

"Nothing. Just a little headache."

Nic wrapped his arms around her. "You're getting a vision, aren't you?"

"No. I'm trying *not* to get one."

"Isn't that kind of counterproductive to what we're doing here?" Ryder asked as he reentered the room.

She shot him a glare. "Easy for you to say. You don't get them." She concentrated hard on eliminating the incessant call of the vision. This one was relentless, and making it go away was doubly hard since Nic was touching her.

"Shay, let it happen." Nic's voice, the feel of his skin on hers, was soothing, lulling her into a sense of comfort and ease. She so wanted to let go, to relax and do what he asked. But still she hesitated, knowing what awaited her on the other side.

"I can't." She shook it off, blinked and pushed out of his grasp. "I just can't go there."

God, she hated that weakness within herself, the fear

that if she went with the vision, it would show her a future, an ending to all this that she didn't want to see.

An end to Nic. Or a complete demonic transformation that would require his destruction.

No, that she didn't want to know about. She wouldn't deliver that kind of news to the demon hunters. She wouldn't betray Nic that way.

Lou stood in front of her, frowning. "Tell me what you've seen before."

She looked at Nic, who nodded. "Go ahead. Say it."

"Nic surrounded by demons in a cave. I'm there, too. He and I are trying to get out, at least in some of the visions, but lately—"

She hated this, hated telling them. Nic's gaze was calm and encouraging, letting her know it was okay.

"The last one I had, Ben was there beside Nic. Nic turned demon, and came after me. He told me I belonged with him, that he wanted me to become like him. I left the vision after that, so I don't know what happened—and I haven't allowed any more."

Nic knew Shay wanted to protect him, but she couldn't. Not from this. He turned to Lou and Derek. "Is that what's going to happen to me? Is Ben going to reappear and make me like him?"

Lou shook his head. "We won't let that happen."

"Lou's right," Derek said. "I fought it. You can, too. Just because Shay can see what *might* happen, doesn't mean it will. We'll change it."

Change the future? Could that even be done? Everything that had happened in Nic's life over the past few days was so far-fetched he didn't know what could and couldn't happen anymore. But he did know one thing for sure. He moved to Derek, pulled him away from the others, and kept his voice low. "I don't want to live that way. I don't want to become like those...things. Like Dad. If it comes to that...you'll take care of it, right?"

Derek gave a sharp nod. "I'll take care of it."

"Thanks."

Nic started to turn back toward the others, but Derek held on to his arm. "But it won't come to that. Trust me."

Powerful emotion swept through Nic as another memory swept across his mind. He and Derek, outside on a tire swing that flew over a lake. Nic was scared to do it. He could swim, but he'd never catapulted into the lake before.

"Come on, Nic, just swing and jump."

"I'm scared."

"Don't be a sissy. It's easy."

Derek stood waist high in the water, having already made his jump. Nic wanted to be like Derek. He looked up to his big brother.

"I'll be here to catch you if anything goes wrong."

"You promise?"

Derek smiled at him. "Trust me."

The memory evaporated, but remained locked in Nic's head.

"I remember you," he said, looking up at the adult Derek. "A tire swing by the lake."

Derek grinned. "You were always afraid to jump."

"You told me to trust you. Did I jump?"

Derek nodded. "Yeah, you did."

And Derek had been right there to catch him, just as he promised.

Would he be there for Nic now? He wanted to believe his brother.

His brother. God, he couldn't believe how much his life had changed in the course of a few short days. This was all real. He had no doubts now.

Derek really was his brother. The memories were starting to come back. He couldn't deny them any longer— didn't want to, in fact. All the years lost. Why had Ben done this to him, to both of them?

Too many questions. He had to have patience, knowing eventually he'd have the answers. Now wasn't the time.

"I had faith that you would watch over me then," Nic said. "I still do now."

It was time to go to the mines and see this through.

Bart stood and waited for the dark-haired beauty to enter his office, waving off the two guards who'd accompanied her.

Aboveground and in the human world, he had to act differently. Pleasant, cordial. She wasn't aware yet of who she was dealing with.

The woman entered and he smiled, tamping down the excitement at seeing her. She had no idea who and what she was, or what she would become. Ah, the plea-sure of manipulation. One of the things he enjoyed most.

"Sit down."

She remained where she was. "I don't have much time. I'd rather stand."

"As you wish. Have you found it yet?"

"No. But I'm close. I've found diamonds very similar to the one you're looking for."

"I'm not paying you to get close. I'm paying you to find it."

"And I will. But if you keep calling me into these meetings it will delay my progress. Can I go now?"

She really was a lovely little spitfire. Raw and un-tamed and rather wild-looking. He'd like to keep her for himself. Too bad that wasn't possible, all things in this matter being preordained.

"You do realize there's a deadline, and a bonus in this for you if you find it before then."

She crossed her arms, her long tapered fingers tap-ping against her skin. "Like I said. You're wasting my time here."

Bart fought back a laugh. Oh, yes, he was definitely going to enjoy her. In as patronizing a manner as he could muster, he said, "My apologies. Do go back to work. I'll look forward to hearing from you very soon."

Her eyes flashed fire. She pivoted and left his office without another word, anger and frustration emanating from her. He inhaled it, absorbed it, along with her sweet scent.

Soon, everything he desired would be under his control. Power, his place in the hierarchy.

And the lovely woman who'd just stormed from the room.

Angelique didn't frighten easily. Bart scared the crap out of her. Now that she knew who and what he was, she was beyond wary.

When his men pulled her out of that tunnel—or rather dragged her forcibly out of that tunnel, claiming she was being "rescued"—she knew better. She was being kidnapped and forced into slavery.

She didn't even have time to scream for help. They'd yanked her by the arms and jerked her through some secret passage—how had she and Ryder missed that before? The wall had immediately closed in front of her, shutting her off from Ryder.

Without a word, they'd spirited her away to Bart's office in the mines. She'd protested and claimed they'd left Ryder there, but Bart told her Ryder had been rescued by the Diavolo security team, and that Bart needed her back on the job she'd been hired to do—finding the black diamond.

At first she'd thought about telling him where to shove it, but knowing what she did about him, about what the black diamond meant to him, she'd reconsidered. She knew they weren't going to let her go, anyway. If she told Bart that she knew who he was, he'd dispose of her, or maybe turn her into one of those . . . creatures.

She'd made a critical error in judgment accepting this assignment. She didn't work for the bad guys—that was Isabelle's territory, and frankly, she was surprised Isabelle wasn't lurking around here somewhere trying to find the black diamond herself. Angelique still wasn't convinced Izzy wasn't here. She hoped not. That's all she'd need to top off what had turned out to be a real mess of a project.

Nevertheless, she'd screwed up. It was her responsibility to make it right. The only way to assure the Sons of Darkness didn't get the black diamond was for her to find it and keep it away from them.

So she kept her mouth shut, played dumb, and thanked Bart for the rescue. She told him she was ready to get back to work, that finding the diamond was essential and she was looking forward to presenting it to the museum.

He'd bought her sense of urgency. After all, she was an archaeologist with a love of history. A find like the black diamond was important to her.

Now if he would just leave her alone long enough to do it.

Unfortunately, she was now guarded. That she hadn't expected, but she'd find a way around that problem when the time came.

First, the black diamond. It was so close she could smell it, could feel the tingle of the find vibrating in her bones. Though it wasn't some kind of magical talent, she had a sixth sense about these things. She knew she was in the right place. Wandering around this cave with Ryder, she had felt something quiver inside her. The way the walls looked—dark, like glittering coal. It was here, she knew it.

She was going to find it, and very soon.

Once she did, she'd figure out a way to get the black diamond into the hands of the Realm of Light.

She'd prove to Ryder that she wasn't in this for money, or power. It was important that he know she was on the side of the good guys.

Chapter Twenty-Two

They were in the mines. Shay was excited, nervous, yet ready for whatever was going to happen. Nic had walked them in through the high-security front entrance and into the offices, where they were given guest badges with full access. Nic was responsible for them, but as one of the owners of Diavolo Diamonds, he had carte blanche. He could take his guests anywhere, including down into the excavation part of the mine itself, no questions asked.

Perfect. No one batted an eyelash as—weapons stored in their bags—they passed through the security offices behind Nic and headed into the harsh daylight of the outer mine area.

They stood in an open pit of rusty orange, with rising steps of rock surrounding them.

"Welcome to the Diavolo mines," Nic said.

"Okay," Derek said, looking around. "Where do we start?"

"Most of our crews are excavating over on the east side, using our traditional open-pit mining, which is all aboveground. I checked the schedule for underground excavation. No one is assigned down there for the next week, so we'll be completely alone."

Nic led them to a massive elevator, large enough for all of them to pile in and still have room for a lot more people. He pressed the button and the elevator started down.

The ride took a while, Shay's stomach doing flip-flops the entire way. She knew it was nerves, and not the ride, causing her anxiety.

Maybe she should have allowed the vision, though it would have probably been the same one again. She didn't want to see it anymore. No matter what her vision told her, that wasn't what was going to happen.

Nic wasn't going to become like his father.

While the elevator descended, they pulled their weapons, strapped on holsters, and loaded extra ammo. By the time they reached the bottom, Shay was fully armed and ready for anything.

She hoped.

It was dark and cold, kind of like being in a cellar. Rather than using their lights, they'd slipped on their night-vision shades in case they ran into demons. Though it was bright daylight topside, they could potentially run into demons down here, since it was cool and dark. Demons wouldn't need to hide out away from the light and heat, no matter the time of day.

Twenty-four-hour demon threat. Great.

They moved along the tunnels, but they hadn't walked for more than ten minutes when sharp pain struck Shay's temples. She halted, blinked, and moved on. But with each subsequent step Shay experienced a profound sense of dread she simply couldn't push aside, like she had with other visions. It was weakening her to the point she had to stop and lean against the wall. She felt closed in, suffocated, unable to breathe.

Something was trying to get at her, through her. A vision that would not be ignored.

Nic was at her side in an instant, grasping her around the shoulders as she sank to the floor.

"Shay, what's wrong?"

She shook her head, trying to pry his hands loose. "Don't touch me." His touch sent the visions careening toward her like a violent storm, dizzying her even more.

He pulled his hands away and she forced normal breathing. In through her nose, out through her mouth. Passing out would be such a bad thing right now.

"Is she all right?" Gina asked, crouching down beside her and pressing a cool hand to her face.

"I think it's her visions," Nic answered.

Shay gazed up at Nic, at the lines of worry furrowing his brow. She closed her eyes to block everyone out. She wanted to reassure Nic that it was nothing, but she couldn't.

"Shay."

Lou's voice was a quiet balm in the storm of her head.

"Shay, listen to me. Your visions are calling to you. You must heed them."

Squinting her eyes harder, she brought her knees up to her chest and hugged them tight. "I know."

It hurt. The pain was like a hot knife in her head. The more she fought against it, the more it sliced through her.

Lou reached for her hands, his touch comforting. "Let me help you. Let me go with you."

She shook her head. "I have to do this alone."

"No, you don't. You just think you're alone. You're not. I can go with you."

"Nic. He—"

"I know, child, I know. Let me see."

Lou's voice, so gentle and caring, so much like her father's, before . . . before he had stopped caring. She let Lou in, and let him take the journey with her.

This time it was different. She stood in front of a door, opened it, and she and Lou descended and traveled through the tunnels. It was as if she knew exactly where she was going. Though they were still in the caves, she found herself in a big room, decorated lavishly, complete with a throne. Standing next to the throne was Nic, his hands on a glowing blue orb, his eyes lost in that demon kind of way that always made her shiver. Demons were all around, focusing on Nic.

And behind him stood Bart, and Ben, their faces also demon, and grinning with pure evil satisfaction as Nic reached out his hand to Shay.

"You belong to me, with me. I claim you."

Shay shook her head, wanting out of this vision now. The force of evil in the room was too intense to bear.

"Wait. Watch. Pay attention to Nic," Lou instructed.

Through the haze of demons, Shay focused on Nic. Much as she hated to see him that way, his face distorted by the demon mask, his fangs dripping, his forehead knotty and bulging, still she forced herself to watch him as he seemed to revel in the demons' adoration.

"I present your king," Ben said to the demons. They cheered while Nic kept his hand on that glowing ball, his expression triumphant and utterly cold.

Nic's gaze settled on Shay.

Then he changed. Something in his eyes, no longer red with evil, but clear blue like a sunlit ocean.

And beseeching her.

That's when she heard him in her head.

Shay, help me. Get me out of here.

He wasn't like them. He didn't want to be there.

Lou turned to her. "He needs you to get through this. Don't lose faith in him."

The vision evaporated, and Shay found herself on the ground with Lou holding her hand. The rest of the hunters looked down on her with a mixture of concern and curiosity on their faces.

She nodded at Lou and he helped her stand.

"Are you all right?" Nic asked, reaching out a hand to her, then hesitating.

Shay slid her hand in his and smiled. "Yes. I'm fine."

"You want to tell us what you saw?" Derek asked.

She'd seen what she needed to see. She knew what she had to do now.

"It's going to be all right," she said to Nic, needing him to know that first. "But it'll get bad before it gets better."

She filled them in on what she saw, but kept her gaze on Nic as she did. His eyes widened as he listened, then he shook his head.

"I'm going to turn into a demon."

"That's what my vision showed."

"I'm going to fight it." He glanced up at Derek. "I *am* going to beat this. They're not going to take me."

Derek laid a hand on Nic's shoulder. "You won't be doing it alone. We'll all be right there with you."

Nic nodded and seemed to relax.

Lou was right. She'd needed to see that vision, to know what was coming. Nic would need her help to get through this, in ways she didn't yet understand.

But no matter what it was, she wouldn't let him down.

Nic was more determined than ever to take control of the situation, especially after seeing what Shay had just gone through. She'd carried the burden long enough.

After she told him what she'd seen, the lines of strain had eased from her expression, and the smile she cast in his direction seemed genuine. She believed he could beat this. That was good. Maybe in her mind, her vision represented a light at the end of all this—a happy ending.

He really wanted that happy ending.

A sense of urgency drove him, as if there was some-
place he needed to be. He pushed on without a word,
letting his instincts guide him.

And his gut told him they needed to go down. But
down where? They were already as deep as the elevators
went, as far as the crews had dug.

There had to be something below this, and some way
to get down there.

"In my vision I saw a door and went through it," Shay
said.

Nic nodded. "Start checking the corners around these
tunnels. Look for a doorway. We need to go down."

"Aren't we already as deep as we can go?" Derek asked.

"That's what I thought. But we need to go farther.
Whatever we're looking for is deeper than this."

He wished he could figure out how he knew that, but
there was definitely something driving him. Almost like
an unbearable itch—and if he didn't scratch it soon, he
was going to go nuts.

They walked the tunnels until there was a split—right
or left.

He looked to Shay.

"Left," she said.

Good choice. They hadn't moved far when they found
a short corridor. They followed it, and found a door.

"That's the one I saw," Shay said.

It took some maneuvering—the door looked as if it
hadn't been opened in ages—but they managed to pry it

loose. Dirt flew out from the other side as they swung it open, creating a cloud around them as they passed through. Nic stayed at the door until they'd all moved inside, then he pulled it shut, erasing any evidence of their being in the area.

The ladder was metal at least, though it didn't look all that solid. The drop was steep, at least a hundred feet. Nic followed them down, taking one step at a time and hoping like hell the damn thing didn't fall apart before he reached the bottom. It wiggled a few times, but otherwise held.

He was grateful for the night-vision glasses when he reached the bottom, because there was nothing down there but utter blackness. The ground was firm and rocky under his feet, albeit a bit dusty. They were in a fairly decent-size, hollowed-out room, no doubt once used to transport ore up to the surface. Long pipes were situated in various spots around the room, as well as containers connected to the bottom of the pipes. Other than that, nothing but a wide shaft leading somewhere else.

"Now what?" Derek asked him.

"We walk."

They moved out of that room and through the shaft, maneuvering between oversize rails that must have been used to transport the trucks of rock.

"They mined down here sometime in the past," Nic said. "Though it looks like this section has been shut down for a while."

Abandoned mine shaft. Good place to stage . . . whatever the Sons of Darkness had in mind.

Nic had a feeling he'd found the right location.

Shay felt the weight of the mountain pressing down on top of her and hoped like hell the ceiling above them was well reinforced. Thoughts of a cave-in were first and foremost on her mind, especially when small trails of dirt and tiny pebbles trickled down in front of her.

Suddenly she couldn't breathe. But it wasn't from fear of being smothered by rocks. She laid her hand on Nic's arm, but before she could get the words out, Lou spoke.

"Demons."

Everyone stopped.

"Quiet," Derek commed. "Get out of sight."

They flattened themselves against the walls. Seconds later, hybrid demons appeared from one of the caverns up ahead. One by one they filed out, each carrying boulders, just like the demons had done at the caves. Shay wrinkled her nose at the stench of them.

What were they doing? Clearing out the room? Hunting for the diamond?

One demon stopped, craned its head in their direction, and stared down the shaft. Shay stopped breathing as long seconds passed. Did it see them?

Finally, it turned and walked down the shaft in the other direction, entering another tunnel. The hunters still couldn't move, though, because once they dropped off the boulders the demons came back and reentered the original room. Now what were the hunters going to do? Go back the way they came, try to slip past that room unnoticed, or engage the demons?

"Get your weapons ready," Derek ordered. "Let's find out what they're doing in there."

And there was her answer. She pulled her laser off her shoulder and rested her finger on the trigger. Heart racing, adrenaline pumping, she was ready. She took a quick glance at Nic, who seemed calm. He was even smiling, as if he was looking forward to what was coming. She shook her head. What was it about men and war games?

Derek pushed off from the wall, Nic moving ahead right behind him with Gina and Shay taking up positions flanking them. The rest of the hunters fell in line, and they stepped carefully, trying not to alert the demons to their presence. Shay hoped none of them came out with those big boulders in their arms. One toss of those monstrous things and several hunters could be crushed.

Almost there; just a few more feet and Derek would make the entrance.

Suddenly, he doubled back, pushing them all backward as demons rounded the corner.

Oh, God. They were going to have to engage in this tight tunnel. Weapons raised, they took position. Shay made careful note of where the other hunters were, as the demons spilled out of the room and moved toward them. She took aim and fired, hitting one point-blank in the chest with her laser. She heard weapons fire around her, but concentrated on one demon at a time, watching one stall, but continue to come at her. She hit it again, this time satisfied when it began to melt.

More were coming, and laser fire was zinging near her ears and around her head. They couldn't let these demons back them up into the room they'd come from. They'd be cornered with no way out but back up the ladder. And the idea was forward progress, not backward. They had to fight them here. With determination she melted one, then another, working two at a time while dipping to avoid laser fire from other hunters.

Nic's arm snaked around her waist and pushed her down, bending over her to fire his microwave at a demon. She pivoted, firing while still underneath him at an approaching demon.

This was insane, but somehow it was working. Every demon that poured from the room was going down. More importantly, the hunters weren't having to back up.

Panting, fighting for breath, Shay and the others waited for more demons to round the corner and come at them.

None did.

Still, they waited, armed and ready for a second round of attacks. When none came, Derek signaled and they stood.

"Let's head in," he said.

Shay realized she was still under Nic. He lifted her, removed his arm from around her. She turned to him, grinning and he planted a quick kiss on her lips.

"We work well together," he said.

"Yeah, we do." It was almost as if she'd been able to

anticipate his movements and make her own accordingly. Pretty damn cool.

Derek edged once again to the entrance of the room. He stopped, peering around the corner, then motioned them forward. They crept into the room, not making a sound. Once in, Shay scanned the entire area. The room was huge, but not empty. Demons were at the far wall, their backs turned to the hunters, allowing them to make entry without being noticed. They seemed to be surrounding something, or someone, but she couldn't make out what it was. More large rocks were scattered to the sides of the room, piled on top of each other. A low rumbling came from the center of the demons, almost as if they were in a huddle, murmuring. Which was kind of odd because as far as Shay knew, the hybrid demons never spoke.

No one moved. Shay supposed Derek was waiting for the demons to turn around and figure out the hunters were there. Her finger hovered on the trigger of her laser, ready to target one of the hulking beasts and blast it to melted death. She knew there were hunters behind her with their backs turned, minding the entrance to this room in case more demons entered. Now it was just a matter of time until the show started.

Finally, the demon pile opened in unison, half of them moving in one direction, the other half in another, perfectly orchestrated, almost like a dance line. She'd have laughed if it wasn't so bizarre.

But the demons didn't come at them, instead lining up against the far wall. And in the center of their group was Nic's uncle Bart. Dressed as he had been earlier, in desert camouflage, he stepped out of the circle of demons and into the center of the room.

Seemingly out of the rock walls, demons appeared. Hybrids, pure, and half demons filled the room. Shay and the others pointed their weapons, but the hunters were clearly outnumbered. Where the hell had the demons come from?

Chapter Twenty-Three

S hit," Nic whispered.

Shay tore her gaze away from the man and looked at Nic.

"I'd like to say I'm shocked to see you, Bart, but I'm not," Nic said, cracking a half smile.

"Dominic, how nice of you to come to me."

"You led me here."

Bart sniffed, lifting his chin. "Of course I did."

Nic wasn't surprised. This whole thing had been preordained by the Sons of Darkness. That's why he'd felt compelled to find the underground. Was it some kind of mind connection with the demons? Were they taking control of him?

If so, he had to fight it. He was stronger than that. Shay inched closer to him, her shoulder brushing his. Derek stepped to his other side. The contact was reassuring.

These were his people, the ones he cared about. He needed to remember that.

Nic held still as Bart moved toward him. The hunters raised their weapons, but Nic held up his hand.

"He's not going to hurt me," Nic said.

"Of course I'm not going to hurt you. We've been worried about you; we couldn't find you after Louis and his minions took off with you. Darkness only knows what they did to you while you were in their grasp."

"Your show of family warmth is . . . interesting, Uncle Bart." Especially considering his uncle was one of the coldest men Nic had ever known.

"You have no idea how important you are to our family, Dominic. We need you here, especially now. I assume they've told you what they did to your father."

"That he's dead? Yes."

Bart nodded, leveling a venom-filled glare at Lou. "They will pay for what they've done." He turned his gaze to Nic and smiled. "But that will occur later. This is your time."

"My time for what?"

Bart reached for Nic but Nic stepped back and Bart dropped his hand. "I'll fill you in on that soon. I'm so glad you're here. And that you brought hostages. They can bear witness to what the Sons of Darkness have planned for you." Bart motioned to the demons nearby. "Guard them while I talk with Dominic. He and I have much to discuss."

"I don't fucking think so," Derek warned, raising his laser.

Nic's gaze shot to Derek. He shook his head. Though he wasn't sure what his uncle was up to, now wasn't the time for battle. Something told him they should wait, that if they tried right now it would be devastating to the hunters. He wanted to find out what Bart's plan was, and if he had the black diamond yet.

Plus, Nic had to protect Shay. And the Realm of Light.

"Don't hurt them," he said to his uncle. "If you do, you'll get no cooperation from me."

Bart's tight smile was less than sincere. "I promise you no harm will come to them."

Nic nodded and followed Bart to the back of the room, the other hunters being herded along behind him. Bart raised his hand and the solid rock wall shimmered, becoming transparent.

Uh, okay. That was interesting. Bart stepped through, motioning for Nic.

Since it appeared the Sons of Darkness had "big plans" for him, it wouldn't be likely they wanted to crush him within a mountain of rock. He stepped through the portal, making sure the others followed. The wall solidified behind them.

Walking through a stone wall was an interesting experience. Kind of a high, actually. This whole otherworldly demon thing was kind of cool. Except for the evil part, of course. Nic felt as if he was dreaming, like this whole thing wasn't really happening. But it was.

The room they occupied now was lavish, completely furnished but still in the cave. Tall, golden columns stood floor to ceiling, reaching up as high as Nic could see. Thick velvet draped from one column to the next. Black, cloth-covered tables were loaded with the most decadent of foods, golden-encrusted, velvet-covered chairs at each table. A roasted pig centered the main table against the back of the room; huge goblets were filled with dark liquid. It looked like they were readying for a feast.

Just like Shay's vision described: the throne room.

"As you can see, we've prepared for you," Bart said, splaying his hand out to showcase the room.

Nic frowned and scratched his head. "Uh-huh."

"Your arrival was timely. Everything is in place."

What the hell. He'd play along. "Good to know."

"After the transition, we will celebrate."

Okay, this was making him crazy. "You do realize I have no fucking idea what you're talking about."

The smirk his uncle shot his way was so goddamn annoying Nic thought about melting him on the spot with his laser.

"Of course you have no idea. You've never known what our plan was for you. That was intentional, ever since your father took you. Though with your father's untimely demise, things didn't quite work out the way we'd planned. Our timeline had to be moved up a bit. We can no longer wait. You must take his place now."

Hearing the affirmation of what Derek told him was like a kick to his stomach. And more bits of memory flashed in his brain, lightning-hot zaps of pain accompanying them. His father's voice waking him up, but when he opened his eyes it was a hideous monster looming over his bed. The feeling of utter terror. Then a hand over his face before he could scream and everything went black. He was starting to remember. "Why?"

"Let's prepare you for the event, then I'll explain." Bart's face softened. "I'm sorry your father can't be here for this. He waited a very long time to bring you into the fold. You were his favorite, and he counted on you to sit as his right hand, Dominic. He wanted to be the one to help you through the revelation." Bart cast a glare at the others.

"Nevertheless, he would be very proud of you right now, knowing you came back to us, that you had fought the Realm of Light to make your way home. You instinctively knew how much we needed you. Your connection to the Sons of Darkness is strong. You're going to be an incredible asset."

Nic didn't have anything to do with their being here. Or did he? Had he inadvertently been leading them here all along? Had he led them all into a trap?

Fuck, he hoped not.

No. He'd led them to this place to fight the Sons of Darkness, to end this nightmare once and for all.

"Everything's in place," Bart said, looking around the room. "We're ready to begin."

"I have questions." And he needed to delay whatever the hell Bart had planned. Because Nic had no plan for escape yet. And getting out of this was paramount. He felt the pull to the other hunters, the need to join with them. Funny how being with his "family" meant being with Shay, with Derek and the other hunters, not with his uncle.

Shay's visions were wrong. He didn't belong with the Sons of Darkness. They weren't going to claim him.

"I'll answer them soon enough. This event will not unfold in a hurry." Bart gestured to the far wall where an ornate, velvet-covered chair sat. "Shall we?"

Although Nic felt like the lamb being led to slaughter, he allowed Bart to seat him on what looked like a throne. But if his uncle put a crown on his head, he was going to have to strangle him. There were limits to the amount of hokey ceremony a guy could put up with.

Bart was going down. Of that there was no doubt. It was just a matter of time. Nic was already antsy enough. Having to endure some kind of bullshit ritual to officially welcome him into the fold was more than he could tolerate. But he'd put up with it until the hunters got the information they needed, figured out what the plan was; then they'd attack.

"Let's bring your friends in closer now, and our family."

Nic assumed by "our family" Bart was referring to the demons. Sorry, no feeling of blood kin there. Just the need for some blood spilling.

"Come closer, everyone," Bart said. "We're just about to start. Please move forward."

Nic noticed the frown on Shay's face and the way Derek's brows arched in confusion. He didn't blame them. If he was looking at one of the hunters perched on this gilded throne he'd wonder the same thing they were probably wondering—had he switched sides and decided to become a Lord of the Sons of Darkness? But he couldn't reassure them right now, because it was paramount Bart believe Nic was part of the demon team.

Nic just hoped the hunters trusted in him. That Shay believed in his ability to get them all out of this.

They stepped forward, the demons surrounding the hunters. Interesting thing was, the demons hadn't taken the hunters' weapons away. Maybe they didn't see the hunters as a threat because they were so outnumbered right now, or maybe they sensed there wasn't going to be a battle.

Not yet, anyway.

"Dominic," Bart started, facing him. "I know you have questions. Ben wanted to make you one of us. But your mind refused to accept what you saw when you were taken by him all those years ago. You blocked it out, refused to recognize the demons around you.

"When he took you, it was . . . traumatic for you. You crawled inside yourself, shut us out. It was as if we didn't exist. After that happened, Ben and I discussed it and felt that when the time was right, you'd remember, you'd accept. Ben wanted to wait until the memories came back to you naturally."

So that's why he'd been uninformed for so long, why he'd never known the truth about his father. And why he had the gaps in memory, why his father had made up the story about his head injury and amnesia.

"Unfortunately, we ran out of time. Your father was killed, leaving the Sons of Darkness without one Lord.

You must take his place. The time is now. We can wait no longer.

"The Diavolo power is yours to control. You were born destined to lead as one of the Sons of Darkness. You were specifically created with this power, a special magic inside you to control this one special event. You need to take the helm, now that your father has been ripped away from us by these heathens from the Realm of Light. These people who claim to be your friends," Bart said, pointing to the hunters, "killed your father. They captured you in an attempt to use you to annihilate the rest of your family. To destroy you. They do not care for you, Dominic. Do not allow yourself to fall victim to their lies, or they will do the same to you as they did to your father. Remember who your family is. We need you. Your father needs you, Dominic."

"Yes, Nic. I need you."

Nic's ears perked up at the familiar voice. He gripped the arm of the chair and looked around, certain he hadn't heard it.

"Nic, I'm here."

"They said you were dead," he whispered. Wasn't he?

"I'm not dead, Nic. Not really. They cannot silence a Lord of the Sons of Darkness."

If his father was alive, Nic wouldn't just be hearing a voice. Ben would be there, in human form. Nic closed his eyes, forcing the voice away. "You're not my father. You're not here. You all are screwing with me."

"The only ones screwing with you are the Realm of Light. Don't listen to them. They don't care about you. I waited forever for this moment. From before your conception I knew who and what you'd be one day. The reason I mated with a human was to create children who could dominate both demons and humans.

"There was a plan, and it was a great plan. One that had you standing by my side."

Nic didn't want to listen to any of this. It was bizarre; it freaked him out; it was way too much like his nightmares. He looked toward Shay, toward Derek, saw them staring at him. Shay was wide-eyed with shock, Derek's gaze narrowed with anger. They heard, too.

"They took it all away from me," Ben continued. "You were supposed to stand at my side and take your place on the throne."

"You're not here." Nic didn't want to believe any of this. He wanted to relegate it to the place where his unconscious mind enveloped the unreality of it all. Where he could blow it off to a dream state and nothing more.

His father's soft laugh was so close it almost felt like it was inside him.

"Of course I'm here. I have to be here to see you transition into one of the Lords. You never did realize how much you meant to me, Nic—you thought I didn't care. But I do care. I took you instead of Derek because I knew how important you were to our cause. I created you. I kept you close to me, let you do anything you wanted, let you have the world—every excess you could ever desire.

"You've grown into a fine man, and I'm so proud of you. You will lead the Diavolo Corporation into unimaginable wealth. You will lead the Sons of Darkness into indescribable power. Take your birthright, Nic. I need you. You are more important to me than life itself."

Ben's words sickened Nic. He felt dizzy, nauseous, closed in. The fact that Ben's blood ran in his veins made him want to turn his laser on himself. He was part demon—that he couldn't deny any longer. His nightmares were coming true. His father really wanted him to stand in darkness with him and lead beside him as some demonic king.

Anguish churned inside him. All he'd ever wanted was to feel needed, to be important and necessary—to feel as if he belonged to the family. To feel loved by a father who had never loved him, never had time for him, never showed him any affection.

Now his father was dead, or some semblance of dead, and he picked this moment to show his love?

Hell of a time for this revelation.

And a lifetime too late. How stupid did Ben think he was? Did he look like a fucking sheep? His eyes were wide open to the truth now. His father wasn't capable of love. Not the kind of love he saw in Shay's eyes. Not the kind of family, the kind of acceptance he'd found with his brother. With Ben he'd known nothing but distance. Loneliness. His uncle Bart had never been anything more than an empty shell.

And this whole mind meld with his father? What a bunch of bullshit.

Nic was no idiot. He might have been able to get a glimpse of the future thanks to Shay's visions, but that didn't mean the future was set in stone. It could be changed.

He *would* change it. What Shay had seen wasn't going to come true.

He opened his eyes and smiled, looking at nothing and no one, as if he were channeling the dead.

"Father. I remember. I know what my place is, where my future lies. I'm ready now."

Shay searched Nic's face, trying to get him to make eye contact with her. But he stared straight ahead, refusing to look at her.

They'd all heard Ben's voice and the conversation Nic had with his father. With Derek's father. Gina had her hand clasped with Derek's, both of them looking a little pale. After the battle they'd fought with Ben on the island, Shay couldn't imagine what the two of them must be going through, hearing Ben's voice again.

Bart bent over Nic, whispering. Shay couldn't hear what they were saying. Ben's voice had gone silent. Did that mean he was gone? Had he ever really been here?

Could the demon dead rise?

"Lou, was that really Ben?" Shay asked.

"Yes and no" was all he said in his typical cryptic way.

"Is this another one of those things like the force?" Ryder asked. "When they die, their essence remains?"

Lou snorted. "Something like that. The evil is always there. Ben's core is gone, but he remains within the Sons of Darkness. He holds no power, can wield no magic, but he can still speak, though only on occasion and with some difficulty. It takes strong forces to amass the dead. I imagine that bringing Ben forth even for such a short period of time has weakened the Sons of Darkness, because he could not return of his own volition."

Relief washed over Shay. "Good to know."

"I'd hate to have to kill him again," Gina said, gripping her laser more tightly.

"I'd be glad to," Derek added. "He's fucking with Nic, isn't he?"

Lou nodded. "In a manner of speaking. The Sons of Darkness are trying to manipulate his emotions, to bind him to them. You know how Dominic was tied to his father all these years. He was the only family Dominic knew."

"But is Nic buying into all this?" Trace asked, his hands tightening on the trigger of his laser. "Is he one of them now?"

"He hasn't changed. He won't change. He's playing them," Shay said to all of them in a harsh whisper. "Don't you see that? He had to accept what we said on faith. Now we have to have faith in him. It's our turn to believe in him, despite what we see."

Even if Nic didn't look her way, she still kept her gaze focused on him. She wanted him to see her, wanted him to know.

"I believe in you, Nic," she whispered. "I know you're on our side."

"If you're ready, Dominic, we will begin," Bart said.

Nic nodded.

A heavy stone table was brought out by several of the hybrids and set in front of Nic.

"Our altar, where we will conduct the ceremony. And thanks to our new friend, we now have the black diamond with which to create the magic."

Shay's eyes widened as Angelique was dragged into the room by two demons. She shook them off, seemingly unafraid of them as she wrinkled her nose. "You bastards stink."

The demons pushed her toward the hunters. She moved by Ryder, shaking her head as if to ask for their silence.

"I'll explain later," she said.

Where had she been all this time? And why did Ryder look so angry?

"Look at the size of that rock," Gina said. "Is that the black diamond?"

"Yes," Angelique answered.

It was the size of a bowling ball, chunky and uneven and dull. Not brilliant and beautiful like Shay expected it to look. And not at all like the glowing, brilliant orb she'd seen in her vision.

"That's mine," Angelique said, glaring at Bart.

"Of course it is. And you will get your hands on it again tonight. You have a destiny, my beauty. That's the reason I hired you. You were meant to be here."

"You told me this diamond was to be taken to a museum. We had a contract."

Bart's lips twitched. "You do not yet understand what is happening, Angelique. You will. Be patient."

"A goddamn treasure hunter," Ryder said, shaking his head at Angelique. "I should have known."

"I am *not* a treasure hunter."

"Where have you been? How did you get out of the tunnels?"

"His men got me out through some secret passage in the hole, then guarded me while I searched for the black diamond. Which *I* found and *I* claim," she finished loud enough for Bart to hear.

Bart didn't respond, just turned his back to her and placed the rock on the table in front of Nic.

"Babe, you have no idea what you've just been thrust into the middle of," Ryder said. "You'll wish you weren't here soon enough, trust me."

"I already wish a lot of things were different." She crossed her arms and clamped her lips together.

"Where did you find it?" Lou asked.

"In a cave near where Ryder and I had been stuck. When Bart took me out of those tunnels and put me back to work to find it, I wanted to grab it and bring it to you," she said to Ryder.

"Uh-huh. Sure you did."

"You have to believe me."

"Why should I?"

"We don't have time for arguing right now," Lou whispered. "We'll settle this later."

Shay's head spun with all that was happening. Nic seemingly under some kind of spell, the black diamond found, Angelique taking part in all of it—how were they going to get out of this?

"Now that we have the black diamond, we can begin," Bart said, capturing her attention once again. "Having Dominic here means the magic can be fully harnessed. Dominic is the catalyst. As Ben explained, Dominic was created with an inherent power to meld with the black diamond and strengthen the demons. We needed someone who was half demon and half human to meld with the diamond."

"What's he talking about?" Derek asked Lou.

"The legend says that the black diamond was forged by a battle between one of the Sons of Darkness and one of the Realm of Light—demon and human—that it contains the essence of both. Its power cannot be triggered by just one or the other, but has to be a combination of both."

Bart stood over the rock, his eyes sharp and wide. "The black diamond will empower Dominic, will make all the Sons of Darkness more potent. The mix of his human and demon blood will allow him to rule over the sons of the earth and of darkness. Once Dominic joins hands with the Queen of Darkness, their touch will finish the Realm of Light. They will harness the power of the black diamond, and the portal between heaven and hell, between good and evil, will belong to the Lords of the Sons of Darkness."

"Oh, shit," Derek whispered. "Who the fuck is the Queen of Darkness?"

They all looked to Lou, his lips set in a grim line. That wasn't a positive sign. Lou was always supremely confident in the Realm of Light's ability to emerge victorious.

Not good at all. She needed Lou to tell them it was going to be all right. The Realm of Light had to win. The good guys always won. The stuff Bart was spouting about Sons of Darkness inheriting the earth and heaven and hell was all bullshit.

Wasn't it? Lou had to tell them they were going to come out on top. He *had* to.

But Lou was fixated on Bart right now, so she turned her gaze back to Nic, trying to get him to look at her.

Please, Nic.

Nothing.

The cold chill of fear crept into her bones.

Bart waved his hand over the rock and began chanting in a language she didn't understand. As soon as he started, Nic's gaze gravitated toward the black diamond. Fixated on it, his eyes widened. Shay willed his attention toward her, but he wouldn't look at her. Only at that damn black rock.

Bart continued to mumble in his strange language, and the demons behind and around them murmured. They didn't speak, just moaned, or hummed, or made some kind of weird noise. It was almost musical in an eerie kind of way. She shuddered, not liking this turn of events.

"Lou," she warned, "we need to do something."

"Wait, Shay. Just wait."

She didn't want to wait. Nic's expression grew more

remote with every passing second. She felt her connection to him weaken. She was losing him.

Angelique watched, mesmerized by what was happening. Ancient rituals had always fascinated her, and the beauty of the singing around her couldn't be denied. Such a lovely sound from such hideous creatures was an incredible thing.

But she had no time to marvel at this. Creatures that could not be real surrounded her, yet in her heart she knew they were. The demons Ryder had described really existed.

She felt responsible for all this. She'd found the black diamond. But what choice did she have? If she hadn't found it, Bart would have eventually.

Her plan had backfired. She'd been so certain of her ability to locate the diamond and turn it over to the demon hunters, to somehow spirit it away and make her escape. She'd gotten out of sticky situations all her life. She'd evaded treasure hunters trying to steal her find. She'd held her own when invaders came upon her at a dig site, trying to claim her artifacts. She'd even outsmarted Izzy a time or two when her sister tried to spirit away a valuable treasure Angelique had uncovered. Angelique thought this was just another situation she could manage to wrestle her way out of. She'd never lost before. She was confident in her ability to uncover the black diamond, hide it, and turn it over to Ryder.

But she was wrong. This was like nothing she'd ever experienced. She was in way over her head.

She'd managed to find the diamond; the guards' backs had been turned. It was huge, but she thought she could load it in the bag of tools and tell Bart she'd never found it. Unfortunately, two hulking demons had come out nowhere, scared the shit out of her, and snatched the diamond right out of her hands. Then she'd been locked up until they hauled her into this cave.

And now this chanting and some kind of odd ritual.

She had to do something to make it right. Bart had his eyes closed and head tilted back. This was a good time to make her move. If she could grab the diamond and make a run for it, she could hope the demon hunters would spring into action. Without the black diamond, Bart couldn't do anything, right?

She eased toward the table, pausing every few steps to make sure no one noticed.

They hadn't. In fact, no one seemed to be paying the slightest attention to her. Even Ryder was in a huddle with his own people. Strategizing, no doubt.

She edged closer to the table. The diamond was within reach now. She could snatch it and head for the exit. And maybe, just maybe, luck would be on her side again. Maybe Ryder and his people would choose that moment to start firing their weapons. Either way, she had to get out of here with the diamond.

Almost there. She reached out, her fingertips grazing the black rock.

But strong arms grabbed her around her middle. Bart's eyes shot open, revealing a hollow blackness that made her shudder and recoil as she was brought to stand before him. And merde, he was so cold! How had she not noticed that before?

"Why, thank you, Angelique. You're just where I wanted you." He turned to Nic. "Dominic, come over here."

Nic moved toward Bart. "Put your hand on the diamond."

Nic placed his palm over the diamond. Angelique's eyes widened as she heard a hum emanating from the rock and felt vibrations under her feet. "What's happening here?"

"You'll see soon enough." Bart's eyes gleamed with dark pleasure as the dirt began to fall away from the rock.

Angelique couldn't believe what she saw. The rock began to transform under Nic's hand, the black changing first to a deep purple, then a midnight blue, and finally to a brilliant, sea blue color. The shape changed, too, from irregular edges to smooth, glassy surfaces, as if she were seeing the diamond cut in front of her eyes, but without benefit of technology. She could see into it, the color swirling and moving within the orb.

It was beautiful. Her breath caught and held, and she felt if she didn't possess it she'd die.

"Lay your hand over Nic's, Angelique."

Anything. She'd do anything to draw closer to the diamond. She'd never seen a treasure like it. Something about it called to her, as if it were a living, breathing thing and she was a part of it. She placed her hands over Nic's, hoping like hell she could take the diamond and run.

But as soon as she touched it, the light within the orb began to dim.

"This isn't possible," Bart said.

Angelique dragged her gaze away from the diamond to look at Bart. He was frowning.

"What are you talking about?" she asked. She wanted, needed to touch that diamond again. She felt cold without it.

"The light within has died." Bart moved closer, grabbing Angelique's wrist in a tight hold and jamming her hand over Nic's.

"Hey. That hurts!"

"Nothing is happening!"

She had no idea what he was talking about. Just as she thought, the man was a lunatic.

"You are the one. You must be . . . but it's not working."

He was beyond insane, his eyes glowing with madness. She tried to jerk away but she couldn't. Fear coiled around her middle, turning her anger to dread. Bart squeezed her wrist so hard tears sprang up in her eyes.

She never, ever cried. But he was hurting her.

"Okay, that's enough."

Ryder. He was behind her, his hand on hers. And she felt safe.

"You are not invited." Bart turned his menacing glare on Ryder. "How dare you put your hand on the diamond?"

"I just invited myself. And she's done here." He slipped his fingers over Bart's. "Let her go. Now."

Ryder's dark gaze met Bart's. Angelique thought for a moment that Bart would strike Ryder. But Ryder didn't flinch or back away. He simply extricated Bart's hand from Angelique's and laced his fingers with hers. His grip felt strong and comforting. Disconcerting.

Bart cursed and pushed her into Ryder's arms. "Take her, then! She is not the one."

Ryder escorted her back to the others; she had never been happier to go where he led. He left his arm around her. No way was she going to shrug it off. She'd never felt so cold before.

"You okay?"

She nodded, her gaze fixated on Bart. "He's insane."

"He's way more than that."

"What's he talking about?" Angelique asked. "What did he mean by 'the one'?"

Ryder shrugged and looked at Lou.

"I don't know yet. Some kind of catalyst for the black diamond's magic, I would assume."

No, Angelique most definitely was not any kind of catalyst. The only magic she knew was the worthless card tricks her mother's friends had taught her as a child.

As far as her being "the one" . . . Bart was mistaken. He'd chosen the wrong woman. But he'd acted as if he expected her to be something or someone she wasn't. A sick feeling twisted inside her. It couldn't be, could it?

Yet even as she thought it, she knew the answer. It wasn't her Bart was after. He'd chosen the wrong woman.

He wanted Isabelle.

Chapter Twenty-Four

S hay had had just about enough of this whole thing. Nic and Angelique, the woman being or not being "the one," whatever the hell that meant. And Nic's eyes still held that hypnotized look, leading her to believe he was under some kind of spell.

Bart had clearly gone off the deep end. He was starting to act frantic, looking first at Nic, then at all of them. He uttered a low growl, then turned back to Nic.

"It doesn't matter," Bart said. "We needed the two of you to merge to bring the ultimate power to life. Hopefully, your strength alone will give us some of what we need, to empower the Sons of Darkness present."

"Lou," Shay pleaded. "What is he talking about?"

"He wanted to use Angelique. He thought she was the Queen of Darkness he spoke of. She wasn't. She had no power over the black diamond."

Why would Bart think Angelique was some queen of

darkness? Shay was so confused her head was pounding. She'd never seen anything like this in her visions.

"You need to push your hands into the diamond," Bart instructed Nic. "Absorb its power. Once you are fully one of us, your unique powers will in turn pass through all the demons, amplifying theirs. Then you will take your place as a Lord of the Sons of Darkness."

Nic shook his head. "Wait." He lifted his hand off the diamond and headed toward Shay. Though his gaze was still vacant, he stopped in front of her, wrapped his fingers around her wrist and dragged her to the table where the diamond stood. "This one has powers. Use her."

Holy crap. What the hell was he doing?

Bart frowned. "What kind of powers?"

"She has visions. She can see into the future."

"Ah. That can be useful, though it won't empower the black diamond. Do you realize what it means to select this human as your mate?" Bart asked.

Nic nodded. "Yes. I choose her, and I'm used to getting what I want."

Bart grinned. "I knew you would embrace your power. You're used to having the finest things in life, and trudging around in the dirt with the Realm of Light isn't going to give you the lifestyle you're accustomed to. Ben knew you so well. As a Lord of the Sons of Darkness, anything you wish for will be within your power. If you want this human woman for your demon bride, then by all means take her."

Shay blinked. She tried to jerk her wrist away from Nic, but his hold was like steel. He turned to her and she knew then that she'd lost him. His eyes were glowing red as he replaced his hand on the diamond.

That wasn't Nic anymore.

"Dammit, Nic, don't you do this. You promised me."

His eyes scared her. They were evil. Dark, bloodred, and vacant, like the demons she fought. Like her vision coming true.

She didn't want to be right. She'd been right about her mother.

Please don't let her visions about Nic come true.

"Take her hand in yours and place it on the diamond. Then enter the diamond with your life force and become one of us," Bart instructed. "It's time for the transition."

Nic grasped Shay's hand between his, and laid them on top of the diamond. It began to vibrate and hum, then whistle, the sound so loud it hurt her ears. Her stomach did flip-flops and nausea rolled. She didn't like this at all.

"Come on, Nic," she urged, desperately trying to wrestle out of his strong grip. "I have faith in you, remember? You're supposed to be on our side. We have to fight this together."

She still believed in him. She was not going to allow him to give up this easily. She knew deep down this wasn't what he wanted, and his will wasn't so easy to control. But how to get through to him?

She finally hauled off and kicked his shin. "Fight this, dammit!"

He didn't even flinch. He looked mesmerized. Out of it. Lost. Dark.

Shay cast a desperate gaze out to the hunters. Derek held up his hand in reassurance. He was talking. She should be able to hear him in her ear comm, but she couldn't. The demons were all humming, the diamond was practically roaring, and Bart was chanting nonstop in that weird language again. Through it all, Nic was looking at her with his red eyes, his hands so tightly held to hers there was no way for her to pull free. And her hand was actually slipping *into* the diamond, the gem's consistency changing to something like gel.

She had a really bad feeling that if their hands went fully into that diamond, something would irrevocably change. She was floundering here, needing help from either Nic or Derek or Lou. She'd never felt so isolated before. Or so petrified.

And her visions swam before her eyes. Nic changing, standing by his father, the two of them laughing at her.

No!

"Nic, help me out here," she whispered, though she was afraid he couldn't hear her. Or even understand her anymore. "You and I . . . we're connected. You feel what I feel and I feel what you feel. You don't want any part of this and you know it. Shake it off, goddammit. Look at me. See me."

No response. She decided she'd just keep on talking. Over Bart, over the hum of the demons and the creepy mystical music coming from the diamond.

"Your father never loved you or wanted you. Not for

who you are and what you can be. The Realm of Light, Derek, Lou and all the hunters—they accept you. They need you. I need you. Did I tell you I'm in love with you?"

He blinked. Reaction or not, she wasn't sure, but she went with it. "I might have failed to mention that. Maybe I let you down, let you think the visions I had about you put me off. They didn't. I was scared, but I was scared *for* you, not scared *of* you. I never once believed you'd become one of them."

He was staring at her, tilting his head to the side as if she was getting through. God, she hoped she was getting through.

"Anyway, I love you, Nic. Demon blood and all, I love you. And I need you. I need the Nic who surfs, and makes me laugh, and who irritates the hell out of me every day. The one I argue with and who makes my toes curl when he kisses me. Not this cold robot with red eyes that they want to turn you into. Not this servant of evil."

She raised her hand and placed it on his cheek. It was cold. She fought the horror at imagining what they were trying to do to him.

"I love you." She raised up on her toes and pressed a kiss to his lips. They were rigid, icy, but she kept her mouth against his, forcing her warmth into him. He lifted one hand, wrapped it around her throat, and squeezed.

She refused to show fear. She wasn't going to lose him.

She pulled her lips from his, but stayed close. "You're not going to hurt me. I know you won't. I still believe in you," she whispered against his mouth. "And I won't let you go."

Nic heard every word Shay said, felt every touch, every brush of her lips against his. Yet he was frozen and unable to move; a part of him already had a foot inside the world of evil.

He thought he'd had this all under control, that his mind, his will, was strong enough to fight the Sons of Darkness. Because he wanted no part of it; he could resist. The problem was, he thought they'd try to strip him of power. Instead, they were filling him with it. And oh, was it seductive.

"Feel it, Dominic."

Bart's voice was part of him.

"It's all yours now. Feel it!"

He felt it all right. Everything. A burning, seething, pleasurable pain filled him. And then his mind cleared. And he saw everything. Remembered it all, from as far back in his childhood as any kid could remember. He recalled Derek. And his mother.

He remembered his mother. His stomach tightened with longing at what he'd lost. Visions of the night Ben took him were so clear he could reach out and touch them. He could even see events he wasn't there for— what happened to Derek and his mother after Nic and Ben left—what happened to her mind. She'd gone insane trying to protect Derek so Ben wouldn't find them.

"She was weak, Dominic," Bart said. "Your father was the strong one. You have his blood. You should be proud."

Proud? He felt sick. He looked down at his hand holding on to Shay's, then back up at her face. And she was smiling at him. God, she was so beautiful.

And what he must look like. He knew the demon inside him was trying to break free. The power of it . . . enormous, frightening, evil power inside him. The power to hurt the people he loved. Sadistic, seductive, it fed like a disease inside him.

Shay's face swam before his eyes. He blinked, trying to focus. His other hand was around her throat. He was hurting her. How could he hurt someone he loved? Is this what their power did to him?

Christ, where was his strength to fight this? Fuck these bastards. They weren't going to take him over. He summoned up his own will, the part of him they didn't yet own, and released his hold on Shay's throat, smoothing his hand down the column of her neck, letting go of her hand at the same time.

"I'm sorry, baby."

She blinked back tears. "You're here."

He nodded.

"I love you, Nic."

"I love you, too." This time the words flowed without hesitation. Effortless. It was important she know, in case something happened to him. Because they weren't out of the woods yet. "My hand's stuck in this diamond."

Her gaze shot down to the blue orb. She withdrew her hand, but he didn't. "What do you mean, stuck?"

He jerked his arm upward, and nothing happened. His fingers were embedded in the middle of the diamond. "I mean like I can't pull my hand out."

"What are you doing?" Bart's shrill voice screamed as he came between them and grasped on to Nic's wrist. "Do not let go of her. Put your hands on the diamond. We must continue."

"Uh, no." Nic arched a brow. "We're done here. I'm not playing anymore."

Bart's dark eyes grew more crazed, anger tilting his brows. "Do not toy with me! You do not know what you're dealing with, young man. You have no power. Do as you're told."

Nic snorted. It was like being a kid again, admonished by his uncle. He felt much more in control now. Nothing was going to make him fall into the lure of that darkness again. But he'd like to pull his hand out of the diamond and get Shay out of there. He scanned the room for Derek.

"I could use some help."

"Two seconds. Dalton's got a little surprise for the humming masses. As soon as he lays down the big bang, I'm there. Hang on."

The funny thing was, neither of them had spoken a word. Yet he and Derek had just communicated. He and his brother had an awesome connection.

Now *that*'s the kind of power he liked.

"Stay still," he said to Shay, hoping to placate Bart for a few more seconds. He nodded to Bart, who studied him for a few seconds as if he didn't believe the sudden acquiescence. Nic went into the vacant look again. Shay began to struggle against him.

"Let me go, Nic, please. Don't do this."

That's my girl.

Seemingly satisfied, Bart looked down at the diamond and began his chanting again. Nic spotted Dalton working on something. The demons were all humming and oblivious as the hunters gathered together.

Dalton pulled out some kind of thick, black-barreled weapon, something Nic had never seen. Whatever the hell it was, it looked like one bad motherfucker. Ryder whispered something to Angelique, inclined his head toward the cave exit. Angelique nodded. Ryder must be telling her to make a run for it when the shooting started.

Nic wrapped his free arm around Shay, pulling her tight against him, ready for anything. If he had to pick up the damn diamond and drag it to the ground to keep Shay safe, he would.

Derek gave the command and the hunters expanded. Dalton swiveled and began to fire, lightning exploding out of the weapon he held. He pivoted back and forth, firing the thing like a machine gun. Bolts flew out of it, striking demons left and right. They sizzled and dropped, frying like eggs on the ground, their bodies jerking and sizzling as flames charred them to nothing but smoke and ash. The other hunters pulled their weapons and engaged the demons near them, leveling them with lasers and microwaves.

But that lightning thing Dalton used? Cool as hell. Or

hot as hell, which is where those demons were being sent back to. He'd obliterated a ton of them.

With the melee going on around them, Derek leaped to the table, firing his laser at a stunned Bart. The force pushed him clear across the room. Bart landed with a thud against the wall. Derek hit him again, a huge hole melting in his chest. Bart didn't move.

"Is he dead?" Nic asked.

Derek shook his head. "He's down, but not out. We're only going to have a few seconds. Let's get your hand out of this thing." He grasped Nic's wrist and pulled. Nic worked with him, but nothing. His hand wouldn't budge. They both tried again. Still stuck.

"Think you can control that demon in you?" Derek asked.

"I can if you can."

Derek quirked a half smile. "We need it to get you out of this. I'm going to stick my hand in there with yours and then we'll both extract."

"Will that work?"

Derek shrugged. "Hell if I know. But two half demons should equal the power of one, right?"

Nic laughed.

"You ready? On three."

"One."

Nic inhaled, pulling forth the darkness. It swirled around him, sick and twisted, like a cloth smothering the light. He held fast to control.

"Two."

He kept his gaze fixed on Shay. He could do this. He

would do this. Power jerked and soared, but he held it at bay. He felt Derek's like a magnet and looked at his brother.

Damn. Derek was fierce. His power was stronger than anything Nic had felt within himself. He drew to Derek's power, let it wrap around him, pull him in.

Now.

"Three."

Derek plunged his hand into the diamond. Nic looked at his brother, felt and saw the demon inside Derek, the control he had over the monster that lived within him. Derek breathed heavily . . . in and out, in and out. His eyes turned deep red, his nostrils flaring.

"Pull . . . out . . . now," Derek managed.

Nic used his strength and Derek's to jerk their hands out of the diamond.

It worked. He was free, the shadows evaporating. Nic finally exhaled.

"My two sons, working together in darkness."

Ben's voice again, swirling through the black mist. It called to him. Nic fought against it, but the lure was so damn strong it was hard to resist.

Shay's hand slipped in his. He turned to her and nodded, absorbing her human strength and her light.

"Nic. I need you with me," Ben said.

Nic sucked in a breath and shuddered.

"Ignore it," Derek warned. "He's not really here, and he has no power."

"But I am and I do!"

Bart flew at them. Derek stepped in front of Nic and

with a low growl took the brunt of Bart's attack, falling backward as Bart landed on top of him. In full demon form, Bart had doubled in size. In human years he might be a middle-aged man, but as a demon he fought with fierce, animal strength, claws extended and tearing into Derek's shoulder, ripping a bloody streak down his arm.

Oh, no. This wasn't going to play out with big brother taking all the flak.

Shay released his hand. "Go." She was already running off to grab a weapon and join in the fight.

He growled, then released the demon inside himself. It rose up, dark and menacing, even stronger than before. He fought it for dominance, careful not to let it take control. *He* was going to manage the damn beast, not the other way around.

When he was confident he had the monster in hand, he dove at Bart, lifting him off Derek and throwing him against the chair. Derek leapt to his feet and the two of them charged after Bart.

"Dominic."

Nic stalled for only a second at the sound of his father's voice. Derek looked to Nic, his eyes an unholy red. He shook his head. "Don't let him get to you."

"He's not." That much was true, though his father's interfering presence was beginning to annoy him.

Bart had already lifted himself off the chair and puffed up, his chest expanding as he approached. "The power of the Sons of Darkness cannot be defeated."

"Yeah, yeah," Nic said, raising his fists and getting into fighting stance. "All the evil leaders say that, I'm sure. Right before somebody cuts their head off." As much fun as it had been to battle hands-on with that demon out in the jungle, beating Bart to a pulp was going to be even more enjoyable.

His father appeared in shadowy form next to Bart—smiling, benevolent, his face one of kindness. Nic knew better than to believe what he saw. Because the feeling of evil in the room just doubled.

And the only way to fight it was to use what he had inside. Strength built within him, and along with it—darkness. He knew it but he wouldn't give up the power. Not right now.

He heard laughter all around him. His father's laughter.

"You will become one of us, son. You like this too much. This thrill, this rush of power. You always enjoyed the seduction of dominance, of having everything you wanted at your fingertips. It can all be yours if you are with us.

"Stay, Dominic. Only you can bring me back to life."

Nic sucked in air, wishing it were crisp ocean air, clean, life-affirming, instead of this dusty cavern. It smelled like death in here. The cave turned black, but Nic could see just fine, even without his night-vision glasses.

Bart was retreating, disappearing into the blackness.

"Uh-uh," Derek said. He stepped forward, Nic with him.

The wall behind Bart shimmered, the rock disappearing. Derek looked at Nic.

"You see that?"

Nic nodded.

Bart stepped into the wall, Ben with him.

"They want us to follow," Nic said.

"It's a trap."

Nic nodded. "Of course it is."

"We're going in."

"Of course we are."

"And we're going with you," Shay said.

Nic whirled to find the hunters behind them.

"Wall's closing," Shay said with a sharp inclination of her head. "Better get moving."

Fuck. No time to argue. He turned and they ran forward, through the invisible wall. As soon as the hunters were through, it materialized to solid rock behind them.

But Bart was nowhere to be found.

Chapter Twenty-Five

Nic and Derek were so far ahead Shay could barely see them anymore. She and the others quickened the pace to catch up, the darkness swallowing the guys. These channels were nothing like the ones in the caves they had explored before. The walls were slimy, something dark and thick and looking like blood ran in rivers alongside them, and the stench was so strong Shay had to fight the urge to cover her nose and mouth with her shirt.

She stopped thinking about where they were or what kind of place this was. It was a cave, that was all.

Panting and out of breath, she and the others couldn't keep up with Nic and Derek. They'd lost them again. She shot a quick glance at Gina, who nodded and rolled her eyes. They pushed forward and ran harder.

Demon blood must have given the brothers super-speed, too. Shay and the others were going to have to hustle if they didn't want to end up lost in whatever the hell place this was.

And no way was Shay going to end up left behind in here. So she dug in her heels, ignoring what was squishing beneath her boots, and ran side by side with Gina. Whether the others were keeping up behind them she didn't know and didn't care. Her first priority was getting to Nic.

She finally saw him. Just up ahead.

God, the darkness in here was unsettling. Even with her night-vision shades on, it was hard to see. No lights, no landmarks, nothing but tunnels and bodies and that god-awful smell. And it was so cold in here she could see her breath in front of her, the only white in a sea of blackness.

"Nic!" She called ahead, but he didn't stop. Maybe he and Derek were close to catching up to Bart. Maybe he didn't hear her.

She'd just have to run harder, but her lungs ached with the effort. She wanted to stop, bend over and rest her hands on her knees, and just take in a few lungfuls of air. Not that the air in here was breathable. She longed for the outside, even if it was a thousand degrees out there. At least outside it didn't smell like death.

They had to finish this and get out of here. The walls were closing in on her. That thought made her step up the pace, drawing closer to Nic and Derek.

Shay and Gina caught up to Nic and Derek, and Shay had a few seconds to replenish her breath and look around. They'd reached a dead end. There were no other tunnels, nothing but solid rock wall on three sides.

And no Bart.

"Well, this sucks," Shay said. "Now what are we supposed to do?" If she thought the walls were closing in on her before, it was even worse now. She struggled to breathe normally. Though she wasn't claustrophobic, this tight fit and everyone packed in with no way out wasn't helping her feeling of being trapped.

Lou arrived, pushed forward, and examined the front wall.

"I saw them," Nic said.

"Them?" Lou asked.

"Bart and . . . my father. They passed through this wall."

"It's solid rock, Nic," Ryder said.

"It wasn't a few seconds ago. Just like the one in the outer cave, it was transparent."

"Then maybe this one is, too." Lou placed his hand on the wall and closed his eyes.

They waited a few seconds, then he turned around and faced them. "But I'm not the one who can go through it."

"I can." Nic palmed the wall. "Just like in the diamond." He tilted his head toward Derek. "You can, too."

Derek shrugged. "If you say so."

They pushed, and their hands melted into the rock.

Nic pulled his out again and his hand was whole. "That's pretty fucking cool."

Lou nodded. "It appears as though you'll be going

in." He pulled his sword from its scabbard. "Take this with you."

Nic examined the sword, gleaming, slender, and vibrating with power. He nodded, and took the scabbard and belt from Lou.

"I wish we could go through there and help you, but it's obvious you two are the only ones who can get in there," Lou said.

"No, I can, too." Shay didn't know how she knew that, but instinct told her she could. She stepped forward and put her hand on the wall, not shocked when her flesh disappeared within the solid rock.

Nic frowned. "You stay here."

She shook her head. "No way. If I can go through with you, I'm going."

"You touched the diamond, too," Lou said. "It must give you some kind of power to surpass the wall."

"Then I'm in, too, because I touched it." Ryder moved forward and put his hand through the wall.

So it was her, Ryder, Nic, and Derek. Either way, she was going. She let her body relax and held her breath, stepping forward and walking through the stone as if it were water.

"Dammit, Shay."

Nic's voice was like an echo in her head. She'd gone through first, afraid he'd try to stop her if she didn't.

"Don't you ever listen?"

He came through right after her, still frowning and still talking.

"No. Not when you don't make sense."

Ryder next, and Derek was last.

"That was fucking weird," Ryder said.

"Understatement," she said, shaking off the heebie-jeebies of walking through a stone wall. She'd rather not think about how they were going to get back.

"Lou, can you hear me?" Derek commed, then waited.

Nic shook his head and tapped his ear. "I'm getting nothing."

"We're on our own."

"Maybe we should have brought a loaf of bread with us."

The guys looked at her like she was talking in a foreign language.

"Bread crumbs? Leaving a trail so we can find our way back?" When they continued to look dumbfounded at her, she rolled her eyes. "Didn't you read fairy tales as kids?"

"Let's get moving. We have a demon Lord to kill," Derek said.

"He's close. I can feel him." Shay was psyched about the ability to sense demons now, feeling as if her talent could be of use. She didn't want to be afraid of it anymore. Hoisting her laser, she asked, "Aren't you going to get weapons ready?"

"I'm not taking him on with lasers," Nic said. "Waste of time." He turned to them. "But you all be ready to fire on any other demons that might be around."

She really didn't like the sound of this. Maybe coming along hadn't been such a good idea after all. Watching him take on Bart with his hands? The thought made her a little ill. Though she'd rather be with him to back him up than standing on the other side of the rock wondering if she'd ever see him again.

Not that she'd wonder. She'd see, she'd have a vision. Now she knew it to be fact. They were irrevocably tied together, no matter what.

The tunnel began to widen, finally opening up into another room, the oppressive weight of evil enshrouding her.

She'd never be so happy to see someone die as when Bart fell.

Though Bart no longer appeared human, Nic recognized him as he stood on an upraised rock platform in full demon glory. Evil emanated from his red-tinged eyes and dripping fangs as he smiled in welcome.

"Dominic, you have used your gifts to find us. Welcome home."

Nic smiled back at Bart. "Nothing I received from Ben was a gift. If I could tear every part of his DNA from me I would."

"I know you don't mean that. You just haven't yet realized what this power means to you."

"If it means I can destroy you, I'll gladly embrace all the power inside me."

Bart's smile flickered for a moment, the look in his eyes giving Nic hope that maybe there was enough power inside him to destroy Bart. Because for a second there, Nic had glimpsed fear on Bart's face.

This entire event hadn't worked out well for Bart. Good.

And standing next to Bart, though he could see right through him, was Ben.

Nic shot a glance at Derek, who nodded, indicating he'd seen it, too. A quick look at Ryder and Shay confirmed it. Okay, so now everyone could see him. He wasn't imagining Ben. Interesting. Now he just had to figure out how to use his strength to kill Bart.

Nic advanced, and Bart took a step back. So far, so good.

"I'm not alone here," Bart said.

Nic kept moving forward. "The remnants of my father don't give you much additional strength though, do they?" Apparently whatever power Ben wielded from beyond had been weakened, because though his mouth was moving, it wasn't reaching Nic's ears.

"I wasn't only talking about your father, Dominic."

Six men stepped through the tunnel on the far side of the room. Dressed all in black and menacing in stature, they took positions behind Bart. Some younger, some older, none of them looked like they'd be a piece of cake to take on. The pure evil emanating from them was like a punishing shot from one of the lasers. Nic found it hard to breathe.

Lords of the Sons of Darkness, no doubt. The most powerful of the demons. Nic felt a surge of dark strength in the room. The balance had just shifted.

"Fuck me," Nic whispered. This couldn't be good.

Bart raised his hands parallel to his body, pointing his fingers toward the ground. "Lord of Darkness, hear my plea. My brothers and I beseech you to give us strength and power to enact your will. Help us to crush the light and bring your children into the fold."

A prayer. A dark one at that. Sickening. As Bart droned on, Nic moved forward. No sense in standing around waiting for them to finish whatever they were doing. It was time for some action.

The sounds of weapons readying behind him alerted him that the others were preparing to fire. Nic had a pretty good idea that facing six of the Lords of the Sons of Darkness meant that chances were the hunters weren't going to survive this battle. They were outnumbered. But he was going to take Bart down before that happened.

He just wished Shay had stayed behind. His eyes drifted closed for a millisecond, long enough to flash on what they could have had together. He didn't want her to die. If nothing else, he'd try to figure out how to get her out of here before the really bad stuff went down. But first, Bart, who stood there like Superman standing on top of the world, looking supremely confident in the victory he assumed he'd already won.

Yeah. Whatever. Nic dropped a shoulder and barreled into him, knocking him off his big fat feet. Bart's putrid breath blew out all over Nic's face as he hit the ground. God, that stench could be a weapon on its own. He sat on Bart's chest and hit him with a series of punches. Blood spewed from Bart's nose and mouth.

Yeah, Bart was some deity. He still bled like a fucking human.

Bart grasped Nic's arms, shredding his clothes and skin with his claws.

Nic winced at the sting but ignored it, channeling what he had within himself to battle this Lord. Bart was no longer his uncle—he was evil, something that had to be destroyed.

"Did you think this was going to be easy, boy?" Bart grasped Nic's wrists and lifted him like he was nothing more than a feather, tossing Nic off him.

Nic flew in the air, but righted himself on his feet.

"Easy? No. But killing you will be a pleasure."

Bart leapt to his feet and grinned, his cheeks puffing out and his fangs extending. What was that slime dripping off his fangs? Disgusting. Bart advanced, his arms raised and claws reaching for Nic. Nic sidestepped him and kicked him in the butt. Now it was Bart's turn to fly, clear across the room. His head hit the wall with a very satisfying crunch.

With a loud growl, Bart flipped around and came at Nic in a run. Prepared for him, Nic sidestepped, but this time something grabbed his arms. Nic tilted his head back and saw one of the other Lords held him.

Shit!

He only had a second to steel himself for the onslaught. Bart barreled into him, claws embedding in his chest. Goddamn, that hurt. And again, that foul breath in his face.

"Dude, you need some breath mints." He turned his head to the side.

Bart dug his claws in further. "Such a silly little game you human boys play."

"Perhaps you didn't have a handle on this as well as you thought?" the man holding Nic said. "Tase said you were losing control."

"I've got it under control," Bart said, anger knitting his bushy brows. "Dominic is ours now."

Nic was fighting for breath, the pain from Bart's claws so intense it was hard to remain standing. The demon Lord behind him had a lock that Nic couldn't break. That is, until he let out a low growl and released Nic. Nic found the strength to push at Bart's chest, hard. Bart's claws retracted and he fell to the ground, allowing Nic to pivot.

Shay was behind him, her dagger embedded in the demon Lord's throat. The Lord's eyes were dark and wide with fury and shock, his hands at his throat. Blood poured from the wound at his jugular and he fell to his knees.

She jerked the dagger out, sheathed it, and backed up, raising her laser to pummel the Lord with a laser array.

"Get back to what you were doing," she shouted at Nic. "I've got this one covered."

He nodded and turned back to Bart. It was time to even the odds and bring his own beast out in the open. Risky, yeah, but he had no choice.

He released it all, whatever was within him, on Bart, concentrating on all that had been taken away from him, all that had been done to him, letting the anger and hatred soar through every fiber of his body.

And when Bart attacked again, he was ready this time, his strength and power multiplied as he tackled Bart to the ground and sat on his stomach.

Bart's eyes widened as Nic wrapped his hands around his uncle's thick throat. He heard the sounds of rapid laser fire but didn't dare break his concentration to see what was happening with the others. First Bart had to die. Then he'd figure out what was going on around him.

Bart clawed at Nic, trying to pull his hands away, but Nic had the leverage. Bart's face began to turn purple, his red eyes bulging. He looked like a tomato about to burst. Nic was going to twist his head clean off, not take any chance this bastard was going to come back to life again.

"Die, you sonofabitch!" he yelled, squeezing hard enough that bones snapped under his fingers. It wasn't enough. Bart was still alive. Struggling, but still alive.

Christ, what did it take to kill one of these things? He dragged him up with his hands still around Bart's throat and slammed him against the nearby wall. Bart's skull made a satisfying crunch as it hit the stone.

A human would be dead by now.

"Nic! Use your sword!" Shay hollered.

The sword Lou gave him. It was sheathed behind him. That's how Ben was killed. Beheading.

No. Nic didn't want to do it that way. He wanted to feel Bart die with his own hands. Anger and hatred filled him and he squeezed Bart's throat tighter.

"Yes. Let those dark emotions rule you, Dominic. They give you such strength."

Great—now he could hear his father talking again. He liked Ben much better when he was mute.

But this wasn't a movie, and he wasn't giving over to the dark side. He was battling it—he was killing it. And if he had to use dark emotions to fight it, he would. He'd use anything he had within him to destroy one of the Sons of Darkness.

"Your soul will belong to us. You have no choice."

His father never knew him, never knew what he was capable of.

"Nic."

The darkness evaporated at the sound of Shay's voice. The one person who *did* know what he was capable of. Light, goodness. Love.

"Finish it, Nic."

Her dagger.

He knew what would work, then. Keeping one hand around Bart's throat he took the dagger, feeling her power in it, his connection to her strength. He palmed the hilt and tightened his grip, focusing on Bart's mottled face, then drove the dagger into Bart's throat.

No anger or hatred poured through him as he stepped back and watched Bart clutch at the dagger, blood spurting from the hole in his throat.

"You have to take his head off or he won't die," Shay whispered behind him.

He nodded and reached for the sword, then pulled Bart forward by his hair. The demon gasped for breath. His last. With a quick swipe Nic sliced the blade across

Bart's throat, effectively extricating Bart's head from his body.

A roar resounded through the room, a howling, unholy moan that made Nic shudder. Nic almost wanted to revel in it, to wrap himself around the evil that swirled like a cold blanket enveloping him. He wanted to absorb it and make it part of him.

But that was the demon side of him thinking, the side of him he didn't want.

Icy wind swooshed around Nic as Bart disappeared in a pile of ash. Nic pushed the beast inside him away, forcing the evil deep within. He closed his eyes, pushing it farther and farther away, using every ounce of strength he possessed. The darkness fought him, compelling him.

But he was stronger. He wanted more than the lure of death and destruction. He wanted the light.

When he opened his eyes, the anger was gone and so was the darkness.

Sweet. He grabbed a cloth to wipe off the blade and sheathed it at his back again, then grabbed the dagger from the ground, returning it to Shay.

"Thanks, babe."

"You're welcome. Now let's kill these things." She handed him a laser and Nic pivoted to see how the others were doing.

Whoa. Not good. Their weapons weren't doing enough damage to the demon Lords. No sooner would Derek or Ryder blow a hole in one of the Lords, than it would close up and they were back after them again.

Nic and Shay rejoined the battle but he soon found the same result.

"We aren't making any headway," he shouted. "These guys are too strong."

"No shit," Ryder shot back.

"Their power is too great," Nic said, knowing what his own power was like, and that he was just an infant in comparison to the Lords. And with six of them and only four hunters, the chances of getting close enough for a beheading were going to be slim to none. He wasn't willing to risk Shay any longer, though she was holding her own. But they were all tiring. And that many demon Lords in one place? Not a good thing, especially not without the other hunters available to back them up.

"Let's keep going," Shay said. "We can beat them."

"No, we can't. We need to retreat," Derek ordered. "We'll finish this fight another day."

Nic had gotten who he'd come for. And while he'd like to take down the other Lords, he had an idea they'd meet them again. "Let's get out of here. Full array now, and then run like hell for the exit."

They blasted the Lords again with all the firepower they had until they were all temporarily down. Then they ran to the wall, hoping they could get through faster than the Lords could recover.

Nic practically threw Shay through the wall. He kept his weapon trained on the tunnel, signaling Ryder through next, then Derek.

"You coming?" Derek asked.

"Yeah. Get going."

Derek went through. Nic was about to do the same when the vision of his father reappeared in front of the wall.

"Dominic."

Damn, he hated this shit. "Why don't you stay dead?"

His father smiled. So benign, so nonthreatening. "Change your mind. There's still time."

Nic took a quick glance behind him to see if the other Lords were coming after him. He should just walk through the wall, walk through his father. But he had to say it, had to have closure. "I don't belong to you anymore. I never did. I'm with the Realm of Light."

Ben's smile died, becoming hard and filled with hatred. "You will not win with them. You will have nothing but emptiness and sorrow."

Nic quirked a smile. "I have family. They need me." And he had love, something he'd never felt with Ben. Something the Sons of Darkness would never understand.

"The Realm of Light will never hold the power."

"Go away, Ben. Back to Hell where you belong."

Nic started through the wall.

"There is another. Just as you. A female—half human, half demon."

Nic stalled, hating that he did.

"She holds the key."

His father laughed and disappeared.

Shit. He walked through and found Shay glaring at him.

"Did you have to push?"

Nothing like a little slap of reality. He grinned. "Sorry, babe. I wanted you safe."

"I'm fine," she grumbled, dusting off her pants.

"Six demon Lords in there," Derek was reporting to Lou. "Bart's dead."

"You killed him with the sword?" Lou asked.

Nic nodded, returning the sword to Lou. "I would have liked to take them all down that way, but the odds weren't good."

"That many Sons of Darkness in one spot are very powerful. There weren't enough of you to take on a battle of that magnitude. We need to leave this place. Now is not the time for that kind of fight."

"Why aren't they following?" Shay asked, her wary gaze flitting to the wall they'd just come through.

Lou shrugged. "They're probably weakened by the combination of summoning Ben, Bart's death, and the battle with all of you. Trust me, we'll see them again."

They made their way through the narrow tunnel toward the room. When they got back to the main room, there were only dead demons. Two very important things were missing.

Angelique and the black diamond.

Chapter Twenty-Six

I should have grabbed the diamond." Ryder shook his head. "But I thought Angelique was on our side. I didn't know she'd come back for it."

Ryder jammed his hand through his hair, his expression filled with anger and frustration.

Shay knew he blamed himself for Angelique's taking the diamond, that he felt his trust had been betrayed. She'd tried to talk to him about it but he'd clammed up tight, refusing to open up about his feelings.

Typical guy. But she read the murderous intent in his expression.

"We were rather preoccupied with other things. None of us was thinking about the diamond at the time." Lou looked around the room at all of them. "No one is to blame for this."

They'd flown back to Sydney, regrouped with the other hunters, and filled them in on everything, planning what to do next. Right now they were temporarily stationed in Nic's house. Plenty of room for all of them, and no Bart lurking nearby any longer to overhear their plans.

"When do we go after her?" Ryder asked. "After the diamond, I mean. We want to get that back, right?"

"Yes, it's essential we start there," Lou said.

"So is Angelique the half demon, the Queen of Darkness that Bart mentioned? If so, and she has the black diamond, that's some really bad shit," Punk said.

"That sums it up rather nicely, Punk, thank you," Lou said. "The problem is, we don't know the answer to that question. That's what we have to find out."

"If she was demon, wouldn't there have been a reaction when Bart put her hand on the diamond? He said she wasn't the one," Shay reminded them. Whatever "the one" meant.

Lou nodded. "Another question we need the answer to. Because if she wasn't who Bart thought she was, then who is? We need to find out who Angelique is, and if she isn't the female half demon, then why did Bart think she was? If she isn't, then who is?"

"Isabelle."

They all turned to Ryder.

"Who's Isabelle?" Derek asked.

"Angelique's twin sister." Ryder shrugged. "Might be nothing and no connection at all, but Angelique said that Isabelle is also an archaeologist. Maybe Bart wanted her instead."

Lou nodded. "That could be. We'll have to look into the possibility."

All these questions made Shay's head ache. And she still hadn't had a moment alone with Nic. She didn't even know how he felt after his ordeal with his uncle in the cave. He'd been crazed in there. Though she'd been intensely concentrating on fighting the demon Lords, she'd caught a couple glimpses of him fighting with Bart, and what she'd seen hadn't even looked like Nic—his face twisted in the visage of a demon: cold, evil, his nails extended into claws. He'd wanted to kill Bart with his bare hands—she'd known that. And maybe he could have. But she had been able to reach him, and that was a good thing. She'd felt no evil or darkness within him when he'd taken the sword and cut Bart's head off.

She still shuddered at the memory. Amazing the things she'd grown used to in her short time as a hunter.

But as soon as Bart was gone, Nic had grabbed his laser and joined her in attacking the other Lords. Just like that. Human again. He seemed to control the transition so easily. Much more easily, in fact, than Derek had. But she wanted time alone to talk to him, to gauge his reaction to all this. To see if he was the same Nic she'd fallen in love with.

A lot had happened.

"I've got the Realm working on Angelique," Lou continued, "though we know very little about her. Still, we've never failed to locate someone we're searching for. We'll find her, too. And we'll investigate her sister."

"And find out if either of them is the half demon that Ben told Nic about," Dalton reminded them.

Lou nodded. "We have much to do."

And at the moment they had no answers, so they couldn't do anything but wait until they received information on Angelique's possible whereabouts.

Shay headed upstairs and turned on the tub, looking forward to sinking in the warm water and soothing her brutalized muscles. She stripped and settled in with a loud moan, closing her eyes and resting her head against the back of the tub.

"Oh, I like that sound."

She smiled without opening her eyes. "What sound is that?"

"You. Moaning."

She lifted her lids and drank in the sight of Nic leaning against the doorway between their bedroom and the bathroom. He looked damn sexy. "You need a bath," she said, purposely lowering her voice.

He looked down at himself. "I do, huh? Well, you're the boss." He pushed off the doorway and removed his shirt, then popped the button on his pants, drawing the zipper down in an agonizingly slow manner that made her lick her lips and watch every tooth of that zipper pull apart. He toed his boots off and shucked his pants, leaving clothes in his wake as he made his way toward the tub.

Just like the first day he'd walked toward her, he took her breath away. She drew her legs up and made room for him in the tub, letting him settle in before fitting her legs on the outside of his. Water splashed over the side and onto the tile floor as he submerged completely, coming up with his hair dripping wet. She didn't care.

Her focus was entirely on the hot man in the bath with her.

"Let me look you over. You're injured." She leaned forward and grasped his arms, noting the marks where Ben had clawed him. The same marks were on his chest. As much as Derek and Lou had warned them about what would happen if they were clawed by demons, Nic seemed unaffected.

He shrugged. "They're fine. Already healing. I guess our demon blood protects us from any adverse effects of the toxins."

She grabbed a washcloth and eased away the blood and dirt, revealing healthy pink marks. The hunters hadn't had time to do more than change clothes, pack up, and head to the plane after they'd left the cave.

But he was right. His wounds *were* healing. Amazing. "Well, aren't you just endowed with superpowers."

He arched a brow. "That's not all I'm endowed with, babe."

Evidence of his endowment was bobbing up out of the water, enticing her to do more than just clean his wounds. "Is that right? Care to demonstrate your incredible . . . prowess?"

"I can't. I'm injured and need nursing care." He leaned back and rested his arms on the sides of the tub.

"Well, then. Let me see what I can do to soothe you." She pushed forward and raised up, crawling over him until she sat on his thighs. Keeping her gaze on his face, she reached for his shaft, encircling it with both hands. "Oh, this is swollen and needs a massage."

He hissed as she stroked him, which compelled her to wind her hands around him if only to soak in his reaction. His eyes went dark when she rolled her thumb over the head. He looked at her like that when he was making love to her. Intense, consuming, the kind of look that made her heart slam against her chest and her breath catch.

Like now. Her pulse kicked in short bursts against her wrist. Just having his body close to hers made her breasts feel heavy and her nipples tighten, and what was going on between her legs was like molten lava underwater. She rocked against him, positioning herself so her sex rubbed his cock. She arched her back, lost in the sensations.

"Shay," he whispered, palming her belly. He moved his hand higher, cupping her breasts and leaning forward to capture one tip in his mouth to suck.

The sensation shot between her legs and she cried out at the exquisite pleasure, tangling her fingers in his hair. Just the touch of skin to skin was so intimate, so much of what she needed with him. Yet she wanted more. She pressed her lips to his and he opened his mouth, touching his tongue to hers.

Like lightning in water. Electrifying, shocking her into a fierce shudder of emotion that left her trembling with need to feel him inside her. He grabbed her ass and lifted her, settling her on top of him. She slid all the way down, wrapping her legs around his back to anchor herself to him. Joining with him was a sweet side of heaven, erasing the days of hell and every battle, every image of darkness she had to endure. He was her light, and all that was good about her life.

He wound his fingers in her hair and tugged, tilting her head back so he could lick at her throat. When he growled and pumped against her, digging his fingers into her hips, she felt the demon that lived inside him. But she didn't fear it.

Because she loved that part of him, too. The wild side that was so much a part of the Nic she'd fallen in love with—the reckless, crazy, primal side that thrilled her. As much as the funny, sweet, tender side that was the human part of him. In combination, they were lethal to her senses.

Lost in sensation, she tilted her head back and let the feelings ride, rising up to grind her aching cleft against him until all she could feel was the spot where they were connected, where he held her and drove into her with relentless abandon until water splashed. She fell forward and kissed him, crying into his mouth as she climaxed, squeezing him with uncontrollable spasms that seemed to go on and on. He tightened, shuddered, and spilled inside her, spiraling her into another intense orgasm.

He held her while she panted and sniffled, overwhelmed by her own emotions. She clasped him tightly, comforted and afraid because she couldn't see the future and didn't know what was going to happen next.

At first she'd hated the visions that zinged her whenever she touched him. Now she'd come to rely on them, and didn't know what to do when she couldn't see ahead.

Nic lifted her out of the bath and grabbed a towel to dry her. She was beyond words at that point, just let him. He carried her to the bed and lay down beside her, stroking her light and easy.

"I love you, Shay. None of us knows what tomorrow holds. I don't really know what I am or what's going to happen with me. What I do know is that whatever happens next, I want to see it through with you."

She let her eyes drift closed and smiled. That was enough, she realized. She didn't need to see any farther than that. Their future—all their futures—were too uncertain to know beyond tomorrow.

"I love you too, Nic. So much it scares me. I worry about losing people I love, which is probably why I never allowed myself to care about anyone. I was afraid to see what might happen, afraid to know in advance that something bad was going to occur."

"Like with your mother."

"Yes." She flipped over and looked at him. He was so beautiful that it caused pangs in her belly. "But I can't let that fear rule me anymore. Touching you, crawling inside the future with you, showed me that I can't be afraid anymore. I did it with you and I survived it."

"We both survived it."

She sighed, the emotion so strong it was overwhelming, but welcome. "I need you. And I've never needed anyone before."

He swept her hair off her face. "It's new territory for both of us. We'll fumble it a little, I'm sure, but I do know that ever since I first touched you, I haven't wanted to be separated from you. We're connected. There's a bond between us that goes beyond physical. I ache when I'm not with you. You're a part of me as much as I'm a part of you."

Her heart swelled, peace and contentment with it. Her demons were banished. "I know that ache. I feel it, too. I don't understand it, but I've come to accept it for what it is. As long as you're by my side, I'm happy."

"I'm not going anywhere, babe. If you ever disappeared, I'd hunt you down."

She grinned. "Same here."

"No chance of that happening," he said, leaning over to press a soft kiss to her lips. "I'm yours forever."

Epilogue

Tase paced the dark cavern, his ire palpable from the waves of heat emanating from his body. He was so hot the temperature was uncomfortable even to himself.

Not that he minded the pain. Discomfort was the least of his worries.

The rest of the Lords kept their distance, not wanting to draw close enough to get singed. He would smile at that if he wasn't so furious.

Aron approached. Obviously the Lord was feeling brave today.

"Our plan, Tase?" Aron asked, licking a dark brow with his overly long tongue.

"The first plan is never to allow our Lords to live in the human realm again."

The other Lords nodded.

"Ben and Bart grew weak and emotional, raising a human child. They grew accustomed to the human lifestyle, to human emotion. They coddled Nic, favored him—I believe that they didn't want to hurt him or traumatize him. That's why they waited so long. And look what happened."

"Ben wasn't the only one of us who has bred with a human, as you are well aware," Badon said.

"Yes, I am aware. And he paid a penalty for that transgression. We must find her, this female. She is the key to our future and she holds great power."

"And we must locate the black diamond as well," Badon added.

"We must do many things," Tase said. "And we should remember first and foremost who and what we are. We have been too soft on the Realm of Light and on these humans. We have allowed them to hurt us. Our demons fall in great numbers because their technology is so advanced, while we foolishly think the strength of our hybrids and the speed and cunning of our purebreds and half-breeds can overpower them."

Tase turned away, looking into the fires. "We have been so imprudent, have allowed our egos to blind us for too long." He turned back to the others. "And look at us now. Two of our Lords are dead."

Anger filled him, his power generating flames that licked around him.

"It's time for the Realm of Light to suffer. And they must suffer mightily."

His gaze was hot as he glared at the other nine remaining Lords.

"The Sons of Darkness must exact revenge! For too

long Ben and Bart concentrated on a small set of the Realm of Light. There are hunters worldwide, yet why do we not target them as Ben and Bart targeted this small set headed by Louis?"

He didn't wait for an answer. "Starting now, we will accept nothing less than the Realm of Light's complete annihilation. If it takes all ten of us to personally hunt them down and kill them all, we will do it. No longer will we sit back and do nothing, expect the mindless to do our bidding. Is that understood?"

He felt the power, the darkness, the evil in the room increase as the anger he sent out multiplied.

Tase had the control now. Bart and Ben had led for too long, and their power had been weak.

If there was one thing Tase was not, it was weak. He had no children within the Realm of Light's ranks, no one he cared about.

He cared about power, about pleasing the Master of all Darkness. His ultimate reward would come with the Realm of Light's downfall. He would enjoy seeing that very much.

The time was now. The Realm of Light's world was about to crumble.

About the Author

JACI BURTON grew up in Missouri, but spent thirteen years as a California girl. Now she's back in the area she loves to call home, this time Oklahoma, where she lives with her husband Charlie and her stepdaughter Ashley.

She is also the author of *Surviving Demon Island*, available from Dell Books.

Read on for a sneak
peek at the next
steamy and
heartstopping
novel in

Jaci Burton's

Demon Hunter Series

The Demon's
Touch

Coming in Summer 2008

The Demon's Touch
on sale summer 2008

Chapter One

Two months later
Sicily, Italy

Ryder was hunting again, and damn, it felt good. To be on his own, with no one to tell him what to do and when or how to do it. He liked the other demon hunters just fine, but he was used to this isolation, to a one-man operation, and this is what he preferred—stalking his prey one on one.

His lips curled as he thought about that prey—Angelique. Lou had known how much he'd wanted this assignment. Maybe a little too much. It was hard to fool the old man, but Lou had let him have it. Ryder knew more about Angelique than any of the others anyway, could complete this assignment better than they could. He'd spent more time with her than they had, touched her, gotten inside her head.

He knew her lies.

It had taken months of searching by the Realm of Light, but they'd located her in Italy. And Lou and his ragtag group of demon hunters, Ryder included, had come to Italy and spread out, looking for her as well as her sister, Isabelle. But Ryder was better at tracking than anyone else, and once they had her location pinpointed to Sicily, he'd convinced Lou to let him go in on his own. Surprisingly, Lou had agreed.

And now that he'd found her, had her cornered, it was just a matter of sneaking up on her and grabbing her, and the black diamond.

If she had it on her, which would be really stupid.

Angelique might be a lot of things, but Ryder didn't think for one second that she was stupid. So she probably didn't have it at the tiny house she'd rented.

It was isolated, but in an open area. He had good camouflage, since there was an abandoned, thickly covered vineyard behind the house, with lots of dense trees and bushes where he'd set up. The house was located in the midst of all this foliage. If not for the narrow road and driveway leading the way, the average person might never locate this place. Perfect spot for someone who didn't want to be found.

Ryder was good at finding people who didn't want to be found. His former job in military special ops had come in handy in locating Angelique, with a little help from all the resources of the Realm of Light. He'd researched her, dug deep, now had details on her background from birth to the present. He knew where her skeletons were buried. He'd vowed to unearth every bit of dirt on her if he had to work twenty-four hours a day to do it. She'd screwed him, and not in the fun way. She'd used him to get her hands on the diamond, and then she'd run.

But not nearly far enough, because he'd found her. And now that he had, he wasn't going to let her go again.

He'd hidden out, waiting to see how populated this area was.

It wasn't. At all. Hardly any traffic traveled this road, so he'd waited until nightfall, then hid his car within a dense area of bushes behind the property.

He'd followed a seldom used footpath leading up toward the house. Thick with bushes along each side, it kept him shielded from the back of the house, though he kept watch to make sure Angelique didn't show up at one of the windows to check out the view. No windows lit the back of the house, so he hoped she was asleep.

The path snaked around parallel to the curved drive, easy enough to keep watch for cars, though judging from the lack of traffic he didn't expect anyone to come this way. He finally found a spot where the house came into view and settled there. It was on higher ground, giving him a great vantage point to see everything. He could see into the back door of the house, and keep his eye on the drive in case Angelique left.

He leaned against a thick tree, figuring he'd just watch awhile, see what she did, get a handle on her routine for a day or so. He'd been single-minded in purpose since Lou had given him the assignment. Single-minded with a vengeance, in fact.

And angry. Damned angry.

It was time to back off, gather a little distance from his subject, and make sure he remained detached from what he was doing.

Just a job, Ryder. She's just a job.

Yeah, right. Betrayal, anger. They seethed inside him. He recognized them for what they were. Emotions. That was bad shit. He liked it better when emotion didn't enter the equation at all, when he could go about his business and not think about anything or anyone but his job. He wasn't his father, imagining slights and insults that weren't there. He'd long ago vowed to never be like his old man. He preferred being grounded in reality. And reality meant a laser in his hand, a demon he could see, and a kill he could verify. His reality was demon body count—not some mental bullshit that screwed with a warrior's reality. He could overcome the weird shit. He wasn't at all like his father. Hadn't he spent his entire adult life proving that?

As long as he remained aloof, with his focus on killing demons, he'd be okay. There was no emotion involved in demon hunting, which suited him just fine.

He'd screwed up with Angelique. He'd let her get close. He'd talked to her. He'd kissed her.

Angelique made him think, made him feel. She'd brought out emotion in him.

That made her dangerous.

He'd convinced Lou he could handle this, find her, figure out where the black diamond was and bring her, and it, back to the Realm of Light.

Ryder had never failed on a mission. He didn't intend to now. All he had to do was wait it out a bit. Angelique would lead him to the black diamond.

One way or the other.

He hadn't seen her yet, other than arriving in her car

this afternoon and going straight inside. The shades were drawn and he'd seen her silhouette moving about in one of the rooms downstairs. He had blueprints of the house, so he knew the layout. Downstairs, kitchen and living room. Upstairs, one bedroom and bath. Small, cozy—room for one or two people, max. His audio equipment picked up everything going on inside. There wasn't anyone else in there with her, and she hadn't used the phone, because he was tracking her cellular calls, too. She didn't even talk to herself.

He heard the sounds of cooking, the shower running, and then all the lights went out about eleven P.M. She'd obviously gone to bed.

He glanced down at his watch. Almost midnight. Good thing it was warm outside. He slid down the tree and parked himself on a thick slab of rock, figuring his equipment would alert him if anything happened. He had to get at least a little sleep or he'd be useless. Though he could go a day or two without any sleep, he preferred to maintain mental alertness, since he had no idea what to expect. As far as the Realm of Light knew, Angelique had already made contact with her sister, Isabelle, and the two of them had planned to do something with the black diamond. And since none of them had managed to find Isabelle yet, they were hoping Angelique would lead them to her. Though the hunters were out searching for Isabelle, too.

It was a waiting game now. Ryder hoped he didn't have to wait too long.

He jerked awake at a sound, immediately glancing down at his watch. It was three in the morning. Shit.

Blinking away the fog of sleep, he listened intently, wondering if Angelique was up. No lights. So what had he heard?

Something crashed inside, like a lamp. He shot up to a standing position, saw a flicker of light, then darkness again. His senses on full alert now, he wondered if maybe she'd just gotten up and knocked the lamp over. Maybe she had a bad dream.

He knew all about nightmares. He'd lived through a few of them. The shit going down around him the past six months seemed like a living nightmare. Sometimes he didn't even want to close his eyes.

He didn't hear anything now. Not wanting to reveal his hand and go running in there, he paused, but grabbed his weapon and readied himself, just in case.

He wished he'd had time to install surveillance cameras inside, but that was going to have to wait until the next time she left the house. Then he'd be able to see as well as hear. Still, his skin prickled with unease, and whenever that happened it meant something bad was going on.

He didn't like this. Something wasn't right. He stood and moved through the bushes, into the vineyards and toward the house, making no sound. Approaching the back door first, he made a slight turn on the knob. It was locked. That was a good thing. He moved to the window, peering in through the sheer drapes, using his night-vision shades to help him discern objects in the pitch-blackness.

No activity. Angelique wasn't downstairs. His ear

comm was connected to his audio equipment, and he could hear her breathing now.

But it wasn't normal, restful breathing like she was sleeping.

It was deep, ragged breathing.

The gasps and whimpers of terror. She wasn't speaking, as if her mouth was covered. He didn't know how the hell he knew this, he just did. She was being restrained, and she was petrified.

Goddamit. He had to get in the house now.

So much for surveillance.

Though he wanted to kick the damn door down and rush upstairs, he couldn't do that. Not without assessing the situation first. Which meant he had to take the time to pick the lock.

Precious seconds ticked by as he grabbed his pick and worked the simple lock. Thankfully she didn't have major armor installed on the door. Bad move on her part, really good for him. In a few seconds, the lock clicked. He winced at the sound and pushed the door open, hoping it wouldn't creak.

It didn't. He left the door open and moved inside, taking each step with care. He headed toward the stairs, wanting to bound up there, but resisting.

Slow. Measured steps. Make sure not to alert whoever was up there.

Patience—something that was in short supply right now. Weapon trained, he reached the top of the stairs and heard the whispers.

"Tell me where the black diamond is. This is the last

time I'm going to ask you. Tell me or I will cut out your heart and eat it. And you'll still be alive to watch me."

Fuck. A dark shadow loomed over Angelique. She was lying in bed, her body pressed to the mattress, the man's hands wrapped around her throat.

But who held her? Was it a demon? It definitely wasn't a hybrid. They smelled so bad he'd have known one was in the house as soon as he walked in. And those foul-smelling, hulking bastards didn't speak.

Angelique didn't utter a single word, her eyes wide as she stared at her attacker, whose face was only inches from hers.

But why hadn't Ryder's equipment picked up the attacker's voice? If he was asking her *again* about the black diamond, that meant he'd posed the question at least once already, but Ryder hadn't heard the guy talk on his comm.

Shit. That wasn't a good thing, because it meant otherworldly. And either way, the bastard was going to die. First thing he had to do was get its attention. He pulled a knife out of the sheath at his belt, took careful aim, and let it sail through the air. It caught the guy in the upper back, right between the shoulder blades.

Instead of jumping up or falling in pain, the creature calmly stood and turned to Ryder.

Well, hell. Its eyes glowed a pale blue. Pure demon, maybe? Ryder didn't remember seeing their eyes glow in the dark like that.

The creature advanced on him.

"Angelique, get ready to run," Ryder said, unable to determine if she was in shock, hurt, or whether she could even hear him. All his concentration was on the thing headed his way.

"She's not going to do anything you say. She's mine now," the dark thing said, inching closer to Ryder.

Without hesitation, Ryder raised his laser and fired a stream of ultraviolet light. Human or demon, it didn't matter. Either one would die.

The light struck the creature and it paused, looking down at the blue fluid spreading over its chest and midsection. Its arms raised out to its side as it frowned at Ryder, then let out a pained growl.

"That hurts."

And then it kept coming. Okay, that was interesting. UV lasers killed demons. And they sure as hell would toast a human. So what was this thing? Ryder braced and fired again, but obviously his laser wasn't going to work. He shouldered it and went for the microwave gun, blasting the creature and hoping to melt it from the inside out.

Again, nothing. The creature seemed irritated, that was about it.

Fuck. Ryder backed up, wanting to draw the thing away from Angelique. He moved down the hallway toward the stairs. The thing kept pace with him, not rushing him, as if it was just toying with Ryder.

Fine with Ryder. As long as he could get the creature away from Angelique, he was willing to play. He backed down the stairs, one slow step at a time, hoping it would follow.

It did.

Ryder continued backward, pulling his silver knife as he did. The high tech weapons weren't working, so maybe something more basic would.

"Come on," he said to the creature, widening his stance and holding the knife out.

The thing looked at the knife, then back at Ryder. "You can't kill me."

"Everything dies," Ryder returned as the creature maintained its distance. It didn't seem to be in any hurry to attack Ryder. Maybe it was waiting for him to make the first move, or maybe it was just confident that it was going to win.

Overconfidence was a bad thing. At least, Ryder hoped so. He was ready for anything.

"You are human," it said. "I can smell it on you, just as I smell it on her."

"Your point?" They were circling each other now, like wrestlers in the ring before the attack.

"I was human. Once."

What the hell did that mean? "You're not human now."

Its lips curled, revealing sharp teeth. Ryder made a mental note to avoid those. "No, I'm not. I'm stronger. I have power. They promised me great things, and immortality." It sucked in a breath, its chest expanding. "I'm tired of this game, waiting for you to move, human. I have things to do."

"Then let's dance."

"The Sons of Darkness have come for what is theirs." The creature lunged and Ryder sidestepped just before it reached him, then he pivoted and shoved his knife in the left side of the creature's back, hoping to hit a vital organ. It tilted its head back and roared an unholy sound. Ryder pulled the knife just as the thing turned around and reached for him.

Ryder glanced at his knife. Blood. Good. If it could bleed, it could die.

The thing came after him again, and this time Ryder met it. It grabbed Ryder by the shoulders and pushed. Ryder went flying, but he held onto the creature, jamming his blade into its heart, using leverage to push the demon up and over him, even as Ryder was sliding backward clear across the room. The thing hit the wall with a loud crash and Ryder slammed into a table. He winced at the pain, but shrugged it off and leaped to his feet.

The creature stood, limping, blood pouring from the wound in its chest. It was weakening and looked up at Ryder, surprise clearly showing on its face.

"What is in . . . the knife?"

"Silver."

The creature shook its head. "They told me I would live forever." It looked down at its bloody hands, let out a roar of frustration, then disappeared in a cloud of smoke.

What the hell? Ryder stalked to the area where the thing had just stood. Nothing. Just a pool of blood.

He'd never seen any of the demons do shit like that before. He walked outside, looked in both directions, saw nothing, then shut the door behind him and hurried upstairs to Angelique. She was lying in bed, exactly as he had found her. She hadn't moved and her eyes were still wide open. She had a vacant look, almost as if she was under some kind of spell. He dropped his weapons, sat on the edge of the bed, and grabbed her shoulders.

"Angelique." He purposely kept his voice low. "Angie, it's Ryder."

She didn't move, didn't acknowledge his presence. This time, he shook her. "Hey, wake up. It's over."

Still no response. He finally lifted her, laid her head in the crook of his arms. "Angie, wake up." He tapped her cheek, then slapped it lightly. "Come on. Snap out of this, goddamit."

When he still didn't get a response, he gave her one hard slap.

She gasped, then screamed, her hands coming up to palm his chest and push, hard. He didn't let go.

"Come on baby, it's Ryder. It's okay, it's over. That thing is gone."

Still she fought him, kicking her legs and feet underneath the covers, her eyes filled with terror. He held tight to her, bringing her up against him, wrapping his arms around her body. Her skin was ice cold. She was shaking and he couldn't imagine what she had gone through, having that creature put some kind of mind hold on her and then terrorize her like that.

Finally, she stopped fighting him, but she was still shivering. She pushed away, searching his face, her breath coming in harsh gasps. "Ryder."

He nodded, realizing that with his night-vision shades on he could see her, but she couldn't see him. "Yeah, it's me. Stay here." She was reluctant to let go of him. "I promise. I'm just going to get us some light." She finally released her death grip on him. He found the switch, pulled off his glasses, and bathed the room in soft light.

Holy Christ. Her hair was a tangled dark mess around her face and shoulders, her eyes wide green pools of fear. The sheet had fallen to her waist, revealing small breasts, pink nipples, and golden skin. His gaze shot back up to her stricken face and he hurried over to her side of the bed again. She was still shaking. He grabbed his jacket out of the bag at his feet and lifted her arms, sliding her into it, though he wasn't sure if it was to warm her or cover her body from his gaping gaze.

"What . . . what was that?" she asked. "A demon?"

"I don't know. Never seen one like that."

"Me either." She was still breathing hard. He slid his fingers over her pulse. Too damn fast. He rubbed his thumb over her wrist. God, her hand was cold.

"He . . . it wanted the black diamond."

"I figured." He should have been pissed. He had a million questions to ask her, should tell her she got what she deserved after taking off with the black diamond. He was here for the same thing—to get it back. But looking at her shaking like this, he couldn't do it. He had to get Angie out of this house, away from that thing and whatever else the Sons of Darkness were going to send her way. He had to contact the Realm of Light, report what he'd seen, gather some intelligence.

He had to protect Angie, before another of those creatures showed up. Or something worse.

He'd been assigned to find and retrieve the black diamond. Find Angie and Isabelle.

He'd found Angie, so one step accomplished. But damn, he'd just stepped into a whole hell of a lot more.

Pandora's Box had just opened, and he had a feeling he and Angie had just climbed right inside of it.

And despite his anger, his determination to keep his emotional distance, here he sat, with his arms wrapped around her.

And dammit, it felt right.

Not good. Not good at all.